D0457904

# A Crazy Little Thing Called Death

**Other Books in the
Blackbird Sisters Mystery Series**

# A Crazy Little Thing Called Death

*A Blackbird Sisters Mystery*

## Nancy Martin

NEW AMERICAN LIBRARY

New American Library
Published by New American Library, a division of
Penguin Group (USA) Inc., 375 Hudson Street,
New York, New York 10014, USA
Penguin Group (Canada), 90 Eglinton Avenue East, Suite 700, Toronto,
Ontario M4P 2Y3, Canada (a division of Pearson Penguin Canada Inc.)
Penguin Books Ltd., 80 Strand, London WC2R 0RL, England
Penguin Ireland, 25 St. Stephen's Green, Dublin 2,
Ireland (a division of Penguin Books Ltd.)
Penguin Group (Australia), 250 Camberwell Road, Camberwell, Victoria 3124,
Australia (a division of Pearson Australia Group Pty. Ltd.)
Penguin Books India Pvt. Ltd., 11 Community Centre, Panchsheel Park,
New Delhi - 110 017, India
Penguin Group (NZ), 67 Apollo Drive, Mairangi Bay,
Auckland 1311, New Zealand (a division of Pearson New Zealand Ltd.)
Penguin Books (South Africa) (Pty.) Ltd., 24 Sturdee Avenue,
Rosebank, Johannesburg 2196, South Africa

Penguin Books Ltd., Registered Offices:
80 Strand, London WC2R 0RL, England

First published by New American Library,
a division of Penguin Group (USA) Inc.

First Printing, March 2007
1   3   5   7   9   10   8   6   4   2

NEW AMERICAN LIBRARY and logo are trademarks of Penguin Group (USA) Inc.

LIBRARY OF CONGRESS CATALOGING-IN-PUBLICATION DATA:
Martin, Nancy, 1953–.
A crazy little thing called death: a Blackbird Sisters mystery / Nancy Martin.
p. cm.
ISBN-13: 978-0-451-22041-7
ISBN-10: 0-451-22041-2
1. Blackbird Sisters (Fictitious characters)—Fiction. 2. Philadelphia (Pa.)—Fiction. 3. Socialites—
Fiction. 4. Missing persons—Fiction. I. Title.
PS3563.A7267C73 2007
813'.6—dc22          2006028084

Set in Bembo   •   Designed by Elke Sigal

Printed in the United States of America

*For Mary Kate*

# AUTHOR THANKS:

To John Minden for scientific input over the hedge.

To *Post-Gazette* restaurant critic Elizabeth Downer for a peek into her world.

To Kathy Sweeney for taking care of a character when he's not on my pages.

To Mary Alice Gorman for many things, including T-shirt slogans.

To Rania Harris for insight into the catering game.

To Deb Foster, our hostess with the very mostest at the Hat Luncheon.

To the Book Tarts, who invite you to visit us at www.TheLipstick Chronicles.typepad.com.

To the whole team at NAL—from Kara to Catherine, Molly, Claire and, of course, the editor who's helped shape the Blackbirds, the wonderful Ellen Edwards.

To all the chicks at the Jane Rotrosen Agency—Annalise, Andrea, X-tina, Kelly and Her Supreme Excellency, Meg.

Bless you all!

## Chapter One

*E*veryone ought to be forgiven at least one mistake.

I gave my nephews Harcourt and Hilton a sum of birthday money I figured couldn't possibly buy anything that might endanger a pair of fourteen-year-old mad scientists. Unfortunately, I hadn't counted on them squirreling away cash for months, because as soon as they ripped open their cards and found the modest gift, they jumped on the Internet and purchased a fetal pig.

When their gruesome investment arrived—in a large carton packed with dry ice and bubble wrap, and clearly marked BIOHAZARD—they rushed over to my house to set up their laboratory in my basement, where they began the pig's long and loving dissection.

"They're weird, Aunt Nora," said their sister, Lucy, already an astute judge of character at the age of six. She had wide blue eyes that saw the world clearly.

In complete agreement, I hugged Lucy and said, "Let's go to a party."

Like all Blackbird women, Lucy had a few eccentricities of her own. She asked, "Can I take my sword?"

I hadn't been able to wrestle it away from her yet, and I didn't feel up to a battle. "Why not?" I said.

Lucy waved the foil. "If we meet any bad guys, I'll give 'em lead poisoning."

When Lucy and I were suitably dressed and accessorized for an outdoorsy Saturday in April, we left the twins and their infant brother in the capable, if slightly distracted, custody of seventeen-year-old Rawlins, who was trying to teach himself Texas Hold 'Em from a book. Lucy and I tiptoed outside to the waiting car and hit the road. In the car, she shared her Hello Kitty lip gloss with me.

Life had thumped me with a few body blows in the last couple of months. A day with my niece felt like good medicine. Even if we were headed to a party celebrating death.

Eventually, we arrived at Eagle Glen, an estate owned by some elderly, eccentric cousins of ours and located in an expensively bucolic enclave outside Philadelphia where green pastures rolled from one exquisitely land-scaped mansion to another. On the tallest hill, Eagle Glen commanded a river view. The neglected estate included a topiary garden with bushes as big as Macy's parade balloons and a green swimming pool full of three-legged frogs. The grass on the tennis court where Billie Jean King once beat the stuffing out of Richard Nixon looked like a wheat field.

Behind the tennis court lay the polo field, recently mowed for the par-ties. The lower lawn, however, was an ocean of April mud, the result of poorly maintained drainage. Surrounded by a profusion of forsythia and waves of naturalized daffodils, it was mud nevertheless. Hundreds of luxury cars were swamped in it. A couple hundred well-dressed Philadelphians had unpacked elaborate picnics suitable for the first annual Penny Devine Memorial Polo Match. It was a pageant to behold.

Each party had a different theme. As Lucy and I picked our way across the swampy grass in our Wellies, we saw a Chippendale table laid with fine linens and silver under one pretty striped tent. Next to it, another hostess had thrown long boards over sawhorses for a barbecue. Champagne cooled in crystal buckets that sparkled in the sunshine, while barrels of cold beer appealed to other guests. One well-known socialite was treating her guests to a circus, complete with cotton candy, a clown on stilts and an organ-grinder with a monkey that fascinated my niece. The scents of chateaubriand and expensive perfumes mingled in the air with the fra-grance of freshly churned-up muck. The mud, in fact, seemed to be the only reason guests were sticking close to their vehicles. If the ground had made better footing, all the parties would have mingled into one spectacu-lar bash.

Lucy pointed at a hired chef in a white coat and toque as he grilled shrimp over an applewood fire. "Look, Aunt Nora. Is that Emerald?"

"I don't think so, Luce."

At the next party, a violinist in tails entertained a party of blue bloods sitting in camp chairs beside a mud-spattered Bentley. Someone had wisely spread out a large blue plastic tarp on the wet ground, then laid a beautiful Persian rug on top of it. They raised their glasses to me and called my name.

Waving back, I thought that half of the city's so-called high society had decked themselves out in designer finery to come watch one another instead of polo.

The competition for Best Dressed was fierce. I spotted two women in Gaultier designs worth more than fifty thousand apiece. Lucy counted six gentlemen in ascots. And there was enough extravagant millinery to give the queen a migraine.

My own choice received a rave review.

"I like your hat best, Aunt Nora. The long feathers look like a fairy's tail."

I simply hoped the damn thing wasn't going to blow off and end up in a puddle. I had carefully unpacked the hat my grandmother wore in the Royal Enclosure the day Princess Diana stepped on her toe—presumably because Grandmama had outshone her.

"Hey, Sis!"

Lucy and I turned to see my sister Emma emerge from a crowd of young men all dressed in matching bow ties—the members of the nearby university's glee club. Emma, of course, wore no party dress or picture hat. Her white riding breeches clung to her like rain on pavement. In one hand, she carried a polo mallet, the shaft resting on her shoulder. In the other, she dangled a helmet by its strap, and her short, punk-style hair stood out in windblown tufts. Her loose polo shirt bore a large paper number on the back, but managed to hint at a figure that would have put Lara Croft's to shame. The entire glee club ogled her butt as she walked away from them.

Tartly, I said, "Are those boys old enough to vote yet?"

"Maybe for homecoming queen. Think I have a shot?" As usual, my little sister had a gleam in her eye. "That's some chapeau you got going there, Sis. How many peacocks died to make it happen?"

"None. They were cockatoos, and all volunteers."

"I see you got my phone message about the mud." She glanced at our boots, hardly a fashion statement, but definitely practical on a day like today.

"Yes, I owe you big."

"Good. Then you can tell me all about your vacation. And"—she lowered her voice so Lucy couldn't hear—"don't skip any details, especially the sexy stuff."

"The vacation was very nice," I said without rising to the bait. Indicating the mallet, I said, "I see you've been playing your own game?"

Emma twirled the mallet and grinned. "One team is short a player. Apparently Homeland Security worried he might terrorize the social set, so they detained him at the airport. Which means I'm an honorary Brazilian today. Raphael Braga asked me to play."

"Raphael—?" I endeavored to keep my composure as my stomach took a high dive.

Emma misinterpreted my expression. "Don't worry about me, Sis. I've got Raphael's number."

"So do half the women in Europe, not to mention South America."

"Think I can't handle him?"

Emma could probably handle an African lion with one hand tied behind her back, so the male animal of her own species was no problem. With her combination of long legs, perfect figure and eyes that glowed with the promise of a dirty mind, I wasn't surprised that a Brazilian lady-killer like Raphael had come calling on Emma.

I said, "Raphael and his friends play world-class polo, Em. The rough stuff. You could get hurt."

"I can ride rings around most of them, even in all this mud. What idiot chose April for a polo match, anyway? The field manager still isn't sure we can play today. It's too wet."

"I suppose Penny Devine's family chose the date."

Emma shook her head. "Penny would never pick April. That crazy old bitch knew there would be too much rain this time of year."

Lucy, who had been slashing at invisible enemies with her weapon, piped up. "Mummy says a crazy bitch is the neighbor's beagle that won't stop barking. Or the lady who's the mother of the president."

Emma ruffled Lucy's blond hair. "Nice duds, Luce-ifer. What's with the sword?"

"It's a foil," Lucy corrected, flourishing the weapon I used on my college fencing team. She also wore her favorite Fair Isle sweater—unraveling at the elbows—and a somewhat tattered tutu. Her outfit had drawn a few smiling glances from the fashion-conscious crowd, but Lucy didn't seem to mind. "I'm learning to fence instead of going to stinky ballet class today. But Aunt Nora won't let me take the button off."

"She's no fun." Emma prudently tipped the foil away from her own ear. "Where's your mom?"

"Mummy had a date last night," Lucy volunteered. "So we all had a sleepover at Aunt Nora's house. The twins got to stay in the basement."

"Chained up like Quasimodo, I hope." Emma sent me a raised eyebrow. "And where is Mummy today?"

"We don't know," Lucy said cheerfully. "Maybe she had a sleepover, too."

I asked, "Have you seen Libby, Em?"

"Nope. What's up? Has she taken a fancy to someone new?"

"Actually, she's been in bed for a week. Alone," I added, "except for her depression. The kids have been staying with me."

Emma frowned. "Anything serious?"

Lucy piped up. "Mummy just likes to take naps sometimes, and read magazines and watch that food channel on television a lot."

I answered Emma's inquiring glance. "Libby's been feeling a little low. The fireman she was dating disappeared in his own puff of smoke."

"But she went out last night? That's a good sign, right?"

"It was a meeting with her accountant. But, um, Lucy says she wore her lucky sweater."

"Oh, boy."

"Exactly."

The Libby Alert System just went to Code Red. In recent weeks, our older sister, Libby, had been a dormant volcano. It was only a matter of time before Vesuvius blew.

Lucy poked the foil at the muddy tire of a Rolls-Royce. "I don't think he's a counting man. Mummy called him hot stuff and maybe her next paramour. What's a paramour?"

"A man who brings expensive presents for little girls," I said.

"I want a sword of my own," Lucy said promptly. "A big one that's sharp, like Captain Hook's."

She executed a lunge and decapitated an imaginary pirate.

Although I dearly loved my niece and her four brothers, I often thanked heaven they were not mine to manage more often than the occasional few days when my sister took her hormones for a stroll.

I caught Emma scrutinizing me. She said, "So you've got the monsters to look after. That must be a dose of reality after your cruise. How was it? Did the Love Machine keep you belowdecks the whole time?"

"We—it was a lovely getaway," I said.

It had been more than lovely, of course. Sailing the Caribbean on a borrowed yacht had been almost heaven. Fourteen days of sun, sparkling waters, azure sky and three meals a day prepared by a private chef had been therapeutic, but endless champagne and long, passionate nights had been a real sojourn from reality. I'd hated to come home. But I told myself it was time to face the world. To get on with our lives.

So I summoned some cheer. "What about you, Em? You haven't been to Blackbird Farm since I got back. Did you find a new apartment?"

"Nah, I figured I'd give you and Mick some space at the Love Shack. You know—in case you want to howl at the moon or tie each other to the headboard once in a while."

"So where have you—?"

"Don't spend any energy worrying about me. I'll be back when I run out of other pillows to rest my head. Anyway, I've been busy. I'm holding down a couple of jobs these days, plus some extracurricular stuff that keeps me on my toes."

I didn't smell liquor on her breath, and Emma seemed quite clear-eyed. But even if she was busy with assorted jobs, there was no telling what kind of trouble she could get herself into. And if Raphael Braga was hanging around, trouble was definitely in the wind.

A mob of little girls suddenly splashed up and engulfed us—a flock of chattering ten-year-olds in breeches and boots and riding helmets. Their nearly identical French-braided ponytails dangled between their shoulder blades, and their freckled faces glowed with excitement. They clamored for Emma's attention, half of them jumping up and down. I stepped back to avoid the mud. If my sister had been the latest teenybopper sensation, they couldn't have been more adoring. Lucy scrunched herself back into me and stared at them with sudden-onset shyness.

"Hold on, hold on," Emma snapped with mock irritation. She towered over the children. "Who let all the elves out of the Keebler factory?"

"Emma, Emma, we want the pony!"

"Can we let Brickle out of the van?"

"You said we could take turns riding him!"

"Not if you're all acting like a bunch of ninnies," she said. "What did I say about staying out of the way of the polo players?"

"But we have, Emma! We've been perfect, just like you said."

"Not one person has yelled at us."

"Except you," one brave little girl piped up.

"We want to ride Brickle!"

"We'll keep him away from the other horses, we promise."

"We promise!"

"All right, all right," Emma said gruffly. "I'll come down and unload him."

"We can do it! We know how!"

"Forget it." Emma was firm. "The last thing I need is for one of you princesses to get her front teeth kicked out in a horse trailer. Go get the tack out of my truck. And make sure it's clean or somebody's head's gonna roll!"

They took off in a pack, running downhill toward the cluster of horse trailers and vans parked below all the tailgaters.

"I'll be there in a minute!" she shouted after them.

"Cute," I said. "Since when did you go back to teaching pony classes?"

She shrugged. "Paddy Horgan needed an instructor, so I took him up on it."

"Sounds promising. The kids obviously love you."

"What little girl doesn't love the person who lets her ride ponies every day?" Emma shook her head. "I'm a glorified babysitter most of the time. But it pays the bills."

"Paddy paid you to bring them here today?"

"Hell, no, I just let them tag along." A slight blush of pink colored her cheekbones, but she wasn't going to admit how much those little girls must have reminded her of herself not too many years ago. She said briskly, "I bought a new pony in case I decide to freelance. Brickle needs some exercise, so I figured I'd take advantage of the free labor. After today, I'll be boarding him in your barn. Hope you don't mind."

Now and then, Emma brought her various rescue projects to Blackbird Farm, where she cured their ills and nursed them back to usefulness. I hadn't heard about her latest patient, but I wasn't surprised. The really good news was that my little sister seemed to be getting her life together since

7

her husband's death. She'd been on a two-year bender. The thought of her teaching little girls to ride made me smile.

I said, "I'm glad you have a steady job again."

"For the moment." Emma raised a skeptical eyebrow. "What about you? Did you put on your party hat today to cover the social set for the *Intelligencer*? Or have you been fired like half the other reporters in town?"

"I'm still on the payroll. The publisher used to be a shopping buddy of Penny Devine, so I'm here to make her memorial—well, memorable in my column."

A few years ago, I might have come to an event like the polo match as a guest of wealthy friends, or even hosted my own small group of pals for drinks and a picnic. But in the last couple of years I had been reduced— thanks to my parents setting out on a mission to blow every last cent of the Blackbird family fortune on a worldwide spending spree—to attending such festivities in my role as the society reporter for a Philadelphia rag.

"So it's officially your column?" Emma asked. "The publisher gave Kitty Keough's job to you at last?"

"Not officially," I conceded. "I still have to prove myself, try not to make mistakes. I'm not a trained journalist, after all."

"What are you going to write about today? The whole concept is kinda tacky, don't you think? A party instead of a suitably weepy funeral service for Philadelphia's most famous kiddie star?"

"Penny loved parties. Almost as much as she loved polo, so I think this was a good solution. And she would have adored the clothes. Besides, there's a charitable angle to the whole thing, so I'll play that up."

The newspaper's owner had insisted I devote serious space to the life and memory of film star and Philadelphia native Sweet Penny Devine. The world-famous actress—best known for her role as Molly, the plucky parlormaid in the Civil War blockbuster *Suffer the Storm*—was an American film icon. She'd been rushed to Hollywood at an early age to begin her career as a tap-dancing child star. After a short awkward period in her adolescence, she'd grown into a decent character actress—often playing the wholesome best friend or the jilted lover of a cad. But she finally received an Oscar nomination (lost to Meryl Streep the year she played Benazir Bhutto) as the maid who looked after Charlton Heston's version of Abe Lincoln.

As her weight grew increasingly out of control, though, Penny had played a few adorably quirky oldsters in romantic comedies. Before her death, she specialized in playing Sandra Bullock's grandmother, and her popularity soared again.

So today, a few hundred Philadelphia aristocrats and film lovers had come out to celebrate the life of one of their own—a local girl who made it big in the movies. My job was to make the event sound lovely despite the mud.

Emma smirked. "Oh, yeah, the charitable angle."

"Yes." I pulled my invitation from my handbag to double-check. "Proceeds from today's tickets go to—here it is—a foundation that helps treat eating disorders."

Emma grinned broadly. "You know what everybody's calling this thing, right? Chukkers for Chuckers."

"Emma!"

From several yards away, a musical voice hailed us. "Darlings!"

Out of the crowd burst a vision of excess estrogen in a leopard-print suit cut down to reveal her bountiful bosom as blatantly as imported cantaloupe in a Whole Foods display. Our older sister, Libby, waved a champagne flute overhead as she waded toward us with what were clearly her son's hiking boots on her feet. On her head she sported a wide-brimmed yellow hat festooned with daffodils—one of which was already trying to curl around her nose.

Emma said, "What are you doing? Getting ready for a mammogram?"

Libby ignored her and cried, "Lucy! My stars, what have you done to your tutu? And who in the world let you have that weapon?"

"Aunt Nora did!" Lucy nearly stabbed her mother through the heart as she flung herself into Libby's open arms. "She let me have ice cream for breakfast, too!"

"Blabbermouth," I said.

"Nice going," Emma muttered to me. "What's next? Showing them how to rob banks?"

"It was all the food I had in the house! How was I to know I'd have to feed the horde, not to mention store lab specimens in my refrigerator?"

Libby chose not to hear me. Bending at the waist, an act that nearly spilled her breasts like a truckload of warm marshmallow fluff, she used a lace handkerchief to wipe a smudge from her daughter's less-than-pristine cheek. "Did you brush your teeth after the ice cream, sweetheart?"

"Aunt Nora ran out of toothpaste."

"Heavens. Well, you won't have to stay there ever again, Lucy."

"You're welcome," I said tartly. "No charge for the babysitting."

Libby straightened and adjusted her hat to dislodge the pesky flower once and for all. "Don't apologize, Nora. I'm sure your mind is scattered after such a long vacation. We began to worry you'd run off permanently with That Man."

"He has a name, you know."

Blandly, Emma said, "You'll notice she's wearing the Rock of Gibraltar again."

Libby seized my left hand and goggled at the giant, emerald-cut diamond ring that flashed on my finger. "Oh, sweet heaven, what have you done?"

"Be careful," Emma warned. "You could endanger the Hubble telescope with that sparkler."

"It's huge!" Libby cried. "It's not stolen, is it?"

"No," I said, "I think he won it in Vegas."

Her eyes widened. "You're kidding!"

"Of course I'm kidding."

She peered more closely. "A diamond that size can't possibly be real."

"You actually gonna marry Mick this time, Nora?" Emma asked.

I took a deep breath. "Yes."

Libby dropped my hand and cried out in anguish. "Nora, think of your family! You can't besmirch our good name this way!"

"Hell, think of Mick," Emma said. "You realize this is his death sentence?"

The Blackbird women all shared such genetic traits as auburn hair, an allergy to cats, and well-documented widowhood at a young age. Emma and I had lost our husbands before we turned thirty, and Libby's marriages—three so far—had all ended in disaster. The joke around our social circle was that the only men interested in marrying us must be suicidal.

I had fallen hard for Michael Abruzzo, however, and he insisted he was strong enough to withstand a little family curse—even one that dated back more than 150 years. I had refused to endanger his life, of course. But after months of holding out, I was finally weakened by too much champagne and a glorious Caribbean sunset. When he'd asked me again, I said yes.

The fact that he was the son of New Jersey's most notorious mob king-pin didn't matter to me anymore. Not much, at least. But our love match was going to turn Philadelphia society upside down. The Blackbird family had been welcomed into sedate drawing rooms since the days of the Continental Congress, and a union with the Abruzzos—known for racketeering, not racquet club memberships—was going to be the scandal of the season.

Libby groaned. "We'll never live this down!"

Emma patted her shoulder. "Take it easy. Maybe the mayor will get caught with a hooker or something."

Libby nodded. "Let's hope there's a catastrophe, so we won't suffer the glare of the spotlight."

"Let's hope," I agreed, only half joking.

"Anyway, where the hell have you been?" Emma asked Libby. "Lucy said you were going to seduce your accountant."

Libby was prim. "We met to review my tax situation, which stretched into the dinner hour, so we—"

"Spent the night getting each other's numbers straight?" I asked.

"Wait a minute," Emma said. "Wasn't your accountant sent to jail for embezzling?"

Libby waved her hand. "Oh, that was a simple misunderstanding. He explained it all to me. What a miscarriage of justice! A man with a soul like Malcolm's is hardly going to cheat people."

"Uh-huh."

"Anyway." She sneaked a look to make sure her daughter wasn't listening, then lowered her voice just in case. "Last night was a one—well, a brief encounter, that's all. I can't be tied down right now, you know, and I've learned Malcolm is a strictly by-the-book kind of person who—well, he's better suited to dealing with the IRS than tending to my more esoteric needs."

"He was lousy in the sack," Emma guessed.

"No," Libby said sharply. "We are simply not suited for an intimate relationship. So I'm at loose ends. Ready for a new challenge! I need a creative project to focus all my energy. It gets pent up, you know, and then I'm all jittery. I need an outlet!"

"Maybe getting reacquainted with your children could be an outlet for all your energy," I said. "You could save yourself the jitters by cooking their dinner tonight, as a matter of fact."

"What kind of creative outlet is that? No, I need something really exciting—something that will engage my mind while making the best use of my social skills and boundless creativity. I want a real challenge! Look around at this wonderful party. Every single hostess here has indulged her fantasies and—" Libby's face lit up. "Why, I have just the idea! It's a brainstorm!"

"Just make sure the rain doesn't start falling on me," Emma muttered.

But Libby was already in raptures and didn't hear.

"I know what I'll do!" she cried. "It's perfect! Nora! I'll plan your wedding!"

I choked.

Emma burst out laughing.

"It will be wonderful!" Libby crowed. "We'll have a tent and beautiful clothes and—oh!—I know just the cleric to conduct the ceremony! She's a Wiccan with absolutely the best karma of any person I've ever known."

"Libby—"

"And flowers! We could construct a Maypole with braided flowers! With the right music, a pagan fertility dance might break out!"

Emma doubled over laughing.

"The Druid tradition of marriage is unlike any other. Nora, you'll simply adore the radiance circle. And the procession to the fire where the man unfastens his flowing white poet shirt as a symbolic opening of his heart to—"

"Libby, Michael won't go for the whole Druid thing."

Emma said, "I want to see him in the flowing white shirt!"

"No," I said. "No flowing shirts."

"I'll talk to him!" Libby cried.

"That won't help. Michael doesn't want a wedding."

"How can you marry without a wedding?"

"He doesn't want a big fuss. It will only create a lot of publicity."

"What kind of man is afraid to declare his love in public? We'll keep everything secret from the press, I promise. Look, I'll come up with a few ideas and make a little presentation. Maybe some sketches to go with my ideas. No pressure, no commitment—just brainstorming. Oh, it will be such fun! We'll bond—the whole family! Can't you see the twins acting as dual ring bearers?"

"Why not?" Emma said. "Just frisk them for weapons first."

"And Lucy in a perfect little pink dress!"

"It'll look great with her sword," Emma said.

"And what about me?" Libby suddenly clapped both hands to her bosom. "I'll need to find an outfit for the occasion! Something beautiful. Something that says I'm adventurous! And available! Do you know what percentage of couples actually meet at weddings? I might meet the perfect mate!"

"If you can't get laid at a wedding," Emma said, "you might as well throw yourself naked into a baseball stadium."

"Don't give her any more ideas," I said.

Emma's cell phone rang, and still laughing, she pulled it out of her shirt pocket. "Yeah?"

Libby said, "Nora, I've had three weddings already, so I know all the pitfalls. It's important to focus on a theme as soon as possible."

"Michael and I aren't exactly the theme-wedding types, Lib."

"Okay," Emma said into her phone. "I've got an opening at midnight. You want me to pencil you in, big boy?"

Libby and I forgot about weddings and turned our stares onto Emma.

"Sure, baby," she said to her caller. "A thousand bucks. In cash, of course. See you then."

She terminated her call, and Libby said, "Lord above, now what are you doing?"

"None of your beeswax."

I said, "You told me you had a couple of jobs. I thought you meant teaching children to ride ponies!"

"That's what I do in the daylight hours. But a girl's got to entertain herself after dark, too, right?"

Our little sister had recently freelanced at a dungeon that specialized in S and M. Heaven only knew what she was doing now. "Em—"

"Hey," Emma said. "Where's Luce-ifer?"

The three of us glanced around.

Sure enough, my niece had disappeared, foil and all.

Looking around, Libby cried, "Nora, you should have kept an eye on her!"

"Do I look like her mother?"

"You were in charge of her today!"

"Why—oh, never mind." Once again, being with my sisters felt like being strapped to a speeding train headed for an exploded trestle. "Lucy's not going to be kidnapped in this crowd. Everybody knows she can make Linda Blair look like a Girl Scout."

Libby's eyes began to tear up. "That's my only daughter you're talking about!"

Emma said, "Oh, for heaven's sake, let's split up. We'll find Lucy faster that way, and the two of you can stop bickering."

It was a bad day when Emma was the voice of reason.

# Chapter Two

*E*mma headed for the horse vans, and Libby marched unerringly off to the refreshment tent. Perhaps the only one who truly felt Lucy should be found—before she injured an unsuspecting bystander—I steamed in the opposite direction in search of my niece.

Naturally, I was waylaid at every vehicle and entreated to join one tailgate party after another. A twenty-something woman wore a hat that looked like the Flying Nun had swooped through a flower garden. It was Betsy Berkin, daughter of the paper-cup magnate and the city's most famous "celebutante." *The* single girl seen at parties all over the city, Betsy had the swanlike grace and burnished glow of a young lady who'd been given every advantage—and expected even more to fall her way.

She waved me over to join her friends from her clique—all young women who reportedly aspired to be wives of professional athletes who could provide glamorous futures. I had heard via the grapevine that they hung around day spas for beauty treatments and spent their evenings in search of prey in bars near the city stadiums.

Betsy made a production of begging me to step into their Ascot-themed party for a glass of champagne. Her young friends were dressed in a flutter of nearly identical chiffon minidresses, all jamming their nearly identical picture hats down over their nearly identical highlighted hair. A king's ransom in ostrich handbags swung from their toned, tanned arms, and each one of them stood posed to entice any passing jock who might throw her over his shoulder and run for a touchdown. The conversation was rapid-fire fashionspeak, however, with a chorus of *"Eeeeww!"* when someone mentioned ballet flats.

Betsy grabbed my arm and drew me to the table. Her buffet included bangers and mash, which nobody was eating. Betsy obviously didn't mind—the food was all for show anyway. She had used a Union Jack for a tablecloth.

"Nora, only you could make gum boots look chic!" Betsy cried when I refused a glass of champagne. "You're the best-dressed person here!"

Her companions turned and didn't seem pleased. But they all tried to look agreeable because—I knew it from the moment Betsy called to me—they were hoping I'd flag down the *Intelligencer* photographer and feature them in my column. Perhaps they thought my society page was regular reading in local locker rooms. I made a mental note to send the photographer straight over. It didn't hurt anyone to make them happy.

Besides, they were all beautiful, and even my stodgy editor liked to see beautiful girls in the newspaper. They had flawless skin and astonishing bodies. Betsy's face was marred by a long, hooked nose that gave her face character, though, and I was proud of her for skipping the nose job each of her friends had opted for. Perhaps she had more depth than her look-alike pals.

"And what do you think of the memorial polo match?" Betsy asked. She dipped her forefinger in champagne and sucked on it. A great way to consume as few calories as possible.

"It's a lovely memorial for Penny," I said.

"Such a nice send-off," Betsy agreed. "That is, if Penny's really dead this time." She slid her eyes at me.

"Well, her family seems certain."

"Do you think they have proof? A suicide note, maybe?"

"I have no idea."

Perhaps my tone was chilly, because Betsy hastily changed the subject. She blathered about my suit and hat, but her beautiful eyes finally widened when she caught sight of my ring. Not ready to discuss it, I made the excuse I was looking for my wandering niece. As I walked away, Betsy's friends put their heads together and began to whisper.

I knew it had to start eventually. News of my engagement was going to race through the aristocracy like a wildfire through a matchstick factory.

At the open trunk of a beautiful Jaguar, Porter "Potty" Devine poured mint juleps for a clutch of fragile, elderly Main Line widows who had all dressed in funeral black. They frowned disapprovingly as a younger blonde I didn't recognize endeavored to perch her unlikely breasts on his arm.

I remembered my mother's cousin Potty as a silly sort of uncle who kept jelly beans in his pockets. My mother had told stories about Potty as a little boy who banged his head on the floor when he didn't get what he wanted. But now his cherubic face showed no hint of a bad temper. With his chubby cheeks and jaunty smile, however, he looked anything but the grieving brother.

"Cousin Nora!" bellowed the master of Eagle Glen. "Don't you look pretty as a picture! Ha-ha!"

"Hello, Potty."

Hard of hearing from years of quail hunting, he shouted, "Have a drink! Join the party!"

"No, thanks," I shouted back. "I'm on a mission at the moment. My niece has wandered off, and we're afraid she might go on a tire-slashing spree."

The various widows looked startled at my joke. The blonde didn't blink. She had a determined lock on Potty's meaty arm.

Potty didn't hear a word I said, either. He flung his other arm around my shoulders. "Nice wingding, ain't it? Penny woulda been proud! Ha-ha! Have you met my friend?"

The blonde presented her hand for me to shake, but it felt like a squishy doughnut in mine. "Hi," she said. "I'm Noreen Winter."

Her name clicked in my head at once. I didn't know her as Noreen, but as "Nuclear" Winter—the famous gold digger. For years, I'd heard she was flitting around country clubs in search of wealthy boyfriends. Dotty old duffers with bank accounts were her specialty, and she pawned their expensive gifts to buy herself enticing clothes and regular liposuction as she upgraded from one rich man to the next. And now here she stood at last— at the center of the blue blood set, literally on the arm of one of the richest old coots in the city. Trouble was, at least two of Nuclear's elderly boyfriends had expired in her arms during what I heard were "intimate encounters." I wondered if Potty's cardiologist knew about his dating habits.

Potty disengaged his arm from Nuclear's grip. He patted the dangerous curve of her rump and said, "Don't run away, honey. But let me talk to Nora."

Nuclear frowned. "But—"

"It'll only take a minute, beautiful."

The endearment prompted a dazzling smile from Nuclear, showing off a set of budget veneers that should have embarrassed her dentist.

Having appeased her, Potty steered me away from the group. "Now, Nora, I can see what you're thinking."

"Not a thing, Potty. I'm not thinking a single thing."

"Well, the other newspaper's having a field day with me. Raking me over their coals. Making me look like a fool for all the young ladies I keep company with. Can you give me a nice word in your column?"

Any man who couldn't see through Nuclear Winter's transparent attempts to snag his fortune had to be foolish indeed. I had read an item in one of the city's other newspapers about Potty socializing with younger women, but I'd had no idea he'd slipped into Nuclear's spiderweb.

He went on. "I'm not opposed to getting a little press for myself, but I sure don't like all the insinuations that I've lost my edge. Ha-ha! I'm still a virile man, you know. I can go for hours."

"I see." Talk about too much information! A change of subject was in order. "It's very charitable of you to allow Eagle Glen to be used for the memorial. Everyone's having a lovely time, and this is a wonderful way to remember your sister."

"Yeah, well, it's a good excuse for a party."

And Potty could afford it. He had built his father's corner drugstore into a pharmaceutical conglomerate worth at least the value of a moderately prosperous Caribbean island. Always focused on the family business or having a good time, he'd dismissed his famous sister, Penny, as unimportant. Now, it seemed, he didn't take her death to heart, either.

I smiled and considered asking him flat out how he knew his sister was really gone this time. I might have tried if we'd been alone. "I'll catch up with you later, Potty."

He gave me a clumsy, cousinly hug, beaming. "Let's catch up later! I want to tell you what my girlfriend said about me last night. I was a tiger! Ha-ha!"

To put some distance between myself and my randy cousin as quickly as possible, I stepped around the open tailgate of an ancient Mercedes station wagon. And found myself abruptly face-to-face with Crewe Dearborne, the restaurant critic for Philadelphia's finest newspaper. He had a messy sandwich in one hand and was trying to wolf it in private while awkwardly keeping the drips from his tie.

"Crewe," I said. "Is that a cheesesteak?"

He froze, and his eyes widened as if he'd been caught committing a crime. Around his mouthful, he said, "Nora, I'll pay a king's ransom for your silence."

I laughed and plucked the paper napkin from the breast pocket of his natty blue blazer. "Be careful what you say, Crewe. I owe a fortune in property taxes, you know."

"But you have a very kind heart." He swallowed his mouthful. "You won't give me away, will you?"

I used the napkin to mop the juice from his chin. "I'm tempted to out the city's most finicky foodie. Who knew you enjoyed a secret cheesesteak now and then?"

"I'm a native son. How could I not love our local cuisine?"

"I read your review of Le Betard last week. Could you have possibly been more insulting?"

"The soup was congealed grease, the fish overcooked, and the custard— well, Nora, I've eaten better desserts at McDonald's."

"And you despise poor service."

He sighed. "The waiter poured a perfectly good pinot noir into my water glass."

Crewe, with a pedigree every bit as aristocratic as my own, was the son of a very rich, famous hypochondriac and her even richer, philandering husband, who was now dead. Both his parents had been snooty types, but Crewe was anything but. He had sandy hair with a high forehead that gave him more of a distinguished air than his not-quite-forty years should allow. His intelligent eyes and rarely bestowed smile had made many women weak in the knees, but he was still single. The fact that he could cut an arrogant restaurateur down to size with very few words made him a fun cocktail-party guest. I'd hate to find him sitting down at my dinner table, though. His culinary standards were dauntingly high.

Today Crewe wore a pair of flannel trousers, and a crisp white shirt with rep tie beneath the standard-issue Brooks Brothers blazer—a uniform for any wellborn Philadelphian. But it was unusual to find him so ordinarily dressed. Better known for the elaborate disguises he donned to prevent wily restaurateurs from recognizing him, Crewe had been spotted in everything from hippie beads and false whiskers to an Arab kaffiyeh meant to confuse an unsuspecting waitstaff.

I, of course, remembered him from our teenage years, when he wore jeans and T-shirts like everyone else, and had a taste for good food even then. He had carefully created a ranked list of the best pizzas, and for Best in the City chose a pie with fresh mozzarella over heirloom tomatoes and fresh basil from a Little Italy kitchen he had sussed out all on his own.

He took another healthy chomp out of the cheesesteak.

I said, "Who dared to serve you something less than caviar and champagne today?"

"My sister's playing hostess," he admitted after a swallow. "It's all the Saks personal shoppers she loves so much. They're here to show off their clothes, so I knew there wouldn't be any real food. I picked up a sandwich on my way."

"Good thinking."

"You'll be a big hit with them. You look great, as always. Shall I introduce you?"

"I'll pass, but thanks."

"Is that suit some designer I should recognize?"

"Only if you were reading *Vogue* as a baby. This was my grandmother's. It's Oleg Cassini, and she bought it in Paris with Penny Devine. Penny bought an identical one. I'm wearing it in Penny's memory."

"You look ten times better than your grandma ever did."

"You never knew her. She was a looker."

"Speaking of lookers, are your sisters here today?"

I didn't realize Crewe knew Emma or Libby. "Yes, they are, as a matter of fact."

"And what about Lexie? Is she around?"

I should have known. Poor Crewe. For years, he'd been carrying a torch for my friend Lexie Paine. And Lexie, who wanted nothing to do with any man on earth, completely ignored Crewe.

"I'm sorry," I said gently, "but she didn't come today. If I know Lexie, she's probably giving advice to the International Monetary Fund, out of the goodness of her heart."

"Where would our economy be without her?" He made an attempt at good cheer.

"Down the tubes for sure."

"Did you know Raphael Braga is here?" Crewe asked suddenly. He tried to be nonchalant, but his gray gaze rested on mine for an instant too long. "He's playing in the match today."

Just the mention of his name gave me butterflies. Crewe's cousin Carolina had married the famous polo player. I wondered how much Crewe knew about my strange connection to Raphael.

"Yes, I—I saw the publicity. I thought I'd get a few quotes for my column and scram before he—well, soon." I managed a smile, but knew I was flubbing the moment. "Meanwhile, I'm looking for my niece, Lucy. Have you seen a little ballerina with a sword?"

Crewe laughed again as he wrapped up the remains of his sandwich in the soiled napkin. "Sounds like a Blackbird, all right! No, sorry, haven't seen her. Do you need help?"

"No, but I better keep looking before she commits a crime."

As I turned away, Crewe put a hand on my arm. "Nora, why don't you come to dinner with me sometime? As long as you don't mind my usual routine, it could be fun. When I review, I try to take a foursome so I get to taste as much of the menu as possible. Want to tag along? We could get caught up, too. You could bring a date."

And maybe Lexie. He didn't say it, but we both knew what he was hoping for. I didn't detect any sly hints about my love life in his invitation, so maybe he was one of the hermits who hadn't yet heard of my entanglement with the Mafia prince. But I doubted it. Crewe was better at faking nonchalance than I.

I smiled. "Must I order braised eel or polar-bear brains?"

Apologetic, he said, "Actually, I do all the ordering. It's the only way I can do my job. But for you, I promise no eels."

"Sounds like fun. Call me."

His smile brightened. "I will. And good luck with the niece search."

I thanked him and left Crewe to dispose of his sandwich without further discovery.

Thinking like a six-year-old, I made an about-face and walked back along the line of parked cars until I reached the area where all the horse trailers were parked.

Here, the fancy parties and beautiful clothes morphed into a very different world. A variety of working trucks and trailers mingled in the mud with polished wooden horse vans as beautiful as yachts. The people who bustled here weren't sipping champagne, but slinging saddles and talking strategy.

A string of polo ponies, saddled and with their tails tightly braided into bobs, had been tied along a makeshift fence beside the most spectacular of the vans. I saw men in riding gear moving among the horses, so I didn't linger. The last person I wanted to see was Raphael Braga.

A Jack Russell terrier, the dog of choice among the horsey set, barked at me from the open window of a truck. Nearby, a couple of female grooms—two sweaty, twentyish girls—sat in camp chairs swigging from plastic water bottles, their work finished for the moment. They wore their breeches and boots and dirty sweatshirts comfortably, without affectation.

Behind another trailer, a heavyset older woman in a saggy turtleneck sweater, breeches and Hermès riding boots might have been a billionaire, but today she looked happy to be among her horses. Despite her years, she wielded a shovel full of manure with ease.

At the last vehicle—Emma's rattletrap pickup and her rusty trailer—the crowd of her young students clustered around a placid Welsh pony. They were combing his tail, brushing his buckskin coat and braiding his mane while one child held his bridle and petted his nose. I didn't see Lucy among them.

But Emma poked her head out of the trailer, caught my eye and pointed.

At the bottom of the field, the estate's landscape disintegrated into a woodsy wilderness that was even muddier than the grass above. I slogged through it, glad to have my boots, but already feeling the cold through the rubber.

I came to the stream that splashed over a jumble of rocks. Sure enough, Lucy was there, poking her foil into the water.

Standing over her, holding one of Lucy's hands to prevent her from falling, was Michael.

As I approached, I heard Lucy say to him, "I don't like toads. The twins keep them in jars, and I hate the way they look. All dead and yucky."

Michael murmured something that made Lucy laugh. Then she turned and saw me.

"I'm okay," she called. "I'm with Mick."

"She's with me," Michael said.

The playful child with blond curls and the pink tutu made a picture standing beside him—a tall and hulking man with a face better suited for a dockyard than a polo match. Neither one of them belonged at today's posh event. Lucy was a kindergarten delinquent, and Michael had probably been one, too. Now he had more sex appeal than six Main Line lacrosse players. His shoulders were delicious, and he had a walk that was both tight and slouchy and often made me think I should wash out my brain with a bar of soap.

His eyes were very blue and discerning beneath their lazy lids, and he saw something in my face that made his interest sharpen.

Then I saw the stitches in his chin, and my heart gave a thump.

"Michael, what happened? You're hurt!"

"Stupid accident," he said, still preventing Lucy from falling as she tilted insistently into the stream. He leaned my way with amusement in his eyes. "Be gentle with me."

I wrapped one arm around him and instinctively lifted my other hand to touch the wound. It was already swollen and looked angry. "What kind of accident? When?"

Michael avoided my fingertips with a twist of his head. "This morning, driving into town. A tire blew, and I went into a ditch." He shrugged. "No big deal."

"I think he hit a porcupine," Lucy volunteered. She pointed her weapon at his chin. "A doctor sewed his skin with a needle. I bet it hurt."

"It hurt like hell, in fact. And it's not going to do my pretty face any favors."

"Is the rest of you okay? No broken bones?"

"I only hit my head, which didn't damage anything important." He smiled. "Forget about it. Lucy wants to see the horses."

Michael had never come to any of the parties I covered. That he had chosen today made me suddenly uneasy. "Did you come to see the horses, too? Or is something wrong?"

"I came to see you. To bring you your new cell phone."

He handed the tiny telephone over, and I blushed. "I forgot it again. I'm sorry."

"You don't really want to carry it, do you?"

"Yes, of course. Well, I know you think it's important."

"Think of it as the quickest way to call 911 when your sisters get into trouble."

"I just can't get the hang of getting a new one every few days. Are you sure it's necessary to switch phones so often?"

"The police want to listen in to everything I say. I don't think they need to hear what you and I talk about, do you?"

"You have a point. But—all right, mostly I feel as if having a cell phone just makes it okay for people to be late."

He gave a disbelieving laugh. "What?"

"If people make arrangements to meet me and they have cell phones, they always call to say they'll be late. But when I don't have a phone, everyone makes an effort to be on time."

"Nora, that's—"

"I'll take it." I began to tuck the phone into my handbag. "I know how you feel about constant communication. And you're right about my sisters. Thank you for getting it for me."

Gently, he said, "It doesn't work if you don't turn it on, Nora."

"Oh, right. How do I do that again?"

He took the phone back and showed me which button to push. I heard a beep and saw a light blink. Michael handed over the functioning phone, and I accepted it sheepishly.

He said, "The guy collecting tickets wouldn't take my money. So I parked up the road and walked in."

"You're supposed to have an invitation."

"I don't think it was my lack of an invitation that kept me out."

No, probably not. Most people took one look at Michael Abruzzo and figured he was the kind of goodfella who left severed horse heads in people's beds.

But not me. When we'd returned from our cruise, Michael had officially moved to Blackbird Farm to live with me. He brought most of his clothes and a couple of cartons of personal things that were gradually finding their rightful places in my house. His fishing rods cluttered my back porch, and his collection of surprisingly fine wines took up half the pantry. Along with his possessions, he brought a lot of laughter.

Late at night when I returned from whatever party I was covering, he cooked supper for us, and we ate in the kitchen and spent a few hours entertaining each other before going upstairs to my bed—our bed now. That was the only domestic routine we'd established. As for the rest of his day, he kept his own hours and rarely told me where he went or what he did. I only hoped he abided by the law. He was neat in the bathroom, but the rest of the house had become one big playpen. He sang lustily on the staircase, sometimes knocked me into a sofa for impromptu lovemaking and had already broken the leg off a valuable chair just because he was six feet four inches of impulsive, active man.

Sometimes it felt as if I were civilizing a wild animal. At other times I wondered how I'd ever lived without him.

And yet, there were still things we hadn't resolved.

"I'm sorry about this morning," I said, "but Libby's kids—"

"Forget it. You had your hands full. I should have been more helpful. But those twins? They creep me out. What's the smell they've got going in the basement?"

"Formaldehyde."

"Jesus. Who are they embalming?"

I smiled. "Don't worry. The neighbors are all accounted for."

He absorbed my smile and seemed to relax. "Nice place, this," he said, casting his gaze along the landscaped property, the many cars parked in the lower field, the throngs of people entertaining among the tents and tables. "It's somebody's estate?"

"The Devine family. They're cousins of mine. My mother's relatives, distantly."

"Lots of land, even for this neighborhood," he noted.

"It's getting a little run-down. The previous caretaker took much more time keeping up appearances."

Michael turned and looked across the stream. "What's behind the big fence?"

"Fence?"

He pointed. "Through the trees there. It's, like, twenty feet high."

"I have no idea. Maybe it keeps the deer out."

"Looks more like a fence to keep things in, not out."

Michael knew about such fences, of course. As a teenager, he'd gone to jail for stealing motorcycles—a sentence extended for his bad behavior once behind bars. When he'd finally gotten out, he'd spent a few years dabbling in his notorious family's businesses, but eventually decided he needed to change his ways or risk going back to prison, a fate that seemed more horrible to him as he grew older.

It had been a long struggle for him, but I thought he'd finally turned his back on his criminal inclinations. He was working to disengage himself from the rest of the Abruzzo family.

"I don't remember a fence," I said. "Maybe it's for security."

He shrugged, accepting my guess. "So what's this shindig all about? Are your distant cousins raising money for a disease or a music hall?"

"Actually, it's a memorial service. For Penny Devine."

He frowned. "That old actress? Sweet Penny Devine?"

"Not so sweet, if the truth be told. In private, Penny was nothing like the characters she played. Before she got into movies, she was famous for pinching her sister black-and-blue and clobbering her brother with his own electric trains. Later, she became a terror in Hollywood. She pushed Dolly Parton into a swimming pool just to show her wet T-shirt to the press."

"How could anybody be mean to Dolly Parton?"

"Penny Devine."

"So everybody's here to pay their respects to an old bitch?"

"Actually, everybody's here for quite a different reason. Secretly, they're all hoping Penny shows up for her own funeral."

Michael frowned. "I don't—oh, is she the one who kept disappearing? And turning up just in time to get her picture taken?"

"After this last disappearance, she didn't come back, though. She stayed disappeared, so her family is having her declared legally dead."

Cocking one eyebrow, he said, "Usually the family keeps hoping their loved ones stay alive. Or is there a reason for all the rush?"

I often thought Michael would make a very good police officer, but when I once voiced that opinion, he had been offended. I said, "They'd rather have her dead, I guess. She shares ownership of a company with her brother and sister. Devine Pharmaceuticals."

Michael whistled. "Her share of that gold mine must be worth a few shekels."

"I imagine so, yes."

"How are they so sure she's really gone? They have a habeas corpus?"

"Nope."

Michael surveyed the estate again, as if calculating its worth. I could see his mind working at various angles of the story. He asked, "Did they check her bank records to see if she's moving money around? Credit cards to make sure she's not staying at the Paris Ritz maybe?"

I couldn't stop myself from smiling. "Professional interest?"

"I like to keep up on the latest techniques for disappearing." Michael slipped his arm around my waist. "Want to run away with me? We could have, whatayacallit, an extended honeymoon?"

Abruptly, Lucy said, "There's my mom."

A few hundred yards away, Libby had slogged to a halt in the mud and was now using semaphore to communicate with us. Either that or she was doing an interpretive dance.

"She looks mad," Lucy said with a sigh. "She doesn't like you, Mick."

"I think she's mad at all of us." I could read Libby's body language from any distance. "Better run along, Lucy."

"Don't run with that damn sword," Michael said. "Give it to me, Luce."

Without a fight, Lucy magically surrendered her weapon to Michael and scampered off to her waiting mother, tutu fluttering.

We watched her go, and I said without looking at him, "A tire blew?"

With an easy motion, he pretended to use the foil as a baseball bat and took a swing at an imaginary pitch. "An accident. No big deal."

"How much damage to your car?"

He hesitated.

"Michael—"

"It was just a bad tire."

"You, of all people, have never had a bad tire. You maintain your cars with more attention than Barbra Streisand gives to her manicure."

"Don't start worrying about your Blackbird curse." He stopped playing with the foil. "There's no such thing. It was just an accident. Besides, I like spilling some blood once in a while. It makes me tougher."

"But—"

He kissed me lightly on the mouth. "You can't scare me off with an imaginary curse. Nice lipstick. It's a new flavor."

"It's Lucy's." I smiled, too. "I don't want to scare you off."

"Good. I was starting to wonder." He stayed close and captured my left hand. "At least you're finally wearing the ring."

With a flash of guilt, I looked at the enormous stone on my finger and didn't meet his eye.

"What's the matter? Still afraid to tell your friends about us?"

"Of course not."

"So tell me what's wrong."

"Wrong?" I pulled my hand from his and tried to laugh. "For heaven's sake, I've never been happier—"

"Is that true?"

"You know it's true."

Behind him, the stream must have continued to murmur, but I no longer heard it. The green, newly leafed-out trees seemed to lean down, enclosing us. Softer, Michael said, "It's not just the ring thing, Nora. You've avoided me for days."

"How can you say that? Just last night, we spent at least three hours—"

"Yeah, I know. And the two weeks of great sex before that was incredible, too. But this morning I figured it out. We're getting naked every chance we can instead of talking."

I turned away. "You must be the first man on earth with that particular complaint."

He caught my arm, then immediately gentled his grip. "You're going through a rough time."

"I'm fine."

Without waiting for me to face him, he said, "I hear you crying in the shower."

When I couldn't come up with a response, he said, "I know losing the baby was bad. It was for me, too. I just—it breaks my heart to see you like this. And spending half the night tussling in bed hasn't made things better."

Months had gone by before we moved our relationship into the bedroom. Although my sister Emma took her frequent sexual conquests in stride, I was more cautious. Michael and I had become intimate in other ways first, and when the sex eventually happened, it meant more. It had been satisfying and fulfilling and exciting. On our cruise, however, after my miscarriage, something else had been unleashed.

I still hadn't come to terms with the loss of the baby in March. Michael was right. Instead of talking, I pulled him into bed every night. And there, perhaps I was taking out my frustrations.

Michael turned me around. "You need help, Nora. More than I know how to give."

I still couldn't meet his gaze. "I don't—let's not talk about it now. I'm working. I've got to get back to the party. I have to find the photographer. I need to interview people—"

"I love you," he said.

I felt hot tears in my throat.

"Is it the baby?" he asked. "Is that what this is about? Or did something else happen when I wasn't paying attention?"

Only a year ago he had been on his own terrible path of self-destruction, but now he knew what he wanted with fierce certainty. He was compelled by that new, powerful love to help me, and I was very grateful.

But I felt as if I were drowning just inches from his outstretched hand. Because asking for help meant telling him things he wasn't going to like.

He said, "I'm not asking you to get over it. That's never going to happen."

"No," I whispered.

"So what do we have to do, Nora? To make things better?"

"I don't know."

"We'll have kids, you and me. It'll happen."

I wasn't so sure. But I couldn't bring myself to say the words.

For a short time after my husband's death, I had started to see a way for myself—a family of my own to take care of. A life with Michael and children. Now that route seemed blocked, as if by huge trees downed by a storm. I needed a map to find my way, and I didn't know where to look for one.

A voice behind us said, "Excuse me!"

We turned, and standing ten feet away was a bedraggled teenage girl in an overly large rain slicker and sloppy wet boots. She had appeared out of nowhere like a somewhat scruffy woodland sprite. Her curly dark hair was caught up in a tangle on top of her head and stuck with a leafy twig she must have bumped into. With a nervous, rapid blink, she said, "You're standing under the vireo's spot."

"I beg your pardon?"

She took a hesitant step closer. "He won't come if he thinks you're invading his territory."

A pair of binoculars hung by a braided leather strap around her thin neck. Beside it swung a heavy old camera on a thick cord. She carried a well-thumbed paperback in hands that were bony, with nails bitten to the quick. The book, I realized, was a bird-watching manual.

"I'm so sorry," I said. "Is this some kind of bird sanctuary?"

"Not exactly." She looked from me to Michael, who made her even more nervous, so she blinked at me again. "It's just a special place. And lately there's been a warbling vireo."

Michael said, "A who?"

She licked her lower lip. "Not a Philadelphia vireo. I'm sure of that. It's the *Vireo gilvus,* the warbler. They're easy to mix up, but I know I'm right. I want to document him, to prove it's really here." She touched the camera.

"You mean a bird?" Michael glanced up into the canopy of trees overhead. "What's it look like?"

A little braver, she said, "It's olive, of course. With yellow-tinged underparts. And a dark spot at the base of the bill. That's what makes him the warbler, not the common Philadelphia vireo. He's not normally found around here, and this is way too early for him, too. That's what makes my discovery so exciting."

"Aren't you Julie?" I asked. "Julie Huckabee?"

She blinked more rapidly at me. "Y-yes."

"You're Juana's daughter, aren't you? I knew your mother when she was alive."

Juana, the housekeeper who worked for years for both Vivian and Potty Devine, had baked plantain cookies for my sisters and me when our mother occasionally paid calls on her peculiar cousins. Juana, with her exotic island accent and thick black locks, had married Kell Huckabee, one of the gardeners at Eagle Glen. Their daughter, Julie, had been a little girl when I'd last visited the estate. I remembered the toddler scribbling in a coloring book while her mother worked at a desk in the corner of the kitchen.

It was odd to see Julie all grown up now. As a child, she'd had a certain biracial beauty—golden skin with a corona of dark hair and surprisingly pale hazel eyes. But now her coloring seemed faded, her appearance unkempt and her anxious blinking a little off-putting. Her jeans were dirty—the kind of dirt that was embedded from weeks of wear. Her mother would have been shocked.

"Yes, I'm Julie Huckabee."

"I'm Nora Blackbird. I knew you when you were little." I shook her hand and found her fingers icy cold and painfully thin. "I was so sorry to hear your mother passed away. She was a vibrant lady—always singing, I remember. And you used to be a dancer when you were little."

The girl toyed with her binoculars. "I don't anymore. I'm not very musical. I'm doing a study of local birds and animals."

"So you're a naturalist."

"Just an amateur."

"Not such an amateur if you can spot a—what did you call it? Some kind of warbler?"

"The warbling vireo." Her narrow face became intense again. "Even though it's early in the season, I knew exactly what it was as soon as I heard its song. It sounds a lot like the purple finch. It's very unusual to find one here because of Dutch elm disease ruining their habitat."

"Right," I said. "Well, I hope we didn't scare it away."

Julie frowned up into the trees. "Me, too. We're not used to having people around. Maybe I better go downstream just in case he felt threatened."

"Sorry. It was nice seeing you again, Julie."

She said good-bye and clomped away, her boots making sucking noises in the mud. She clutched her binoculars and craned to scan the branches overhead.

"Well," said Michael. "There's another well-adjusted teenager. Think she eats nuts and berries? If she eats anything at all? That is one skinny girl."

I didn't answer. I was busy thinking about Julie's mother and how little her daughter resembled the vibrant, laughing woman I remembered.

"Nora, you're frowning."

"What? Oh, sorry. I was just—I thought Juana would always be here at

Eagle Glen. She held the place together, if that makes any sense. Things have gone to pot since she died a few years ago. It's even more sad to see Julie so—well, bereft. I should have contacted her after the funeral."

"What about her father? Where's he?"

"I don't know," I said. "He's some kind of general maintenance person for the estate. He grew up here, never left. I remember him as a man on a mower when I was a kid. Except . . ."

"Except?"

"He had a very bad temper."

I found myself recalling an afternoon long ago at Eagle Glen. While our mother conducted some kind of family détente in another room, Emma and I had played a board game at Juana's kitchen table, and little Julie had toddled around the kitchen clapping wooden spoons together. I recalled the smell of limes and baking, and Juana singing.

But Juana's husband Kell had burst through the back door, furious about something Juana had asked him to do.

"You bossy bitch!" he'd hissed, grabbing her wrists.

He was a small man—shorter than Juana by a few inches—but bristling with anger all the time. It was as if there was a bigger beast fighting to get out of that diminutive body. His short hair stood up at the back of his balding head, and his clothing—a hunting jacket and rough trousers—smelled of grease and gunpowder. He kept shotgun shells in the little pockets under his sleeve, and the sight of those frightened me. I pulled Emma deeper into the breakfast nook.

Kell slapped Juana across her cheek, but she didn't flinch. Her face was impassive, and she stared down at him until he backed off.

"You're not the boss of me," he snarled at her, then slammed out through the door again, banging it on its hinges. Little Julie had burst into tears.

Michael had been watching my face as I flashed back on that afternoon. He said, "Don't tell me you're going to take this kid under your wing."

"What? Of course not."

"You've got enough going on right now."

He was right, of course. I said, "Yes, I know."

"It's time to think about yourself for a while."

Yes, perhaps. But it was easier to think about other people's problems.

I looked up at Michael and saw his concern. "Look," I said, "I know we need to talk. I'm just not ready, Michael. I don't know what's going on in my head, but I—I need time, I guess."

Michael put his hand on the back of my neck and squeezed gently. "We've got all the time in the world."

A throng of men on horseback cantered down the slope, in a rush of hoofbeats, friendly shouts and snorting animals. They were headed for the upper field by way of the streambed, to make a grand entrance for the waiting audience. But some of the helmeted riders swarmed toward us, swinging mallets teasingly, warming up for their match while they taunted us for canoodling by the stream.

Michael didn't see the humor and drew me close. When the ponies jostled even nearer, he spun me behind him to keep his body between the animals and me.

"Hey," he snapped to one rider who reined closer yet.

But the rider circled us and came back to bump us again aggressively, and this time Michael fended off the pony with a stiff-armed shove and a curse.

"Nora?" The voice of the rider had a thick accent. "Nora Blackbird?"

I looked up, shielding my eyes from the dappled sun with one hand, but I couldn't make out his face. The pony threatened to step on my toes, and once again Michael pulled me out of harm's way.

With an impatient phrase, the rider dismounted and held the pony's bit to steady her. He was long-legged and broad-shouldered with a lithe, athletic horseman's build accentuated by perfectly tailored breeches and a pair of boots clearly custom-made in Italy. With a flourish, he unsnapped his helmet and took it off, revealing a cascade of beautiful black hair and a very tanned, familiar face.

"Raphael," I said in a strangled voice.

Raphael Braga seized my hand and bowed to kiss it—his lips warm but featherlight on my skin. When he straightened, his dark eyes swept up my figure to rest appraisingly on my face. "I thought it was you. How beautiful you've grown up!"

Of course I knew he'd come to Philadelphia. The prememorial publicity had been crowing his name for weeks. But seeing him like this—so close, so forbidden—threw me for a loop. Again, I could only say his name.

"This man." Raphael turned to give Michael a haughty stare. "This very big *patife*—he bothers you?"

"No, of course not. Raphael, this is Michael Abruzzo. Michael, this is Raphael Braga. He—he married a friend of mine many years ago."

Michael had bent to pick up the foil he'd dropped. He straightened to his full height. Raphael hesitated for only an instant before extending his manicured hand. "How do you do?"

"Yeah." Michael's tone was surly.

Handshake exchanged, Raphael zeroed back on me with the intensity of a man who cut to the chase when it came to seducing women. "You have come to watch me play?"

"Actually, no, I—"

"It's all right," he said graciously. "I enjoy my fans. Have you heard from Carolina lately?"

"Not for years," I said, aware that we appeared to be exchanging inanities. "You?"

He threw up his hands, causing the pony to jerk her head away. "Not for years also. We live apart now. But she loves Brazil, so she stays. I hear she raises orchids and hikes in the mountains, the silly bitch."

Years ago, I had been close friends with Carolina Moreno-Penn, Crewe Dearborne's Florida cousin who had been my roommate for a year at Barnard. Descended from a noble Spanish family on her mother's side and fascinated by her own heritage, Carolina enjoyed backpacking in Spain and Portugal during semester breaks. She spent her holidays at their home in Palm Beach, though, where her father played the most expensive amateur sport on earth—polo. It was only natural that pretty Carolina fell in with groups of the international tournament players who often visited their home. Eventually lightning struck.

After our junior year, she met Raphael, son of a wealthy Brazilian industrialist. Raphael was a world-class polo player with a lucrative gentleman's business in training and selling ponies. He also had a history of sweeping some very sophisticated women off their feet.

That a playboy of Raphael's reputation might fall for a studious, backpacking American girl like Carolina—no matter how rich her father was—seemed unlikely at first. But they married in a romantic whirlwind and moved to Brazil to live with his family on a ranch that had once been featured in *Architectural Digest*. When her own father died shortly thereafter, Carolina committed herself to pleasing her in-laws and became a traditional Portuguese wife while her husband continued to play on the world's most prestigious polo fields. And bedrooms.

Despite our early close relationship, I saw Carolina only a couple of times after their wedding. She preferred to stay in her adopted country, and I was not invited to visit. There were other issues, of course.

But now here was Raphael.

Aware that my voice sounded unnatural, I said, "It's very nice that you came today to honor Penny Devine's memory. You knew her, didn't you?"

"Yes, of course, Penny was a great *patrone* of polo. She came to many tournaments." Raphael's dark brows twitched into a sorrowful frown. "I am sorry to miss her now. She was a great lady. You knew her also, I think?"

"Penny was a friend of my grandmother. They shopped for clothes together."

"In Paris, yes," Raphael said. "I see some of the grandmother's taste is yours, too, Nora." He cast a glance down my suit and ended at my rubber boots, and he smiled. "But not all. You are a sensible one, too."

Uncomfortable under his scrutiny, I said, "I'm sure Penny's friends and family appreciate your coming today."

"It is for a good cause," he replied. "One close to Penny's heart—or stomach. She was a pig, Penny. She loved to eat. Such a pig."

The rest of the players had ridden up the hill toward the polo field, but one circled back to us. When she came closer, I realized it was Emma, handling her borrowed pony with ease.

"Hey, Mick," she said, reining near to get a good look at his chin. "What happened to you? Cut yourself shaving?"

Mick shot a sour look at Emma. "Something like that."

Raphael appeared amused. "So the *patife* is not so *roji* after all?"

Emma laughed. "Rafe," she said, "let's go. We've only got a few minutes to warm up."

"You are a taskmistress, Emma," Raphael replied, but he obediently swung up onto his mare again.

On impulse, I caught his stirrup. "And your daughter, Raphael? How is she?"

His black gaze rested on me. His face hardened as he settled into the saddle. "Yes, Mariel. She lives with my mother now. They are devoted to each other."

"Does Carolina . . . ?"

"No, she stays away." His voice was suddenly cool. "Mariel lives with my family. It is best that way." He put on his helmet with a practiced, one-handed maneuver, then spurred his horse across the field.

Michael muttered, "I hope nobody lights a match too close to that guy's hair. With all the grease he's got on, it might explode."

My heart was beating very fast as I watched them ride away.

"Nora? You okay?"

"Hm? What? Sorry."

"Oh, great," Michael said. "Tell me he's somebody you slept with years ago. Am I going to have to whack him?"

"That's not funny. He married a friend of mine, that's all."

"Yeah, I figured out that much. What is he now? Some kind of gigolo?"

"Heavens, no. He's—well, Raphael. Wealthy, successful."

I didn't want to talk about him, certainly not with Michael. The time would come when I would have to explain everything. But not yet.

I said, "I should get back to work. Once the polo match starts, it will be harder to interview anyone."

"Sure," he said, watching my face.

"Would you like to come along? I could introduce you to some friends of mine."

He smiled and shook his head. "I might frighten their horses."

My heart turned over. "You'll have to meet them eventually. Why not today?"

"I've got things to do at the garage. I wanted to bring your new phone, that's all."

I stretched up on tiptoes and kissed his cheek, taking care not to bump his chin. "And I love you for it. We'll talk, I promise."

He slipped one hand to my hip and accidentally jostled something out of my pocket.

He bent to pick it up. "What's this?"

An envelope, we saw.

"I don't know. I didn't have it when—" Instinctively, I slit the vellum envelope open and discovered a sheaf of money inside. Several one-hundred-dollar bills. Astonished, I said, "What in the world?"

"Looks like you hit it big at the casino," Michael said, amused.

I reached for my pocket, half expecting to find more surprises within, but there was nothing else secreted inside. "I can't imagine where—oh, for heaven's sake. Potty!"

"Uh—"

"Porter Devine," I corrected. "He must have slipped it into my pocket while we were talking."

Michael took the money from my hand and flicked it expertly. "That must have been an interesting conversation. There's a thousand bucks here."

"He was telling me about the bad press he's gotten for having a young girlfriend. Good grief, do you suppose he's trying to buy space in my column?"

"If he needs some favorable publicity, I'd say that's exactly what he's trying to do. Congratulations. Consider yourself bribed."

"I can't accept this!" I flushed. "It's unethical!"

"Surely every newspaper writer in the world has been greased at least once. I'd say it's a career milestone for you." He slid the money back into the envelope.

"You aren't suggesting I keep it!"

"Hell, no. Give it back. Or give it to an orphanage. But don't get bent out of shape about it. A little graft is no big deal."

"It is to me."

"I know," Michael said fondly. "I think it's cute."

"I need to find Potty right now and return this money."

"Suit yourself."

I stuffed the envelope into my handbag where it would be safer. Michael walked me back across the grass toward the cars. I reached for his hand, and he guided me around the worst of the mud. I don't remember what we talked about—something about dinner that evening, I think. But my mind was on Potty's attempt at bribery.

And, of course, I thought about Raphael.

So I didn't see it until we nearly stepped on it in the grass.

At first, I was sure it wasn't real. But we stopped together, halted by the sight of it, and we looked down at the thing lying on the muddy ground.

"Jesus," Michael said.

A human hand.

Severed above the wrist.

Drained of blood, it was gray. Still fleshy but mottled, with chubby fingers and acrylic nails painted pink. A wristwatch glittered on the wrist.

It was so bizarre and so horrible—there in the mud on such a beautiful day.

I felt the trees start to spin around me. Michael had his cell phone out, and I knew he was calling the police. He pushed me back, but I could only stare at it—a dismembered bit of a human being in the sunshine. A black swirl washed around my ankles, and then it swept upward to engulf me. I passed out cold, into Michael's arms.

# Chapter Three

The police, of course, took Michael away.

"Why would they arrest him?" Libby demanded in an uncharacteristic show of protectiveness. "He didn't cut off somebody's arm and then call the cops to report it!"

"The police always react this way." I hugged the plaid stadium blanket she had produced out of the flotsam in the back of her minivan. "They assume because he's an Abruzzo that he's mixed up in any crime committed within ten miles of where he's standing."

"That's hardly fair," my sister sniffed. "Why didn't they question me in more detail? That one officer had an intriguing aura. I sensed a potential connection."

"Libby—"

"I might have been helpful, that's all. I certainly know as much as That Man of Yours. Maybe more."

We were sitting in the backseat of her minivan with all the doors open, still parked in the muddy field. Lucy napped in the front passenger seat, contorted in the boneless, tangled way only children could sleep. The other guests had long since walked up to the polo match, and we could hear a muffled voice on a loudspeaker announcing the action. Occasionally, the crowd gave a collective, "Oh!" So far, not many were aware of the police presence in the lower field. Around us were parked several cruisers and a forensics van. The police had strung crime-scene tape, and now the long process of analyzing the ground was under way. If they didn't finish before the polo match was over, there was going to be one very big, well-bred traffic jam.

A few chauffeurs and some of the catering staff stood behind the crime tape, watching and talking in low voices.

"Michael hasn't been arrested," I said. "They're just asking him routine questions."

"I hope he has a good lawyer."

Michael had a dozen good lawyers. I sipped from the cup of tea Libby had procured for me from someone's tailgate party. The delicate cup was Wedgwood, hand painted with violets. The tea was cold.

"Was it really gross?" Libby asked. "I mean, did you see a lot of blood?"

"No blood." I had fought down the nausea that came after fainting, but here it came again. I pulled the blanket closer.

"And it was a woman's hand?"

"Most certainly. Nail polish. A lady's watch."

"Do you think . . . ?" Libby asked. "Could it possibly . . . ? Oh, for heaven's sake! It makes sense, you know."

"It makes no sense whatsoever, Libby."

"Things may seem to happen by chance, Nora, but actually, it's the wings of a butterfly in northern Africa that cause the hurricane in Mexico."

Even on my best days, I had a hard time comprehending Libby's latest cockamamy theories. "What are you trying to say?"

"That it's Penny Devine's hand, of course! What are the chances Penny disappeared, and a year later someone else's severed hand turns up on her family's estate?"

"Libby—"

"And where's the rest of her, may I ask? Has she been divided up into bite-sized pieces, or—"

"Oh, God."

"You're thinking the same thing—admit it!"

A truck with a bad muffler roared up beside us and stopped. It was an old pickup truck with a ragged tarpaulin tied over the cargo bed and a kind of winch attached to the back. The vehicle was beaten with age and coated with dust.

As soon as the engine died, we were overcome by a terrible stench that wafted from the back of the truck. I stared at the large lump covered with the tattered blue plastic tarp. From underneath it thrust the leg and hoof of a dead animal—probably a deer.

"Good heavens," Libby cried, clapping one hand to her nose and mouth. "What is that smell?"

A light, brisk knock sounded on the side of the minivan, and an instant later, an elderly face appeared in the doorway. "Eleanor Blackbird? Is that you?"

"Vivian! Oh, I'm so sorry about all this."

"No apologies necessary, you poor lamb. I understand you found the—er—remains? What a terrible shock for you. Here, would you like a cookie? It might revive you."

She extended a small brown paper bag that bulged with cookies. Automatically accepting her offering, I peeked inside and noticed they were all cut into animal shapes—cats, in fact—and sprinkled with fragrant cinnamon.

"Uh, thank you, Vivian."

Vivian Devine looked little like her famous sister, Penny. Where the actress had been petite and struggled with her weight, her older sister, Vivian, had given up the fight long ago and now looked as plump, kindly and sweet-tempered as Mrs. Claus. They had the same face—rounded cheeks and a pointed chin with china-doll eyes—but Vivian's wrinkles and jowls lent her face a cozy sort of expression. Penny had often looked as if she'd been drinking vinegar.

Over her rounded figure, Vivian wore a shapeless green jumper with a Peter Pan collar showing at her neck and long sleeves demurely buttoned at her wrists. On her tiny feet were white socks and red plastic gardening boots in the shape of Dutch wooden shoes. In her arms she cradled a thin, sickly little cat.

From behind Vivian came a nervous Brittany spaniel, white with chestnut-colored ears and filthy legs. The animal put his muddy forepaws into the van by my feet and stretched his speckled pink nose to sniff me.

"Get down, Toby," Vivian said, and the animal shied from her as if she'd jabbed him with a Taser. "I'm sorry about the behavior of the dog. He belonged to our caretaker and never received any proper training. Are you very shaken up, Nora? Can I bring you some tea to go with the cookies?"

"I have some tea already, thank you, Vivian. Yes, it was me who found—her—it."

"What a shock, you poor lamb. Have you spoken with the police?"

"Yes. They asked me to wait a little longer."

Libby said, "It's so inconvenient. Nora should be at home in bed by now."

Vivian said, "Of course she should. Oh, this is very distressing. Did the police identify the . . . ?"

"I imagine that process will take weeks."

"I know what they're thinking." Vivian glanced over at the forensics van. She seemed oblivious to the awful smell that hung over her truck. "It's what everybody's going to think, isn't it?"

"That's what I said," Libby muttered. She took the bag of cookies from me and peered inside.

"I'm afraid so," I said. "Is it possible Penny could really be . . . gone?"

"Oh, she's dead, all right," Vivian said, surprisingly blunt. "No sense pussyfooting around that. We have a suicide note."

"Penny left a note?"

"She sent it by UPS. She said she planned to end it all. We gave it to the police months ago, but they didn't believe it had come from Penny. Today's discovery should end their doubts, don't you think?"

"Well, I—Vivian, I'm terribly sorry."

Vivian stroked the cat in her arms. "It's for the best, I suppose. Penny was an unhappy person from a very early age. For years, our mother devoted herself to pleasing Penny, but she was never satisfied."

A state trooper slogged up to Libby's side of the minivan and bent to look inside at me. He was very tall, and his chin strap seemed barely large enough to contain his strong jaw. "Miss Blackbird? You're free to go now. And thank you for your cooperation."

Libby perked up as if someone had waved smelling salts under her nose.

"Don't worry about my sister, Captain," she said, hastily swallowing a mouthful of cookie. "I'll look after her."

"I'm perfectly capable of looking after myself—"

"I'm not really a captain, Miss—uh?"

"I'm Libby." She dusted off some cookie crumbs and put out her hand at an angle that made it hard for the trooper to discern if he was meant to shake it or kiss it. My sister smiled brightly. "You have a very appealing aura. Has anyone ever told you that?"

While Libby made her next conquest, I threw off the blanket and climbed out of the minivan to stand with Vivian. Toby, the spaniel, crouched on the ground, watching us warily.

The smell of Vivian's truck was even worse close by, and I tried not to look into the cargo bed. But the deer inside was definitely dead, and just a quick glance told me there might be more dead animals under the plastic tarp, too.

Vivian made no explanation, and she seemed impervious to the smell. Instead, she tenderly cradled the little cat.

I said, "I'm very sorry for your loss, Vivian. Penny will be terribly missed."

"Not by anyone who spent more than five minutes in her presence." Vivian rubbed the little cat's head. The animal looked bleary-eyed and weak. "You know as well as I do, Nora, lamb, that my sister was no day at the beach."

"She had an artist's personality."

"Be careful, young lady, or you'll get yourself nominated for the eulogy."

I smiled, too. "This memorial polo match was a good way to celebrate her life."

"Well, it wasn't my idea," Vivian said. "My brother thought of it. Potty hates a funeral as much as I do. He'd rather be out shooting defenseless birds, but he insisted we needed to mark Penny's passing. For her public, of course. Certainly not for ourselves. And I didn't even plan to come down here today."

I refrained from glancing at her clothing. Her jumper hardly seemed appropriate for a polo match or a funeral. "No?"

"Goodness, no. I saw the police cars and assumed some poor soul got a car stuck in the mud. I only wanted to make sure no one was hurt. Now that Penny's dead, it doesn't make much difference if I watch a polo match, does it? All I can think about is the poor horses. Polo is such an exhausting game for them."

Vivian's concern for the animals certainly exceeded her feelings for her sister, I noted.

I tried to remember what I knew about the three Devine siblings. Potty was the oldest, Vivian the middle child, and Penny had been the baby—the pretty one with all the spunk and sparkle her brother and sister lacked. If I remembered correctly, their mother had whisked Penny off to Hollywood, essentially abandoning her other two children to help make Penny's movie career happen. I wondered if they harbored ill feelings toward their sister for capturing their mother's attention so completely.

I looked past Vivian's shoulder and spotted a police detective making his way toward us. He had already seen me, so there was no escape.

"Detective Bloom," I said. "It's been a long time."

"Miss Blackbird. May I have a word? Excuse us," he said curtly to Vivian, taking my arm.

There was no avoiding him, of course. His touch was familiar, and I knew that tone in his voice. Detective Benjamin Bloom and I had met nearly a year earlier when he investigated the murder of a dear friend of mine. At the time, both of us toyed with creating a more personal relationship, but that had ended abruptly in the fall. We hadn't spoken for months.

As he propelled me around the back of Libby's minivan, I said, "You should have let me introduce you. That was Vivian Devine."

"I'll get to her," Bloom said. "But she didn't find the body. You did."

"I wasn't alone at the time."

"I heard," he said shortly. "You're still seeing that criminal?"

"Detective—"

"It's none of my business, I know." He stopped short and released my arm. "But I'm sworn to protect the public. That includes you."

"I assume you were the one who had Michael arrested just now?"

"He's not under arrest. He's being questioned in this matter."

"This matter has nothing to do with him, and you know it."

Ben Bloom still looked like a teenager in a too-large black trench coat that hung on his lean frame like a crusader's cape, which I had decided long ago was no accident. He was the kind of cop who liked to think he was a superhero. But his thick brown hair and soft brown eyes combined with a callow kind of awkwardness to give him the air of a kid on a first date rather than that of an experienced cop.

He checked his watch with purpose. "I'm sure Mick Abruzzo knows how to make a few hours fly by in a jail cell. Maybe it'll give him time to think over his current situation."

"Situation?" I asked.

"Hasn't he told you? About the latest Abruzzo family feud?"

I knew things weren't peaches and cream among the various branches of Michael's family. But the dynamics of the Abruzzo clan had always been an off-limits topic between us. I relied on the newspapers to keep me up-to-date. Lately, I knew the family was at odds over the shooting death of

Michael's uncle, Lou Pescara, by federal agents, not to mention the disappearance of Little Carmine Pescara. Little Carm was presumed dead by just about everyone, but I had seen him with my own eyes, happily ensconced in his own restaurant and Jet Ski rental business in the Caribbean. Thanks to Michael, the boy had been freed from life in a crime family.

Most of the family presumed Michael had killed Little Carm. Apparently, so did the police.

"You'll get nothing out of me, Detective," I said blandly. "Until I have a lawyer present."

He shot me a look at last, exasperated. "You're not a suspect, Nora. Whoever you found didn't die of natural causes. This is no time for joking around."

"I already told the officer what we saw. And I must admit I wasn't very observant. I fainted, you know."

"I heard." He hesitated, then asked, "Are you okay now?"

"Yes, thank you."

The air between us hummed with unspoken tension, and I found myself thinking of a kiss we'd shared in a moment of temporary insanity. I felt a blush rise to my face. "You look well, Ben."

He gave me a closer inspection, also. "You look good, too, Nora. Very pretty." He glanced from my suit to my boots, but refrained from remarking on them. "I know you told Officer Harding what you saw. But I hope you have more useful information to share."

"Such as?"

"You know these people. Maybe you can help us understand what's going on here today."

"It's a polo match for charity."

"And some kind of memorial for a movie star," he prodded. "A movie star who maybe isn't dead yet."

"You think the hand is Penny Devine's?"

"We don't know yet." He sighed and rubbed his hair with one hand like a sleepy kid trying to fix a bed head. "The crime scene's completely contaminated. It's going to take a lot of work to figure this one out. We'll send the hand—the arm—whatever—to the coroner's lab for testing. But already her brother's kicking up a fuss. He's demanding his sister's remains immediately. He's yelling at my superior right now."

"You're the police. You can do what you like, right?"

"Normally, we'd send the hand for tests and get results in a couple of days. But those egomaniacs in our local morgue are on some kind of a walkout."

"Oh, heavens, I'd heard about that!" Various employees were on strike in some suburban communities, thanks to a political scandal.

"We don't know when they'll be back to work. So we have to count on the family for a preliminary identification." Bloom swung around and took another look at Vivian, who was talking to Libby. "That's the sister, you say? Is she as loco as her brother? Think she'd be capable of making an ID?"

"She seems comfortable with the possibility that the hand is her sister's." I decided not to say more.

But Bloom caught a change in my tone, and he looked at me sharply.

"It's a strange family," I said. "A little eccentric."

"No surprise there." He shoved his hands into the pockets of his raincoat. "I haven't met one of these Main Line dynasties yet that isn't full of maniacs."

"Vivian's not a maniac."

"You know that for a fact?"

"She's—okay, I might as well tell you. They're my mother's cousins."

His eyes widened. "You're related to these people?"

"We haven't been close, but I've known them all my life."

"No shit. Did you know Penny?"

"A little. After she left town for the movie business, she returned only a few times. I remember she came to my grandfather Blackbird's funeral. I know her siblings better."

"What can you tell me about Vivian?"

"She's Penny's older sister. That's her truck parked over there. The one that smells so awful." When Bloom turned to look, I said, "Her brother, Potty, is an executive with the family pharmaceutical company. It's the family trade."

Bloom continued to squint at the disgusting truck. "What's Vivian's story?"

"She's an animal lover. To be candid, I think she devoted herself to animals, not humans. She hasn't had many friends, as far as I know, and she never married."

"Any history of family squabbles?"

"Doesn't every family squabble?"

"Not to the point of dismemberment."

"Don't start thinking one of her siblings killed Penny. That's ridiculous. They're ancient."

"I've got to start somewhere. Look, I'm going to need more info about your wacky relatives. Call me tonight." He fumbled in his coat pockets and coolly handed over a card printed with various phone numbers. "We have a lot to talk about."

## Chapter Four

*L*ibby drove me to Blackbird Farm, blathering the whole way. She talked about Penny Devine at length, even quoted some famous lines from *Suffer the Storm* until I stopped listening. I finally tuned in again when she said, "As if we don't have enough troubles already, now we've got Emma to worry about!"

I forgot about the thoughts that tumbled around in my head, and finally tried to focus on Libby's latest rant. "We have to worry about Em? She hasn't been drinking. I thought she looked pretty good."

"Of course she looks good! That's what an active sex life can do for a woman! She's walking proof of the benefits of estrogen surges."

"So what's the problem?"

"You heard her phone call! What is she doing?"

"Libby, I'm sure what we heard was nothing more than—"

"Than Emma making appointments to see men! Late at night! Alone! For money!"

"Calm down. Emma may have a healthy libido, but she wouldn't do anything—well, tacky."

"Oh, no?"

"No. Of course not. Look, don't blow a simple phone call out of proportion. She was probably just joking."

We arrived at the farm, and Libby left Lucy dozing in the backseat while she came inside to collect the rest of her family. With a great martyr's intake of air, she gathered her courage and went down to the basement to tell the twins it was time to pack up their fetal pig and go home.

While Libby negotiated with her mad scientists, I talked to Rawlins for a few minutes in the kitchen. At seventeen, he had finally gotten through the long period of wearing black clothes and facial piercings. Now he could hold an intelligent conversation with an adult, if necessary. And he seemed surprisingly comfortable babysitting his infant brother, Maximus.

Maybe because of losing my own baby, I hadn't bonded with Maximus as I had with my other nephews. Rawlins seemed uncannily aware of my reluctance to hold the baby, and he managed not to drop his little brother while dealing himself a hand of playing cards.

I fondled the sleeping baby's hair. "How's the poker coming?"

"I think I'm ready to play a hand. Want to try me?"

I gave my nephew a kiss on the cheek. "I'll wait until you have some experience. When I clean out your bank account, I want to do it with a clear conscience. Are the twins under control?"

"I didn't have to break out the straitjackets. They're busy playing with their new pet. Only Harcourt and Hilton could love a dead animal, right? You okay? Mom called on her cell to tell me about Thing."

"Thing?"

"You know, the hand." He held his own hand up to show me and wiggled all his fingers. "Pretty gross, Aunt Nora."

"Very gross." I sat down at the table.

"Oh, and your editor called, too. Mr. Rosencrantz?"

"Stan Rosenstatz. What did he have to say?"

Rawlins screwed up his face to remember. "He wanted to know if you'd call the city desk. Something about contributing to a news story. Does that make sense?"

I nodded. Of course, the story of Penny Devine's death was going to hit the media very big. The *Philadelphia Intelligencer* didn't often have the inside track on breaking stories, but this time the reporters had an eyewitness to the whole thing—me. But I was also connected to the family, which made me hesitate. What were the journalistic rules in this case? Did I have to talk to my fellow reporters?

While Rawlins rocked the baby, I picked up the phone and called Stan to ask him.

"Of course you don't have to answer their questions," my editor said. "But I figured maybe you'd want to contribute to the story. You know, to give yourself a little career boost."

Judging by Stan's tone, I guessed my career in journalism was once again in need of such a boost. I'd been hired by the previous owner of the paper, and lately I was receiving more and more hints that the industry cutbacks might soon include me, too. Nobody's job was safe anymore.

I thanked Stan and hung up, still not sure I wanted to talk to the press—even if it meant getting my byline on the front page. After I put the receiver down, I realized I should have asked Stan if there was a company policy about returning bribes. I had Potty's envelope in my handbag.

Half a minute later, Libby rushed up the basement stairs, looking pale. "Harcourt and Hilton say they're at a crucial moment in their dissection. They can't possibly leave the pig right now." She took a handkerchief from her purse and pressed it to her mouth. Then she said, "Honestly, I wonder if they were switched at birth."

Rawlins said, "Only if the Dahmer family is missing someone."

Libby gulped. "Nora, they want to know if your severed hand showed any signs of freezer burn."

Although I should have been appalled, I found myself seriously contemplating the question. If the hand indeed belonged to Penny Devine, there was a good chance she'd been dead for nearly a year. And where had the hand been for those months? I frowned, trying to remember some details of our grisly discovery. "I'm not sure. The flesh was wrinkled and—I guess kind of spotted."

Rawlins grinned. "The twins are gonna love that information. What else? Any claw marks? Signs of werewolf attack? Maybe a few maggots?"

"Rawlins, please!" Libby gasped and dabbed her forehead. "You see what I have to put up with, Nora? Rawlins is bad enough, but the twins can hardly wait until summer. They're going to forensic camp, you know. They've been promised a look at a human cadaver."

Rawlins began to slide Max into his hooded sweatshirt. "I wonder if every well-meaning guy who donates his body to science really knows what he's getting into. I wouldn't want the monsters to get their grubby hands on me—even in death."

I said, "Should I be worried about what they're doing in my basement?"

Rawlins laughed. "Wait till you see what they cooked in your frying pan!"

Recovered, Libby stuffed her handkerchief away. "Really, Nora, you should enjoy having your nephews around a little more. They love you so dearly."

"Forget it, Libby. Drive them home. I refuse to take them off your hands."

"How about just until tomorrow night?" she wheedled, gathering the baby from Rawlins. "I need to get started on the wedding plans!"

I groaned. "Libby—"

"I have brilliant creative ideas bursting to get out of my head. You'll thank me! Just keep the boys for the rest of the weekend."

"Out of the question."

"Okay, okay! I'll come back first thing in the morning, I promise." She fished out her car keys and edged for the door. "Come on, Rawlins. Nora, order a pizza for the twins, will you? They're starving."

"Better hurry," Rawlins advised with a grin. "If the pizza doesn't come in time, lock yourself someplace safe and call 911."

I considered dragging Libby back inside by her hair and forcing her to take the twins with her. But she was remarkably quick for a woman who carried a few extra pounds. She beat me to the driveway by a good fifteen yards.

Rawlins waved from behind the wheel as the minivan spun gravel and roared for the highway.

I went back inside and dialed the number for pizza delivery. As the phone rang, I heard creepy laughter coming from the basement. "Better make it two," I told the pizza shop.

While waiting for the delivery, I tried telephoning Detective Bloom for the promised talk. He didn't answer, so I left a voice mail. Then I scrubbed out my sauté pan. Whatever the twins had heated in it, I didn't want to know. It smelled like eggs left in the sun.

Or the back of Vivian Devine's truck.

I squirted more detergent into the sink, thinking of the dead animals that Vivian kept covered up in the truck. What was that all about? Why was the sweet old lady who gave out cookies driving around in a Deathmobile?

Thinking about death in general, I segued to the shooting of Michael's uncle Lou Pescara. It had been a terrible night for Michael, who'd loved his uncle despite the crimes the man had committed.

Eventually my thoughts strayed to my own loss—the baby I'd carried for less than three months before miscarrying on a night that was among the worst of my life. Since then, I'd alternately tried to shove all thoughts of that lost child out of my mind or found myself listening to a whispering inner voice. It had been my fault that the baby died. I should have been more careful. I should have protected my child.

I had long wanted children of my own. The need tugged at my heart so hard it sometimes hurt. It was Michael's wish, too, to have kids. I knew we were both trying to do the same thing—create a family because the ones we'd been born with hadn't fit the bill. That desire was perhaps what had first drawn us together. And since then, I often felt as if we kept coming back to each other because a happy future with children was what we both wanted most.

But with Raphael Braga in town, things were even more complicated.

Michael phoned around seven with apologies that he wouldn't be home in time for dinner.

"Are you still with the police?" I sat on my bed, having changed into jeans and a sweater. I pulled my loafers on as we spoke.

"No, they turned me loose about an hour ago. Are you okay?"

"I'm fine."

"You talked with Detective Gloom, I hear. Did he ask you for a date?"

I heard the amusement in Michael's voice. "Detective Bloom was pretty much all business."

"Did he warn you about me?"

"Yes," I said. "You're still America's Most Wanted."

"And he'll never quit hoping he can be the one to send me to jail again."

My heart contracted. "Michael—"

"Sorry," he said at once. Then, "He's got a thing for you."

"Not anymore."

"No?"

"Today he seemed more interested in the Devine family."

"Good thing. His department's had budget cuts. And his boss doesn't like him. If he doesn't take care of business, he might lose his job."

I said, "Where did you hear that?"

"Around." Michael had ways of learning inside information that sometimes put Detective Bloom to shame. "He's got to prove his worth. And fast. So it's no wonder he's concentrating on the case. Did he ask you a bunch of questions?"

"About the hand we found? Yes. Did you hear anything about it? Do the police have any theories?"

"Plenty. They all seem to involve a dead movie star. They assume we found what's left of Penny Devine."

"Michael," I said slowly, "when we found her—it—whatever—did you notice any—well, freezer burn?"

A short silence. "You're kidding, right?"

"It's just a question the twins asked."

He laughed. "Consider the source!"

"It got me thinking. . . ."

"Nora, sweetheart, please, this is a case for the police to solve. I think you can safely forget about it, okay?"

"But—"

"Don't do this to yourself. Let the police take care of it. Hell, you'll be giving Gloom some job security."

"I thought I might be helpful."

"The person you need to help most right now is yourself. Take the night off, why don't you? Have you had anything to eat?"

I hadn't been able to choke down the pizza I'd ordered for the twins. "The idea of food isn't very appealing since our afternoon discovery."

"I hear you. Well, get into the bathtub and read a book. Relax. I'll be home soon, but I've got some things to take care of first."

I thought of Ben Bloom's warning that the Abruzzos were having some family problems. "Anything I should know about?"

"Not unless you're interested in changing the oil in a couple of cars. I'm sending some vehicles down to the muscle car auction this weekend."

"That's what you're doing? Working on cars?"

"And a few other things. Spending the afternoon with your pal Bloom put me behind the eight ball."

Michael ran several businesses now, and all of them required his frequent supervision. His chain of gas stations, Gas N Grub, were popping up all over Pennsylvania, New Jersey and Delaware so fast, I couldn't keep track of them all. But there was always more happening behind the scenes than he wanted to share with me.

"All right," I said, unwilling to ask more questions. "See you later."

"Before midnight," he promised.

I shut off the phone, but it rang in my hand again.

"Sweetie!" Lexie Paine cried when I answered. "Have you had dinner yet? How about a girls' night out?"

I smiled. Just hearing my dearest friend's voice was enough to lift my spirits. "I'm babysitting Libby's twins tonight."

"Is your life insurance paid up?" She gave a raucous laugh. "Forget that. Listen, I'm in my car," she reported. "I met with a whole convent of nuns this afternoon, and I'm on my way home. How about I pick up some take-out and stop by your place?"

"Nuns?" I asked. "Lex, have you had a spiritual awakening?"

"I have it every morning when they ring that opening bell at the stock exchange. Can I come over, or not?"

"Of course. Michael's out, and I can lock the twins in the basement if they make you nervous."

"I'll be there in fifteen."

It was more like half an hour before the headlights of Lexie's sleek BMW flashed on my kitchen windows. She sailed into the house dressed in red and bearing a pizza box.

"I got the works," she reported, handing over the warm container. "Even extra cheese because you need to put some meat on those bones, sweetie."

I kissed her cheek. "You're so thoughtful. And look—you put on your red dress for the nuns. I take it you weren't auditioning for a place among them?"

"Not yet. They're my clients." She slipped an elegant black coat from around her shoulders and tossed it across the back of a kitchen chair. Her long-sleeved, high-necked dress, the color of claret but beautifully designed to downplay her sex appeal without blotting it out entirely, was a ladylike masterpiece. Her black hair was smoothed into her usual ponytail. Her makeup was light and perfect.

Lexie said, "I manage a stock portfolio for the old dears, and I make a pilgrimage to the convent every six months to report to them."

"I thought nuns took a vow of poverty."

"But the church hasn't. And there's more money in religion than any-thing else, darling."

I had already opened a bottle of pinot gris, and I poured a glass for my friend. "What do nuns invest in? Am I allowed to ask?"

"I'm not allowed to tell. But let's just say they take a dim view of risk and prefer their chips bright blue. Oh, thanks, sweetie, that's just what I need. Good Lord!"

She grabbed my hand and stared at the ring on my finger. "My God, is that an ice cube straight from your freezer?"

"It's my engagement ring," I said. "Michael's idea of a love token."

"You weren't wearing it when I saw you on Monday. Did he just propose? Again?"

"We talked it over on our vacation. I haven't gotten accustomed to wearing it yet."

"No kidding." She was still turning my hand this way and that so the facets of the diamond sparkled in the light from the chandelier over our heads. "It must be like carrying around an asteroid on your finger." She skewered me with a closer look that communicated her true concern for my well-being. "Sweetie, are you happy?"

"Very. I think it's right for both of us."

Lexie gave me a swift hug. "I hope so, too, darling. After what you've been through, you deserve something truly wonderful."

My throat closed abruptly as I hugged her back. She had been my best ally from elementary school, through college and during the long, punishing years of my marriage to Todd. Even when he'd hit rock bottom of his drug addiction, she'd stuck by me, helping me cope, allowing me to vent, enabling me to get back on my feet after his death. Most recently, after my miscarriage, she'd finagled two weeks' worth of time aboard her mother's yacht for Michael and me. If not for Lexie, I might have lost my mind a dozen times. Someday I planned to do something good for her in return.

"Thanks, Lex. I appreciate your support."

"Let me guess." She took the point of my chin in her hand so she could look me square in the eye. "Your sisters disapprove?"

"Libby does. Emma thinks Michael's risking his life."

Lexie laughed. "The Blackbird curse, of course! Is Michael worried?"

"Not a bit. But," I said, "he had a car accident this morning. Not serious, but enough to send him to the hospital for a few stitches."

My friend linked her arm with mine. "Sweetie, if any man can survive the Blackbird curse, surely it's Michael Abruzzo. He has more lives than a wily cat, don't you think? A little fender bender won't put a dent in your knight's armor. Wait, you're not the one who's worried, are you?"

"No," I said at once. "Well, not much."

"Sweetie, that curse is just an old wives' tale."

"Right," I said. "I know that. It's completely silly. I'll only make myself crazy thinking about it."

"That's the spirit. I'm a firm believer in the positive effects of denial. Let's have some pizza, shall we? I'm starved."

"I've laid a fire in the library. Want to have our supper there?"

She gathered up the plates and napkins I'd already prepared. "Lead on."

I'd inherited the whistling caverns of Blackbird Farm when my parents ran off with all the family trust funds they could scare up, and I was still reeling from the winter heating bills. Built over two hundred years ago and added onto whenever one of my ancestors felt the need for a little more elbow room, the house had started out as a pretty good example of grand Georgian architecture, but now resembled the kind of farmhouse typical of Bucks County—a pile of fieldstone that rambled in several directions, all under a leaky slate roof and surrounded by giant oak trees that threatened to crash through the dormers during the slightest thunderstorm.

But the library was positively cozy with its book-lined shelves, a cheerful fire and the comfortable leather furniture that had belonged to my husband years ago. I tossed a newspaper onto the coffee table and put the pizza box on top of it and the bottle of wine within easy reach.

"Tell me more about your nuns."

Lexie kicked off her shoes and sat on the sofa. "They're all darlings, of course, but sticklers about their money. They rake me over the coals. They don't want to support any industry that damages the environment or sends Third World tyrants to drink champagne at the Cannes Film Festival. All very politically correct. I'm always reassuring them that they're not sending flammable baby pajamas to poor neighborhoods in India."

"Who would do such a thing?"

"You'd be surprised, sweetie." Lexie slipped open the pizza box and dug in. "I have to spin the truth a bit to keep them happy."

I sat opposite her in the wing chair and took one sip of wine. "You're lying to nuns?"

"In business, truth is a matter of perception. If I didn't bend the facts a little, they'd take their investments down the street to some money-grubbing bastard with fewer principles than I have."

"Lex," I said, "you sound like your father."

She stopped short of taking a bite of pizza. "Lord help me, you're right. Have I become a stone-cold bitch?"

"Of course not."

"I need a life, don't I?" She picked off a mushroom and nibbled it. "Something besides the NASDAQ to give me perspective. I guess that's you, sweetie. There's nothing like a good girlfriend to set a person straight."

"Hm," I said. Despite the flippancy of her remark, I decided to take it seriously. "Is that why you're here? To set me straight?"

"Well," she admitted, "I thought you looked a little wan on Monday. Not like a woman who'd spent two weeks relaxing in the Caribbean sun."

On Monday, I'd heard Raphael was coming to town. But I said, "The Caribbean was wonderful. Just what the doctor ordered."

"But?"

"But all good things must come to an end." I smiled. "Guess who I saw today?"

"Who?"

"Crewe Dearborne."

She raised a cool eyebrow. "Sweetie, you're not going to be one of those women who gets engaged and thinks everybody in the world should be similarly delirious with matrimonial joy? It's so tiresome."

"He's crazy about you, Lex."

"Crewe Dearborne is crazy about food. Now, I appreciate a man who loves his work, but that doesn't mean I want to throw myself into his arms and discuss china patterns. Have you chosen your china, by the way? I'd love to see Michael in Tiffany's. Promise you'll let me tag along to watch." She took a healthy bite of pizza and dragged a long string of melted cheese away from her mouth with her fingers. "Mmm. Delish. Have a piece."

"Don't change the subject," I said. "Crewe is a kind, thoughtful and in-telligent person. I think he has a heart worth exploring."

"I've put away my crampons and my spelunking equipment for good. No exploring for me."

Lexie had inherited her father's financial empire at a very young age and managed it with expertise, guts and style, so that it was now one of the most respected in the nation. She was a community leader, the chair of the museum board and a charitable virago. But the sexual abuse she'd experienced at the hands of a cousin when she was a young teenager had scarred her in ways she still hadn't been able to overcome. She avoided men the way most women avoided saturated fat.

I wanted to help, of course. But I knew better than to force the issue.

So I said, "I saw Crewe at the polo match. And you won't believe what happened."

"Tell, tell."

I described how Michael and I found the severed hand on the grounds of the Devine estate, and Lexie nearly dropped a gooey slice of pizza in her lap.

"You're kidding!"

I told her about Detective Bloom, Michael's nonarrest and how I'd spoken with Vivian Devine, too.

"How gruesome!"

"It was pretty shocking," I admitted.

"When will the police know for sure if it's Penny's hand?"

"I don't know. There's some kind of strike at the morgue."

"Surely Penny Devine would get the red-carpet treatment, even in death. I bet they rush the results. That whole suicide disappearance theory didn't entirely convince the police, right? A lot more people will want to know if she's really dead or not."

"What people?"

"Nora, you really must start reading the financial pages. You know about Devine Pharmaceuticals, right?"

"Of course," I said.

She cocked one eye at me. "About their new product?"

"Uh . . ."

"It's a new drug for erectile dysfunction. Like Viagra, only it lasts a whole weekend and doesn't have any side effects. Good grief, every late-

night comedian in the country has been talking about it for weeks! It's called MaxiMan."

"And it's a Devine product?"

"Well, yes and no. There are patent issues. Another company came up with something very similar. Lawsuits are flying. Devine is thinking of buying the other company, which would make the patent problem disappear, and MaxiMan could hit a pharmacy near you and make everybody rich right away. But the board of directors of Devine Pharmaceuticals is divided on the buyout subject, because some directors think they can win the lawsuit and take all the prize money for themselves. They've been waiting for Penny Devine to reappear so she can break the tie vote. Half the board believes she's still alive."

"Penny Devine was on the board of directors? What did she do for the company? Tap-dance on the boardroom table?"

"Even movie stars can serve on corporate boards. It's her family's company, and besides, if it hadn't been for Penny, Devine Pharmaceuticals would have gone bust forty years ago. She used a lot of her *Suffer the Storm* paycheck to bail out the company."

"So they put her on the board?"

Lexie laughed. "That's what makes the world go round, sweetie. She's probably the youngest person on that board, too. This group is especially geriatric. They all act like electricity is a newfangled invention that can't be trusted. I know the CEO, and I hear he serves Metamucil at board meetings. Claims it calms everyone down. They have terrible fights."

"Why doesn't he ask the troublemakers to resign?"

"Because together they own massive amounts of stock."

"Like Potty, you mean?"

"He's the chairman of the board, and the chief nutcase. He throws jelly beans when the fighting starts. With all their squabbling, it's a wonder a company can function like that in the modern business world."

"I imagine pharmaceuticals would be a pretty cutting-edge business, too."

"Yep. New developments happen all the time. Devine must have some really good scientists behind the scenes. Or else they've been very, very lucky, considering."

"Lucky up until now, you mean." I found myself frowning into my wineglass. "How would Penny vote if she were alive? And who was on the opposite side of the argument?"

Lexie grasped my meaning at once. "You mean, who has a motive to kill her?"

"I assume the purchase of another pharmaceutical company means millions of dollars in somebody's pocket."

"Maybe billions. Definitely a reason to kill somebody." She took another bite of pizza and spoke around it. "Nora, you're not getting mixed up in this murder, are you?"

"Heavens, no. I'm curious, that's all."

"Me, too," Lexie admitted. "If that was Penny's hand you found, I'd like to know not only who bumped her off—"

"But who was furious enough to cut her up afterwards?"

Lexie abruptly put down her slice of pizza. "Now I understand why you haven't been eating."

"Have another glass of wine?"

She shook her head, applying her napkin to her mouth. "I still have to drive home. Or do you want me to spend the night? Should you be alone this evening after finding—well, pieces of Penny?"

"I'm not alone. The twins are downstairs. And Michael will be back soon."

She nodded, studiously wiping her fingers on the napkin. "He moved in?"

"You didn't notice the fishing rods on the back porch? Yes, he moved in."

"Well, that's nice."

I eyed her, reading deeper into my friend's thoughts than she intended. "Is there something on your mind?"

"Is there something on yours?"

I blinked, surprised. "Like what?"

Lexie busied her hands by closing the pizza box, but gave up trying to keep her concern to herself. "Sweetie, you know I love you like a sister."

"Lex—"

"And I like Michael, I really do. He's been wonderful for you. We were all so worried after Todd died."

The months after my husband's death had been a very dark time. I didn't respond to Lexie, just remembered how terrible I had felt—as if I'd failed Todd, failed saving him from the drugs and the life that got him killed in the end.

Lexie sat forward. "You fought Todd's addiction every way you knew how, and I know his death nearly killed you, too. And when you moved out of the city to this—to the farm, we were even more terrified that you—well, that we couldn't help you out of your depression. But Michael came along, and I give him credit—he really brought you back to life."

Quietly, I said, "You're probably right."

"Now, though, I wonder if maybe he's the—what is it called? The Pilot Light Lover? The one who lights your fire again so you can try other men?"

"Lex—"

"Nora, you're my dearest friend, and I respect your intelligence. If he's the man of your dreams, I'll shut up and never say another word against him. But you've only known him a few months—"

"A year," I corrected.

"A year, then," Lexie acknowledged. "Is that enough time? To figure out if you're still in that romantic-infatuation, lusty stage? Or have you had the time to progress into a truly mature relationship?"

"This? From you?"

She flushed. "Just because I choose not to dive into the pool doesn't mean I don't know how to swim. Is Michael really the one? Nora, do you have the same—well, family values? Or are the two of you still trying to make each other into what you need most?"

"What do you think I need from Michael?"

"He can protect you," Lexie said. "Your father is an idiot, and Todd was the loosest cannon on the pirate ship, but Michael is strong—stronger than you really need, perhaps. He thinks like a man in another century. Whatever it takes, he's going to protect you and—listen, I'm not saying he wants to control you exactly, but maybe it will come to that someday."

I didn't say anything.

"Have you had enough time to figure out who you really are, sweetie? What you truly want your life to be? You just started an interesting career, but you haven't had a chance to explore what your work is all about or where it can take you."

"It takes time."

Lexie nodded and considered me for another moment. "I know. But this mystery about Penny Devine. Have you wondered why it intrigues you so much?"

"I'm curious," I said. Then, "But maybe I'm putting off thinking about my own situation."

Lexie reached for my hand. "Maybe so."

I put my wineglass down.

She squeezed me. "Darling, I don't want to hurt your feelings. But I know you're vulnerable right now. Losing the baby must have been awful. I'm glad I could help a little by letting you get away for a while, but that wasn't nearly enough. Maybe it's time to slow down. To pull yourself together before you take the next big leap."

"Thanks, Lex," I said. "I appreciate how much you care."

"But?"

I shook my head. "No buts."

"What does Michael say?"

"We—I haven't been able to talk about it. He's—I love him, Lex. I really do. I don't want to hurt him."

"He's strong. And he's smart. He'll listen."

There was more, of course. And I could talk about Raphael Braga with Lexie.

But we heard a noise in the hall, and suddenly Michael was there in the doorway. Still in his coat, his car keys in one hand, a pizza box balanced in the other. "Who'll listen?" he asked. "To what?"

Lexie got to her feet in a flash and crossed the room to him. "Sweetie!" she cried. "How nice to see you looking so tanned. Did you have a lovely cruise?"

She kissed him on the cheek, and helped him out of his jacket. Michael thanked her for arranging our vacation for us.

"What happened to your chin?" Lexie asked.

"Little accident," Michael replied, looking rueful. "Nothing to worry about."

I kissed him gently on the mouth and took the warm pizza box and put it on top of Lexie's offering. He and Lexie talked, and I poured him a glass of wine, wondering how much he'd heard. He betrayed nothing, just relaxed, ate some pizza and laughed while Lexie told stories of cruising on her mother's yacht.

I listened with only half an ear. The rest of my attention strayed back to what Lexie had said. That perhaps our family values were different. That I was using anything that came along to divert my thoughts from exactly the questions I should be carefully thinking over. That solving the puzzle of Penny Devine's disappearance might be more savory to me than the conundrum my own life had become.

And I found myself thinking about Raphael, too.

# Chapter Five

Later when Lexie had gone home, I stowed all the leftover pizza in the fridge and put away the groceries Michael had brought—staples and toothpaste and a lot of food obviously meant to keep the twins happy. He was the one who braved the basement to make sure Harcourt and Hilton planned on taking a break from their experiments. When he came up again, he reported the twins were sleeping in their dungeon.

Then, when we were alone upstairs, Michael tried to talk. "Nora," he began.

I knew the tone of his voice. But I locked the bedroom door and turned off the lights. I took off my clothes and pushed him down on the bed. He resisted for about ten seconds, then gave in and let me unfasten the buttons on his shirt.

We didn't speak at all. We didn't even kiss. I trailed my lips down his chest until he caught my hair in his hands to stop me. But I unsnapped his jeans and slipped my hand inside first and followed with my mouth, and he surrendered with a noise that never quite made it out of his throat.

After that, we wrestled. Feverish, we were quick at first, writhing and pushing until finally he was six fathoms deep inside me and we both lost our heads.

We had been to many dark places before, but that was perhaps the darkest of all. Only this time it wasn't Michael who took charge, but a woman I didn't know. A woman who seemed to want to use my body—and his—to avoid thinking about anything else.

In the end, exhausted and maybe a little frightened by what we'd done, we said nothing, but slept pressed back-to-back against each other. In the darkness, I listened to Michael breathe for a long time. I knew I should have opened up to him, tried to figure out what I was feeling. But part of me was afraid of what I might discover once the sex was over and we had to find out what lay beneath it.

In the morning, I woke in the tangled bedclothes and listened to Michael in the shower. Usually he sang, but this morning he was quiet.

I slipped on my bathrobe and went downstairs to make coffee, not eager to start this particular day without benefit of caffeine. Or breakfast. I was starving.

Intent on cinnamon toast, I went into the kitchen and stifled a scream.

"Don't sneak up on me like that!" Libby cried, spinning around as if menaced by a psychopathic killer. "Oh, I thought you were the twins."

"Libby, what the hell are you doing here? At this hour?"

My sister heaved an enormous bulletin board up onto the kitchen counter. She wore a lime green velour exercise ensemble that concealed the fact that she never exercised. She had pulled her hair up in a clip with little stars poking out of her head, making her look as perky as a cheerleader.

"I've started the wedding plans! I need peace and quiet to kick-start my creative process!"

"Why does it have to be my peace and quiet?" I demanded.

"Nora, your nuptial bliss is my fervent desire. I need to concentrate, to focus all my energy on making you happy."

"You can't concentrate at home?"

"It's bedlam at my house. Rawlins spent the night playing poker with his friends and making a mess of everything. Lucy's in one of her moods. So I fed Maximus and rushed over here to get started. See? This bulletin board will soon become the centerpiece of your life."

I didn't look at the blank bulletin board. "The twins are downstairs, in case you were wondering. Have you checked on them yet?"

"No." She stole an uneasy glance at the basement door. "I'm sure they're fine."

I could see she wasn't eager to find out what atrocities her homicidal offspring were contemplating. Neither was I. Without further discussion, I pulled out the toaster and found the loaf of raisin swirl bread Michael had brought home last night.

"If the truth be told," Libby said, coming clean, "I have a houseguest."

"Who?"

"My mother-in-law."

"Which one?" I plunked two slices of bread into the toaster and pushed the lever.

"Mary Marie. My second. The twins' grandmother. Which might explain a few things."

I reached for the coffeepot and tried to recall which of Libby's three mothers-in-law was Mary Marie. "Is she the golfing one? Or the one who likes vodka gimlets?"

"Neither. She's the clean one."

"The one with the braid around her head like a Swedish masseuse?"

"Exactly." Libby sent me a dark look. "As soon as she arrived last night, she started climbing around on chairs and taking down all my draperies. Today she's delivering them to the dry cleaner, and then she's going to wash all my windows."

"Well, that's rather nice, don't you think?"

"Nora, the last time she visited, she refinished all my hardwood floors—on her hands and knees! I nearly broke my ankle when I slipped on the fresh coat of polyurethane she put down in the dining room!"

"Libby, it's really very generous of her to—"

"It isn't generous. It's obsessive-compulsive! She's a neat freak! And she's making me feel like a positive slob!"

"She won't stay forever," I soothed. "And when she leaves, your windows will sparkle."

"It's not like I haven't washed my own windows, you know." She glowered at me. "I do them every spring. Well, every other spring, maybe. So why should I be made to feel like I live in a pigsty by Mrs. Tidy?"

Libby wasn't the best housekeeper on the planet. But pointing that out might cause a sisterly meltdown. As the aroma of toasting raisin bread wafted up from the toaster, I filled the coffeepot with water from the tap. "Maybe a day or two of cleaning is a good thing."

"Day or two? She's going to stay for a week! So you can understand why I came over here this morning, can't you? Oh, get that look off your face. I won't stay overnight. This place is getting too crowded, anyway."

"Too crowded?"

"That's Emma's truck parked outside, right?"

I rushed to the door and yanked it open. Sure enough, Emma's pickup sat on the grass outside, one front tire leaning against the porch steps as if she'd cruised in and jumped out in a hurry. I closed the door with a bang I hoped was loud enough to be heard on the second floor. "Where is she?"

"Upstairs, I presume."

"Is she alone?"

Libby and I shared a glance. Of course Emma wasn't alone.

My toast popped.

I grabbed both slices and slapped them on separate plates. "I wonder what time she got in."

"You didn't hear her?"

"Uhm, no."

"She had an appointment at midnight, remember? You heard her on the phone."

Whatever Emma was up to this time, I was pretty sure I didn't want to hear about it. And I was equally sure Libby wanted all the details.

Libby opened her handbag and pulled out a package of multicolored pushpins. "Well, you can be sure I'm staying until she shows her face downstairs. I want to know who the cat dragged in last night. Meanwhile, we can start our plan!"

"Plan?"

"For your *wedding*, of course! Where is your mind these days?"

I refrained from screaming.

Libby said, "I might object to your choice of spouses, but I'm a firm believer in allowing people to make their own mistakes. Meanwhile, we might as well make your wedding picture perfect!"

The thought of Libby at the helm of my nuptials gave me the sensation of being strapped to the railing of the *Titanic*.

Full of enthusiasm, she went on. "As far as I'm concerned, the worst-case scenario is the traditional New Jersey Mafia wedding. And considering That Man's family, we run the risk of the full gamut of horrors—tight satin bridesmaids' gowns, big hair, and fistfights in the parking lot."

"But—"

"So, Nora, if we don't get cracking, you're liable to end up with a reception at one of those tacky Atlantic City banquet halls with a Frank Sinatra look-alike for a doorman."

"I don't think Michael wants—"

"Your last wedding was a disappointment, I must say. Hardly more than a blip on the social scene. Lovely, of course, but too small. This time, you can invite all our friends and family!" She had grabbed a stick of butter from the refrigerator and was lavishing a large smear of it on her slice of toast. "It could be the event of the year!"

I swallowed hard.

"First things first," Libby said firmly, pointing the stick of butter at me. "Vera Wang. The three of us should go to New York next week to scout out the dress possibilities. It's going to take some real effort to find a bridesmaid gown that will look good on Emma and stunning on me. What date have you set?"

"Actually—"

"It's best to be flexible about venues, of course. I'll call all the best reception sites and find out what's available. There's an inn in New Hope that would be perfect—they have two darling pet monkeys that wear little tuxedos for special occasions. Doesn't that sound adorable? But I'm not sure how many guests they can accommodate."

"We really haven't discussed—"

"Of course," she said, bustling around my kitchen, "if That Man of Yours is going to foot the bill, maybe I should find out if the Du Pont estate is available?"

"We're not getting married at the Du Pont estate."

Libby had found a bag of chocolate chips in the pantry and opened it. She sprinkled a dozen on top of her toast, then popped a few extra into her mouth. "We need to brainstorm! What about a destination wedding? That's really the cutting edge, you know. Hawaii? No, no, Bermuda! Oh, but you can't beat Paris. Maybe we should go to France to check out a few—"

"Libby," I said sharply enough to get her attention at last. "Stop right there."

I would rather endure Chinese water torture than allow my sister to plan my wedding.

She paused, the slice of toast halfway to her lips. "What?"

Faced with explaining that I wasn't ready to contemplate a marriage, let alone a huge ceremony and reception, I chickened out.

"What's the matter?" Libby came over and seized my hand, her brow squinched in sympathy. "Darling, he's not insisting on something ghastly, is he? Not—heaven, help us—not menu control?"

"Calm down," I said. "We haven't discussed anything yet."

"What a relief!" Libby heaved a sigh and clutched her heart. "For a moment, I had visions of rigatoni and pigs in a blanket! Surely you'd rather have trout, maybe with a nice champagne reduction? So classic!"

I rubbed my forehead. "It's too soon to be making these decisions."

"Oh, darling, I agree completely! We can't rush into anything. Decide in haste, repent in—well, later. What we need is a timeline! And that's why I brought the bulletin board—to create a schedule for planning the whole thing so we don't miss a single detail. General Schwarzkopf used this method during Desert Storm or something."

"You don't get it, Lib. I'm not ready to think about this yet. The wedding might be a long way off. And anyway, it's definitely going to be small."

She looked dismayed. "How small?"

"Very small. I think it's going to be very, very private."

"Why? Are you afraid your friends will be judgmental?"

"N-no. We're just the quiet types."

She stewed for a moment. "Maybe we should have some prewedding parties to get everyone accustomed to the idea of you married to a mob boss." Despite my choke, Libby cried, "That's it—I'll throw you a wedding shower!"

"Libby—"

Emma shuffled into the kitchen in riding breeches and a dirty sweatshirt, with socks on her feet and a yawn on her face. "What the hell is all the noise about? Libby, I could hear you all the way upstairs."

"Good morning!" Libby trilled. "You're just in time to help plan a wedding shower for Nora."

Emma scratched her stomach and blinked at me. With her hair standing out on her head, she looked like an electrocuted woodpecker.

I said, "Is that a love bite on your neck?"

She rubbed the spot and grinned. "You should see the one on my butt. Is there any coffee?"

"In a minute," Libby promised around a mouthful of toast. "Meanwhile, you can tell us who's upstairs in your bed. The man who telephoned for the midnight appointment?"

"Nah. Somebody else." She waggled her eyebrows.

"Oh, Em," I said. "You didn't."

"Polo players make the best lovers," Emma replied. "They play hard and walk away with a smile."

My heart began to pound. "Please tell me you didn't bring Raphael Braga into my home."

"What's it to you who I sleep with?" Emma threw herself into a chair, legs splayed. "At least I don't make the kind of noise you two were making last night. Jeez, Nora."

"What kind of noise?" Libby asked.

"Big noise," Emma reported.

"Vocal expression can be an exciting part of lovemaking, you know. I once knew a Nepalese gentleman who chanted—"

"You have to get Raphael out of here," I said. "I can't have him in the house, Em."

"Raphael Braga?" Libby used her forefinger to wipe a dribble of chocolate from her lower lip. "Isn't he that handsome one from Brazil?"

"He can't be here." My voice went up an octave. "It's important, Em!"

"What side of the bed did you wake up on? Or isn't there any bed left after last night?"

"Please, Emma. If Raphael is here, will you please, please get rid of him right away?"

She looked at me at last and frowned. "What's wrong with you?"

"I don't want him here!"

"He isn't here," she said shortly. "I brought—oh, here he is."

Into my kitchen walked an extraordinarily handsome young man. He wore low-slung jeans and a tight white undershirt, which defined the masculine curves of his body in a way that brought a whimper to Libby's throat. His smile was bashful. He had tousled blond hair, deep dark eyes that pooled with shy sensuality and a generous, supple mouth that seemed to be permanently smiling. The rest of the inventory was the stuff of female fantasy: a strong throat, broad shoulders, sinewy arms, narrow hips and long, long legs. He was the perfect blend of Tarzan and Bambi, standing in my kitchen.

"Hello."

"This is Ignacio," Emma said. "He doesn't speak English. Which comes in surprisingly handy, let me tell you."

"Good morning," I said to him, hoping my thundering heartbeat couldn't be heard by everyone. "Would you like some coffee?"

"Hello," he said again, still smiling.

Truly, I was sure I'd never been in the presence of a man so beautiful. His eyelashes were like velvet. His hands looked strong and sensual. For a moment, I thought Libby might have suffered a stroke. She still hadn't blinked.

Emma patted the chair next to hers, and Ignacio slipped into it, beaming her the kind of adoring gaze a beagle puppy might give its master. I noticed his perfectly tanned neck sported, not one, but two vicious-looking love bites.

I got up, poured several cups of coffee and distributed them around the table. Ignacio accepted his without tearing his attention from Emma.

Which was the moment Emma's cell phone rang. She pulled it out and answered by saying curtly, "This is too damn early to call."

And she hung up.

Libby finally blinked and switched her stare to Emma. "Who was that?"

"I dunno. What's it matter?"

"What if—well, it might have been the dentist calling to confirm your teeth cleaning."

"If my dentist calls this number, it's not about cleaning my teeth."

"What on earth are you doing?" Libby gave up the pretense of concern for Emma's dental health. "I was never more relieved than when you quit working at that awful Dungeon of Darkness, but if you've gotten into something even more appalling, Emma—"

"What? You'll disown me?"

Libby summoned a long-suffering expression. "I will be very, very disappointed."

"So what else is new? My phone calls are my business." Emma sent me a wink.

"Exactly what kind of business—that's what worries me."

The wink told me Emma planned on tormenting Libby for as long as possible, and if I joined the discussion, I was only asking for more frustration in my life.

"So what happened," I asked Emma, changing the subject, "after yesterday's polo match? Did the police interview everyone on the field?"

Emma gulped her hot coffee. "I heard you discovered the body. The remains. The hand—whatever you call it. Did you faint?"

"She certainly did," Libby said from the counter.

"Feeling okay now?"

"Fine, thank you." I bit into my toast, which was delicious. "What happened after I left?"

Emma put a socked foot into Ignacio's lap. At once he began to give her a massage, which she ignored. "The cops talked to a lot of us—everyone who'd been around the horse trailers. Asked what we'd seen, which was nothing. I think somebody might have noticed a maniac tossing amputated body parts on the lawn, right?"

"How long were you detained?"

"An hour or so. They let me go early because I had all those pony-club kids with me. Is anybody going to make more of that toast?"

Libby dropped two more slices into the toaster. "I don't know why we have to talk about body parts over breakfast. It was bad enough yesterday."

Ignoring her, Emma said to me, "Pretty gross, huh?"

"Very."

"Everybody assumed the hand belonged to Penny Devine. Guess that means she didn't die of natural causes."

Libby shook her head and sighed. "What is the world coming to? Who would murder a movie star?"

"Anybody," Emma said. "She was a bitch on wheels, remember? She called Daddy a pea brain at his father's funeral."

"I met Penny a few times." Libby began to sort the pushpins by color and stick them into the blank bulletin board. "And she was very rude to me, too. She asked if I knew how to spell *cellulite*. I still haven't decided if she was insulting my intelligence or my weight. Potty gave me some jelly beans to stop my crying."

"Potty's a dirty old man," Emma said.

"How can you say that?" Libby asked. "He was very sweet."

"Maybe while you were jailbait. When I was practicing at Eagle Glen with the polo team this week, he followed me around the grounds, and he wasn't offering jelly beans. What a lech."

"He had Nuclear Winter on his arm yesterday," I said.

Libby got interested. "Did you really see her? Did she have her new breasts?"

"I wouldn't know her new breasts from her old breasts, Lib. Is there something extraordinary about them?"

"She sued her doctor because the implants he gave her were too small—said he'd made a mistake by not giving her the ones she picked out. She complained to anyone who'd listen—including a local magazine that printed a story about plastic surgeries gone wrong. To shut her up, the doctor gave her a new set for free—at least, that's the rumor down at Bellissima."

"The spa?"

"It's her regular place," Libby told us. "A friend invited me there for a chocolate body wrap last month. It was so sensuous! Except I must have gotten some up my nose. I've been sneezing Hershey's Kisses ever since. Anyway, it's Nuclear Winter's hangout. She's always getting beauty treatments there."

"And it's next door to the Towpath Club," Emma said.

The Towpath Club was a venerable Philadelphia institution for men who worked in the financial district, but not exactly the kind of place young lions wanted to join. I had once heard the joke that in order to be eligible for membership, a man had to be old enough for Medicare. It was better known around the city as the Tar Pit Club because it was where the dinosaurs went to die.

"Maybe Potty gave Nuclear a few jelly beans on the sidewalk in between. She had her hooks in him pretty deeply yesterday."

"I wouldn't worry about Potty." Emma traded one foot for the other, and Ignacio eagerly continued rubbing.

I said, "Let's hope she doesn't kill Potty."

"He seemed confident he could make me happy. So he's probably not afraid of Nuclear."

"Maybe he uses MaxiMan," Libby said.

"You know about MaxiMan?" I asked. "I thought it wasn't on the market yet."

"It's easy to get," Emma said, "if you know where to look."

"Where?" Libby asked, with perhaps too much energy to be mistaken for idle curiosity.

"Under the table. The prototype is all over the club scene."

"How do you know that?" Libby demanded. "Could you buy it?"

Emma shrugged. "If I wanted some, I know who to ask. Fortunately, I don't know anyone who needs it." She patted Ignacio on his head, and he smiled.

I asked, "Is it legal?"

"To buy it in the clubs? Of course not. Roofies aren't legal, either, but they're everywhere. In fact, I heard there's a new flood of it since some of the Brazilian boys hit town."

"The Brazilian polo players? They have roofies?" Libby looked askance at Ignacio.

"Not all of them," Emma said. "It's a fad among some of them, that's all."

"A fad?" I repeated. "Gummi bears are a fad."

"Okay, bad choice of words. It's a trend. Same with MaxiMan. Obviously somebody inside Devine Pharmaceuticals is making a few extra bucks outside the workplace."

"Do you know who?"

"Nope. I imagine whoever it is would be in a shitload of trouble if he—or she—got caught. Why do you want to know?" She shot me a grin. "Mick's not having a problem, is he?"

Libby saved me from answering by bringing buttered toast to the table. Ignacio never wavered from massaging Emma's foot. Em grabbed both slices and smacked them together like a sandwich before taking a huge bite.

I said, "Anybody know anything about Vivian? What's with that horrible truck of hers?"

Emma laughed. "You mean Roadkill Mama?"

"What?"

"Oh, she's big into all that animal rights stuff, but she also cleans up roadkill—you know, dead animals on the highway. Paddy Horgan calls her if one of his horses dies, too. She takes the animal somewhere for a decent burial. She's a real nut."

"Her truck smells to high heaven," Libby said. "Roadkill explains it."

"I thought men like Horgan would sell dead animals to the glue factory."

Emma shrugged. "Vivian pays better than the pet-food companies."

"She actually pays money for dead animals?"

"Right. Out of respect. Her brother spends his money on jelly beans and women, and she spends it on animals."

So much for wondering if Vivian had some nefarious reason for driving around with dead animals. I should have known she had an altruistic reason for doing so.

"Do Vivian and Potty live together?" I asked.

"I don't think so. Potty's living in the mansion at Eagle Glen. I heard he kicked Vivian out years ago."

"I looked after Vivian's cats once when I was a teenager," Libby said. "Vivian called Mama to ask if I'd house-sit while she was in the hospital."

"You stayed at Eagle Glen?"

Libby shook her head. "She had a small ranch house at the time. It was incredibly adorable. Like a little storybook house with kitty-cat art everywhere. A zillion little cat figurines. And at least two litters of kittens—real ones. She must have had two dozen cats in that place. They were everywhere, some of them wild. Actually, I was afraid they might gang up on me."

"Vivian is a cat lady?"

"She used to be," Libby said. "That was years ago. She even had a lion cub in a special cage. He came from a petting zoo that was shut down."

"She had a sick-looking kitten with her yesterday. And a dog." I remembered the skittish spaniel that had unwillingly trailed after Vivian at the polo match. Had she said the dog belonged to the caretaker?

"She just had cats then. Lots and lots of cats."

"Where was the house?"

"I don't remember exactly. Somewhere near here in Bucks County."

"Was that the time she was in the hospital after Potty shot her?"

Emma laughed. "I'd forgotten about that! He was hunting quail, and she intervened to protect the birds. He shot her accidentally."

Libby said, "Nora, what does all this have to do with Penny dying?"

"I don't know. It's just interesting family lore, I guess."

"You don't think Penny's siblings had anything to do with her death, do you? Those dotty old dears?"

"I'm just asking idle questions, that's all."

Around a mouthful of toast, Emma said, "Wasn't there an old rumor once that Penny had an illegit child?"

Libby sat down at the table with us. "Sweet Penny Devine got herself knocked up? Now, that would have been a scandal! Like Shirley Temple getting busted for cocaine."

Emma frowned as she tried to recall. "Didn't she? I can't remember where I heard that story. Maybe from Mama? She was always letting things slip when I was around."

"You used to eavesdrop on her phone conversations."

Emma grinned. "Yeah, I did. Maybe that's where I heard it. Something about Penny having a baby when she was supposed to do a movie. So she gave it away."

"I never heard that," Libby said. "I love celebrity gossip, don't you? It makes them so real!"

"They are real," I said. "Do you know anything else about Penny, Em?"

"Penny liked horses," Emma said. "She bought horses as fast as she bought clothes and jewelry. It's common knowledge she supplied polo ponies for Raphael Braga."

At the mention of his name, I swallowed my last bite of toast and pushed the plate away.

Emma took note. "So what's up with you and Raphael, Nora?"

"Not a thing."

"I hope you're not pining for him. I heard he had a date with Betsy Berkin last night."

"Good for Betsy."

My response just made Emma more curious. She asked, "How do you know him?"

"I think Ignacio needs some toast, don't you? Would anyone like some cereal? I think there's yogurt in the fridge, too. Ignacio? Breakfast?"

He smiled at me. "Hello."

I got up and bustled around the kitchen.

Emma and Libby exchanged a look.

Which was when we heard a terrible crash and a muffled yelp from far away.

"What the hell?" Emma cried. She got up and led us all running for the living room.

At the bottom of the staircase lay Michael. He was sprawled on the floor, stunned.

"Michael!" I rushed to his side. "Are you all right?"

He used one hand to gingerly touch the back of his head, then looked at it dizzily. No blood. Sounding astonished, he said, "I slipped and fell."

"Nice going," Emma said. "Maybe you ought to join a ballet company."

He squinted up at her. "Hey, Em."

"Don't try to stand," I said. "Have you broken anything?"

He tested one wrist and flexed his left leg uncomfortably before shifting his weight to get off the floor. "I don't think so."

I helped him to his feet.

"How the hell did you fall?" Emma asked, hiding a smile.

"I don't know. One minute I was—"

"Here." Libby held up a child's toy truck. "I think you must have stepped on this."

The toy was small and dark, easily missed on the staircase when the chandelier was turned off.

"Where did that come from?" I took it from Libby. "Does this belong to the twins?"

"They outgrew trucks years ago."

Michael stretched his neck carefully. "Lucy must have left it there yesterday."

Emma said, "How come none of the rest of us slipped on it?"

"Just my luck today, that's all."

"Hello," Ignacio said cheerfully.

Michael took a limping step forward and shook his hand. "Hey, sorry. Mick Abruzzo. How y'doin'?"

"Hello," Ignacio said again.

"Mr. Lucky." Emma patted Michael's shoulder. "Now that you're marrying one of us, you'd better get used to accidents, big guy."

# Chapter Six

Emma and Ignacio had plans to pick up another pony to add to Emma's collection. But it appeared that Ignacio had accidentally locked the keys in Emma's pickup truck. Michael went outside to assess the situation.

"Hope you don't mind," Emma said to me when we were left alone in the kitchen. "Last night I put Brickle in the barn with Mr. Twinkles. There's room for a couple more ponies. I figured I might cut Horgan out of the loop and give some lessons here."

"Sure," I said. "I like having kids around."

Emma nodded. "We're going to look at another pony today."

"Bring some carrots home so I can make friends with them."

"Sure." She lingered, giving me a curious once-over. "You okay? After what I heard coming from your bedroom last night—"

"I'm fine. We're both fine." I realized I was blushing.

Her cell phone rang, and Emma took the call.

"Ten o'clock sharp," she ordered her client. "And don't be late or I'll give your place to somebody else."

Of course I wanted to know what she was up to. But Michael came in to report he'd popped the truck door open—a maneuver he'd managed to accomplish in thirty seconds, I noticed—and Emma bolted.

Libby came in from the porch and watched them leave. "I have a bad feeling about this."

"About Ignacio? Don't worry. Emma's not an idiot."

"She has very poor judgment sometimes." Libby's frown had given way to something more like longing. "Especially where men are concerned."

*Look who's talking* was the phrase that nearly slipped out of my mouth, but I managed to keep it to myself.

Libby decided she needed color-coded index cards for the wedding bulletin board, so she got into her minivan and roared off. Michael and I carried coffee and the Sunday newspapers into the library, where we read the front-page report of the grisly discovery at the polo match.

In the *Philadelphia Inquirer*, Michael was mentioned only as "a person of interest who was detained for questions and released after two hours."

"Three," Michael said. "But who's counting?"

The *Intelligencer* had no qualms about naming names.

"Convicted criminal Michael Abruzzo, son of reputed mob boss 'Big Frankie' Abruzzo, was questioned by police." No mention of his release.

After reading that, neither one of us felt much like relaxing, but I made a pretense of skimming the rest of the newspapers. Michael read the business section and the sports pages, did the puzzles with a felt marker, then pulled out the manual for a telescope he'd bought when we came home from our cruise. While on the yacht, he'd become interested in the big telescope that belonged to Lexie's mom, and he was slowly figuring out how to assemble one for himself. As I turned the pages of the newspaper, I thought how easy it was to pretend nothing felt wrong between us as long as we were reading.

Then I found an article about Ben Bloom's suburban police department and became absorbed in the politics that seemed to be tearing apart the local government. The police were being accused of slacking off just as the grisly discovery of a dismembered hand clearly indicated a murder had occurred in their fine community.

Michael tossed down his book first. "I think I'll go check on my car."

I looked up from the police story. He meant the car he'd wrecked the day before. "Where is it?"

"The guys are working on it down at the garage."

"On a Sunday?"

He grinned. "The beauty of owning your own business is the preferential treatment."

"Shall I come along? We could have lunch afterwards."

He shook his head. "Better not. I don't know how long this might take. There could be complications. Plus I'll go to Mass on my way. You're just going to stay here today, right? Relax and take care of yourself?"

"Who could relax with Libby coming back any minute?"

"Promise you'll stay in?"

"No promises," I said, but I think he assumed I was joking.

I noticed that Michael's mind had been elsewhere all morning, and I was fairly certain he wasn't really worrying about his car. But I refrained from asking any questions when he kissed me good-bye.

To be honest, I had other plans, too.

As soon as he was out of the house, I got on the phone and called my driver, Reed Shakespeare. I asked him if he was free to take me into the city.

"Now?" Reed asked, startled.

"Well . . . if you're not busy."

"I'm taking my mother to church."

Rozalia Shakespeare, a God-fearing woman of profound faith, never missed an opportunity to sing in the choir. Her voice could rattle the stained-glass windows of the AME Church.

"Oh," I said. "Sorry. Maybe another time."

"No," Reed said, sounding relieved, "I can pick you up in an hour."

"You sure?" I didn't want to be the one to tempt a young man from his religion.

"An hour," he said, and hung up.

Just enough time to shower and dress and make a plan.

I was decked out in a pink suit with a pencil skirt when Reed arrived in the black town car. Fortunately, Libby returned in time to make sure the twins didn't set off a bomb or commit any crimes against nature, so I dashed down the back porch steps and met Reed at the rear passenger door. He carried an open umbrella to protect me from a fine April mist that filled the air.

"How nice to see you back, Reed." I wanted to kiss him on the cheek, but I knew he'd disapprove. He liked to keep his distance. We settled on a handshake. "How was London? Did you enjoy your semester abroad?"

"It was okay," he said, stone-faced as always. "Food was terrible."

"It's amazing the British Empire didn't bring home a few good recipes while they were off conquering the world, right?"

"Uhm." He helped me into the backseat and closed the door.

When I'd first been hired on at the *Intelligencer* by the newspaper's owner, an old family friend, part of the deal was that I would receive the services of a driver in addition to my small paycheck. I'd worked for a grand total of three days before the real reporters began making fun of me and my chauffeur. I had no idea journalists weren't driven around to their assignments. But since I couldn't hold a driver's license due to my tendency to faint—the Commonwealth of Pennsylvania took a dim view of losing consciousness behind the wheel of a vehicle—I continued to rely on Reed for transportation. His schedule of classes at the community college was fortunately flexible enough to mesh with my own odd hours, so we spent a lot of time together.

But Reed still refused to be very friendly. The social stigma of a young black man driving a white woman around the city of Philadelphia infuriated him. I think he lived in dread of being spotted by his friends.

"Where we going?" he asked when he'd gotten behind the wheel.

"To a Sunday brunch." I gave him the address.

He made no judgment about our destination, turning on the radio to a Sunday gospel show to prevent conversation, and we were off.

I couldn't help noticing Reed had gotten himself a new haircut since returning from his trip to England. Rather than the close-cropped, no-nonsense style of before, his hair was neatly trimmed into sharp angles around his ears and across his forehead. For the first time, I detected a small show of ego in the young man. Which had to be a good thing.

Within the hour, Reed slid the big car into the well-to-do Chestnut Hill neighborhood. He nosed the car to the curb in front of a narrow storefront on an upscale street. A few droplets of rain spattered the car's windshield.

"Don't get out—I won't get wet. Come back in an hour?"

Reed shrugged. "I can stick close."

As I got out of the car, he shut off the engine and reached for a book he kept in the door pocket. Given any free time, Reed studied. I still hadn't figured out what classes he was taking, but I gave him credit for being so diligent.

Shouldering my bag, I quickly crossed the wet sidewalk and ducked through a door with the name of the restaurant, Vernacular, painted in gilt letters on the glass. Someone had tied a damp golden retriever to the bike rack beside the door. The dog stared mournfully into the restaurant.

The front room was crowded with tables where the single men of the neighborhood drank their coffee behind newspapers and peeked at the women who walked through. A large dour man in shirtsleeves and a skinny tie sat on a stool behind the cash register counting receipts. He didn't glance up as I passed by.

I knew the way and cut through the coffee shop portion of the restaurant and down two narrow steps before ending up in another world—a high-ceilinged room with skylights, flowers on the tables and a piano in one corner. The clientele was definitely more refined here, with a scattering of couples among the many well-dressed women.

The man at the piano spotted me immediately and paused in his rendition of "Stormy Weather" to say into his microphone, "Hey, it's Nora!"

And half the room turned to greet me warmly.

I had lived around the corner just a few years earlier, so I knew most everyone there. The Sunday regulars were all accounted for. Babe Mallick, the opera singer best known for taking an accidental swan dive into the orchestra pit when a set gave way under her weight during a performance of *Aïda*, sat with her friend Joanie Parsons, the tulip heiress. Ajole Ada looked like an African prince at a table with his brood of five giggly daughters, who appeared to be passing some electronic gadget under the table to one another while their father, eyes closed, intoned a long prayer. Garrett Steinbrecker, who was ninety years old and looked every single day of it, still came out for brunch once a week to drink Bellinis and listen to his much younger partner, Winston Washington, play the piano.

I gave Joanie an air kiss, noted Babe was plowing through a double portion of French toast, and allowed Garrett to kiss my hand as I made my way through the crowded tables. I was glad to be snug among the group I knew so well.

"Dilly," I said when I got to the corner table. "Order me one of your special Bloody Marys, will you? No olives."

"Nora, we were just talking about you!"

Ever the courtly gentleman, Dilly Farquar got to his feet and kissed me on both cheeks. His white hair was perfectly combed off his high forehead, and he smelled very subtly of a sedate cologne. He wore a fine cashmere sport coat over immaculate gray trousers and a pair of classic Cole Haan woven loafers, no socks. His striped shirt was crisp, his bow tie and matching pocket square ice-blue. But, of course, looking good was what Dilly breathed. He was the city's foremost fashion columnist, and even out for brunch, he looked every inch the part.

Holding my hand, he said, "I don't believe you know Kaiser Waldman, do you? Kaiser, this is Nora Blackbird."

I kept my composure, but I'd never been so thankful that I'd left my blue jeans at home in favor of one of my grandmother's most treasured garments—the pink Chanel suit. I'd even thrown a Fendi scarf around my shoulders, and my shoes were a respectable pair of Ferragamos I scrupulously maintained. I knew I'd see some of the city's most fashionable citizens here, but I never imagined this.

Kaiser Waldman, Paris designer of international fame, took my hand from Dilly and gathered up my left one, too, then bowed over them as if bestowing a blessing. He practically clicked his heels. When he opened his eyes, he stared at the diamond on my finger before meeting my gaze.

"It is my pleasure," he said in his impossibly German- and French-accented English, "to meet the lovely girl on the rainy Sunday morning."

Coming from the man who dressed more Oscar nominees than Givenchy, such a compliment was either genuine flattery or complete bullshit. I chose to think it was genuine. "I'm honored to meet you, monsieur."

"Call me Kaiser," he purred. "All my ladies do."

The chances of becoming one of Kaiser Waldman's clients—one of his famous "ladies"—were as slim as winning the Irish Sweepstakes, but I smiled and thanked him and hoped the Chanel didn't look thirty years old, which it was.

"Please join us." Dilly pulled out the extra chair at their small round table.

"Am I interrupting? You must be conducting an interview for the newspaper."

Years ago, Dilly had grown tired of being a wealthy heir with nothing to do but shop, and he began writing for the premier newspaper in the city. Very quickly, he'd made himself into the arbiter of taste in Philadelphia. His column was well read.

He said, "We finished the interview two days ago. Please join us."

"You wear the elegant piece of jewelry." Kaiser had been unable to stop staring at my ring.

"Thank you."

"It is the famous design, but of course you know that."

Surprised, I looked at the rock on my hand. "No, I didn't, as a matter of fact."

"Oh? It is done by Calvetti, the colleague of mine. He does work for the jewelers in New York and Rome. May I ask how you came by the ring?"

"It's an engagement ring from my—from the man I'm going to marry."

Dilly coughed discreetly. "Shall we sit, Nora? I was telling Kaiser about you just a few minutes ago."

"I can't imagine why."

"Kaiser worked with Penny Devine," Dilly said. "We were speculating about whether or not she's actually dead."

We sat down and the waiter appeared to take my order, which Dilly managed to convey merely by circling their two Bloody Marys with his forefinger and winking. It gave me time to slip the Fendi from my shoulders and settle into my chair.

Kaiser sat back and crossed one leg grandly over the other. His trouser cuff lifted to reveal black, low-cut boots with three-inch heels. He was wearing a four-button suit of silver wool with a black turtleneck underneath, perhaps to hide the jowls that had begun to appear beneath his renowned square jaw. He had very dark brows and a mane of iron gray hair worn swept away from his face and surely sprayed to keep it in place. His skin glowed as if from a recent peel.

He braced one elbow on the arm of his chair and held a swizzle stick between his first two fingers as if it were a cigarette. Tilting his chin up, he said, "Penny was the bird. Always flitting from one thing to the next, but never happy. Never satisfied."

Dilly sent me a look to communicate that we must be patient with Kaiser's grandiose poetry. "We heard you found the—er—remains."

"Yes."

"It must have been awful," Dilly said coolly. "But now that you've had time to reflect, do you think the—I mean—was it Penny?"

"I can't be sure." The police had not asked me to keep any secrets, so I said, "But there was a wristwatch. Studded with small diamonds. Something Penny would have liked, I'm sure."

"Well, then." Dilly shook his head. "This is very sad news. I'm sorry she's gone."

"You knew her, didn't you, Dilly?"

Vaguely, he said, "We were friends once, many years ago, that's all."

"I knew her." Kaiser sighed grandly. "The discerning customer. The perfectionist with her wardrobe. And with her weight never the same from one season to the next, preparing her order was the trial for everyone."

"You must have created many garments for her," I said. "She always looked so beautiful."

He waved off the suggestion. "I made the few things for Penny, but not all her clothes. Because of her eating, I could not keep up with the demand. Sometimes she would be thin—sometimes she had the ass of a washerwoman. Many of us sewed for Penny Devine."

"Her collection must be astonishing," Dilly murmured.

Carefully, I said, "It's hard to imagine that someone like Penny could have had enemies."

"Then you haven't much imagination, my dear," Dilly said.

"She was evil," Kaiser agreed.

"Well, all right, she was nothing like her brother and sister. But who could hate her enough to kill her?"

Kaiser said, "From time to time, I contemplated strangling her myself. I despised the woman. I hate the ungrateful. She was worse than the rock-and-roll singer with the pointy breasts."

"Was Penny so disliked in Hollywood, too?"

Kaiser waved off the seriousness of my question. "She was despised on at least three continents."

My drink arrived along with a plate of toast points and foie gras surrounded by an artful display of caviar. Kaiser dug into the caviar with fury.

Dilly raised an eyebrow at me.

I said, "But she must have been murdered here. By someone in Philadelphia. Unless someone from Beverly Hills brought her arm here in a suitcase."

"I have the alibi," Kaiser said at once.

"I wasn't suggesting—"

"Of course you weren't," Dilly intervened. "You're simply wondering who could have committed such a heinous crime."

Kaiser made a rude noise with his mouth full. "Or service to humanity."

"Uhm," I said, "Penny may have been unlikable, but that's not necessarily a motive for murder. Since she spent so little time here, I've been wondering who she could have had relationships with in Philadelphia."

"Old friends?" Dilly suggested. "Or rather, old enemies?"

"I'd like to know about her past, that's all."

He smiled. "So you came to me because I'm so damnably old. Yes, Penny and I did grow up in the same era, same social circle. In fact, I may have been one of the few people who actually liked her. She was unpleasant from time to time, but hardly anyone understood the pressures she was under. Staying thin was very difficult for her, for example, but necessary to remain employed."

"Did she keep in contact with Potty and Vivian after she became successful in Hollywood?"

"Who wants to keep in contact with the viper?" Kaiser muttered.

Dilly hid a smile. "Actually, there's hardly anyone I can think of who stayed in touch. Well, maybe your grandmother, Nora, but how long has she been dead? Penny burned a lot of bridges when she left."

"Is it true Penny had an illegitimate child?"

Dilly's face froze. "Why would you say such a thing?"

"Emma overheard it once—probably my mother gossiping on the phone. Is it true? Penny had a baby? Or was it just a rumor?"

"Where there is the smoke," Kaiser said solemnly, "there might be the conflagration."

Dilly wrestled with his conscience for a moment.

"Dilly, I don't want to pry. If you're uncomfortable, I apologize—"

"No, no." He toyed with the skewer of olives from his Bloody Mary. "It was many, many years ago. Perhaps forty years now. She confided in me that she was—well, expecting."

Kaiser shook his head. "It is very inconsiderate, the having of babies. If my ladies get with the pregnant, I tell them not to return to me until their children are in school five years. It's just too hard on my nerves to do so many fittings."

Kaiser reached for the plate before us and helped himself to a generous swab of foie gras. "Can you imagine the kind of mother she might have been? Better the child spent no time with such the parent."

"When did you say this happened, Dilly?"

"Forty years, at least."

Kaiser said, "And who was the insane person who slept with her? Who was the father?"

We heard a small commotion across the room, and Babe Mallick got up from her table at the urging of people around her. The large woman majestically made her way to the piano. Applause erupted from the patrons, and Babe bowed her head and feigned a falsely modest smile. Then she consulted with Winston in a businesslike fashion, and he obediently trilled a few chords on the piano. Babe launched into an operatic version of "What Is This Thing Called Love?" A few notes wavered.

Kaiser leaned across the table to Dilly. "When I get too old to do my work well, tell me to stop. I hate making such the fool of myself."

We listened to the performance for a while, all of us stirring our drinks. Kaiser might have pondered the eventual decline of his career, but I found myself thinking about Penny Devine's love life. It was a little like imagining how Tasmanian devils mated. I wondered how I could find out the identity of her lovers in her younger days.

Babe concluded her song, then launched into a show tune from *Rent*. Dilly rolled his eyes. The five Ada daughters began poking one another and giggling even louder than before.

Which, thankfully, caused Babe to frown and decline to perform anything else. She sailed back to her table to more applause. Winston mopped his brow with his handkerchief and went to join his partner for a Bellini.

"What about Vivian?" I asked. "Did she know about Penny's love life?"

"Perhaps, but I doubt it. They despised each other, as far as I could see."

"I can't imagine Vivian despising anyone."

"It must have been hard having a sister so well-known, so lovely, so talented. And you know, their mother took Penny to California and never came back to her other two children. Any sibling would resent such abandonment."

Still I couldn't envision Vivian being anything but a kindly old lady who loved animals. "What about Penny's friends?"

"She hardly had any. She had teachers and coaches. I remember she spent hours every day learning to tap-dance in the dining room at Eagle Glen. It had a marble floor, you see. She worked very hard, especially with her mother so determined that she learn to perform. But friends? None that I recall."

"Except you."

Dilly smiled slightly. "Except me, I suppose. But, of course, we lost track of each other eventually."

We were interrupted as two ladies I didn't know approached the table to beg an introduction to Kaiser Waldman. Rising to his feet, Dilly did the honors, and Kaiser stood and responded coolly, but graciously, to the gushing.

It was clear that the rest of the people in the dining room had simply been waiting for Kaiser to begin receiving his adoring public, so I murmured my thanks to Dilly and picked up my handbag.

"What's your interest in this, Nora?" Dilly asked as Kaiser spoke with his fans. "Why so worried about Penny Devine's death?"

"I don't know. I can't explain it."

He smiled gently. "Well, perhaps it would be best for you to let the police take over."

I smiled, too. "I will. Thank you for talking with me."

"I hope we might have a different conversation soon. We were going to discuss your career, weren't we?"

"I'd like that. I could use a mentor." I told him about receiving an envelope of money from someone asking for preferential treatment in my column. Without mentioning Potty's name, I told him I planned to return the money immediately.

Dilly shook his head. "It happens. Even now, people try to bribe me for my good opinion. You're right to return the money as soon as possible."

I gave him a kiss on the cheek. "Thanks, Dilly. It's nice to know you're in my corner."

We promised to have lunch together soon, just the two of us, and I left the restaurant. Despite my agreement to forget about the investigation, my mind was still full of Penny Devine. Although she'd been famous and successful, her life sounded very empty. How sad that she had left her only friend behind forty years ago.

Perhaps the news that she'd borne an illegitimate child made her more real to me. What had become of it?

On the street, the rain had stopped, and a brilliant April sunshine glinted off the wet pavement and the tightly parked cars. Chestnut Hill looked beautiful, as always, with its genteel old homes flying patriotic flags and sporting window boxes filled with spring pansies. I paused and put my hand up to shield my eyes so I could see where Reed had parked the car.

I hesitated for only an instant. A man in running shorts jogged past, which might have distracted me for just a heartbeat.

Then suddenly someone jostled me from behind. I hadn't seen him or heard him coming. Instinctively, I started to turn, then grabbed my handbag closer to my body.

But that wasn't what he was after. A second person—someone bigger and rougher—collided with me, and together they sandwiched my body between them. I caught a glimpse of the second man's face. I didn't know him, but I recognized the intent in his expression and was hit by a lightning bolt of fear.

Without thinking, I jabbed my elbow into the nearest stomach, but the blow wasn't hard enough to dislodge me from either man. Besides, they were already propelling me toward the curb, toward a car. I knew they were too strong to fight off, so I twisted and doubled over fast, and they lost their momentum. The three of us stumbled.

I shouted. One of them grabbed me around the waist and tried to jam his hand over my mouth. In that instant, I felt the solid object stuck into his belt. A gun. I bit him and lashed out a kick that connected with his knee.

One of them said, "Goddammit."

The other growled, "Get the door open."

I wasn't getting into a car with them. I wasn't. As he tried to get a grip around me, I dropped my handbag, cocked my right hand into a position I'd practiced so often in self-defense class that it came automatically. I jabbed the first man under his nose as hard as I could. His head snapped back, and his clasp loosened.

I must have yelled as soon as the attack began, because suddenly the jogger was back. He leaped and grabbed one of the men from behind, locking his arm around his throat. They grunted together and struggled.

Then Reed arrived, swinging a long plastic ice scraper. He clonked the second man over the head with it. The ice scraper broke on impact, and my attacker backed off, clutching his bleeding nose.

He snapped, "The hell with it!" and he ran for the driver's door of the waiting car.

The first man twisted and punched the jogger in the stomach. My rescuer let out a curse on a gasp of air and dropped to his knees.

Then both attackers clambered into their car and pulled out. Tires squealed. A horn blared. We heard a crash and a tinkle of broken glass, but the car didn't stop. It peeled out and barreled up the street.

On foot, Reed followed the car for half a dozen paces, trying to read the license plate.

The street tilted under me, and my legs felt like seaweed. I had lost one shoe somehow. But I caught my breath and staggered over to the jogger. I put my hand on his shoulder. "Are you all right? Thank you so much! I don't know how I would—Crewe!"

Crewe Dearborne looked up from clutching his stomach. "Nora—I thought it was you."

"Crewe, you were wonderful! Thank you!"

Reed came back. He grabbed me under my elbow and pulled me away from Crewe. "You okay?"

"Yes, I'm fine. I just—it happened so fast."

Crewe was still breathing hard—whether from running or the blow to his stomach, I wasn't sure. His face was red. He shook his head like a wet dog coming out of a pond. "I think they tried to kidnap you!"

In my ear, Reed said, "Get in the car. I'm taking you home."

"I'm okay. This man is a friend." I pulled loose and together we reached down to help lift Crewe to a standing position.

A small crowd had stopped to watch the whole thing, and a young couple approached us tentatively. The man offered his cell phone. The woman returned my shoe.

"Call the cops," Reed told them, and they obeyed. The other onlookers dispersed quickly, not wanting to get involved.

Reed went out to the street again to speak with the man whose car had been struck.

I slipped on my shoe. Then Crewe and I helped each other over to the bike rack where the golden retriever had been tied earlier. The dog was gone, so we leaned against the rack, recovering. Crewe was dressed in running shoes and tall socks that emphasized the length of his legs so much that he looked like a racehorse. A cloud of steam rose from his shoulders, too, which were encased in a UPenn T-shirt, soaked in sweat. His running shorts were loose and faded. He looked dazed and nauseated.

Concerned, I said, "Are you badly hurt? We'll take you to the emergency room."

He half sat on the bike rack and braced his hands on his knees, shaking his head to refuse my offer. "I'll be fine as soon as I catch my breath."

"You got more of a workout than you intended."

He allowed a rueful smile up at me. "I thought I was in better shape than this. A restaurant critic spends half his time eating and the other half trying to burn off the calories. I figured I was pretty strong. But that guy was like a bull."

"You were wonderful, Crewe. I can't thank you enough."

"Don't mention it." He pretended to be offhand. Then he gave up and grinned a little. "Okay, you can mention it once in a while, but not too much. I'm a little embarrassed. He brushed me off like a fly. Who were those guys?"

"I haven't a clue. Reed, did you get the plate number?"

Reed returned to us, frowning. "It was a Delaware plate, coated with mud. Or some kind of brown paint. Real mud would have washed off in the rain. They were keeping their identity a secret."

"Why? Who in the world—?"

Reed stopped my questions with a squeeze of my elbow.

Crewe muttered, "I'm not ashamed to say, they scared the hell out of me. This neighborhood is usually very safe."

The young couple came over and reported that the police were on their way. They asked if we needed anything else, and Reed had the presence of mind to ask them for their names and phone number. They obliged—the woman had a notebook and pen in her shoulder bag. Then they headed off up the sidewalk while Reed tucked the sheet of notebook paper into the pocket of his Windbreaker.

A city patrol car arrived in less than five minutes. The driver of the car that had been bumped in the fender bender was furious and made a scene, which the police gradually quelled before turning to us. Reed gave a succinct report while Crewe and I acted like a couple of shaken teenagers. The senior officer made a radio call while his younger partner took notes on what happened.

"You didn't know the guys?" he asked me. "Can you describe them?"

"Both late thirties. One had a blue jacket. The other wore a—a sweat-shirt, I think."

"The jacket was green," Crewe said, then frowned. "At least, I think it was."

"About the men themselves. Black? White? Tall? Short?"

"Tallish," I said. "Weight lifters, I think. They had strong upper bodies. I think they were . . . Mediterranean."

"What does that mean?"

"Greek or Spanish maybe."

"Italian?"

"Maybe. I mean, they were Americans. They didn't have accents."

We managed to come up with little more than that general description, and eventually the police decided we couldn't give them any more assistance. They promised someone would be in touch and asked if we needed medical attention. When we refused, they got back into their patrol car and left.

I told Crewe we'd take him home.

"I live right around the corner." He hugged himself, chilled in the spring air. "Besides, I was on my way over to visit my mother. I put her trash out on the street every Sunday so she doesn't have to touch it. Her house is just a couple of blocks from here."

"Let us drop you."

"No, no, I'll just get sweat all over your upholstery. Besides, I need to warm up again." He executed a few leg stretches, regaining his manhood once the incident appeared to be truly over.

"Well, then, thank you again," I said. "I owe you a huge favor now."

He grinned. "I might take you up on that."

"Anytime," I insisted.

A thought struck him. "Have dinner with me tonight."

"Tonight?"

"If you're not too shaken up. I have reservations for eight o'clock. It's just for two, but why don't you invite your fiancé? I'd like to meet him."

"I don't think he'd—"

"Maybe you could invite Lexie, too. We'll make it a foursome. It'll give me a chance to put the reservationist through his paces."

I smiled, aware that his real motive wasn't an evening spent in my company. "So you review more than just the food at your restaurants?"

"Of course. Everything from the person who answers the phone to the wallpaper in the lavatories. How about it? If they can't make an adjustment to my reservation, I scratch a black mark in my little book."

His light tone gave me the opportunity to politely decline. A last-minute invitation assumed a lot—especially if I was burdened with managing to get two more dining companions to show up in a few hours. And convincing both Michael, who had avoided meeting more than a small handful of my friends, and Lexie, who had more issues than half a dozen neurotics, to come out for dinner with Crewe sounded like Mission Impossible.

But I said, "I can hardly refuse, can I?"

We exchanged the important details of our dinner that evening and parted. Reed bundled me into the backseat of the town car.

He said, "I'll have you home in half an hour."

"I'm not going home, Reed."

He swung around from the steering wheel and put his arm on the back of the seat to glower at me. "You know what just happened, right?"

"I think I was mugged."

"Damn straight. So let's get you home and see what the boss says."

"We're not telling Michael anything. At least, not yet. Reed, I'm not a delicate flower. See?" I put both hands up. "I'm perfectly fine. Let's go to my office, okay? I have some phone calls to make."

Reed argued with me, but eventually he obeyed and drove me to the Pendergast Building, home of the *Philadelphia Intelligencer.*

The offices of the Lifestyle Section were nearly deserted early on a Sunday afternoon. I waved at Skip Malone, the sportswriter, who was watching a videotaped basketball game with the sound off as he worked at a computer. He tilted his head back in greeting, but didn't break from typing.

I slid into the swivel chair at my desk and phoned Lexie Paine first.

"Dinner?" she said. "Sounds fabulous, sweetie!"

"I'm glad you're free," I said. "Because it's Crewe Dearborne who invited us."

"Damn you, Nora. You know how I feel about—"

"I owe him a huge favor, Lex, and I'm afraid you're his reward."

"What favor? What's going on?"

I told her about the mugging, and she was properly horrified. It was a relatively easy matter to convince her that dinner was the only possible way I could recover from the ordeal.

Next I phoned Michael's latest cell phone number.

"Hey," he said. "I just called your house. Your sister said she couldn't find you. I was afraid the twins had you trussed up for dissection."

"I went out after all. Brunch with Dilly Farquar." If I told him more, he'd come roaring into the city to my rescue, so I said, "Michael, listen, I need your help."

His tone changed. "What's wrong?"

I took a deep breath. "We owe Lexie an enormous debt for arranging our vacation on the yacht."

"Whatever she needs, you know I'm there."

Lexie needed a lot of things, although she'd never admit it. I said, "I'd like for us to have dinner with her tonight."

Michael was smart, of course, so he said, "What's the catch?"

"We'll be going out with Crewe Dearborne, the restaurant critic for the other newspaper. He's a very nice man, Michael, and I know you'll like him—"

"Nora—"

"He has a crush on Lexie, and I actually think they'd be good together, but they need a little help."

"Are you playing matchmaker?"

"No, never that. Well, not much. Please come. It will mean a lot to everyone."

He groaned.

"I wouldn't make you do anything you'd really hate. Meet me at Caravaggio at eight."

"Caravaggio?" He laughed shortly. "You're kidding! That's where you want to have dinner?"

"Yes, Crewe is going to review it. He'll probably be in disguise, so we'll have to play along. Will you come?"

He sounded pained. "Caravaggio?"

"Yes. Do you know it?"

He sighed. "It's my father's favorite spaghetti joint."

# Chapter Seven

Still at my desk, I tried phoning Potty Devine next to explain to him that I could not accept his money. I was surprised when Vivian answered just as I'd decided nobody was at home.

"Hello?" she sang, sounding cheerful but harried. I heard a dog barking behind her.

"Vivian? It's Nora Blackbird. Am I catching you at a bad time?"

"Nora? No. Yes. Oh, goodness, just a minute." She covered the receiver. I couldn't make out her words, but I got the impression she was talking to people as well as animals.

At last she came back. "I'm so sorry, lamb. There's a lot happening here."

"Oh, I don't mean to bother—"

"The truck carrying Penny's things arrived this morning. They're unloading now."

"Penny's things?"

"Yes, the lease on her house was up last week, and there's no sense paying rent when we know she's not going back, is there? So we had all her furniture and clothes and belongings shipped here."

"I see. Well, I won't keep you. I was hoping Potty might—"

"It's a terrible mess. I'm a little overwhelmed."

"Can I help?"

"As a matter of fact, some of it is supposed to go to you."

"What?"

"Why not come over and have a look? See if you have enough space for it all?"

"Heavens, I can't imagine—"

"Come now, if you like." I heard a crash in the background, then more barking. Vivian said, "Oh, goodness. Someone just dropped

96

Penny's collection of exercise videos. They're all over the floor. Must run!"

And she hung up on me.

I phoned Reed, grabbed my handbag and headed for the elevator. An invitation to Eagle Glen meant I'd be able to see Potty and return his envelope.

The afternoon had warmed, although a few gray clouds still skimmed the sky as Reed drove me out to Eagle Glen.

At the estate's gate, I was surprised to see a cadre of television vans and SUVs marked with the logos of various radio and TV news stations. A paunchy rent-a-cop stood guard at the gate, refusing entry to all of the reporters. When Reed pulled up, however, the rent-a-cop saw a black man behind the wheel of a town car with a white woman in the backseat, and he waved us through.

Reed muttered under his breath, and I didn't dare say a word.

The driveway split, and we headed for the house by making a wide circle around the polo field. From the high vantage point, we could see down into the lower field, where a team of workmen was disassembling the large party tent. We could also see up the slope to the mansion where Potty lived. I couldn't help noticing that the grass of the front lawn had grown weedy and long. I wondered who was managing the estate for the Devines now that Juana Huckabee was gone. Whoever it was should be fired.

An enormous moving van blocked the driveway behind the mansion. The truck's rear door yawned wide, and we could see the shapes of furniture and large boxes inside. A steamer trunk and a rack of fur coats sat in the sunshine, the first things unloaded. Two men backed down the truck's ramp carrying a pink velvet fainting couch. As if it weighed no more than a table lamp, they briskly carried it into the open door of the carriage house, not into the mansion.

Reed and I got out and stood on the lawn beneath the gently whispering trees, which rained down a fine snow of blossoms.

"I won't be long," I promised.

Reed nodded. Normally, he would have gotten back into the car to study, but since the episode after brunch, Reed had clearly decided to be extra vigilant. He put on his sunglasses and leaned against the hood of the town car.

I intended to follow the movers into the carriage house, but I heard Vivian's quavery voice coming from behind a badly neglected hedge, so I followed the sound and discovered a ragged garden out back. It was surrounded by a corroded chain-link fence. A large, rusted mobile home was parked inside and looked extraordinarily out of place beside the estate's original Georgian mansion.

The Brittany spaniel that had followed Vivian around the polo grounds lay in the dirt of the garden, watching me. He barked once, warning me not to come closer. But I said his name, and Toby changed his mind. His short, wispy tail began to wiggle as I approached. I rubbed his velvety soft ears, and he rolled over on his back. But a swarm of fleas roamed in the thin white hair of his tummy, and I pulled my hand back hastily.

"Poor puppy," I said.

He leaped up and followed me to the mobile home, oblivious to the many cats that populated the garden. Some sunned themselves in the grass, while others crept among the bushes. A sign printed with the likeness of a smiling cat and the words KITTY KROSSING tilted crookedly in the dirt. Two black toms chased a calico kitten under the mobile home, and I could hear them screeching at one another there.

About ten yards from the door, the dog sat down and waited for me.

The door of the mobile home was closed. On either side of the doorway, however, two brackets were mounted as if the owner sometimes had occasion to bar the door from the outside with the stout piece of wood slightly larger than a baseball bat that lay on the ground beside the step. A cat sat on the step.

I could hear Vivian talking inside—cooing, really, as if speaking to an animal.

Suddenly I realized that the cat on the step was no ordinary house pet. It was a very large cat, and it watched me without blinking its large, oval eyes. My heart gave a thump when I realized it was not a pet at all. It had very long ears with black tips, and its long, graceful limbs were more the length of a medium-sized dog's.

The cat glared at me.

It was some kind of wild animal, I realized, taking an instinctive step backward. Not as big as a bobcat or a mountain lion. A serval cat, perhaps. Its speckled coat was as distinctive as a leopard's. The small head swiveled as it looked from me to the spaniel, clearly debating which one of us might make a tasty meal.

"What are you doing in here?" Vivian asked sweetly as she opened the door. The serval cat leaped away and disappeared under the mobile home. Immediately, six other smaller cats bolted out and disappeared into the grass.

"I—I thought I heard your voice, Vivian."

"Be careful!" she cried. "You're stepping on Socrates!"

I lifted my foot instinctively and found an ugly striped tom cunningly trying to snatch the heel of my shoe as if it were a mouse.

Vivian came outside and closed the door firmly behind herself, cradling the same listless kitten she'd had at the polo match. By now, however, the little cat's condition seemed much worse than before. It appeared to be barely conscious. Vivian's adorable jumper was covered by an apron emblazoned with the face of Garfield, the cartoon cat. But the fabric was spattered with a brownish substance that might have been blood.

"I was making dinner for all my darlings." Vivian came down the steps. "These are my rescue cats. People abandon them out here in the country, and what are the poor things to do? They can't survive on their own. So I take them in. This is a sanctuary."

"But, Vivian, there are so many!"

"I try to find homes for them." She glanced sadly at the animals that waited in the grass for their meal. "But people don't want full-grown cats. They want kittens like this little darling. So I give the rest love and affection. That's all an animal really wants, you know."

Just one glance at the desperately thin cat in her arms told me that these animals needed food as well as love. And veterinary care. Yellow mucus ringed its half-closed eyes. I had never seen a more miserable creature.

I said, "How do you manage by yourself?"

"Oh," she said vaguely, "Julie helps out now and then, but mostly, it's me." As one cat jumped out of her path and crouched in the grass, she added, "You'll have to forgive their manners. They're not accustomed to strangers."

"You must really love cats."

"I do," she said with a beatific smile. "Any animal in need of affection—that's my specialty."

With the kitten in her arms, she led the way out of the garden, through the fence gate and back to the carriage house. The spaniel followed us warily, keeping an eye on Vivian and staying a stealthy few yards behind me. The door to the carriage house stood open to the April air. Once large enough to house horses and several vehicles, it was now crowded with piles of old newspapers and heaps of trash bags. It looked like a dump site. Upstairs, I knew, was the apartment where Julie and her parents had once lived. Perhaps she still lived there with her father.

We arrived inside just as the movers carried the pink couch to a vacant corner.

"No, no, not there! Put it in the other corner!"

The whole garage was full of junk, however, and the movers hesitated in confusion. There wasn't an open corner to put anything else.

"On top of those boxes," Vivian directed.

With sighs, the men heaved the fainting couch near a heap of similarly colorful and feminine furniture. I caught a glimpse of a sunny yellow armchair, a tufted footstool, a curvy lavender headboard and a flowered love seat. The movers balanced the couch on top of the other stuff and headed back to the truck for more. If Vivian intended the entire truckload of furniture to fit into the remaining space in the carriage house, they had their work cut out for them.

The spaniel came over and poked his nose against my leg.

I couldn't bring myself to pat the flea-bitten little fellow, but I gave him a kind word, and his tail shivered.

"People drop off puppies all the time out here, too," Vivian said, noting my interest in the dog. "But not like the cats. I'm always rescuing cats."

"Have you always loved animals?"

"Oh, yes. From the time my dear mother gave me my first kitten. I remember it clearly. She had packed her bags to move to California with Penny, but she took the time to give me a darling kitten. I called him Dandelion." She took a worn lace hankie from one pocket and dabbed the corner of her eye. "Shall we take a look in the truck?"

I followed Penny to the doorway of the carriage house.

"It's jammed to the ceiling with Penny's things," Vivian said. "Really, she had the most ridiculous furniture I've ever seen. Look at this—who'd buy a yellow chair? You'd spend all your time cleaning a thing like that, wouldn't you?"

I said, "It may be impractical, but Penny lived differently than the rest of us. A movie star of her era could hardly be expected to live simply."

Vivian shook her head and flicked imaginary dust from Penny's furniture. "The silly fool."

I finally heard a tinge of sadness in her voice. "I'm sorry for your loss, Vivian."

Vivian's face had turned pink. "Well, the only good thing that's come out of this is that I can sell some of this junk to buy supplies for my darlings. Penny's gone, and that's that. No sense wasting time with the dead. Those television people are calling me all the time, wanting details about my sister—what a waste of energy. She didn't exactly bring world peace, you know."

"Penny belonged to more than just her family. I suppose many people felt they knew her through her movies. They're bound to wonder what happened to her."

"She died, that's what happened."

"But how? I wonder. Vivian, you must admit, finding her hand like that was—well, gruesome, but also very troubling. Don't you wonder what must have happened to her?"

"I don't wonder at all." Vivian set her jaw to control her emotions. "How she died doesn't matter. It's best just to bury her, and forget about the circumstances."

The movers returned, this time lugging a large buffet with graceful legs and inlaid ivory. Still flushed, Vivian turned away from me to direct the men where to place it, and I decided that trying to penetrate Vivian's refusal to discuss Penny's death would only upset her further.

One of the movers wiped his perspiring face with a bandanna. "Ma'am, we've got that big table to come inside next. I don't know if it ought to be sitting out here in a garage. Is there a room we could put it in? Somewhere it won't get damaged?"

"What are you talking about? It's perfectly dry in here."

"I don't know much about antiques, ma'am, but the table looks valuable to me. Maybe it belongs someplace a little safer."

"What nonsense," she said. "Let me have a look."

She led the way outside. The movers exchanged a glance, then followed her. I tagged along with Toby hugging my shadow.

Outdoors, Vivian and the movers got into a heated discussion about the table. I eased away, and glanced around for Reed. He had disappeared, although the car hadn't moved. Down the driveway, three of Vivian's tomcats chased the female in heat.

I took a few more steps, and suddenly I could see around the moving van.

Reed was there, roughly wrestling with a slender young girl. To free herself, she hit him across the shoulder and kicked his shins.

I broke into a run. "Reed!"

He managed to push the girl far enough away to avoid her kicks, but he kept a tight hold on her right arm. In it, she gripped a can of spray paint.

"Let me go!" She tried to wrench away. "You're hurting me!"

"Stop it," he said. "You can't go around ruining other people's stuff."

"Reed!"

As I ran up, I realized the girl was Julie, standing beside the rack of fur coats. A splash of orange paint had been sprayed across the front of the first coat.

I skidded to a stop at the moment Julie jammed her finger down on the can and sent a gush of orange down the sleeve of Reed's blue Windbreaker. He dropped her at once.

"Aw, damn," he cried, "why'd you have to go and do that?"

From behind her, I knocked the spray paint out of Julie's grasp. It clattered onto the driveway and skittered underneath the moving van.

Julie swung around, her face set with fury. "Leave me alone!"

"Julie!"

As if I'd slapped the girl, her face went blank. Then she shoved her hands into the pockets of her long cardigan sweater. Her knee-high rubber boots and loose khakis looked as if she'd just come from an extended hike. Her hair was pinned tightly away from her face, emphasizing the sharp cut of her cheekbones and the hollow around her eyes.

"Did you see what the crazy bitch did?" Reed held out his sleeve for me to see.

"Watch your language, young man."

"But she—"

"There's no need for name-calling. Julie, I understand your cause, but this is the wrong way to go about it."

"Why?" she asked, lower lip poking out. "Fur coats should be destroyed to honor the animals who died so stupid women can parade around wearing death on their backs."

"Okay," I said. "You have the right to your opinion. But you can't destroy property."

"I don't care what happens to me. Go ahead. Have me arrested!"

I managed to keep my calm. "I'm sure that's not necessary. But you owe Reed a new jacket, I think."

She sent a resentful glare at Reed, but I saw her expression soften when she saw his genuine dismay. "Sorry," she mumbled.

"You should be," he grumbled back.

They were close to the same age, I realized, both still awkward in their own skins. Standing next to Reed, Julie was more obviously biracial. I could see her Jamaican mother's curly hair and golden skin quite clearly.

"Really," she said. "I'll get you a new one."

"Damn straight."

I sent him a warning glance.

"Darn right," he corrected.

"I get carried away," she said. "I have a passion for creatures that can't speak for themselves."

"That feeling is admirable," I said. "But surely there are more creative and useful ways to protest. You should join an organization, maybe. Go on the Internet and do some research."

"I don't have a computer. I don't use the Internet."

Reed looked aghast. "What planet are you from?"

"I'm from right here," she said, indignant. "I prefer to commune with nature, not machines."

"You're nuts," he muttered.

"Reed."

Vivian came around the side of the moving van. "What's going on here?"

Reed didn't answer, and Julie didn't speak, either. I said, "Julie registered a protest."

Vivian took in the sight of the ruined furs, but appeared to be more offended by the coats than the damage done to them. "Killing animals for fur is disgusting. People might as well move back into caves. Except they could never live without their air conditioners and their plastic water bottles."

I was beginning to see where Julie had acquired her adamant views on animals and the environment. I glanced at the girl and saw her nodding vigorously.

Vivian swung on Reed, eyeing the sleeve of his jacket as she held the cat in her arms. "And what happened to you?" she asked Reed, more forcefully than I'd ever seen.

"There was a little accident with paint," I explained.

"I'll pay for it," Julie whispered.

"Yes, you will," Vivian replied, surprisingly cold. "I'll take it out of your allowance, in fact, to make sure this young man doesn't suffer."

Reed's face hardened. "No way I want her in trouble."

"She got herself into trouble," Vivian replied just as heartlessly as before. "So she'll pay the consequences. I'll see you are reimbursed for your coat immediately, and she can repay me. Is that arrangement satisfactory?"

Reed glanced from Vivian to Julie, who stood with her head down now. Reed said, "This is between me and her, not anybody else."

"Don't be silly," Vivian said. "Do you want to walk around looking like a clown? Or do you want to have your jacket replaced?"

"I don't want her in trouble," he insisted.

"Must I repeat myself? I'll pay for a new coat."

Reed closed his mouth and made his expression go blank, putting an end to the discussion. Julie looked down at the toes of her boots.

"Very well." Vivian gentled her tone at last. "Then the matter is closed, and I don't want to hear another word about it."

Julie trembled, but said nothing. Reed stared at the girl as a tear rolled down her cheek.

Vivian seemed unaware of Julie's distress. "Nora, this truck is full of my sister's old clothes."

"Yes, I assumed the fur coats were Penny's."

"Coats and a lot of other frilly things she bought in Paris and Italy. It's yours."

"I—what?"

I was sure I had heard wrong.

But Vivian said, "Penny's will originally stipulated that her clothes were to go to your grandmother. But she revised her will after your grandmother passed, and these things are to go to you now."

"I—I don't know what to say."

"Did you come in a car? That one?" She pointed at the town car.

"Y-yes."

Vivian didn't notice my stunned reaction. "Well, there's too much of it to fit into a vehicle like that. I can have the movers drop it off at your home later today."

"Vivian, I'm overwhelmed."

To say the least. Penny's collection of couture was museum quality. I had as much right to it as I had to the *Mona Lisa*. My brain did a dizzy little dance in my head.

"Well, don't get too excited," Vivian said. "I think it's a bunch of old rags. I've got to get back to preparing food for my darlings now."

"Of course. Thank you, Vivian."

She turned and headed back to her mobile home, her tiny feet quick in the grass.

Julie stayed where she was.

"Hey," Reed said. "I'm sorry she yelled at you."

Julie couldn't speak. She turned and rushed away, heading for the trees.

When Reed and I went back to the car to leave, I got into the front seat.

Surprised and disgruntled to find me beside him, Reed slid behind the wheel and closed the door.

"Before you start the car, Reed, I just want to say that I was not happy with the way you spoke to Julie. I know you were upset about your jacket, but that's no excuse."

He glared out the windshield and didn't answer.

"But I must admit I was proud of you," I went on, "for not taking any guff from Vivian."

"That old lady needs—" He stopped himself. "She's not very nice."

Until this tiny incident, Vivian had seemed more than nice. She had been almost too sweet to be believed. But perhaps her focus on the animals—coupled with her blindness when it came to their genuine needs—made her incapable of seeing Julie's predicament. The girl had clearly tried to act on Vivian's beliefs about fur coats, but Vivian had coldly punished her for those actions.

Reed said, "She's got that girl bullied. What is she? Her grandmother or something?"

"No, just—well, Julie's mother was Vivian's employee. I don't know what their relationship is now."

"That girl needs to get away from this place."

I didn't disagree with Reed. I had seen a hint that Vivian wasn't as kind to people as she was to her animals. The old woman's behavior puzzled me.

Only when we reached the city did I realize I hadn't found Potty to return his money.

# Chapter Eight

*T*he Caravaggio restaurant was located in a pair of row houses along an unsavory street in what real estate agents called a mixed neighborhood. There was a gas station on the corner and an Italian bakery next door with a plastic wedding cake in the window. A line of grimy row houses stretched deeper into South Philly, and in the opposite direction I could see an abandoned elementary school with padlocked gates and signs warning trespassers. Hints of gentrification included a Dumpster parked on a sidewalk in front of a house under renovation, and that universal sign of an up-and-coming neighborhood, a Starbucks.

Caravaggio stood across the street from the coffee shop. Reed escorted me to the restaurant's door.

"Thanks, Reed. I'll ride home with Michael."

I went into the dark vestibule and found a customer arguing with a maître d' who stood behind the safety of a large reservations desk.

I nearly didn't recognize Crewe. I heard his voice as he complained to the annoyed maître d'. Crewe wore—of all things—a Kansas City baseball cap. With an earring and round tortoise-shell eyeglasses. And pleated khakis with a loose sweater that didn't quite match and gave him the appearance of a potbelly. By not removing the baseball cap, he had undeniably marked himself as a tourist, and the maître d' clearly didn't like him.

"I changed the reservation several hours ago," I heard Crewe complain. "What's the problem?"

The maître d' endeavored to hide his pained expression. "We'll have a table open soon, sir. Meanwhile, you can wait for the rest of your party in the bar."

"We shouldn't have to wait," Crewe fumed.

"The bar is that way, sir."

Crewe turned and found me standing behind him. He took my arm and steered me away from the reservations desk. In a lowered voice, he said, "Sorry about the act. I'm testing the reservations policy. I'm glad you could make it."

"Lexie and Michael will be here any minute," I promised. "In fact—yes, here's Lex now."

Lexie came through the door dressed in a severe black suit buttoned up tight under her chin and belted sharply at her waist. Normally, she wore her hair pulled back from her face in a ponytail, but tonight she looked as if her hair had been cranked in a vise before being pinned at the back of her head. Her expression said she was determined to have a lousy evening.

She gave me a brisk kiss on the cheek. "Hello, sweetie. Are you feeling okay? No aftereffects?"

"None at all. It's Crewe who was injured. He came to my rescue, did I tell you?"

Lexie faced Crewe as if he were a firing squad and she were a martyr prepared to die for a worthy cause. Then she got a look at his disguise. "Crewe, what in the world are you wearing?"

Crewe didn't melt under her glare. "Hello, Lexie. It's part of the job, I'm afraid. Does it embarrass you?"

"Not in the least. Why should I care? But must we look at that hat all evening?"

"Are you planning on wearing that frown all night?"

"I might," Lexie said dangerously. "Do we have a table?"

"There's been a mix-up with the reservation," I said. "We're waiting."

"What nonsense," she said. "I'll take care of this."

Crewe caught her by the hand before she could march over to the reservations desk to make her demands. "Take it easy," he said. "I hope Nora explained you have to play by my rules tonight. I'm on duty, which means you have to cooperate or the staff will figure out who I am. Can you do it?"

Quickly, I said, "I think it's going to be fun. I've never had dinner with a restaurant critic before." For good measure, I pinched Lexie.

She jumped, then glared at me. "Oh, all right. If we're forced to wait, we might as well get a drink, at least."

My first impression of Caravaggio was that it had been designed by an avid Andrew Lloyd Webber fan who'd seen *Phantom* far too many times. Red velvet wallpaper was punctuated by flickering sconces and a lurid painting of Paris or Venice, impossible to tell which. A connoisseur of great art, Lexie gave it a glance and shuddered.

The doorway from the vestibule to the dining room was barred by a set of iron gates, entwined with fake grapevine and firmly closed against us.

We went into the bar, which was even darker than the vestibule. Tall tables, jammed together with black lacquered stools, were decorated with cheap votive candles that barely illuminated the gloomy faces of other patrons who had been denied tables.

We ordered drinks—a scotch for Lexie, a martini for me, and Crewe asked for a Diet Coke, which triggered a barely suppressed sneer on the bartender's face.

"I'm beginning to get it," Lexie said when our drinks arrived and the bartender compounded his bad service by dribbling mine on the table. "This could be fun after all."

I attempted to make small talk, but the evening had started out tense and seemed to be sliding rapidly downhill. Lexie stared stonily at the awful art on the wall, and even Crewe appeared to be losing his courage. After five agonizing minutes, he went out to check with the maître d' again.

"Lex, the least you could do is be polite."

"I can't help it," she said. "I'm just not interested in being set up. With any man, which you know perfectly well."

"Don't think of this as a setup. It's just a night out with friends."

"I hate to wait," she grumbled, glancing over her shoulder. "Can't he even get us a table?"

"Under normal circumstances, probably. But he's doing his job. Let's see what happens."

"I notice Michael hasn't shown up yet. Clever fellow."

I had stopped checking my watch every few minutes, but of course I also noticed Michael was late. Very late. I started to worry that he had decided not to show up at all.

Crewe returned. "No table yet."

"You'd think they'd offer us a little amuse-bouche to keep us happy," Lexie muttered. "I'm hungry."

"Maybe we'll get something," I said. "Look, those people are being served an appetizer."

We looked over at a couple seated at the bar who nibbled from a small plate of tidbits that had been offered to them by an apologetic waiter.

"Hm," said Crewe. "Looks like Caravaggio has two levels of service. One for the regulars, and one for the tourists."

"Will you mention that in your review?"

"Only if the differences become markedly obvious."

"So far," Lexie said coldly, "this place deserves a scathing review."

Crewe sipped his Diet Coke. "I don't do scathing, as a matter of fact. I am cognizant that a lot of restaurants are run by local guys trying to make a living, paying a mortgage. So I try to be diplomatic. If you're a foodie who reads my reviews all the time, you know I have my codes for poor service and lousy food."

I quoted a recent review I had read. " 'If you like salads made with iceberg lettuce, this is the restaurant for you'?"

"Exactly. In good conscience, I can't put an honest restaurateur out of business."

We finished our drinks, and I began to wonder if we'd ever be seated. The couple at the bar was escorted into the dining room. A few other waiting patrons had given up and departed. Eventually, we were the only party left in the bar, and the maître d' behaved as if we were invisible. He disappeared, and the bartender drifted off to sleep with his chin propped in his hand.

Which was when the front door slammed and Michael came in. He glanced around the vestibule. I slid off my stool and went out to meet him. He had put on a pair of black trousers, a black shirt and a black leather sport coat as if he hoped to blend into the darkness of the restaurant.

"Sorry I'm late," he said when I kissed him. "I was putting out a small fire."

"Oh, really?" I smiled at his joke. "Anything serious?"

"I am serious. Your sister set the house on fire."

"Michael!"

"Take it easy. We got it out. The twins even helped. They're not bad in a crisis."

My heart was pounding. "What happened? Is Libby okay?"

"She's fine. I can't figure how she did it. She put a stack of index cards on the stove, and they caught fire. So she blew them out and carried them out to the back porch to put in the trash later. The next thing we knew, there were flames."

"Oh, my God!"

"It's okay. There's a little damage to the porch, but nothing that can't be fixed."

"At my expense," I said dolefully.

"She offered to pay. Between sobs."

"So she's really upset?"

"About losing her cards, that's all."

"Is she still at the house?"

Michael's smile was wry. "I thought it might be best if she went home to calm down. Besides, the twins have school tomorrow. So I drove them all home, then brought Rawlins back to the farm to pick up her minivan. It took longer than I thought."

I hugged him. "Thank you. The whole house might be destroyed if she stayed any longer. Come meet Crewe. And Lexie's here, in a foul mood. This may be a long night."

I introduced Crewe and Michael, who didn't bat an eye at the baseball cap. Crewe looked intrigued to be meeting the son of a famous mob boss.

Lexie eyed Michael suspiciously. "Are you limping?"

"I slipped on the stairs." Michael accepted her kiss. "Nothing serious."

"Your chin still looks awful, too. Does it hurt?"

"Not much."

"We're having a lousy time," Lexie reported. "They won't give us a table, so I'm getting ready to go in search of a McDonald's before I faint from hunger. Are you with me?"

"I might have a stick of gum." Michael patted the pockets of his coat. "If you're desperate."

The maître d' had returned to the reservations desk, and when he glanced in our direction, he dropped his fountain pen and came rushing into the bar.

"Mr. Abruzzo! I had no idea you were waiting! Please forgive me. Have you ordered a drink? On the house, anything you want!"

"Uh," said Michael.

"Please, please." The maître d' snapped his fingers at the sleepy bartender. "A drink! The scotch we keep especially for your father—"

"No, thanks," Michael said. "I don't need a drink."

"What can I get you? Whatever your pleasure. Oh, you want your table, of course. Right this way, sir."

Crewe's eyebrows had disappeared up into his baseball cap, and Lexie looked highly amused as we were ceremoniously ushered through the gates and into the much more elegant ambience of the dining room. No pictures of gondolas here, just subdued upholstery, beautiful lighting, plenty of flowers. The scent of well-coaxed herbs wafted in the air. A small number of tables were grouped in the main room, all occupied by well-dressed couples and foursomes of patrons who were quietly enjoying their food.

Through another doorway lay another room, obviously reserved for uncouth tourists who were noisier, and badly dressed, and had even brought along children, who scattered the floor with crumbs. There, every table was full. As we passed the tourist room, the maître d' held our menus aloft, perhaps hoping he could protect us from the mob.

In the main dining room, he found us a secluded corner table where we could survey the rest of the patrons, but where our conversation would not be overheard by anyone else. Expertly, he assisted Lexie and me into our seats, then guided Crewe into the corner chair and Michael into a spot with his back to the wall and an unobstructed view of the whole room.

"I hope this is satisfactory, sir," he murmured to Michael as he distributed the menus. "Allow me to send a bottle of wine to apologize for your inconvenience."

Already, waiters had begun a silent, swooping ballet of removing and replacing glassware, delivering a basket of crusty bread and, in less than two minutes, a plate of antipasto glistening with artichokes.

"Sorry about this," Michael said to Crewe. "I think I just ruined your night."

"Not at all." Crewe smiled generously. "The good news is that I haven't been recognized. All they can see is you. I guess that means I can discard the disguise."

He removed his baseball cap at last, and the eyeglasses went, too. The earring remained, however, and gave him a rakish air. "Good thing I didn't go to the trouble of wearing my false teeth."

"But Crewe," I said, "this way you're not going to get an average dining experience."

"No, but I'll have to come back at least once more anyway, so this will be a good baseline—at least where service is concerned. It'll be interesting to make comparisons."

Lexie opened her menu. "How do we proceed?"

Crewe took over, explaining apologetically that he would order for all of us and be the first to taste every dish.

"And it's time for me to turn on my recorder." He displayed a small microphone that he concealed in his sleeve. "Since I can't take notes without being spotted, we'll have to talk about the food. That way, you see, I can record my impressions."

"Are we allowed to have opinions?" Lexie asked.

"Of course." He was in professional mode, all joking aside. "But I don't have to agree with you."

We nibbled on the antipasto and studied the menu together. The flustered sommelier arrived, and in rapid Italian, he apologized profusely to Michael for keeping us waiting. He provided the wine list, made a few murmured suggestions in Michael's ear and bowed away. Another waiter arrived with a tray of small bites sent by the chef. There were tiny rolls of succulent prosciutto, shaved truffle, a morel-scented puff pastry and an array of tiny fish delicacies.

Then the chef himself arrived, hastily buttoned into a clean white jacket with his name embroidered on the breast. He conferred with Michael about the menu, suggesting we sample various items from the tray before making our final selections.

"Well, well," said Crewe when the chef bowed and went away. "So this is how the other half lives."

He chose our orders for us so that our selection of dishes ranged widely across the menu. The waiter appeared at exactly the right instant, and he memorized our requests—even the special preparation of the scallops Crewe requested to test the chef's flexibility. The waiter disappeared without taking a single note.

"That always makes me nervous," Crewe said darkly. "I'm afraid something will be forgotten."

"I have confidence they'll get it right." Lexie gave Michael a bright smile.

He sighed and shook his head. "They think they're going to sleep with the fishes if they get something wrong, don't they?"

Crewe and Lexie rushed to assure him that the staff simply wanted to give him the pleasure of a nice evening, and together they started a lively conversation to make Michael feel at ease. I wanted to kiss them all.

We had calamari first, and I remember a squid ink soup that Crewe crowed over. Michael found a bottle of Produttori del Barbaresco 1996 on the menu, a rare bottle at a bargain price that impressed Crewe no end. Then came a parade of dishes I didn't think were normally served in traditionally Italian restaurants. A swordfish with tomatoes and capers, sardines with the intense flavor of wild fennel, an eggplant rollatini with crisply burnt edges to counterbalance the creamy ricotta inside. Crewe reported the scallops were so-so, but the rest of us loved them.

By the time the cheese tray had come and gone, and our desserts were shared and discussed—a small but delicious crème brûlée, a merely average apple tart, a lemon cake with crunchy, lemon-infused sugar, and a chocolate mousse with raspberries that, in my view, was the perfect end to any meal—we turned down the offer of cognac and settled for a round of espresso.

And finally our conversation diverged from food.

Lexie wanted to know more about the probable murder of Penny Devine.

"What do you think, Nora?" she asked. "Who do you suppose murdered the old girl?"

Aware that Michael watched me, I said, "The police seem to be focused on the family first. Then I suppose anyone who had business dealings with her. You thought her connection to the board of Devine Pharmaceuticals might be important."

My friend clearly wasn't prepared to talk about that in public, so she asked, "Have you learned anything else?"

"Well . . ."

Michael guessed, "You learned something from Dilly Farquar."

"One interesting tidbit: Penny might have had an illegitimate child."

Crewe coughed and abruptly set down his cup.

The three of us looked at him while he tried to recover himself.

Lexie said, "Let me guess. Your father had a fling with Penny."

Crewe flushed.

I knew as well as Lexie that Crewe's late father had been a serial philanderer. One of the city's most notorious adulterers, in fact. My mother often told an amusing anecdote of Topper Dearborne trying to seduce her at a Halloween party. The tale included a French maid's costume and Topper dropping a monocle down her cleavage.

I wouldn't have dreamed of saying anything about Topper in front of Crewe, but Lexie smiled coolly. "Well, Crewe? Did Daddy ever climb into Sweet Penny's four-poster?"

"I have no idea." Crewe stared into his espresso.

Lexie put her elbow on the tablecloth and leaned forward. "Oh, there's no need for secrets here. Nora's father is no angel, and we all know how my mother spent her Saturday nights. Michael, you've met your share of ne'er-do-wells, right?"

"Lexie," I began, painfully aware of Crewe's discomfort.

"Oh, come on. Did Papa poke Penny or not?"

"It's possible, I suppose."

"Likely," she guessed.

"Perhaps. I—my mother—well, she made her objections known behind closed doors. But I may have heard her mention Penny's name once or twice."

Lexie sat back in triumph. "See? Doesn't it feel good to come clean? Did your parents throw china and yell about their assignations?"

"My mother never had assignations," Crewe snapped.

"Of course not. I know how she hates germs. But she knew all about your tomcat father, right?"

"Yes," he conceded.

"Did she keep a list?"

"Lex," I said again, more sharply.

Crewe looked Lexie square in the eye. "She knew about all his affairs. My father kept no secrets."

"Neither did mine," Michael said.

All three of us immediately forgot about Crewe's discomfort and shifted our attention to Michael. He looked surprised at himself.

He surrendered personal information very rarely. I crossed my fingers and hoped he might say more. Here was a chance for him to open up to friends, perhaps encourage a kind of intimacy besides what he'd managed to forge with me.

Michael noted my encouraging expression. Slowly, he added, "I'm his son by his mistress. But his wife—my stepmother—raised me."

"No kidding." Lexie looked intrigued. "Did you—forgive me for asking—did you ever know your real mother?"

"Sure. I see her every couple of months. She still keeps in touch with my father, too. But—well, she's not the motherly type."

Lexie leaned both elbows on the table this time. "What's she like? Tall, like you? Pretty?"

Michael shrugged. Once he'd managed to distract Lexie's attention away from tormenting Crewe, he clearly wasn't sure he wanted to keep talking. "She's tall."

When we waited, obviously interested to hear more, he volunteered, "She likes to gamble. I take her to the track once in a while. Or to Atlantic City."

"Have you met her, Nora?"

"Not yet. I hear she's a character. Didn't you tell me she was a Rockette?"

Michael smiled. "That's what she claims, but I don't think her dancing was that high-class. She still looks great in fishnet stockings, though."

The rest of us picked up our espresso cups and gulped.

"Well, well," Lexie said finally. She turned to Crewe. "I'm sorry. I shouldn't have pushed."

Crewe shrugged in a passable imitation of Michael's controlled calm. "No harm done."

"Look," Michael said. "Maybe my family is more screwed up than most. Maybe my mother didn't raise me, but I'd be—you know, upset if she died."

I said, "You're thinking of Penny Devine's child?"

"Yeah. Somewhere out in the world, there's a kid whose mother's gone."

"A forty-year-old kid," I said.

He shrugged again. "Doesn't matter. Where is she? Who is she? Does she even know who her mother was? Or his mother?"

Lexie mused, "So somewhere in the world there might be a person who's sorry mean old Penny is dead?"

We had all leaned close, but the waiter returned one last time and we sat back in our chairs.

Crewe said to him, "A terrific meal. Thank you. I'll take the check."

"No," Michael said. "It's mine."

Although most waiters might have paused until the argument was settled, this one didn't hesitate. He gave the small folder to Michael.

When the waiter went away, Crewe said, "Really, you've got to let me pay. It's newspaper policy."

Michael shook his head. "It's my pleasure."

Lexie drained her espresso. "Oh, let Michael pick up the tab. He owes you, Crewe, after what you did for Nora this afternoon."

I sat still and held my breath.

Michael glanced up from the bill. "What?"

"It was nothing," Crewe said jovially. "It's an honor to come to a lady's rescue."

Michael looked mystified.

I pushed my espresso cup away. "Uhm . . ."

Crewe said, "She was mugged this afternoon."

Lexie added, "Crewe happened to be there."

"One of the guys punched me in the stomach." Crewe rubbed his belly. "It's still sore."

Feebly, I added, "Reed was there, too. It was over in the blink of an eye—"

Michael turned to me. "When the hell were you going to tell me?"

"It wasn't a big deal. They tried to grab my handbag, that's all."

"No," Crewe corrected. He still hadn't seen the thunder gathering on Michael's face. "They were trying to kidnap her. They grabbed her and tried to shove her into a car. We fought them off. Nora probably broke one guy's nose. And the kid was a hero. Hit the other guy over the head with a tire iron."

"It wasn't a tire iron. It was an ice scraper. Really, Michael, I was just—"

"Who were they?"

"I don't know."

"Did they say anything?"

"Nothing I remember."

"Did you see their faces?"

"Not really. Please, they drove away, and it was over."

"Did Reed get the license number? Did you call the cops?"

"Of course. I mean, no, Reed didn't get the number. He said it had been smeared—"

"Intentionally smeared," Crewe added. Then Lexie must have kicked him under the table because he winced.

"We did call the police. They came and took a complete report." I soothed, "Really, Michael, it was nothing to get upset—"

He got up from the table, already pulling his cell phone from his pocket. "I'll be right back."

He left the dining room, which was almost deserted by now. On his way past the waiter, he shoved the check and a wad of cash into the startled man's hand.

Anxiously, the waiter said, "I hope everything was satisfactory, Mr. Abruzzo—"

Michael brushed past him.

The waiter tiptoed over to us.

"Don't worry," I said to the disconcerted man. "Our dinner was lovely."

"If there's something we can correct," the waiter began nervously, "I hope you'll give us a chance to make things right. We want Mr. Abruzzo to be happy."

"It's me he's not happy with right now," I said. "Don't worry."

He went away reluctantly.

"Sorry, Nora." Lexie reached for my hand. "I should have realized he'd go all Rambo when he heard."

"I'm so sorry," Crewe chimed in. He looked as shaken as the waiter. "I didn't mean to upset him. He's furious."

"It'll pass," I assured them.

But I wasn't looking forward to the ride home.

# Chapter Nine

"*T*his is completely unnecessary," I said once we were alone. "You're acting as if I'm in mortal danger."

"Two guys tried to kidnap you. You don't call that mortal danger?"

"Honestly, Michael, I think it was simply a purse snatching. I'm carrying a Balenciaga worth at least five thousand dollars. It would be worth ten thousand now if Spike hadn't peed in it that time—"

"Your average purse snatcher doesn't know the difference between your whatever and one from Wal-Mart. Besides, kids snatch purses, not guys with cars." Michael's hands were tense on the steering wheel. "I don't want you going anywhere without checking with me first."

"I have a job! I can't report my whereabouts every five minutes—"

"Then I'll go with you."

"Fine. Tomorrow night is the ballet fund-raiser. You'll need a tuxedo."

Michael ground his teeth as he drove. At last, he said, "All right, I'll admit I can't be with you all the time. But Reed takes you everywhere from now on, got that? And where's your cell phone?"

With a guilty swallow, I said, "At home. I left it on the kitchen counter."

"Nora—"

"Okay, okay, I promise I'll be more careful. Look, I can't imagine why anyone would want to hurt me."

"You've been asking questions about Penny Devine's murder."

"Only among my close friends."

"What about Farquar?"

"Oh, heavens, Dilly didn't even know I was coming today until I tapped him on the shoulder. I'm perfectly safe."

"Why are you so determined to pretend this didn't happen?"

My worst fear was that the men were connected somehow to whatever Michael was up to. He was dabbling in his dark arts again, I suspected, and perhaps the attack on me was some repercussion I didn't understand yet.

Michael said, "It's like you're trying to prove something."

"To myself maybe," I murmured.

"What does that mean?"

"I don't know," I said.

"Nora—"

"I don't know! I can't explain how I feel! I'm upset!"

Maybe I'd had too much wine, or maybe all the day's excitement finally boiled over. I found myself hyperventilating, and my voice rose, quaking with frustration I couldn't define. "I want my life to be easy, and it's not! I want a home and a family and you—but I—I can't have those things, can I? Everything keeps going out of control! But figuring out how Penny died—it keeps my brain from going places I don't want to go. From making the wrong decisions!"

Michael had listened to my little tirade in silence. At last, he said, "What kind of decisions?"

"I don't know! I'm just—I'm afraid, Michael. I'm afraid of doing something stupid, of making another bad choice that—that ruins everything again."

"Are we back to the miscarriage? Because that wasn't your fault."

"It's not that."

But the miscarriage was part of it, of course. I so wanted a family, and Michael did, too. But my body wasn't cooperating.

If I brought it up, though, I knew what he'd say. Everyone was saying it to me. That I had lots of time. Plenty of chances to get pregnant again. Women got themselves pregnant all the time, and I shouldn't worry about it.

I didn't want to hear the platitudes anymore.

Nor did I want to hear what he was doing late at night when he wasn't home with me.

"Getting married," Michael said. "Is that a bad choice?"

"No," I said.

"You don't sound convinced."

"I'm completely convinced. I know it's what I want. Unless . . ."

"Unless what?"

"Unless it means you die."

He drove another mile and then said more quietly, "Nora, I'm not going to die."

"Already you've had one car accident. Plus a fall down the stairs. And now a fire!"

"That was your crazy sister's fault, not mine."

"None of it's your fault! It just happens!"

"Todd's cocaine addiction didn't just happen. He did it to himself."

"I'm not talking about Todd. I'm talking about you. And you've been having accidents that—"

"Accidents." Michael reached for me. "That's all, just accidents."

I seized his hand and gripped it hard. "I'm sorry. I'm being crazy."

"You have reason. You were attacked today. Yesterday you found a severed hand. A few weeks ago—"

"I know." I didn't want to hear any more. I forced a laugh, but it sounded hollow. "I'm sorry I'm such a wreck."

At home, he parked beside Emma's pickup truck, and we got out to stare at the charred remains of my back porch. It had been more than a small fire, I saw at once. The lawn was gouged by the tires of multiple fire trucks, and the blackened pillars of the porch stood forlornly pointing at the sky. What was left of the roof lay in a crumpled heap on top of my rose-bushes. The floorboards were scorched, but usable.

I slid my arm around Michael and stood with my head against his shoulder, looking at the mess. It was a miracle the whole house hadn't gone up in flames. I knew whose quick thinking had saved the old derelict.

"Michael," I said, contrite. "I love you. I know you're trying to protect me. I'll be more careful, I promise."

He kissed the top of my head. "Thank you."

Upstairs, we paused on the landing. From the bathtub down the hall, we heard Emma's husky laughter. We went into my room and closed the door.

Michael sat on the bed, gingerly stretching his sore leg. Despite our lovely evening with friends, he suddenly looked exhausted, and I thought with guilt about our searing lovemaking the night before. Quietly, I undressed and hung up my clothes.

We had more to talk about, but neither one of us knew where to start. And neither one of us wanted to initiate another night like last night.

Watching me hang up my clothes, Michael said, "I liked your friend Crewe."

"Did you? I'm glad."

"But what's going on with Lexie? She was a bitch tonight."

I slid into a wisp of a nightie and sat beside Michael on the bed to help him out of his shirt. His ribs were black-and-blue from his fall down the stairs. Folding his shirt into my lap, I told him about Lexie's teenage years and the cousin who raped her. It was a long story, and an ugly one. I explained why Lexie didn't like Crewe or any other man, really. Michael forgot about being sore and listened.

I finished by saying, "After what happened, I don't know if she'll ever allow any man in her life."

"Crewe's got it pretty bad for her, though."

"He has for a long time. But I don't think she'll ever get over what happened to her."

"She doesn't have to get over it," said Michael, who had survived an awful childhood, too. "She just has to find a way to work around it."

We went to bed and allowed an evening of too much food and drink to put us to sleep. But I drifted off thinking of Crewe's father and Penny Devine. Had they had an affair? From the look on Crewe's face, I was sure they had. Was Topper Dearborne the father of Penny's child?

# Chapter Ten

On Monday, Libby arrived before nine, bursting into my house in a screaming pink velour suit with matching sneakers and a T-shirt that said ROLLER COASTER in sequins. Before she had even slammed the door shut, she demanded, "You don't think Emma has become a call girl, do you?"

"Libby, for crying out loud, have a little faith." I was in the scullery folding laundry.

"Well, what else could it be? She's taking phone calls from men around the clock, making appointments for late at night. What am I supposed to think?"

"You're supposed to think about giving Em the benefit of the doubt."

"In this family?"

"Has it crossed your mind that she's not telling you what she's doing because it drives you nuts? And Emma loves pushing your buttons?"

"She's just ashamed of herself, that's all."

I didn't think Emma had looked the least bit ashamed of whatever she had going. All I knew was that every minute Libby spent fuming about Emma was one minute she wasn't making me crazy with wedding plans.

"Want to tell me what happened to my porch last night?"

"What a disaster!" Libby leaned against the dryer while I matched socks. "I don't know what's wrong with your stove, Nora, but it's very dangerous. No sooner had I dropped a few index cards when they burst into flame! At first I thought it was the twins tormenting me again. Did I tell you they moved their collection of snakes in jars to my bedroom because theirs gets too much sunlight? They're just too disgusting, so I brought them over and put them in your fridge. Fortunately, I saved the timeline."

"Timeline?"

"From the fire! The bulletin board with our list of tasks to accomplish before the wedding. You have a string of things to do, by the way, so you should check it and get busy." Without pausing to draw a breath, she said, "Did you see *Excess Hollywood* last night? There was a big story about Penny Devine."

"I missed it."

"Well, they had a psychic who thinks Penny went to Alaska and is hiding out among the Inuits eating whale meat!"

"Even you couldn't have come up with that one."

"What does that mean?"

"Just—"

"I'm a creative soul! I have bursts of inspiration! But I'm not psychic."

Thank heaven for small favors, I thought. But I said, "Yes, you're very creative, Libby."

"Thank you. I've been thinking about cake."

"Oh?"

"Wedding cakes, of course. It's very popular to have exotic flavors these days, did you know? So I thought we could experiment a little."

"Can't we just buy a cake when the time comes?"

Libby blew an exasperated sigh. "Nora, when are you going to get into the spirit of this wedding? If you don't put your heart and soul into the planning, you can't expect the most wonderful day of your life to be meaningful!"

At that moment, I was simply hoping my wedding day might not include a house fire. "I'm not sure I find cake flavors very meaningful, Lib."

"You will," she said ominously. "Look, I've bought everything we need. I thought we could bake this morning."

"Your mother-in-law is driving you up the wall," I guessed.

"She's making me crazy," Libby agreed. "So let's bake some cakes!"

I gave up trying to save my own sanity. "Fine."

"Oh, wait. Here. Lucy sent this for you."

Libby handed me a piece of construction paper on which my niece had drawn some figures on an ocean of green grass dotted with flowers.

"It's a self-portrait," Libby explained. "One of her best representational drawings. That's Lucy riding a pony, and you picking flowers."

The flower looked more like a severed hand to me, but I didn't say so.

"I don't know why I shouldn't just bring her over here and let you raise her," Libby said. "You're all she wants to talk about."

With a smile, I put Lucy's drawing on my refrigerator, anchored with a magnetic bottle opener. My first refrigerator picture.

"Now," Libby said, "where are your measuring cups?"

"The twins were using them downstairs. Why don't you go down and get them?"

"Why don't we just improvise!"

While I puttered, taking care of household chores, Libby mixed and baked a cake. Without burning down anything.

"Have you seen that dog-whisperer guy?" she asked. "I wonder if I could hire him to retrain the twins?"

Around noon, the insurance adjuster arrived. I met him at the front door, and we walked around the outside of the house to the porch. A shy man with a clipboard, he resisted my attempt at small talk until we reached the backyard. There, he shook his head sorrowfully over the ruined structure and asked if the fire department had sent an arson investigator.

"The fire was caused by a wedding," I told him.

"A wedding?" He made a note. "Well, that's a first."

Libby must have finally noticed I was in the company of a man, because she came out onto the porch. Over her pink velour suit, she had added a frilly apron, and she looked like a Stepford wife dressed for an Easter egg hunt. With pot holders, she carried a cake pan.

"Hello!" she yodeled.

The insurance adjuster took off his reading glasses and put one hand up to shield his eyes from the blinding sunlight. Or perhaps the mesmerizing power of my sister's bosom. "Uh, good afternoon."

"I'm Nora's sister Libby. And you are?"

Politely, he went up the charred steps of the porch. "I'm Gerald Hopkins. From the insurance company." He moved to shake her hand, but belatedly became aware that she was carrying a hot pan. He stepped back as if it might burst into flame at any moment. "Is that the cause of the blaze, ma'am?"

"Certainly not. This is fresh out of the oven. It's mango lemon. Doesn't it smell heavenly?"

"Uh, yes, it does."

"I was hoping to get an unbiased opinion. Do you see anything extraordinary on the top of this cake?"

Mr. Hopkins put on his reading glasses again and peered down at the surface of Libby's confection. "Looks pretty much like a cake to me."

"Are you sure? You don't happen to see a likeness?"

"A likeness?" I went up the stairs, too. "Libby, you're not seeing the Virgin Mary or Elvis or some such nonsense, are you?"

"Of course not. That would be sacriligious, not to mention very tacky. No, look, Nora, don't you think the top of this cake looks rather like Tom Cruise?"

"The movie star?" Gerald Hopkins peeked at the cake again. "My wife loves Tom Cruise."

Libby's face fell. "Your wife?"

"Ex-wife," Gerald corrected unwillingly, as if forced to reveal an ugly fact about himself. "We used to cook together. Until she developed an allergy and switched to all raw foods. I don't know about you, but that raw diet just about ruined my insides."

"How thoughtless of her! You poor man!"

"I'm better now." He blinked as if finally becoming aware of more than my sister's physical attributes, then caught himself staring and looked down at the cake again. "Come to think of it, I do see a profile there. And it does have Tom Cruise's nose, doesn't it?"

"And his chin," Libby said. "Look again."

"You should take a photo and put it on eBay. My wife made a fortune on eBay. Sold my old saxophone in two days. Before I had a chance to bid myself, it was gone."

"Ex-wife," Libby corrected. "Right?"

"Right, right."

"EBay," Libby said. "What a brilliant idea."

I went into the house. I figured Mr. Hopkins would find me when he finished talking to Libby.

Michael had been making phone calls all morning, but now he was assembling a hasty sandwich in the kitchen.

He ate hurriedly at the sink.

"You're trying to get out of here while Libby's distracted, aren't you?"

"Think it's going to work?"

"Eat faster," I advised.

But too late. Libby came back inside, carrying her cake. "What a charming man!"

"Don't ask," I murmured to Michael. "Libby, you're incorrigible."

"Why? Whatever do you mean?"

"Did you make a date with him?"

"No." Her smile twinkled. "But he's coming back tomorrow to have a second look at the—um—damage. Oh, good, you're both here! We can get some wedding planning done!"

Mouth full, Michael sent me a frightened look.

"Libby, I don't think we—"

"Let's start at the beginning. Have you discussed a date?"

Michael swallowed hard. "A date?"

"Of course, a date! For the ceremony! We need to narrow down our reception choices." She located her bulletin board and propped it on the kitchen counter beside the coffeepot. Then she opened a pack of index cards and reached for her pushpins. "And, of course, the size of the wedding makes a difference. How many guests were you planning to invite?"

"Do we need guests?" Michael turned to me. "Can't it just be us?"

Libby exploded. "I'm dealing with amateurs! No, it can't just be the two of you! It's—it's illegal or something. You need witnesses! Friends and family to toast your future! Bridesmaids in beautiful gowns!"

"Libby—"

"What kind of wedding did you have in mind?" Libby asked Michael.

"The usual kind, I guess."

"In a church? Under a tent? At a hotel? In a garden, perhaps?"

"Uh—"

"I envision a lovely landscape—with water, perhaps. Swans, flower petals cast upon the waves, that kind of thing. Maybe children blowing those gigantic bubbles into the air. I'm not a fan of doves, though. They look like pigeons to me."

Blankly, Michael said, "Pigeons."

"We don't need any of that," I said in a rush. "There's no earthly reason why we can't have a quiet, private little—"

"I know what's wrong," Libby said. In a voice full of authority practiced during years of motherhood, she commanded, "Sit down, you two."

We sat.

"Now, look," she said, standing over us with a pushpin in each hand. "I understand you have been through a difficult time. God knows, I've had enough trying experiences for more than one lifetime, but my personal tragedies have given me wisdom and insight that I'm only too happy to share. You can't allow the loss of your unborn child to color the rest of your life together."

"Please, Lib—"

She held up one hand to silence me. "It's very painful, I know. I've been there, and miscarrying was one of the most devastating events I've ever suffered. I feared I might become inadequate in the eyes of my lover. I feared I might never experience the rapture of childbirth. And perhaps most agonizing of all, I feared I would never enjoy the passion of lovemaking again without dreading the loss of the baby we might be conceiving. It was terrible. So I sympathize."

"Thank you," I said. "But—"

She closed her eyes and took a deep breath. "I am channeling all your worst fears, Nora. I know exactly how you're feeling. Which puts me in the perfect position to help plan your wedding."

"Maybe," Michael said, half rising, "I should run along and let the two of you—"

"The man's input is vital!" Libby thundered so loudly that Michael was catapulted back into the chair. "How can we possibly decide the color of the table linens without hearing your thoughts? If left to our own devices, we might accidentally choose something that reminds you of a terrible childhood trauma!"

"Well, I don't recall any color traumas—"

Libby gave me the pushpins and laid a consoling hand on Michael's shoulder. "You're suffering, too," she said soothingly. "The loss of a child isn't just a female tragedy, is it? But you can't allow one bump in your road to happiness to ruin everything. Think of your wedding as a renewal—an opportunity to begin again, to open the door to a new chapter in your life."

"Sounds great," Michael said, "but—"

"There will be more children," Libby assured him. "In today's world, nature and science can work wonders together."

"I really don't think we're going to need any—"

"In fact," Libby went on, "if Nora finds herself incapable of carrying a child to term, I volunteer my own womb to help you."

"Uh—"

She was beaming. "That's it! I'll be your surrogate, Nora! God knows, I've delivered each of my five children as easily as a Chinese peasant drops babies in a rice paddy, so I'm the perfect candidate! Just think! The three of us could attend Lamaze classes together! And the birthing room will be one big family party!"

"Lib, you're very generous, but we don't need to think about extreme measures right now—"

"We don't need to think about extreme measures at all," Michael said. "We're not going to make any Frankenstein babies, so you can forget it."

"But—"

He was on his feet. "Look, the two of you can talk weddings as long as you like, but I've got things to do."

"Michael," I began.

He kissed me hard. "I'll be back tonight."

"Well!" Libby said when he'd slammed out the door. "He couldn't get out of here fast enough, could he?"

"Who wouldn't be scared of the things you were saying?"

"I don't think That Man is fully accessing his emotions, Nora."

"Good grief, it's a wonder he didn't faint with all that rapture in the rice paddies!"

Libby seized my hand. "I meant what I said, Nora. I'll be your surrogate mother! After the wedding first, of course. I want to look good in my bridesmaid dress."

# Chapter Eleven

tried phoning Detective Bloom that afternoon, but no success.
A skim of the newspapers revealed no developments in the
Penny Devine case, and the six o'clock news was nothing but con-
tinued media hysteria. I tried to put the murder out of my mind.

On Monday evening, Reed was engaged to drive me to a fund-raiser
for the city's ballet company. What I didn't expect was Reed's companion.

One of Michael's minions, Aldo, a former prizefighter who obliged the
Abruzzo family when called upon, stood with Reed beside the car when I
went outside. I saw the flash of his pinkie ring as he opened the car door
for me. Aldo wore an ill-fitting tuxedo with a white silk scarf around his
neck. The ensemble smelled strongly of mothballs.

"Aldo—"

"Yeah. Howya doin'?"

I gave his clothing a cursory inspection. His cummerbund didn't look
up to the task of containing his belly. "Who put you up to this, Aldo?"

His face was impassive. "I'm supposed to keep an eye on you."

"That's a very handsome tuxedo you're wearing."

"You think so?" He stroked the lapel. "I got it for my daughter's wedding. Still looks good, don't it?"

I had never contemplated the possibility that Aldo might have offspring.
"Very nice," I said.

"You look good, too."

Although I heard the false note in his voice, I said, "Thank you."

I had put on a Dior dress of my grandmother's: a Greek-column
evening gown in green silk—not my best color, but not bad, either—that
was a series of pin pleats that fell straight from a high bodice trimmed with
seed pearls. The dress fit me beautifully now that I had lost a few pounds.

It was sleeveless with a demure stand-up collar, which Aldo apparently didn't seem to care for. I carried a jeweled Dior stole over my arm.

"It wouldn't hurt to show a little skin," Aldo said. "On a special occasion like this, I mean."

Reed shouldered him aside and hustled me into the car.

"What'd I say?" Aldo asked, mystified.

The drive into Philadelphia was long and tortured. Every thirty seconds Aldo adjusted his collar and sighed. Reed shot him uneasy glances.

The ballet fund-raiser was just getting started when we arrived at the Merriam Theater. I had plenty of time to conduct a few early interviews during the cocktail hour. Tonight, money was to be raised for the orchestra that played for the Pennsylvania Ballet, always a good cause. The board of the organization had decided to try a Chinese auction instead of the usual dinner or preview party. Various individuals, local businesses and a few corporations had donated items, and guests were invited to bid on the prizes.

A law firm I knew had donated a trip for four to a Caribbean resort. In addition, my friend special-events coordinator Delilah Fairweather had donated her services for a private party for twenty-five guests in the home of the highest bidder. Other smaller donations included a pricey bottle of wine, some autographed baseballs from the Phillies and a watercolor painting by a famous local artist, plus several restaurant dinners by chefs who volunteered to prepare and serve the meals personally.

A number of television trucks idled outside the theater. I was surprised to see them. The ballet rarely attracted extensive media coverage. I wondered if a celebrity might make a surprise appearance later to add to the festivities.

Reed stayed with the car. It was Aldo who escorted me into the landmark theater, where the ballet often performed. Aldo labored up the staircase, huffing for breath and moaning every time his bad knee creaked. When we reached the marble floor, a throng of perhaps a hundred guests already mingled, while waiters circulated with trays of champagne glasses and canapés. I saw sashimi in delicate white cups, skewers of shrimp that smelled spicy and exotic, as well as long spears of asparagus baked in phyllo and sprinkled with Parmesan cheese.

Members of the ballet company whisked through the crowd decked out in costumes from the recent performance of *Coppelia*. A string quartet played a lively gavotte in one corner. Overhead, thousands of tiny lights had been strung like stars against the darkened ceiling.

"Why don't you wait here, Aldo?" I snagged two champagne flutes from a passing waiter and urged him into a corner to catch his breath. "You can keep an eye on things from this spot. See? A great vantage point. I have to interview a few people, but I'll be in plain sight the whole time."

"Yeah, good."

He looked relieved to be spared rubbing shoulders with the balletomanes, so I left him gulping champagne and went in search of the party hosts for quotes.

Instead, I found Detective Bloom. Or rather, he found me.

"I figured you'd be here," he said.

"Hello, Ben. Are you enjoying the party?"

"I'm not here for any damn party."

Without further explanation, he took my elbow and propelled me across the floor away from the crowd. He glared at a young woman in one of the many mechanical-doll costumes from the *Coppelia* production. She dashed back to her comrades for safety.

As Aldo launched himself across the lobby toward us, Bloom said, "I see you've got one of the Abruzzo goons playing babysitter."

I gave Aldo a don't-worry-about-me smile, and he stopped in his tracks. Glowering at Bloom, he reluctantly retreated.

"Not by my choice," I said to Bloom. "Smile so he doesn't come over and break your kneecaps. What are you doing here?"

Bloom took me seriously and plastered a stiff smile on his face for Aldo's benefit. "Investigating a murder, and you know it."

"I tried calling you after the polo match. Several times."

"I just heard about the attack on your life."

At once, I said, "Somebody tried to grab my handbag, that's all."

"Bullshit. Abruzzo obviously knows it was more than that, or you wouldn't have his attack dog along tonight."

Attack dog? To me, Aldo was more of an overweight mutt that slept on furniture and smelled bad.

Bloom said, "I already talked to the cops who took your statement. Now I want the details from you."

"Why? What possible connection could a purse snatching have to Penny Devine's murder? It is Penny who's dead, by the way, isn't it? Have you made it official yet?"

Bloom sighed shortly. "No, not yet. We're still having a problem with the morgue. We're not the city of Philadelphia," he added with heat, "so we have to play Mickey Mouse games. But today the brother and sister identified the wristwatch as definitely Penny's. They're making a fuss to have her body—what's left of it—returned so they can bury it."

I heard the bitter note in his voice. More than anything, Bloom wanted a job on the city's homicide squad, but he'd been stuck in a sleepy suburb for a few years now, and the constant exasperation took its toll. Tonight Bloom seemed more agitated than usual. His modus operandi was to play a Boy Scout in search of points for his next merit badge, but this evening I could see tension vibrating in him.

I softened my tone. "Can you blame the family? The longer it takes, the more publicity there will be. It's all very ghoulish for them."

He snorted. "Yeah, wait till you see *Entertainment Tonight*. They had a camera crew all over the Main Line today, shooting footage. A cop brought his lunch in a paper bag, and the cameraman zoomed in like we were smuggling in body parts with the Quiznos sandwiches."

"Do you have any theories about how she died?"

He surprised me by telling me the truth. "Yeah, maybe. An employee of the Devine estate who disappeared a few months ago. Kelly Huckabee, a gardener or something."

"Kell disappeared?"

"Yeah, do you know him?"

"A little. I wondered where he was. No wonder the place looks so terrible."

"He was lousy at his job?"

"He grew up on the estate. His parents were live-in servants of the Devines. And he married a woman who came to the estate when she was hired as the household manager. But she died. If he disappeared, this is a big development, isn't it? Do you think he—good heavens, did he kill Penny?"

Bloom shrugged. "Nobody knows where he is. The Devines say he took off last fall and didn't come back."

"Could he have left around the time Penny died?"

"The autopsy will tell."

"He killed Penny and left town?"

"That's the idea."

I considered Bloom's theory. Of course, it made sense. Kell Huckabee's bad temper made him an obvious killer in my imagination. But why a gardener would kill his employer's famous sister—that question was beyond me.

Bloom shoved his hands into his pockets. "I ran Huckabee's name through the system and came up with a couple of assault charges against him."

"I'm not surprised. He was a good candidate for anger management."

"There was one complaint he filed, too."

"Against whom?"

"Some newspaper writer."

"Anyone I know?"

Bloom hesitated, then clearly decided he had nothing to lose by telling me. "Guy named Crewe Dearborne."

I tried to maintain a neutral expression, but my insides did a flip-flop. I had no idea Crewe even knew Julie's father. "Kell Huckabee filed a complaint against Crewe Dearborne? For what?"

"A fistfight, from the look of the report. Doesn't seem like Huckabee was totally innocent in the altercation." Bloom sighed and rubbed his face. He muttered, "If I could forget about sleeping, I'd get to the bottom of it. I hate looking like Barney Fife on national TV."

I touched his arm. "I'm sure it's not as bad as that."

He glanced at my hand. When things with Michael had been at their worst, spending time with an officer of the law had seemed like a good idea. At least I didn't have to worry about him going to jail on a regular basis.

And Bloom had been interested in me, too. But eventually I had realized all he really wanted was to get himself noticed by the city police force by nailing Big Frankie Abruzzo's son. I discovered Bloom's primary fascination with me had been to get himself an informant.

I pulled my hand away.

He allowed his gaze to skim my dress before saying, "Tell me about the guys who tried to grab you."

"Neither one of them was Kell Huckabee. I'd have recognized him."

"So describe them."

"I already—okay, okay. Two big men, both with strong upper bodies, dark complexions—"

"The report said you used the word 'Mediterranean.' You meant Italian?"

"Or Spanish, maybe. Dark hair. Olive skin."

"Brazilian?"

My interest sharpened. "Why do you ask?"

"Did you hear any accents?"

I shook my head. "They sounded local. New Jersey, maybe. Why do you ask if they might have been Brazilian?"

He shrugged. "I want to cover all the bases."

"Some of the visiting polo players are from Brazil."

"I know. I tried to interview a bunch of them. But do you know how hard it is to find a Portuguese interpreter on my budget?"

"Sorry. Did you learn anything?"

"Not much," he grumbled. "Penny Devine bought a lot of horses for polo players."

"Like Raphael Braga."

He heard the change in my voice and shot me a look. "You know Braga?"

"A little, yes. A lot, actually."

"How? What's your relationship?"

"He married a college friend of mine. I did them a favor a long time ago."

"What kind of favor?"

At once, I was sorry I'd mentioned it. I didn't want to get into it with Detective Bloom, who would get even more wrong ideas than Michael. So I told him the bare minimum. "Nothing to do with Penny Devine's death. Penny was Raphael's patron, though. Which means she paid some of his expenses. That might lead you somewhere."

Bloom studied me, puzzled and intrigued. "She gave Braga a hell of a lot of money over the years, in fact, in the form of horses. I'm trying to figure out how much, but again, my budget doesn't allow for a simple phone call to Brazil, let alone an international audit. I was thinking . . ."

I met his gaze and said nothing.

"I was thinking maybe you could help me out," he finished.

The last thing I wanted was for anyone to start digging around Raphael Braga.

But I heard myself ask, "What do you need to know?"

"Braga's connection to Penny Devine. Was it purely business? I mean, if he got horses out of it, what did she get?"

"I don't know. You're thinking their business arrangement might have gone bad somehow."

"Maybe. It was a very sweet deal for Braga. But it looks one-sided to me."

"Maybe they simply enjoyed each other's company."

"She was forty years older than he is!"

"They had a common interest in horses."

Bloom squinted at me. "Are you defending him?"

"God, no."

"This favor you did for him. What's that all about? Does it mean you've got some emotional tie to the man?"

I shook my head. "It's not like that at all. What else have you learned about Potty? Or Vivian?"

He hesitated, trying to find a way to ask the same questions again. He shot a glance across the marble floor at Aldo, who stood glowering at us.

"All right." Bloom gave up at last. "The old guy's coming here tonight."

Startled, I said, "Potty's coming out this evening?" That information explained the number of television trucks outside the theater. "So much for being afraid of bad publicity."

"He cut short my interview this afternoon because he had to go home to get dressed for this damn thing. He seemed pretty anxious to get here in time for the free drinks."

"The drinks aren't free. Everybody here has donated at least ten thousand dollars to help fund the ballet's orchestra. Potty's been a big donor over the years."

"Still, I'd like to know why he'd brave more television cameras to come tonight. Why's it important for him to show up?"

"I have no idea. Many people simply write a check and stay home. Do you want me to find out why he insisted on coming this evening?"

Bloom stopped watching Aldo and turned to give me a long stare. "I can't help noticing you're awfully willing to help this time. Except for Braga, you're almost eager, in fact. I haven't even threatened to arrest Abruzzo to get you on my side."

"There's no need to make a threat we both know is empty."

Bloom frowned. "But you're volunteering to help me out. What's changed?"

"Nothing," I said. I had my own reasons to want to corner Potty. I still had an envelope full of his cash. "Look, here comes Potty now."

From the windows, we watched Potty Devine get out of a new Cadillac and hand the keys and a cash tip to the valet-parking attendant. Television lights blazed on, and cameras followed him across the sidewalk. A reporter rushed forward, brandishing a microphone. Potty irritably waved him off and shoved through the door to the theater.

Bloom and I left the window and went to the balustrade to watch Potty labor up the marble stairs. He wore evening clothes with a light overcoat and a black hat tilted at an angle that looked positively jaunty.

At the top of the stairs, a woman squealed and ran down two steps to fling her arms around Potty. She nearly knocked him down the staircase with the force of her affection. I recognized Nuclear Winter. Potty reached around and gave Nuclear's bottom a squeeze.

Sounding surprised, Bloom said, "He's a dirty old man!"

"Potty does enjoy young women," I said on a sigh. "That's Noreen Winter, better known as 'Nuclear' Winter. She's rather famous around town."

"For?"

"For pursuing rich men who—uhm—don't always survive."

"She kills them?" Bloom sounded startled.

"With love," I said. "Two of her former partners didn't have sufficient cardiac stamina to withstand her affections."

"Devine doesn't look worried."

"No, he doesn't, does he? Shall I go talk to Potty now? What would you like to know?"

Bloom continued to frown. "Ask him about his relationship with his sister Penny. Just see where the conversation leads."

"Aye, aye, Detective."

I cut across the lobby to head off Potty at the bar.

# Chapter Twelve

Tonight Nuclear Winter looked like an escapee from *Girls Gone Wild* in her slinky strapless dress that barely clung to her breasts. She towered over Potty in shoes high enough to require a strobe light to warn low-flying planes. Potty, standing three inches shorter than his Amazonian companion, handed her a champagne, and they clinked glasses and giggled together.

"Potty," I said, but he didn't hear me. I touched his arm.

He turned and shouted, "Nora! Don't you look pretty tonight! Ha-ha!"

In the crowded party, it was going to be hard to communicate with him without sharing our conversation with a hundred people.

I raised my voice anyway. "Hi, Potty. Are you having a good time?"

"Yes, it's delicious wine!" he bellowed. "Can I get you a glass?"

"That would be lovely, thank you!"

Beaming, he toddled after the waiter.

Which left me standing with his date. Nuclear had been pretty once, I could tell, but her lips were ballooned out of proportion now, and the implants in her cheeks, her chin and her breasts made her look as generic as any aspiring starlet.

"Get lost, honey," Nuclear said to me. "I saw him first."

"Honey," I said, "I'm not here to stop you from landing the big fish. Just give me ten minutes alone with him first, please?"

"What for?" Nuclear drank a slug of champagne. "You gonna write something nice about Potty in the paper? I keep telling him he needs a press agent, but he says he can do it his way."

His way, I knew, meant bribing journalists. "Trust me," I said. "I'll do everything I can for Potty. How about giving us some time to talk it over?"

She gave my dress a withering look and clearly decided she didn't have to worry about competition from me. Then she spotted the ring on my hand, and her eyes bugged out. "Okay, ten minutes. I have to go to the little girls' room, anyway."

She made an about-face and wiggled off in search of the nearest bathroom.

The string quartet took a break as Potty elbowed his way back to me through the crowd. "Did you meet Darlene?"

I accepted the glass of champagne he offered and tried putting my mouth close to his ear. "I thought her name was Noreen."

"I'm not sure," he admitted with a twinkling grin. "Maybe it's Charlene. Or Marlene. I get them all mixed up after a while."

He reached into his ear and adjusted the mechanism on his hearing aid.

"You're very lucky with the ladies, Potty."

"It's not luck. It's money, dear girl. Ha-ha!" He laughed, no illusions.

"Money can't be the only secret to your success."

"Oh, I know how to make snappy conversation with the young ones. Get them talking about themselves, that's what works."

I smiled. "You're a lady-killer, Potty."

"Truth be told?" He slipped his hand past the silk lapel and into his jacket. "I have my little jelly beans to thank."

But it wasn't candy that came out of his pocket. Potty held up a small, clear vial and shook it, showing me half a dozen little blue pills.

It was the kind of small bottle Todd had used to bring his cocaine home from the street. I took the vial from Potty and looked more closely at the pills inside. "What are they?"

"MaxiMan." Potty laughed heartily at my expression. "Oh, don't be shocked, Cousin Nora. You look like a young lady who enjoys her bedroom. Those little beans changed my life."

"I thought MaxiMan wasn't on the market yet."

"It's not. It's in the testing phase. And who better to test them?"

"Potty, are you sure it's safe for you to—"

"These pills are the safest of their kind. Don't worry about me. I've used them a hundred times, and I am here to tell you that satisfaction is guaranteed."

"How . . . nice for you."

"Nice for you, too," he promised, folding my hand more firmly around

139

the vial. "Take those home. Find some fella who'll swallow one, and you'll end up in paradise."

"Potty—"

"No, no, I insist. Take 'em. I have plenty more where those came from."

So Potty was the Devine Pharmaceuticals insider who was passing out MaxiMan so freely.

Rather than argue with him, I tried to change the subject. "Potty, you and I have had a little misunderstanding, and I want to set the record straight. At the polo match, you slipped an envelope into my pocket, and that was very naughty of you."

He winked. "I'm a naughty man."

"Thing is, Potty, I can't accept money from you. And I certainly can't promise to give you favorable treatment in my column."

"Nora, that envelope was a gift! You could use a little financial help, right?"

"That's very kind of you, but we both know it was not a gift." I had the envelope out of my handbag by that time, and I pressed it into his palm. "I must return the cash, Potty."

He grinned. "Is it all there?"

"Yes, of course."

"You sure I can't convince you to take it?"

"Absolutely not. I know you're upset about Penny's death, and no doubt that clouded your judgment. It must be a terrible shock—"

"Oh, not such a shock." Potty amenably slipped the envelope into his breast pocket. "We've known for some time she was dead."

"Because of the suicide note."

"What? Oh, yeah, the suicide note. And those runaway trips of hers— eventually one of 'em was going to end badly."

"Why do you say that?" I asked. "Didn't she hide out at spas? That seems safe to me."

"Spas?" Potty scoffed. "Not unless they had hot and cold running men. Hell, Penny didn't go off to lose weight."

"What?"

"Younger men, that was her real addiction—ha-ha!"

"Are you sure?"

"Sure, I'm sure! The old girl surrounded herself with young fellas—the

140

younger the better. All bought and paid for. That's how she spent her money, you know. Buying affection. Those good-looking polo players? That's who she ran away to."

"Do you think—I mean, could one of her boyfriends have killed her?"

"During some kinky sex?" Potty asked with a knowing wink.

"No, that's not what I—"

"You're blushing again, Cousin Nora. No, my bet is that Penny's heart gave out. What a way to go, right?"

"But why would she end up—Potty, this is very hard for me to say, but why would anyone—"

"Cut her up into pieces afterwards?" Potty took a swig of champagne and eyed me, his expression turning cold. "Let me ask you this, young lady: Do you think sex is all about hearts and flowers? Lovey-dovey whispers in the dark? Hell, no, it can be angry, too, right? Rage and frustration and anger channeled into the physical act of procreation."

My throat dried out. "So you believe Penny's last lover might have been furious enough to . . . ?"

"Divide my sister into manageable chunks? Yes, I do. Penny was an infuriating woman. And I know all about infuriating women. Sometimes?" He leaned closer until I could smell his breath mint. "Those girls I screw? I just want to punch their lights out afterwards."

I looked into Potty's face and decided of all the people I'd encountered since Penny died, this was the man who was most capable of killing another human being. He grinned back at me with no soul in his twinkling blue eyes. A cold shiver of revulsion slid down my back.

"Ha-ha," he said.

We heard the clack of high heels, and turned to see Nuclear Winter had come out of the little girls' room. She marched straight over to Potty. She towered above him, running her long fingers up and down the stem of her champagne glass. Potty made no bones about looking at her décolletage.

I took the opportunity to excuse myself.

"Enjoy your evening," I said as I slipped away. I wanted as much distance as possible between me and the couple that seemed to deserve each other.

I mingled in the crowd for a while, making inane conversation to forget my distasteful encounter with Potty. I nearly disposed of the vial he'd given me, but in the act of leaving it on a busboy's tray, I hesitated. Perhaps the pills were evidence of some kind. I slipped the vial into my bag and got rid of my half-full champagne flute instead.

Looking around for an interview, I happened to catch the moment when a portly matron in a floor-length dress approached Aldo. Her silver helmet of hair was sprayed into a tall sculpture. They spoke for a moment, and then I stared in fascination as Aldo led her to the dance floor. Like a recent graduate of Arthur Murray, he gathered up his partner and began to dance. And he was astonishingly graceful. Aldo guided the woman around the marble floor in precise, yet florid, box steps. Apparently, his daughter's wedding had required more than just a tuxedo. The woman in his arms seemed to float along with him. She looked familiar to me, but I couldn't place her.

Gradually other party guests turned to watch, sipping champagne, and they enjoyed the mature couple dancing smoothly to the music. Soon the whole party had stopped to admire their performance. Aldo never faltered, just continued to sweep his partner around the floor with fluid dignity.

When the music came to an end, everyone broke into spontaneous applause. The woman blushed, but Aldo bowed chivalrously to her. She pulled her hand from his and slipped into the crowd. Aldo became himself again and went back to his potted palm.

Members of the theater staff circulated with trays bearing rolls of numbered tickets for the Chinese auction.

The photographer for the *Intelligencer* appeared beside me. Dave was still a teenager, moonlighting during his sophomore year in college. The paper had fired several experienced photographers in a round of budget cuts, and I found myself—not long on the job, either—leading most of the new freelancers by the nose. Fortunately Dave had grown up in a cultured family in Gladwyne and knew his way around a party scene. Briefly, we conferred on the photos he should snap for the paper. He promised to come back to me, then cruised into the theater, camera ready.

I bought a few Chinese-auction tickets to be polite, but I paused before entering the theater, where the items that had been donated for the cause were on display. I scanned the crowd.

Sure enough, Betsy Berkin came up the staircase in a long, surprisingly juvenile dress the color of cotton candy. She wore a white wrap around her bare, Florida-bronzed shoulders. I had taken a chance she'd come to the ballet fund-raiser.

Holding her arm was the perfect accessory for the girl who had it all, Raphael Braga.

"Betsy," I said when they walked within speaking distance. "Would you like to have your photo taken for the *Intelligencer*?"

"Nora! How nice of you to ask." She blushed with pleasure. "I'd be delighted."

"The photographer's waiting inside." I indicated the theater. "You'll look wonderful in my column this week."

Betsy slipped her wrap off her shoulders. "Rafe, will you hold this for me?"

I held my breath and hoped I didn't look as tense as I felt inside.

"Honored," Raphael murmured. When Betsy had rushed into the theater, he turned to me. His dark eyes glittered with laughter. "That was clumsily done, Nora. If you wanted to speak to me alone, you simply had to ask. Betsy is very young, though. Maybe she would be jealous."

His smile was amused, but something dark lurked at the back of his gaze.

I said, "Technically, I'm not supposed to speak to you at all."

"That was Carolina's foolishness, not mine. She was afraid."

"I know."

We looked frankly at each other.

Raphael was even more handsome than he'd been ten years ago. His English was more polished, his manner more sophisticated. He had combed his luxurious black hair away from his temples, and he wore sharply cut evening clothes. His shirt studs were inlaid with pearls. Instead of evening shoes, he wore flamenco boots with heels that did not give him an effeminate air in the least.

"I was wondering when you last saw Penny Devine."

He laughed attractively, and made a business of winding up Betsy's wrap and placing it formally over his arm. "And what is your reason for wondering? Are you concerned for Penny's health?"

"Aren't you?"

"She has disappeared before."

"Not for this long. And not when—well, part of her may have been discovered on Saturday."

"By you, I understand. How unsettling."

"It was, very. But you don't seem terribly worried, Raphael, even though you were her friend."

His smile faded. "Let's get a drink, shall we? Then I'll tell you what I think of Penny's disappearance."

He took my arm and drew me in the direction of the bar. Except for Aldo, who remained stolidly beside his tree, the rest of the crowd had filtered into the theater. Even Bloom had disappeared. Raphael and I were the last guests to ask for drinks. Raphael ordered a vodka, straight up. He also asked for a glass of champagne and bowed as he gave it to me.

We carried our drinks away from the bar. I sipped the champagne and found it bitter—a cheaper vintage than what I'd enjoyed earlier.

"Ten years have agreed with you, Nora," Raphael said as we strolled along the balustrade. "I like a woman with a little experience in her eyes."

"Is that a polite way of saying I'm getting old?"

"Only in the way a good wine ages."

"Speaking of clumsily done," I said lightly. "Why don't you tell me about Penny and skip the Latin-lover routine?"

"I have not seen her since last summer. Which I told the police. If you must know, she phoned to say she had visited a farm and seen some quality polo ponies. She wanted to show them to me."

"Did you go?"

"To California, yes."

"And?"

"When I arrived, there were no ponies. I discovered she had lured me there."

"What for?"

"She wanted me to fuck her." Raphael smiled into my eyes to gauge how shocked I might be. "I declined. Shortly thereafter, she went on one of her trips. She disappeared."

"Because you wouldn't sleep with her?"

He laughed again. "Penny could pay for lovers as seasoned as myself, and even at her age, men would have lined up to take her money. I doubt my rejection set her off."

"Had you slept with her before?" I asked.

"She was very old, Nora."

He didn't answer my question, I noted.

He had not sipped his drink while we spoke, but suddenly knocked back the vodka with a swift tilt of his head. He savored it, looking into the empty glass. "I have not seen her in nearly a year. Nor have I seen my wife in that time."

I drank another swallow of champagne, then said cautiously, "I'm sorry to hear you and Carolina are not together anymore, Raphael."

"We are not together, but I have not divorced her," he corrected. "I will not do so while my father is alive. He's old-fashioned."

"Do you plan on divorcing Carolina someday?"

"Why do you ask?" he said.

"I'd be sad for my friend. For you."

He used the rim of his empty glass to trace the line of my cheek. "Don't be sad, Nora. Not for me. I have many things to keep me happy. My daughter, for instance."

Why I allowed him to touch me—even with the glass, not his hand— I'm not sure. But I held still and waited until he slipped the cold surface down my throat before I turned my head away. I felt a little tipsy, I realized. As if my drink was stronger than champagne.

Quietly, Raphael said, "We should go somewhere and talk, you and I. We have things to discuss, and I don't like crowds."

He liked crowds very much, I thought. He enjoyed the cheering and the adoration he received on the back of a horse, swinging a mallet, running down his opponent and trampling him, if he could. As he leaned closer, I felt my head lighten. His cologne was suddenly very strong.

"The man you were with on Saturday. The tall one. He is your bodyguard?"

"No," I said.

Raphael allowed a derisive smile. "I see. Your lover, then."

I sent a glance across the marble floor to Aldo. He hadn't taken his attention off me since the moment Raphael walked up the staircase.

Raphael said, "Does he give you children?"

"No."

My heart had begun to beat very fast. I wanted to ask Raphael a direct question, but I couldn't form the words.

"Are you all right, Nora?" he asked.

I put my hand to my forehead and was surprised to find it damp.

"You don't look well," he said. "Shall I take you out for some fresh air?"

Fresh air sounded wonderful. Raphael put his arm around me. I stumbled. My ears had begun to ring. Then I discovered I could not put one foot in front of the other without wobbling.

"Come along," Raphael said. "We haven't much time. I must have the truth."

I wasn't sure I could think, let alone talk. I hadn't felt so drunk in years. The buzz in my ears heightened to a clang, and I couldn't see straight.

But then Aldo arrived, not the least out of breath despite coming across the lobby faster than I expected he could move.

"Shove off, bub," he said to Raphael. His voice sounded distorted. Distant.

Raphael stepped back to get a better look at the picture Aldo made— a heavyset old boxer dolled up in a tuxedo with wide lapels. It was a hard decision to conclude whether or not Aldo should be taken seriously.

"Hey, puppy dog," I said to Aldo. "Dance with me."

I fell into his arms, which felt all wrong, but somehow the right thing to do at the time. My head spun, and I began to laugh.

I remember that Raphael chose to smile at me. He said, "She doesn't need your help, Nora. So stop your questions before you get hurt."

I danced with Aldo. Or else we left the Merriam, I wasn't sure. I vaguely remember Aldo taking me down the stairs. "You okay?" he asked. "You drunk? Or did that bastard slip you something?"

# Chapter Thirteen

*I* don't remember anything about the rest of the night. Maybe Emma was around. And there was coffee, I think.

In the morning, Michael was in bed with me, sleeping with a Sudoku book on his chest, as if he'd stayed awake as long as possible. I tried to dig into my brain to recall some detail of the night, but all I found was darkness—a frightening blank. I pulled the covers closer and trembled. What had happened? What had I done? Said?

Then my stomach erupted, and I bolted out of bed and ran for the bathroom, whacking my head on the doorjamb and the edge of the toilet before upchucking whatever poison was in my stomach.

Michael came into the bathroom and mopped my forehead and held me there on the floor while I forced my mind to function.

"What happened to me?" I finally blurted out.

"Emma thinks you were doped," Michael said. "The polo player slipped you a roofie."

"I'd never fall for that!"

But I had. I pieced together the few snippets of memory that I could dredge up. The ballet event. Bloom. Aldo dancing.

"Michael?"

"Hm?"

"Did I do anything to embarrass Aldo?"

"He'll get over it."

I groaned and put my cheek against the cool tile floor. "Did I make a fool of myself?"

"You were pretty out of it."

"What did I—did I do anything awful? Say anything?"

He patted my bottom. "Don't worry. We took care of you."

I spent the whole day sicker than I could ever remember. Emma came back late in the morning to take over looking after me, and Michael went off to do whatever he was doing. Libby came for her shift later in the afternoon.

"What was it like?" she asked, sitting cross-legged on the bed while I languished in agony under the blankets.

"A complete blank." A terrifying blank.

While trying to unscramble my brain, I remembered the vial Potty had given me before I encountered Raphael at the party. "Lib, would you look in my handbag for me, please?"

She brought the bag to my bed, and when I opened it I found the vial of MaxiMan, but also the damned envelope I'd given back to Potty. I held it up to show her. "Look at this! Dammit, Potty gave me back all the money!"

Libby looked sympathetic. "Darling, you're still delirious, aren't you?"

"No, listen." I explained to my sister how Potty had tried to bribe me once and didn't appear to be taking no for an answer. I wasn't sure Libby believed me, either.

She heated up some chicken soup for me, the first food I could choke down, and afterward I felt a little better. She gave me a get-well card that Lucy had drawn. It featured me in a huge bed with a thermometer in my mouth. My eyes appeared to be crossed, too. Which felt surprisingly accurate.

By evening, I was capable of making a phone call, so I telephoned Detective Bloom from my bed.

"Okay," he said when I'd told him what I'd learned about Potty. "We already know the old codger has a yen for younger women. But not that he had such a mean streak, too."

I sipped the last of the soup from a mug Libby had brought to me before she left for home. "That doesn't mean he killed his sister, but he certainly gave me the willies. And I don't believe the suicide-note story anymore."

"Why not?"

"I don't know. He looked confused when I mentioned it. Or maybe I'm the one who's confused."

"You okay, Nora?"

I had debated about whether or not to tell Bloom about Raphael drugging me with Rohypnol. But I didn't want to reveal anything to him about my relationship to Raphael. So I said, "I'm fine. What's next on our agenda?"

There was a pause in my ear before he spoke. "You're red-hot to do this, aren't you? You want a deputy badge?"

"I was thinking I should call on Nuclear Winter."

"Okay. What are you going to talk to her about?"

"Maybe she knows when Potty last saw Penny."

"Good plan."

"Did you find out anything about Kell Huckabee's disappearance?"

"His daughter tells us he took off last fall. He was some kind of interim caretaker of the estate, but Potty fired him for running some other businesses for himself and neglecting the place. Now the guy seems to have disappeared. We're trying to find him, but—well, do you know anything about him?"

"I can ask Julie. Maybe she'll tell me more than she told you."

"That kid is scared to death of everything."

"What did Vivian say?"

"She doesn't know where Huckabee is either. She seems glad he's gone. I get the impression nobody liked the guy."

I asked, "Did you see that mobile home where Vivian keeps her cats?"

"God, yes, what a mess inside."

"Really?"

"The stench just about knocked me over. I took one look inside from the doorway and called Animal Services. They're busy with a case involving a puppy mill right now. It may take them a couple of days to get over there to clean out Vivian's kitties so we can search the place for evidence."

"You didn't go inside?"

"Nope. And I'm not going to until some of the cat mess is cleaned up. I hate those cat ladies—the ones who hoard animals. They always talk like they're saving the world, but who can stand the smell?"

I remembered Michael's first impression of the Devine estate and asked, "Ben, did you find a big fence on the property?"

"Yeah, around the back. A big enclosure of some kind."

"Nothing's there? No animals?" I thought of Libby's recollection of a lion cub.

"Looks like they raised livestock there once. Cows or something. The old lady said something about the caretaker raising calves, but I got the impression the work was overwhelming. Why do you ask about the fence? What are you thinking?"

"I don't know." I could feel my headache returning, and I fumbled on the nightstand for more aspirin.

Bloom said, "There's a break in the morgue situation, by the way. We might get a prelim tomorrow."

My pulse quickened. Who knew what kind of secrets might be revealed once various tests were conducted? "Let me know what you learn."

"Sure thing. Are you really okay? You sound—I don't know—not so good."

"I'm just a little hungover." I tried to make it a joke.

He didn't believe me. "Everything okay at home? I mean—with him?"

"We don't need to talk about this," I said.

In a different tone, he muttered, "I hate what he's done to you."

I said nothing.

Bloom let the silence grow, and then said, "You used to be happy. And now—look, it's none of my business, but he's made you miserable, Nora."

"I'm not miserable. And it's not his fault."

"If I can stop him, I'm going to do it," Bloom said.

I didn't want to hear more. For a while, I had sensed Ben Bloom's frustration, but now he sounded truly angry.

I heard footsteps on the staircase. Not wanting to be caught talking to Bloom, I turned off the phone just as the bedroom door opened.

It was Emma, not Michael, and she had her polo player in tow. Also a bottle of wine in one hand.

She laughed at me. "Don't start playing poker with Rawlins, Sis. You have guilt written all over your face. Who were you talking to?"

I put the phone back on its cradle. "Ben Bloom, as a matter of fact. Hello, Ignacio."

"Hello!"

"You were talking to the boy detective, huh?" She pulled Ignacio into the bedroom. "What did he want? A date for the prom?"

"He wanted some information."

Emma plopped onto the bed beside me. "Does Mick know you're having phone sex with Bloom?"

"I'm not having—look, it was police business. But just the same, I'd ap-preciate it if you didn't go blabbing."

"Oho," said my little sister. "Keeping secrets from your fiancé doesn't sound like the right way to start a marriage."

"I'm not keeping any more secrets than you are. Ignacio, would you like to sit down?"

He truly was a beautiful specimen of a man. He could have been a model. That perfect tan, those delectable shoulders, that angelic face. The melting brown eyes.

"Hello," he said cheerfully, standing at the foot of the bed and admiring Emma beside me. He carried two wineglasses in one hand.

Emma's half-empty wine bottle had a cork stuck in it, and she used her teeth to pull it out. She spit the cork on the floor. Ignacio held out the glasses, and she poured generously. "Feeling better?"

"Not much. What are you doing?"

"What does it look like?"

"Like you're drinking again."

"A glass of wine before bed doesn't constitute drinking. I can handle it."

"Em—"

"Hey, do I look out of control? I'm having a social drink, that's all. Iggy likes to relax with a glass of wine. I don't need you playing cop, okay?"

But she hesitated, her nose poised at the rim of the glass to inhale the bouquet of the wine. She didn't drink, though. Instead, she gave the glass to me. I didn't smell alcohol on her breath. I wondered what brought on her sudden urge to have a drink.

"Okay," I said, relieved that she'd stopped herself. "Did you buy another pony?"

"Two. And I'm going to start a beginners' class in June. I've got three students signed up."

"Wonderful." I noted that Emma seemed pleased despite her offhand manner. I said, "Thank you, by the way, for looking after me last night."

My little sister grinned and leaned back into the pillow. She patted the bed, and Ignacio sat beside her. He rubbed her thigh. "Hey, you were in no shape to be left alone. Aldo couldn't wait to unload you. Good thing I was here to take over. You don't remember any of it, do you?"

"Zilch," I admitted.

"Well, you were ready to party, Sis. None of your usual inhibitions. I didn't think you had it in you."

I looked into the wine in my glass. "It's a terrifying drug, isn't it?"

"The real question is why a guy like Raphael Braga feels he needs to drug a woman to get laid."

I didn't answer. But I felt sure Raphael hadn't drugged me for sex. He had wanted information.

Emma said, "Do you think you were Raphael's original target? I heard he went to the party with Betsy Berkin, the twenty-two-year-old virgin. Maybe he planned to party with her. Thanks to you, she can still wear white on her wedding day."

"Em, have you heard anything about Raphael using roofies on women before?"

"Not Raphael. But I heard some of his teammates talking about it. It's all over the place. In fact, I know some women who've used roofies on men."

"You're kidding."

"It's one way of waking up with the man of your dreams, I guess."

"Before it happened, I talked to him about Penny Devine. He told me his relationship with Penny was more than business. He as much as admitted they slept together."

That news startled Em. "Wow, that must have been some performance on his part."

"I should ask Bloom to test the hand I found for drugs. If there are traces of Rohypnol in her remains, maybe we'll know if Raphael had something to do with Penny's death."

"That won't prove he's a murderer."

Ignacio moved his massage higher up on Emma's thighs. He set his wineglass on the nightstand, then put his other hand on my leg.

Emma and I looked at each other. I said, "Is this one of those situations where the language barrier might be a problem?"

She reached down and removed Ignacio's hand from me. She patted him to show all was forgiven, and he smiled. No harm, no foul.

"I love the language barrier," she said. "This way we don't have to know a thing about each other. Just take off our clothes and have wild monkey sex. But you and the Love Machine, Sis? Is there a language barrier there, too?"

I folded down the top of the sheet and smoothed it flat in my lap. "Of course not. I was just talking to Ben on the phone for a minute, that's all—"

"Forget the kid cop," Emma said. "I'm not blind, you know. Or deaf. You and Mick—there's something going on. Is it the whole baby thing? Your miscarriage? You're not trying to sweep it under the rug, are you?"

"No, we talk about it."

"Because you could get some counseling, you know."

I laughed. "Can you imagine Michael in counseling?"

"Yeah." Emma was serious. "I can imagine him doing just about anything to make you happy. Look, Sis, I don't want to tell you how to run your life—"

"Good."

"—but since you have no qualms about giving me advice all the time, let me just give you my two cents on the Love Machine subject: Don't blow it, okay?"

"I'm not. I'm marrying him!"

"Don't do that, either," Emma said.

"What?"

She lay back and stared at the cracks in my bedroom ceiling. "I know it's stupid! But how can we not believe in the curse? Hell, Mick's already been in a car accident, plus the fall down the stairs, and then the whole house almost burns down around his ears—"

"Those were accidents."

"Yeah, and any one of them could have been fatal."

"What are you saying? I should break it off with him?"

"Hell, no. Just break off the engagement. Before he gets killed. Then you can live happily ever after, but safely outside the bonds of matrimony."

"Emma, I never expected this from you."

"I know." Her grin was embarrassed. "Me, neither. But it's hard to ignore the evidence when your house is in flames, right?"

I looked up at the ceiling, too. "I can't break off the engagement. It would hurt him, Em. He wants to be married. He's really a very traditional person."

My sister rolled over on one hip and pulled a smashed pack of cigarettes out of her hip pocket. She shook one out of the pack, but made no move to light up. "It's the Catholic thing."

"He wants a wedding."

"So does Libby," Emma said on a laugh. "I heard her on the phone earlier. She's found somebody who will rent her a chocolate fountain. With an attendant who wears a G-string."

"Why would anyone want a woman in a G-string at a wedding?"

"It's not a woman, Sis."

I groaned. Libby and her wedding plans were putting my stomach in knots. I had a lot on my mind, and a night of crazy, drugged-up behavior hadn't made any of it go away. So I said, "Stick with Ignacio, Em. He's very sweet. Sweet and uncomplicated."

Looking up from his massaging, Ignacio smiled very sweetly indeed.

"Thing is," she said, "sweet and uncomplicated doesn't exactly float my boat."

Before I could ask her to share more, her cell phone rang. She dug into her pockets again to find it.

"Yeah?" she said to her caller. Then, "Sorry, I'm all booked up tonight. Try again tomorrow."

She terminated the call and found me watching her. She grinned. "You going to give me the third degree?"

I knew she was sleeping with a man who satisfied her need for sex without intimacy. And that she was buying ponies so she could teach little girls how to ride. So I figured there couldn't be anything else going on that was too awful.

So I said, "Rock on, baby."

We heard Michael's car arrive, and in a couple of minutes, he came up the stairs and found the three of us in bed together.

Ignacio sat up abruptly, cheerful and willing. "Hello!"

"Not a chance," Michael said.

Emma laughed as he bent to kiss me. "I figured you for the more adventurous type, Mick."

"He doesn't worry me," Michael said. "You're the scary one." He had brought up a slice of cold pizza from the fridge. Seeing Ignacio's hopeful expression, Michael gave the pizza to him. Then Michael pulled an unopened can of beer from the pocket of his leather jacket. He stripped off the jacket and dropped it on a chair. "How are you feeling?" he said to me.

"Like I've been kicked in the head," I answered. "But better than this morning. Look at the get-well card Lucy sent me."

"Cute." He smiled a little, cracked the beer and sipped off the foam. "But your eyes aren't so crossed anymore. I want to wring the bastard's neck, you know."

"I want to let you," I said lightly. "I haven't felt so hungover in years."

Emma said, "Let's plot some really good revenge."

"Sounds good to me," Michael replied.

With Emma watching, I decided to come clean. "I talked to Ben Bloom tonight. I saw him last night, too, before I turned into a raving lunatic."

Michael took a long, relaxed swallow of his beer before responding. "I heard."

"Aldo reported to you?"

"Yep." He made no apologies for checking my whereabouts. "What'd you learn from Gloom? He making any headway on the dismembered-movie-star case so he can get his promotion?"

"He doesn't want a promotion. He wants to get onto the city's homicide squad."

"When he grows up," Michael added, then caught my look. "Okay, okay. I assume he wanted your help."

"Yes."

"And he threatened to have me deported or executed so you'd cooperate?"

"Don't even joke like that, Michael."

"Sorry." He came back over and ran one finger underneath my jaw. "What did you learn from Bloom?"

"He has a suspect. A gardener from the Devine estate who disappeared back in the autumn. Kelly Huckabee."

Emma glanced up. "Huckabee? That son of a bitch is gone? What's going on? Serial disappearances?"

"They say he was fired and left the estate, but the police can't find him. I think I could find out more about Kell if I asked Vivian Devine. Gently, of course."

"The dead woman's sister, right?" Michael said.

"The cat lady," Emma said.

"The one with the big fence in her backyard," Michael reminded us.

"I asked Ben about that fence. He says there's nothing behind it. He figured they might have raised some farm animals there at one time."

If Michael noted my use of Ben Bloom's name, he gave no sign. He drank a little more beer.

I said, "So I've been thinking about what Libby mentioned. About Vivian's house where she had all those cats years ago here in Bucks County. I wonder if she still lives there."

"Me, too," said Emma. "Libby's such an idiot, she couldn't remember where the house was. But I got to thinking about a map in Granddad Blackbird's collection—"

To Michael, I explained, "Emma was our grandfather's favorite. She spent hours with him. He collected clocks and mechanical toys."

"And maps," Emma said. "Are they still here?"

"Yes, of course. In the library."

Emma stood up. "Let's have a look."

I put a bathrobe over my pajamas, and the four of us trooped down to the library. From one of the lower bookcases, I hauled a large bound book of maps. It was so heavy that Michael stepped in to carry it to the long library table, where his telescope was laid out in pieces. He set down the book on the opposite side of the table.

Emma unfastened the ties expertly and opened the book with care. She smoothed the covers flat. Inside, a selection of maps lay in sleeves, each one carefully folded. She let her fingers walk through the index tabs until she located the one she wanted.

It took a full minute to unfold the dry paper of the map without damaging it.

Emma said, "These really ought to be stored flat now. They're getting too old to keep folded like this."

"I don't have room."

"They ought to go to the museum, then."

Emma hadn't been a particularly good student, and she had lasted only a semester or two before dropping out of college, so her continued interest in cartography surprised me. Her passion had clearly been learned at our grandfather's knee.

"Here," she said, smoothing the heavy paper. "See?"

We all leaned close and tried to read the fine drawing.

She said, "Here's the Delaware River, and here's New Hope."

She went on to point out landmarks we knew. Michael found the site of his own house across the river on the New Jersey side.

"And here's Blackbird Farm."

Our family's estate was so old it warranted a grand label on the map.

Emma's finger ran lightly down the river from the farm, cut westward through the hilly contours of the county and came to rest on a spot I didn't recognize.

"See this?" she said. "From the description Libby gave me, I think this is Vivian's property."

I said. "It's isolated, isn't it?"

"More than you think. It's really hilly. See these lines? That's the topography. This looks like a cliff. See how fast it drops to this creek? The place wouldn't be much use as a farm."

Michael said, "You could find out who owns the place by looking at the tax rolls. That's public information at the courthouse."

I said, "I wonder if that information might be online, too."

While they continued to study the map, I went for my laptop. I took it back to the library, plugged it into the phone line and went on the Internet. In five minutes, I'd found exactly the information I needed.

"Vivian Devine still owns the house."

Michael grinned. "These newfangled inventions sure make crime a lot easier."

"Crime? You're thinking maybe we ought to pay a visit?"

"If you feel up to a little excursion." His smile broadened. "Get your coat."

"Now?" Emma asked, startled.

Michael smiled. "We'll do a drive-by. Nothing fancy."

# Chapter Fourteen

*I* put a raincoat over my bathrobe and pajamas and exchanged my slippers for a pair of gardening boots.

Then the four of us piled into one of Michael's muscle cars—a streamlined convertible with a gleaming white top—and he drove for about twenty minutes with Emma navigating from the backseat. Ignacio, clueless about our mission, seemed to be enjoying our late-night jaunt. Perhaps he thought we'd gone out for ice cream.

In the dark, Michael drove slowly by the old farm.

"There's a split-rail fence." Emma pointed. "That's probably the beginning of the property line."

Beyond the fence we could see a tangle of underbrush—darkness prevented us from seeing through it—and in the distance rose a rocky hillside, covered with scrub trees made visible by thin moonlight.

The house was a low ranch-style place, probably built in the early fifties, made of yellow brick that looked dingy. A carport was jumbled with old trash cans and a flatbed trailer. An electrical wire sagged from a pole on the road to the corner of the house roof.

No lights shone from inside the house. I could barely make out tufts of grass growing up through the asphalt driveway. A stand of weeds nearly concealed the mailbox.

"House looks empty," Michael murmured.

He cruised up the road a little farther, turned around and went back even more slowly, this time with the headlights turned off. He didn't pull into the driveway, but crept past the house and stopped the car along the fence.

Quietly, he said, "There's a flashlight in the glove compartment."

I found the light and rolled down my window. The night air was cool, but dry. Flicking on the flashlight, I pointed it through the fence and into the overgrowth. The looming bulk of a barn was little more than a shadow.

"What are we looking for?" Emma asked, low-voiced.

The flashlight picked up a long, gleaming structure beyond the barn. I squinted, trying to discern what it was. I said, "A place where Kell Huckabee could be hiding."

"I think it looks deserted," Emma said. "Some of the windows on the house are broken. Nobody's been here for ages."

Michael pulled the car along a little farther and slipped it into a sandy spot on the shoulder of the road. He cut the engine.

"What are you doing?" I asked.

He put out a hand for the flashlight. I could see the gleam of excitement in his eyes. "Taking a closer look."

"Not alone, you're not. If Kell is here, he could be dangerous. He may have murdered Penny."

"He's not here. Nobody's here. The place is deserted. Stay put, Nora."

I popped my door and stepped outside. "You're too accident-prone to go alone."

He got out of the car, too. "How are you going to explain that getup if you get arrested for trespassing?"

"That I'm sleepwalking. What about you?"

"Hell, we'll all go," Emma snapped, climbing out of the backseat. She hauled Ignacio out, too. "If we get arrested, at least we'll have a foursome to play bridge in jail."

Emma was in favor of jumping the split-rail fence, but in deference to my bulky outfit, the group followed the rails until we came to a break where a post had been knocked down—probably by a winter snowplow. We stepped gingerly in the clumpy grass. Michael flashed the light to and fro, and he found a recently fallen tree that had cut a swath through the thick brambles as it fell. We climbed over it.

"Are you sure you want to do this?" Michael asked me.

"Stop asking. I'm fine."

He pointed the flashlight at the barn. Its dilapidated shape leaned precariously southward. The moon shone down across the broken tiles of the old roof and revealed a gaping hole with a broken rafter poking out. As we watched, a pair of bats flickered out of the hole and disappeared into the sky.

"Hello?" Ignacio whimpered. He stepped closer to Emma.

"There," I said to Michael. "Shine the light a little farther over."

He followed my direction, and the flashlight suddenly picked out the criss-cross pattern of a tall chain-link fence. It stood fifteen feet high and stretched far into the darkness.

"What's that for?" Emma asked. "To keep deer out?"

"Nope, look. Razor wire." Michael aimed the light higher. "See?"

Emma cursed softly at the sight of coils of dangerously sharp concertina wire fastened to the top of the fence. "What's back there?"

Nobody suggested we find out, but we all moved forward as if drawn by the same magnet. We followed the tall fence for as much as fifty yards before we reached a ravine where it made a turn and ran along the rocky ledge. Below, we could see the gleam of water and hear it rushing over rocks. We couldn't walk along the narrow ledge, so we turned back the way we'd come.

And heard a low, long rumble.

"H-hello?"

"It's okay, Ig," Emma whispered.

The sound floated to us through the darkness. It reverberated in the air—softly, yet with menace. The back of my neck suddenly prickled, and even Michael froze still as a statue until the sound died away.

"What was that?"

"A motor of some kind?"

"Don't laugh, but to me it sounded like a great big stomach growl."

"A growl?" Michael said.

We retreated more quickly than we'd come and at last arrived at the beginning.

"I gotta pee," Emma announced. "Whatever we heard, it went straight to my bladder."

Ignacio was also hopping from one foot to the other in the universal language of urinary emergency.

"Go back to the car," Michael said. "I'll just be a minute."

"Okay, hurry."

Emma grabbed Ignacio's hand, and they hustled across the grass toward the parked car.

"I'm going with you," I said to Michael.

"I can go faster by myself."

"One of the foundations of a good marriage is compromise."

He smiled in the moonlight. "Okay, let's go."

Together, we crept rapidly through a copse of trees, and ended up in the backyard of the house. A patio faced the fence, and a lone plastic outdoor chair sat on the pitted concrete with a bucket beside it. It could have sat there for a day or ten years. Impossible to guess. More trash cans were lined against the back wall of the house.

Here, the fence had a large gate. It wasn't locked, just latched and tied with a short length of dirty nylon rope.

More than the gate, I noticed the smell. A heavy, moist, dog-kennel smell.

"What do you think?" Michael asked.

"Do you think Kell's been living here?"

"Check the trash barrels. If he's been here, he'd have left garbage."

I hiked across the yard to the large plastic cans and found them all fastened tightly shut and secured with sturdy bungee cords, probably to keep raccoons and other pests from getting into the contents. Risking my manicure, I unfastened one of the elastic cords and pulled the lid off. Inside, I found, not garbage, but dog food. Lots of it. I replaced the lid with care.

Which was when I became aware of the mess beneath the carport. Someone had set up a pair of sawhorses with a sheet of plywood balanced on top. The plywood was stained, and so was the floor. My boots stuck to the dark, sticky substance on the concrete. The smell made my stomach roll.

In one corner of the carport, someone had created a heap of garbage. I looked closer and realized it was a tangle of antlers and animal limbs. Pieces of bone, the leftover bits of carcasses.

I backpedaled out of the sticky carport. The gunk on the floor was blood.

When I rushed back to Michael, he had already opened the gate and was inside the enclosure.

I ran, stumbling in my clumsy boots, across the grass to him. "Are you crazy?"

"Stay outside," he commanded. "I'm just going to look around."

"Don't, Michael, please."

"There's another fence inside this one. Like a pen or something. I'll be okay."

I followed him. But he was inside, and I was outside. I trailed him as he progressed along the new fence, casting the flashlight upward to note that there was no razor wire here. Instead, the inner enclosure was topped by a kind of chain-link roof. Michael shone the light into the interior pen. Nothing.

Then suddenly, I heard a terrible metal clang and Michael stifled a yell. He cursed, lost his balance and fell headlong into the tall grass. The flashlight flew into the air, tumbling, and went out, extinguished with a crack of plastic on rock.

"Michael!"

I knew he was alive because he began to curse even louder.

"Michael!"

More cursing.

I ran back to the gate, my heart near to exploding in my chest. My hands—cold now and clumsy—fumbled with the latch for a terrible half second before I managed to jam it upward, and the gate squealed open. Inside the inner enclosure, I doubled back, heading for Michael's now-strangled bellowing. I hitched up the bulky coat and bathrobe and tore through the grass, shouting—I don't know what, but shouting just the same.

I found him thrashing in a patch of brambles.

He panted with pain. "Jesus Christ, it's a trap!"

An iron animal trap. Clamped around his ankle and drawing blood. I could see the wet shine.

The two of us tried prying it off, but the thing had snapped shut with incredible force and was now impossible to budge. With my hands, I found the chain in the dark and felt blindly along its length until I located the juncture where the chain had been welded directly to the metal fence post. Only a blowtorch could have unfastened it. Michael sounded as if he was hyperventilating.

"Michael, Michael, I have to go for help."

"Go," he said, clenching his teeth to get control of himself. "It's not so bad."

But it was.

He didn't tell me to hurry. There was no need for that. I got up, and ran back toward the gate, toward the car, toward Emma. I pounded along the grass. My breath was coming in sobs. Then my boot caught again, and I nearly fell. I grabbed the fence to catch myself. My cheek slammed against the chain link.

And then I saw it.

His yellow eyes first, and then the unmistakable black and orange mask, the wide mouth, the long, long teeth. A cat.

A tiger. The sleek body striped with orange was unmistakable.

Six feet away from me, with his gaze locked on mine.

And I heard him rumble again—the low, rolling purr of a hungry carnivore.

He took a pace toward me with one enormous paw. His head never moved, but his body eased forward like liquid. His shoulders looked as strong as a bull's, and his body was nearly as big. He was very, very big.

I could not move. But the adrenaline in my veins was suddenly screaming in my ears. My hands, curled around the heavy chain link, felt like blocks of ice frozen in place.

A tiger.

Then Emma was beside me, yanking my hands, calling my name. The tiger leaped clean off the ground, smooth and silent as a bird, his paws outstretched, his giant claws unsheathed. He soared, growing more enormous, more powerful.

I pulled free and pushed back, taking Emma with me.

The tiger hit the fence just as we hit the ground, safe but nearly hysterical with fear.

The tiger opened his mouth and gave a kind of scream. Not a roar, but something louder, deeper and even more bloodcurdling.

Then he turned and leaped away, disappearing into the darkness of his prison.

Emma babbled, her hands still locked around my wrists.

"Go see what tools are in the car," I said. "A tire iron, anything!"

I had just realized Michael had his cell phone, so when Emma took off running for the car, I raced back to find him again.

He was still on the ground, but stretched out on his back, and straining to get as far from the fence as he could manage. On the other side now were two more tigers. Both sets of eyes were fixed on him. One of the animals sat at the edge of the fence, the other paced in agitation.

"Jesus," Michael said, and it didn't sound like a curse anymore.

"Emma's coming. Do you have your phone? Michael, your phone!"

"I dropped it. It's here somewhere, but—"

The sitting tiger had begun to work her paw beneath the fence. She made hideous, throaty hisses as she clawed, trying to reach Michael's foot, trapped just half a yard from those deadly claws. The second tiger threw himself at the fence with that scream-roar ripping the night air. They were so enormous, their slashing claws so lethal.

Michael dug backward, trying to stay out of range, but held fast by the trap. The tiger worked her incredibly muscular foreleg under the fence. I could see now why the outer enclosure had been laid with traps. Because the inner fence couldn't hold the animals.

I fumbled through the grass to find Michael's phone.

Emma arrived, tire iron in hand. She yelled and used it to bang the fence, causing the tigers to back off for a moment. Ignacio came, too, lugging the car's spare tire and a tool kit wrapped in canvas. Emma took the tire and jammed it against the fence where the trap was fastened. It provided some protection from the tigers, which were back, hissing and pacing closer and closer.

Michael grabbed the tool kit and struggled to open it. While he scrabbled through the pathetically small objects, Emma wedged the tire iron into the trap. But there was nothing to provide leverage.

"Iggy," she snapped.

Ignacio obeyed her gesture and grabbed the tire just as one of the tigers hooked a fang into it through the fence. They wrestled, and somehow Ignacio won. He fell down next to the trap, and Emma kicked the tire into place. Together, they jammed the iron into the trap, and I heard Michael gasp back another grunt of pain. He dropped the tool kit.

How they did it, I'm not sure. I was still trying to locate the phone when Emma called to me, and I threw myself down beside Michael to help drag him out of the trap. Emma released the tire iron, and we heard the trap bang closed again.

The tigers followed us along the fence—three of them now, snarling and hurling themselves at the chain link—as we struggled to get Michael back to the car.

At last, we heaved him into the backseat, and I scrambled in with him. Emma and Ignacio climbed into the front seat. We locked the doors and sat panting, stunned and shaking with fear.

Ignacio burst into tears.

"Tigers," Michael said, sounding amazed.

And then he passed out in my arms.

Emma leaned over the back of the seat to look at him. She shook her head in wonder. "Mr. Lucky."

# Chapter Fifteen

At the hospital, I didn't faint until the doctors had stopped the bleeding, pumped Michael full of a powerful painkiller and taken him away for an X-ray of his broken leg.

"It's not a compound fracture," a very jaunty young doctor told me later when I could sit up and absorb information. "Although that's what normally happens when a human steps into one of those animal traps. Nasty things, those. I didn't think they were legal anymore. Where did you say this happened?"

"On a farm," I said weakly. "We were out walking."

He looked at my raincoat-and-pajamas ensemble, now a torn, muddy ruin.

"It's a long story," I added.

"What about all the other injuries? The bruises? The wound on his chin?"

"He was in a car accident a couple of days ago."

"Wow. What is he? Cursed or something?"

"It's a long story," I said again.

He seemed less interested in my story than in telling me more about leghold-trap injuries. Trauma from leghold traps sometimes caused animals to chew off their own limbs, he told us cheerfully. And he had heard about a dog that sniffed a steel trap that snapped closed around its neck and killed it instantly. In med school, he had watched a surgeon remove the toes of a child who had stepped in a trap set for muskrat.

"Anyway," the doctor said when the infomercial was over, "there's no compound fracture here, but it's a pretty spectacular break that's going to require surgery. I've called about getting him to an OR right away for an open reduction and internal fixation. We'll install some hardware—a pin and a few screws. Trouble is, we won't be able to cast it because of the risk of infection to the puncture wounds. So he'll need to see a wound specialist, who will probably prescribe IV antibiotics for six or eight weeks. And tetanus. He should also have a boost of tetanus just in case—"

I didn't hear any more. I fainted again.

Emma and Ignacio took me home, and gave me a shot of brandy before seeing me into bed for the second night in a row.

In the morning I felt much less woozy. After a restorative piece of cinnamon toast, I put on jeans and a turtleneck sweater from Target. I packed up Michael's razor, some clothes and his telescope book. Emma drove me back to the hospital.

We found Michael drugged and sleeping in a private room. Aldo sat on the uncomfortable visitor's chair reading a newspaper and making a cup of Starbucks coffee last. Instead of his tuxedo, he wore one of his more customary outfits—black sneakers and a red tracksuit, unzipped partway down to show the logo of a weight-lifting gym on a black T-shirt. A gold chain gleamed on his thick neck.

"Hey, little lady," he said to me as he lumbered to his feet. "Howya doin'? Feeling better?"

Perhaps I was still feeling too emotional. I felt my eyes overflow, and I gave Aldo an impulsive hug.

"Hey! Don't start that stuff again!" He pulled away, startled, then turned sympathetic when he saw my face. "Hey, the boss is gonna be just fine. Just fine. See? They got him breathing on his own and everything."

Aldo put a fatherly arm around my shoulders, and we looked down at Michael in the bed. He had electrical leads stuck to his chest and running to a beeping monitor, IV tubes in both arms, and a contraption under his leg that prevented the bedclothes from touching him. He slept soundly. Even with rough stubble and the cut on his chin, he looked young.

"I took the oxygen tube out of his nose," Aldo confided. "It looked undignified, you know?"

"But if he needs the oxygen—"

"Nah, a doc came in and said it was just a precautionary thing, so it's all good." He held up a palm-sized gadget that was attached by a wire to Michael's IV stand. Aldo poised his thumb over the button. "I been giving him a little jolt of painkiller now and then. Keeps him comfortable. You okay? You had some breakfast?"

"I'm fine, Aldo, thank you. And thank you for coming last night."

"Hey, you did the right thing, calling me. There was a newspaper guy came by, but I ran him off."

I hadn't expected that, but of course reporters would be interested in anything that happened to the son of a known Mafia kingpin. I said, "Thank you. I didn't want to leave Michael alone, but—"

"But I made her go home," Emma said. "She was a mess, and Mick wouldn't have wanted her here like that."

"Aldo, do you know my sister Emma? Em, this is Aldo."

"Hey," said Aldo. "We met last night. Thanks for taking over. You must be the horsey one, not the crazy one."

"That's debatable." Emma grinned. "You must be the knee breaker."

Aldo looked humble, but pleased. "I help out when I can."

While they talked, I put my hand on Michael's forehead, checking for fever, I suppose, or maybe just to reassure myself that he was alive. His skin was dry and warm to my touch. I had an ache in my chest, and I leaned down to kiss him.

He woke up about half an hour later. He shifted in the bed and squinted at me. His voice was hoarse, but strong. "Tigers?"

I patted him, and he went back to sleep. Aldo went out for more coffee. Alone, Emma and I stood at the window and talked in sickroom murmurs.

"So," she said. "What the hell? Tigers in Vivian Devine's backyard?"

"I guess Vivian graduated from collecting house cats to big cats."

"Very big cats." Emma glanced at me quizzically. "Puts a whole new light on Penny Devine's death, doesn't it?"

"Em!"

"Oh, come on. You thought of it, too."

I hugged myself and looked out the window. "That Penny might have been killed by tigers?"

"And maybe eaten."

We looked at each other, and she grimaced.

"Tell me again about the hand you found. Was there any sign . . . ?"

"Of teeth marks? No. Actually, it looked as if it had been—well, amputated. The cut was clean." I laid my hand karate-chop-style across my own forearm to show her where the cut had been. "It was just a hand and a wrist with a small amount of—I can't believe I'm saying this—a small amount of arm showing. I noticed the wristwatch and the nail polish, but nothing more than that."

"Have you called Bloom yet? To tell him about Vivian's backyard zoo?"

"I tried before we left the house this morning. I got his voice mail, but I didn't leave a message. I figure he might not believe me."

"Do you have the cell phone Mick gave you?"

"Oh, heaven! It's at home on the kitchen counter again!"

Em shook her head. "You weren't meant to live in this century, Sis. I'll bring it to you tonight after polo practice. Or Libby can bring it earlier, if you want."

"Let's not call Libby just yet, all right? She might want to drag the twins along, and I don't want Michael waking up and finding those two standing at his bedside."

She laughed. "Suit yourself."

"Thank you, Em. For last night, too. I can't thank you enough."

She gave me an affectionate punch on my arm. "I'll save your boyfriend's life anytime. Just tell him I think he ought to call off the wedding before he really gets hurt."

As Emma gathered up her coat to leave, Michael came around again.

Emma poked him on the shoulder, the only part of his body that wasn't bruised. "You look pretty good without your shirt, Mick. Purple suits you."

He frowned at her, but couldn't gather his thoughts to respond until she was gone. Then he shifted his somewhat bleary gaze to me. "I'm gonna live, right? That look on your face says otherwise."

"You're fine." Gently, I tugged the sheet up higher on his chest and smoothed it gently. "You'll be home tomorrow."

"Why don't you bust me out of here now?"

"Because they have to teach you to use crutches before you can leave."

He sighed. "How hard can that be?"

I squeezed his arm. "Don't be in a rush."

He rubbed his face to try to clear his head. "Was Aldo here?"

"He went out for coffee."

Michael nodded, glad, I think, to have the protection of his trusted co-hort. He dozed again.

I sat in the bedside chair and read Aldo's newspaper. Reporters rehashed Penny Devine's murder in the light of Kell Huckabee's disappearance. There was plenty of overblown prose written about her, too. Several Hollywood actors were quoted saying stupid things about her life and death. One ditzy starlet who played Penny's granddaughter on a maudlin episode of *ER* blathered about the Tibetan custom of hacking up dead bodies and scattering them for the birds to eat.

"Penny was a spiritual woman," the starlet said. "She would have wanted to be with the birds."

I dropped the newspaper in the trash can.

And then I remembered Ben Bloom saying the autopsy might happen today. I checked my watch. I glanced at the phone on the bedside table. I should try to phone him again.

"Go," Michael said from the bed.

He was conscious again and had been watching me. I got up and went to him with an encouraging smile. "Ready for some Jell-O?"

He shook his head. "You don't need to play nurse."

"I'm not playing. I want to be with you."

"You want to be in the city, too," he said. "You're thinking about how a tiger could kill an old lady."

"Michael—"

"And you probably want to talk to Detective Gloom about it, too. So go. I don't want you here, anyway. If you start treating me like an invalid, you'll never look at me the same again."

"That's what being together is all about, baby," I said. "Taking care of each other. Let me do it this time around."

"See? Already you're calling me a baby."

We smiled at each other. I felt the tears coming again, but I fought them down. The last time we'd been in a hospital, I had lost our child. We'd wept together in the dark, and I didn't want him to remember that just now when he needed to get well.

I said, "You'll be chasing me around the bedroom again in no time."

He managed another smile—rueful this time. "Hold that thought.

Meanwhile, Aldo will find somebody to watch my back. Take him with you. Go find out what the police policy is about keeping tigers as pets."

I kissed him with more oomph this time, and an attendant came in. She handed Michael a menu he should fill out to select his meals, and we looked at the choices. Oatmeal seemed the most exciting thing on the list.

Michael said, "It's hardly Caravaggio, is it?"

A nurse arrived next. She wore a smock with pink teddy bears, but her attitude was one of military precision. She took his vital signs, then ticked off a long list of hospital personnel who'd be arriving soon—a physical therapist, a respiratory therapist, the wound-care nurse and the orthopedic surgeon, all before noon.

"So let's get you cleaned up," she said at last. "Make you presentable. I like a man with a clean shave."

That sounded like my cue to salute or leave, so I said, "I'll wait outside until Aldo gets back. Then I'll see you later this afternoon."

Rolling up her sleeves, the nurse said, "We'll keep him busy until at least five o'clock."

When I bent to kiss him good-bye, Michael whispered, "You sure you won't bust me out? She makes me nervous."

I called Reed from a phone at the nurses' station. Then Aldo came strolling back with some magazines under his arm. He had a book in one hand and another cup of coffee in the other.

He said, "They got a nice gift shop downstairs. Good selection of paperbacks, too. You like detective stories?"

"Love them," I said. Then I told him I was leaving and would return in time to have dinner with Michael.

"Good idea." Aldo nodded. "Maybe you better not see him like this. You know, before the wedding."

"Uh—"

"Hang on a minute. I'll go with you."

"There's no need for you to tag along with me, Aldo. I'll be careful what I drink."

"I'll come," Aldo said, no-nonsense. "I just gotta find Delmar first."

"Delmar?"

"Guy from Big Frankie's outfit. He'll look after the boss while I'm with you."

"No, Aldo, truly, I'd be so much happier if I knew you were here with Michael."

My blatant flattery did not deter Aldo. He shook his ponderous head. "Delmar, he does good work. You'll be real happy."

I was stunned. Delmar turned out to be half-man, half-triceratops. His narrow hips widened into the biggest shoulders I had ever seen on a human being, topped off by a head shaved and polished to a bulletlike perfection. Except he had a dent in his forehead as if someone had clobbered him with a sledgehammer. He seemed to have most of his wits, though. He accepted Aldo's assignment with a shrug and a nod, and he went into Michael's hospital room. I saw a telltale bulge under his tracksuit and knew it was a weapon.

"Let's go," Aldo said to me, politely holding open the elevator door.

On the first floor of the hospital, I recognized two of Michael's regular crew loitering purposefully near the elevators. Outside, another of his posse was slowly smoking a cigarette by the front door. All the men gave Aldo impassive nods as we went by.

In the car, I borrowed Reed's cell phone and tried calling Detective Bloom again. He didn't answer, so I left a voice message—vague because Aldo made no secret of eavesdropping.

Reed delivered me to the newspaper office first. Aldo waited in the lobby at the security desk while I spent an hour working alongside my busy colleagues. I went through the fresh batch of party invitations that had arrived by mail and e-mail.

As usual, I received far more invitations than I could possibly accept. Choosing which parties would receive space in the newspaper was tricky—a combination of political importance, social significance, personal favors and sometimes simple cachet. One enterprising charitable organization tried to encourage my attendance at their annual dinner by sending me a bunch of silver balloons. I only wished they'd try to be more creative with their dinner party. I couldn't allot precious newspaper inches to a dull event that didn't lend anything special to my column.

I tied the balloons to my desk chair and wondered if I had the courage to take them to Michael in the hospital.

I wrote notes and e-mails, made a few phone calls. When my work space was cleaned up again, I phoned the other newspaper and asked to speak to Crewe Dearborne. I still couldn't get my brain to accept Bloom's information that Crewe had been in a fight with Kell Huckabee before Kell disappeared.

Crewe wasn't at his desk, so I was put through to his voice mail. "Crewe," I said when the recording beeped at me, "Michael and I had a wonderful time Sunday night. Thanks so much for hosting us. I hope to catch you soon so I can thank you properly. Bye-bye."

Short and sweet. I'd tell him about Michael's injury later. And I'd find a way to learn about his altercation with Kell when we could be face-to-face.

Next I dialed Lexie Paine's office.

Her office assistant said she was still in a meeting. "With Mr. Dearborne. I believe they're having lunch."

"Crewe Dearborne?" I said, unable to keep the amazement out of my voice.

"Yes." The assistant realized he may have said too much, so he hastily asked if I wanted to leave a message or a voice mail. I chose voice mail again.

"Lex," I said when I heard the beep, "it was nice to see you on Sunday evening. We've had a little excitement since then." I decided not to give her the details. Nor did I want to demand an instant report about her lunch with Crewe. Not over the phone, anyway. So I said, "I'll tell you all about it soon, I hope. Maybe a drink this week? If you're not—um—already busy. Call me when you get a chance."

One more time, I tried Detective Bloom. No answer. I didn't leave another message.

I sat at the desk and drummed my fingers. There had to be something I could do to get more information for Bloom. I dug the phone book out of a desk drawer and flipped through it for an address, finding exactly what I needed.

"Where we going?" Reed asked when Aldo and I climbed into the car a few minutes later.

"Bellissima," I said, and gave him the spa's address.

Aldo wasn't happy about letting me go inside alone, but the steady parade of female patrons through the famous pink doorway unnerved him.

"I guess you'll be safe in there," he told me.

"Take my cell just in case," Reed said. "Use it if you need us."

Obediently, I accepted the loan of Reed's cell and took note of Aldo's phone numbers.

Inside the spa, I tried to book a manicure, of course, because the fastest way to learn anything in the city was with my hands in a warm bowl and a chatty nail technician to talk to. But all the manicurists were busy. While the receptionist flipped through her book of available services, I peeked at the sign-in book to see what customers were already enjoying their various treatments. Halfway down the page, I saw the scrawled signature I'd hoped to find.

Nuclear Winter was in the sauna.

"How about a sauna?" I said to the receptionist. "That's just what I need today."

In minutes, I was in the locker room and taking off my clothes. Another woman was there—a chunky, elderly woman with her hair wrapped up in a towel. I didn't recognize her face. She turned away from me, perhaps shy about stripping off her bathing suit in my presence, so I murmured a non-committal hello and slipped past her, wrapped in my own fluffy pink Bellissima towel. A quick shower later, and I was ready to step into the steamy fragrance of the sauna.

"No more than twenty minutes," the gum-chewing attendant said. "I'll set the timer because I'm going on my break. Bathing suits are optional, you know."

I hadn't planned on coming to the spa, so I didn't have a bathing suit. Hugging my towel, I stepped inside the warmth of the sauna and peered through the steam. Another woman I didn't know got up hastily from the bench, wrapping her towel around herself. She scooted past me with a murmur about her time being up, and I took her place.

The sauna was barely twelve feet across with two benches on either side of a hissing pit where the attendant had placed a bowl of herbs over the steaming coals. As I sat down, someone splashed more water on the coals, and a fresh cloud of steam boiled up into the air. I inhaled the delicious scents and thought perhaps I'd made a good decision coming here. A little relaxation might help clear my thoughts.

"I hope you don't mind," said a voice, "but I like it very hot."

"Noreen?" I tried to sound surprised. "Is that you?"

Nuclear Winter lay supine on the bench opposite mine, her towel loosely draped across her body. Both of her long, golden legs were exposed to the heat, and the towel had slipped from one of her breasts. She sat up on one elbow to peer myopically at me.

"It's Nora Blackbird." In an effort to sound friendly, I said the first thing that popped into my head. "Is that a nipple ring?"

"Yes. Do you like it?" She cupped her enormous breast to better show me the gold hoop.

"Very nice," I said, cursing myself for choosing that particular vein of conversation as an opener. Obviously, I still hadn't regained all my wits.

She sat up and let the towel fall completely into her lap to reveal both of her full, naked breasts, both ornamented with delicate gold hoops weighted with a small jewel at their centers. "They're pretty, aren't they? I wonder if I should show you my other piercing."

"Probably not," I said. "I'm squeamish. Did you have a pleasant evening with Potty the other night?"

"Not too bad. I just wish he'd quit playing those damn Sousa marches before I have to salute the flag, if you know what I mean."

"Uhm."

"I saw you with that polo-player guy Monday night. He's good-looking. His date was pretty pissed, though. She heard you left with him."

"That's not exactly what happened. We didn't go home together."

Nuclear nodded and took a slow swipe of sweat from her torso. "He's not your type, huh?"

"No."

As the steam wafted between us, she used her towel to swab the perspiration from her thighs. "Frankly, I'd rather put up with a soft old guy than a young one, you know? Less bother."

"Potty seems . . . pretty energetic."

She shrugged. "He's okay. If I get a chance, I break those damn pills of his in half. You know, to ease up on the dosage."

"I see."

She got up, moving as smoothly as a python, and sat on the bench beside me. She tossed her towel onto the floor, and leaned into the hot steam to inhale a deep breath of it.

"About Potty," I said. "Do you think he knows anything about his sister Penny's disappearance? More than he's saying in public, that is?"

"I'm just glad the sister is out of the picture." Nuclear smiled at me. "I hear she was a bitch."

"You didn't know her?"

"No, but Potty's told me everything. I mean, who doesn't want to hear about movie stars? Even old ones. But he hated her guts. Something to do with a vote at a board meeting."

"Potty must have disagreed with Penny about a lot of things."

Nuclear stopped breathing the steam and gave me a frank look. "I'm not as dumb as I look, Nora. I've got an MBA that cost more than these implants, so I can see what you're trying to do. I don't know anything about Potty's sister, and that suits me just fine. It's Potty I've got in my sights, and I'm not doing anything to jeopardize the progress I've made so far. Get it?"

"I—yes, I get it."

Nuclear turned her body toward me and lifted one limber leg over the bench so that she was straddling it. I tried not to look, but I couldn't help catching a glimpse of more jewelry in the smooth, hairless curve between her legs. In a huskier voice, she said, "You know, you get the best benefits of the steam if you drop the towel."

"Nuc—Noreen—"

"Let me help."

I gripped the edge of my towel as firmly as I could manage. "Maybe I've miscommunicated here."

"You have beautiful skin. Very soft."

"About Potty. I'm sorry if I implied that you—hey, just a second."

She had one hand on my arm, and before I knew it, she was sliding her other hand between my bare knees.

I clamped my thighs together and suddenly figured out that Potty Devine's money was the only thing Nuclear found attractive about the man. Hastily, I tried to talk my way out of the embarrassing moment. "Noreen, I've made a mistake. I have nothing against—you know, who you are, but it's just not who I am."

She had used the knee maneuver to distract me. Because in the next second she had her other hand under my breast and was squeezing me gently. "You feel great," she murmured.

I grabbed my towel closer. "I'm sorry if I gave you the wrong cues." I heard my voice going unnaturally high. "But really, Noreen, you've got to stop—please."

I stood up, and she dropped both hands into her lap. She pouted. "I thought you were different."

"No," I said. "I'm not different. I'm perfectly ordinary. Completely, utterly ordinary."

"We could try, you know. Just experiment a little. You'll like it, I promise. I have a double-jointed tongue."

I headed for the door.

Nuclear caught the tail of my towel and stopped me. "Slow down," she said in a different tone. "Let's talk. You wanted to know about Potty, right?"

I hesitated, torn between running shrieking for the locker room and learning something useful about Penny Devine's murder. I pulled my posture stiffly erect and said, "I think it's best if we keep our hands to ourselves, Noreen."

She smiled again. "Okay, deal. Why do you want to know so much about them, anyway? Penny's dead, so that means the cash goes farther, right? So you're in the clear."

"I don't think the cash, as you call it, has anything to do with me."

That information seemed to satisfy her. "What do you want to know?"

"About Kell Huckabee's disappearance."

"The caretaker? Potty says he left last fall, but I don't remember that."

"What do you remember?"

"The Huckabee guy hasn't been around since I started seeing Potty last summer. But now Potty's claiming he fired the guy in November. It didn't happen that way, because I would have noticed."

"What else did you notice? What's going on between Potty and Vivian?"

She shrugged. "They stay away from each other. He doesn't like her in the house because she's such a slob. Give her five minutes in a room, and she'll start a collection of newspapers to use for her smelly cats. So he forbids her to step into his house."

"Where does she live? Good grief, not in that awful little mobile home behind Potty's mansion?"

"Yep."

"Alone?"

"I've never seen anybody else go in that hellhole."

"What about Julie?"

"The kid? She lives over the garage. She doesn't talk much. She's a little spooky, don't you think?"

"Yes, I do."

"You're okay," Nuclear said, after staring intently into my face. "I didn't expect that. I figured you came around hoping to get some of Potty's dough."

"That's not my concern," I said. "I just want to know what happened to Penny."

"So I have a shot at the whole enchilada?" Nuclear asked.

"As much as anyone, I guess."

"I can keep Potty happy," she said. "As long as I get the kind of sex I like someplace else."

At which point she opened my towel and planted a hot, wet, sloppy kiss on what's gently known as my bikini line.

I fled.

# Chapter Sixteen

*F*ully dressed and partially recovered, I staggered out into the street, pulling Reed's cell phone from my handbag. I tried Lexie first.

Her assistant said she was back in her office. "But she's leaving for home in a minute. She asks if you'd meet her there."

"At home?" Startled, I checked my watch and found it was only midafternoon. Lexie never left her office until the end of business on the West Coast. "Is she sick?"

"No," the assistant said carefully. "Shall I tell her you'll meet her?"

"Yes, by all means."

When I disconnected the call, Aldo appeared at the back of the town car and gallantly opened the door for me. "You're all pink," he said.

I directed Reed to Lexie's place, and he took a circuitous city route to avoid the worst of the traffic. His strategy didn't work. Reed muttered, but drove sedately through the jam. We got off the expressway and crossed the river, which was dirty and swollen with spring rain, then wound our way down to Boathouse Row, where Lexie lived.

At a curve in the river, several boating clubs still maintained the Victorian-style boathouses where they kept racing shells, kayaks and canoes. At night, the picturesque houses were illuminated with strings of white lights that glowed on the surface of the river. On warm weekends, the clubs were thronged with members who enjoyed water sports on the river.

"Nice," Aldo said. "Classy."

Reed pulled into Lexie's narrow driveway. Although the other buildings on Boathouse Row had been long since grandfathered in for boating clubs, Lexie had managed to acquire one of the more fanciful houses for her own. I often wondered how she finagled that astonishing real estate transaction, but I didn't dare ask. I assumed strings had been pulled somewhere along the line. Her family, city leaders and philanthropists for generations, had not been above asking for a favor now and then.

Lexie was climbing out of her BMW when we arrived. She carried a bulging briefcase and wore her darkest glasses. Her face, I noted, was paper white.

And she didn't greet me with her usual exuberance. "Sweetie," she said when I got out of the car, "I don't know whether to kiss you or kill you."

"Lex, what in the world is wrong?"

"Come inside," she said, "and I'll open a few bottles of scotch. I plan on getting good and drunk."

I gave her a hug. "Honey, whatever the problem is, I'm on your side."

Lexie's house might have been adorably quaint on the outside, but the interior was sleek and modern—the better to display choice pieces from the art collection she had amassed on her own and inherited from her mother, a formidable collector of international stature. My friend liked to rotate her favorite paintings and sculptures, and today her living room gallery was dominated by a Gauguin. The hot, tropical colors slathered on the sarongs of island women seemed to echo Lexie's mood.

"Samir!" she bellowed. When no answer came, she muttered, "Where the hell is that man? I didn't hire him to spend his time playing tiddly-winks!"

Lexie's houseman—as efficient as an English butler and less chatty than a samurai warrior—usually appeared like smoke when Lexie got home from work. But today, the house was silent.

I said, "I didn't see his car in the driveway. He must be running errands."

She kicked her stilettos off onto the white carpet and threw her brief-case down onto the white slipcovered sofa. A glare of afternoon sunlight streamed into the room from the tall windows that overlooked the river. We could hear the rush of the water without opening the French doors. The sound seemed to fuel Lexie's temper.

She headed straight for the kitchen. I caught up with her just as she was pulling an expensive bottle of scotch from her liquor cabinet. Her expression was stormy.

I took the bottle from her and put it back. "Lex, booze isn't the answer. Let me make some tea, and we'll talk. It's Crewe, right?"

"Goddamn right, it's Crewe. Who the hell does he think he is?"

"Your friend?"

"Bullshit!" She paced the kitchen.

"For crying out loud, tell me what happened! I heard you went to lunch with him. What could he have done to—"

"He kissed me, that's what he's done! And I don't appreciate being manhandled by a—a horny goat with delusions of fairy-tale love!"

"Crewe manhandled you?"

Lexie stalked out of the kitchen, too infuriated to explain. I followed her doggedly back across the living room, down the hallway to her bedroom. There, her sterile white sanctuary was graced by a tall John Singer Sargent painting of Lexie's great-great-grandmother and her teenage sister. Both women wore white dresses, which looked charming next to the billowing white curtains at the nearby windows.

I sat on the bed while she slammed open the door to the walk-in closet. I thought about Crewe's assault charge and wondered if there was a side to the charming restaurant critic I hadn't seen yet.

When Lexie snapped on the closet light and disappeared inside, I called, "What happened, exactly, Lex? Was he really rough with you?"

I heard her slapping hangers on the rod. At last, she said, "He wasn't rough."

"What, then?"

She came to the closet doorway and stripped off her suit jacket. "He wasn't rough. He surprised me, that's all. And I hate that."

"Where did this happen?"

"In Louie's."

"In a restaurant? He kissed you in a restaurant?"

"Where else?" she snapped. "He never goes anywhere except restaurants! At least this time he wasn't dressed in one of his ridiculous disguises!"

"Lex—"

"I told him I have no intention of starting a relationship. Not with him, not with any man. My life is busy. Very busy. I run a large financial concern, and I have no time for personal issues."

She ripped her silk sweater over her head and threw it on the floor. Then she bent to snatch it up again and went back into the closet. She shouted, "I'm not an available woman! I told him that!"

"And he argued?"

"No, of course he didn't argue! He just—He said—oh, hell!"

I waited, and in a moment, she came out of the closet wearing a pair of yoga pants and her bra. She carried a black sweater.

I grabbed her hand and pulled her to sit on the bed. "Just tell me," I said calmly. "Tell me what happened, and I'll help. Take a deep breath."

She sat down obediently. And she breathed. Then she said, "He asked if he could kiss my hand."

"He—? Lex," I said, "that doesn't sound so bad."

"After I clearly stated I wanted no part of a relationship? For him to act like that?"

"It wasn't exactly the act of a—what did you say? A horny goat."

"Well, where does he get off doing the Sir Walter Raleigh routine? I don't want a man in my life!"

"I know, honey. I'm sorry."

"You put him up to this!"

"Lex, I felt sorry for him. I feel sorry for you! I'm sorry he feels so much, and you feel so—differently. I'm sorry, sorry, sorry. But you can hardly be angry at him for asking permission to kiss your hand. Really, doesn't it show how considerate he is?"

"He knows, doesn't he?"

"Knows what?"

"That I was raped."

"I never told him."

"But he knows. I can see he knows."

"Lexie, it doesn't take Sam Spade to figure out that something caused this—this extreme unwillingness to have anything but professional, business contact with the opposite sex."

She fell back onto the bed and put her arm over her eyes. "Oh, damn," she said unevenly. "Damn, damn."

"Do you want me to talk to him? To tell him you really aren't interested?"

She lay unmoving on the bed for a full minute in silence. Then, "No."

"Tell me what I can do," I said. "I want to help."

She sat up finally. There were no signs of tears on her face. She was in control again. "I don't know what anyone can do."

"Is it time for more therapy?"

She shuddered. "God, no. I've been therapied so much I know all the lines by heart. No, it's up to me. I just don't know. . . ."

I hugged her around the shoulders. "Take it slowly."

"How can I? One lunch date, one kiss on my hand, and suddenly I can't finish my day at the office? This is no way to do business, Nora."

"I bet you have a few people at the office who can take up the slack."

She sighed. "I don't know how you do it."

"Do what? I'm not running an investment firm, looking after millions entrusted to me by my clients."

She grimaced. "I know. But weaving the threads of your life. You're always coping with twenty different things at once. That's all beyond me."

"A few things are beyond me, too," I said, thinking of my trip to the sauna with Nuclear Winter. "But most of the time you don't have a choice. At least, I don't seem to."

She looked into my face finally. "I heard Raphael Braga is in town."

"Yes."

"You didn't mention that when I stopped by your house."

"I was going to. Then—well, Michael came home."

Lexie absorbed that information and noted my expression, too. "And you've seen Raphael, haven't you? Spoken with him?"

"I—yes."

"Sweetie, is that wise? I remember the contract you signed. You have a legal obligation to stay miles away from him."

"He wasn't supposed to come back to Philadelphia, either, so he's in violation of the agreement, too."

My friend studied me askance. "What did you say?"

"Nothing important. At least, not before he drugged me." I told her all about drinking the spiked champagne.

"Oh, my God!"

"I'm okay. I was rescued before he could—before anything happened."

"Thank heavens. That's my worst fear. Did you—well, did you ask him about Carolina?"

"He says they're separated."

"And the child? It's a girl, right?"

"She's with Raphael's parents in Brazil. Her name is Mariel."

Lexie frowned. "Nora, when you helped Carolina when she couldn't get pregnant—I know it was a time in your life when these things weren't so important to you."

At last I could discuss it. Here was Lexie, who'd been through it with me back in college. She knew the whole story, and had helped me figure out what to do then. Perhaps she could help me now, too.

"It seemed so easy," I said. "I went to the hospital, and a doctor took some of my eggs, and it was as simple as having a routine exam, almost. And the legal contract—the promise that I'd never try to meet the child or have any communication with her—it didn't seem so earth-shattering."

"You were twenty years old! And doing something nice for a friend who needed help."

I nodded. "His parents were so insistent they have children right away. And when Carolina discovered she couldn't, Raphael demanded a divorce. She was so crazy in love with him. It all seemed so romantic at the time."

"Seems downright medieval now, doesn't it?"

"But to a college girl—one like me, who always thought true love conquered all . . . I don't know. I wanted to help."

"And now," Lexie said, "you've had two miscarriages. And you want children of your own."

"I do."

"And Michael." Lexie smiled. "I suppose he wants a whole platoon of little Corleones, doesn't he?"

I found myself trembling then.

It was Lexie's turn to hug me. "Oh, sweetie."

"Thing is, Lex, I'm afraid to tell Michael. I haven't told him about helping Raphael and Carolina have a baby."

"Darling, why?"

"Because of something he said. Libby—oh, you don't have to hear the whole story, but in one of her nutty moments, Libby said she'd be happy to be a surrogate mother if we decided to have children that way—"

"Oh, dear!"

"And Michael said—he said he didn't want any Frankenstein babies."

Lexie winced. "Ouch."

"I know. It was awful."

"Nora, if he didn't know, if he was simply responding to Libby—"

"He said something similar months ago. Underneath everything else, Michael is a devout Catholic. He still goes to Mass, to that church with the ultraconservative priest. He's had it beaten into his head there's no other way to have children except how God intended."

"Well, God wouldn't have let man invent the wheel if He didn't think we'd come up with a few other ideas on our own."

I shook my head. "I don't know."

"Are you going to tell Michael? About Raphael and Carolina's kid?"

"My kid," I corrected. "He's going to think of her as my kid."

"Well, yes, but . . . not really. What you did for your friends has no bearing on your life with Michael, does it?"

"I don't know. I don't know how he'll react if I tell him, so maybe I should keep it a secret. He doesn't really need to know. And yet," I said slowly, "I may not have any other children, Lex. That little girl in Brazil might be the only child I'll ever have in the world."

Seriously, she said, "But you've agreed to stay away from her."

"I know." I put my hands over my face. "I start thinking about all this, and my brain just goes in circles. Things are different now. Carolina and Raphael aren't together."

"So that gives you the right to swoop in? Darling, you must be Raphael's worst nightmare."

"What do you mean?"

"If he thinks you're going to steal his daughter—Nora, it's a wonder he didn't try to poison you! He's probably scared to death of you."

That possibility hadn't occurred to me. Maybe Raphael was only protecting his daughter. I said, "I don't know what to think. My hormones are still making me crazy."

Sounding amused, she said, "Maybe we need that drink, after all."

"What a mess," I said. "When did our lives get so damn screwed up?"

Together, we sat in silence, contemplating our situations. Then she said, "This calls for hot chocolate."

"With marshmallows."

Lexie put on her sweater and a pair of velvet slippers, and we went back to her immaculate kitchen, where she pulled two white mugs from the cupboard. I found skim milk in her perfectly clean refrigerator, and we combined the cocoa and sugar in a saucepan on her stove. We took the finished product out onto her deck overlooking the river, and we sat in a pair of teak chairs, wrapped in cashmere shawls she had brought outside.

We turned our faces up to the afternoon sun, and I told her about Michael's broken leg.

"Oh, my God," she said. "Tigers! In the middle of Bucks County!"

I told her everything I had pieced together so far.

"So Vivian Devine keeps tigers on a private preserve?"

"She collects all kinds of cats, in fact. I saw a serval cat in her house, too. We knew she'd been collecting dead animals, and turns out, she's got a whole zoo to feed."

"It's a wonder Michael wasn't eaten! Have you told the police?"

"I've been trying to reach Ben Bloom all day. He doesn't answer. I assume he discovered something interesting at the autopsy of Penny Devine's—uh, hand. But I'll tell him about the tigers right away."

Lexie quelled a shiver by sipping hot chocolate. "The whole Devine story gets more peculiar every day. I did some research for you, too."

I sat up straighter. "Tell, tell."

"You know the whole history of Devine Pharmaceuticals, right? That the three siblings inherited their grandfather's drugstore, and Potty built it into a pharmaceutical giant. Well, he needed capital to do that."

"So he borrowed money from Penny."

"He didn't borrow it. He gave Penny a fifty percent interest in the new company. All three siblings own the original Devine Pharmaceuticals, and Penny owned half free and clear. Then, like other companies, they wanted to grow bigger yet, but even Penny didn't have the millions to make that happen. So they issued stock, and the company went public."

"But Penny still owned a big share, right?"

"The biggest. It was assumed those shares would revert to Vivian and Potty upon her death, but a little bird in the legal community tells me that Penny's will says something completely different—that her shares are supposed to go to her son."

"Son?"

"You heard right. Her illegitimate son, the child she gave away."

"So who is her son?"

Lexie shook her head. "My lawyer friend won't say. Whoever he is, he's going to inherit Penny's gigantic share of Devine Pharmaceuticals."

"You're suggesting he—whoever he is—might have killed his mother to get it?"

"Do you think it's possible?"

"I know this is a crazy idea, Lex, but do you think . . . ? That Crewe?"

Lexie paled. "No!"

"His father did have an affair with Penny. And Dilly Farquar told me that the child was born about forty years ago. Isn't Crewe thirty-eight or thirty-nine?"

"Crewe's mother would never have raised another woman's child."

"No? Not even if it saved face somehow?"

"Crewe wouldn't kill for a share of Devine Pharmaceuticals. He loves his work. He's got plenty of money of his own."

"Plenty isn't necessarily enough sometimes, Lex."

"It's a crazy idea," Lexie said. "He had nothing to do with Penny's murder."

I almost told her about Crewe's fight with Kell Huckabee, but I held my tongue. I needed to find out on my own if Crewe had any role in Kell's disappearance.

I fervently hoped Crewe was innocent. For Lexie's sake most of all.

# Chapter Seventeen

$I$ was in the car with Reed and Aldo, fighting traffic again, when I finally reached Detective Bloom by phone.

"I've been trying to contact you." His voice was low and tense, as if he was being overheard. "You're supposed to keep your cell phone turned on!"

"I don't have it with me."

"Then how are you—? Never mind. Where are you?"

"Right now?" I looked out the window. "In a car, passing the art museum."

"Pull over at Logan Circle. I'll be there in ten minutes."

"Ben—"

He had hung up.

Reed obliged me by pulling into a parking space in the looming shadow of the public library. In less than five minutes, a city police cruiser slid to a stop beside us, and Bloom bailed out of the passenger seat. He spoke to the cop behind the wheel, then slammed the door. The departing cop gave a friendly *whoop-whoop* with the cruiser's siren.

In one hand, Bloom carried a cup of coffee with a plastic lid. He sloshed a few drops as he opened the rear door of the town car.

Aldo said, "I don't like the looks of this."

Bloom got into the backseat with me. "Hey, kid," he said to Reed. "Take a walk. You, too, fella. Or do I have to arrest you first?"

Expressionless, Reed glanced at me in the rearview mirror. Aldo gave Bloom a steady stare.

"I'll be okay, Reed. Thank you, Aldo. Do you mind? I need to speak with the detective alone."

Reed sighed and got out of the town car. After a moment, Aldo did the same. The two of them stood on the sidewalk where they could see me through the window. Aldo pulled a cigar from his pocket and stuck it into his mouth.

"Don't mind them," I said to Bloom. "They take their babysitting very seriously."

"Good." One-handed, Bloom pulled a paper napkin from his pocket and mopped the spilled coffee from his raincoat.

"You must have big news," I said, "if the Philadelphia police are chauffeuring you around. Is it the autopsy?"

"It's a lot of things."

Normally, Bloom liked to pretend he was a cool, experienced cop who had his emotions under control. But not this afternoon. He stuffed the napkin in his pocket, then pulled out his cell phone. He checked the screen.

"Should I brace myself?"

He put away the cell phone and didn't smile. "The hand wasn't Penny Devine's."

"It—?"

He shook his head. "Not unless she shaved the hair on her arms and grew a Y chromosome."

"What are you saying?"

"The hand belonged to a man."

"A *man*? But—the nail polish! The wristwatch!"

"The nails were fakes. The wristwatch could have been bought by anyone at a department store."

"The family claimed it belonged to Penny."

"Yes, they did. They also wanted to bury the hand as fast as possible. They fought us every step of the way on the autopsy. They must have known all along the hand wasn't really hers."

"Could the hand belong to Kell Huckabee? The missing gardener?"

"That's what I'm thinking. Hang on. There's more. The hand had been frozen. We're sending away blood and tissue samples for more information. But get this: There was a gunshot wound, too. Bird shot passed clean through the palm of the hand."

I had seen how mottled and disturbed the flesh looked. I realized now that some of the discoloration could have been small wounds. "Could such small puncture wounds in the hand have been the cause of death?"

"No. It was a defensive wound—through the palm. Makes me think the victim could have been shot several more times in other places, too. Hard to know exactly what the cause of death is until we get our hands on—well, more of the body."

I sat back in the leather seat, trying to make sense of what he'd just told me.

He drank a little coffee. "You seem surprised."

"I'm stunned. Aren't you?"

He shrugged. "I wondered, that's all. That maybe you knew some of this already."

"Why would I? What's going on, Ben?"

He shook his head. "You've been helpful on this case, I'll admit. But the other family stuff is beginning to bug the hell out of me. It makes me think you're lying about a lot of things."

"About the Devines? I have no family loyalty to—"

"What about Abruzzo?"

"What?" I couldn't make the mental turnabout fast enough. "Are we back to that? Michael has nothing to do with Penny's—with the disappearance of whoever we found at the polo field. You know that as well as I do."

"Forget the polo field for a minute. I want to hear what you know about Mick."

"All right," I snapped, exasperated. "I've been leaving messages for you all day. I was going to tell you everything first thing this morning, but you didn't answer your phone. Look, I know we should have called someone first, but it was a hunch, that's all. An impulse. So we were walking in tall grass where we didn't have any business, and he didn't see the trap. It was dark, and—well, it snapped shut and broke his leg. The doctors at the hospital say—"

"What the hell are you talking about?"

I finally noticed Bloom's blank expression. "What the hell are *you* talking about?"

He said, "The hit."

I forgot about tigers and Michael's broken leg. "The what?"

"There's a contract out on his life."

I felt my whole body turn cold. "A contract? On Michael's life?"

He scowled, disbelieving. "You don't know about it?"

I could hardly catch my breath. "Tell me. What's going on?"

"The Pescara kid. His family figures Abruzzo killed him, so they've taken out a contract. They want Mick dead."

I couldn't absorb what he was saying. "The Pescaras want to kill Michael?"

"That's the word on the street. That's why you were kidnapped the other day."

"I wasn't—wait a minute." My hands were suddenly shaking so badly that I jammed them between my knees. "Tell me everything, from the beginning."

Bloom scanned my face, looking for clues to a mystery I still didn't understand. As if speaking to a soon-to-be hysterical woman, he said carefully, "The Pescara branch of the Abruzzo family thinks Mick kidnapped the kid and executed him to squeeze loose a confession in last winter's cop killing. Only the kid was innocent—so the Pescaras claim—and he didn't deserve to die. So they've hired a couple of wiseguys to kill Mick. It's payback. They opened fire on him the other day and missed. He went into protection mode, so they wanted to snatch you to bring him out into the open again. Only you fought off the goons."

"Oh, my God."

Now I understood why Aldo was with me night and day, and why Reed was under orders to keep me in plain sight every minute. And it explained why every member of Michael's usual posse was standing guard at his bedside in the hospital.

But I still asked, "Are you sure about this?"

Bloom shrugged. "It's big news among all the regular snitches—here in the city as well as my neighborhood, and believe me, we don't get the top secrets up there, so this news is out big-time. Mick's a marked man. The Pescaras want to take over Big Frankie's operation, and Mick is the only obstacle in their way. By killing him, they get the business, plus their revenge."

I felt as if I might choke. I needed fresh air. I opened the car door and got out onto the sidewalk. "Reed," I said. "Aldo!"

They materialized beside me, and Reed gripped my arm. "You okay?"

"Is it true? Somebody's trying to kill Michael?"

The boy released me and backed up a pace, then realized his mistake and grabbed me again. I felt the sidewalk shift beneath my feet. Reed pulled me over to a park bench near a flower bed.

I sat down on the bench. "Tell me the truth, Aldo."

The big man shook his head. "This is nothing I'm supposed to talk about."

"But you knew? And you didn't tell me?"

"That's not my job."

"His car accident wasn't an accident at all, was it? Someone tried to shoot him that day."

Aldo didn't answer, but his face told me the truth.

"What else?" I asked.

"Not for me to say."

Bloom had followed me out of the car, and he came over to the bench. He threw his coffee cup in the direction of an overflowing trash can. "Somebody tried to shoot him Saturday morning in a parking lot. Bullet hit a passing car, which just happened to be a state trooper, who's been telling everybody he saved the life of Big Frankie Abruzzo's son just by—"

"Stop it," I said. "Don't try to be funny about this."

Bloom put his hands into the pockets of his dark raincoat. "Sorry."

I tried to massage some logical thoughts into my head. "The hand we found. Does it have any connection to the—the hit on Michael?"

"I doubt it."

"He came to the polo field after the attempt on his life, just to make sure I hadn't heard about it somehow. After someone tried to kill him? Saturday morning?"

Bloom nodded. "Broad daylight. In the parking lot of a diner. Pretty bold, if you ask me."

I checked my watch. "Reed? I'd like to go now."

"Wait a minute." Bloom blocked my way back to the car.

"I need to see him."

"This hit," said Bloom. "It's serious, Nora. You're in danger now."

"And you're going to protect me, is that it?"

"I can. You shouldn't be with him, Nora. Every day he's in your house, you get dragged deeper into his business. Unless somebody can stop him."

"And that's you?"

"Yeah, I think so. Unless you warn him about me."

I cut around him, heading for the car. "He already knows about you, Detective."

Aldo put his arm out to bar Bloom from following me.

Bloom called, "Take care of yourself, Nora."

A minute later, the three of us were on our way to the hospital. The traffic was terrible, so the trip took more than an hour. I didn't speak. Now and then Aldo gave me a look, and Reed glanced into the rearview mirror.

More of Michael's posse loitered around the parking lot, the lobby and the hallways. I didn't recognize most of their faces, but I knew who they were—men connected to the Abruzzo family. Today they had been called upon to keep Michael safe.

I bulldozed my way past the young man standing outside his room and pushed through the door so fast that the two men inside jumped up from their chairs as if I'd fired a rocket through the window. Delmar dropped his crossword puzzle.

Only Michael seemed unperturbed by my entrance. He was sitting up against a stack of pillows, cell phone to his ear. He glanced up and saw my face. "Donnie," he said into the phone, "I'll have to call you back."

I took the phone from his hand and punched the off button.

"Hey," he said easily. "You're a sight for sore eyes."

"I feel like giving you a sore eye right now." I dropped his phone into the trash can beside the bed and threw my handbag into the nearest empty chair. "Gentlemen, step outside."

"Fellas," Michael said, "take a coffee break."

The two thugs hustled out faster than Kentucky Derby contestants.

The room looked like a fraternity house after a weekend bender. Two pizza boxes lay on the floor. Open sections of newspapers had been abandoned on every horizontal surface along with Styrofoam cups, a book of crossword puzzles and a vase of flowers the size of a Christmas tree. The television muttered the evening news. I reached up and slapped the TV off.

"Who told you?" Michael asked.

"Ben Bloom, as a matter of fact."

"I have a broken leg," he said. "Doesn't that buy me a little mercy?"

"Two broken legs won't get you off the hook for this, Michael. Somebody's trying to kill you! When were you going to mention that to me?"

"I didn't want to upset—"

"Well, I'm plenty upset now, buster!"

"Nora—"

"Bloom is delighted, by the way. He's hoping to make points with his superiors, so if you can manage to get yourself murdered when he's on duty, you'd be doing him a big favor."

"I'm sorry," Michael said. "What do you want me to do? Tell you every time some knucklehead wants to punch my lights out?"

I exploded. "You mean this happens often? It's a typical week in Mafia Land?"

"Jesus. No, this is a—will you stop pacing? I'm pumped full of so much painkiller that I'm already dizzy."

"Good!"

"Nora—"

"I can't help it. I'm angry. Somebody shot at you! What about the porch fire? Did Libby really start it? Or do I have criminals creeping around my backyard, flicking their Bics at my home?"

"I don't know about the fire yet. We're working on it. But it's likely the Pescaras were responsible."

"And your car accident? That wasn't an accident at all, was it? Tell me the truth!"

He shook his head. "A guy ran me off the road. When I got out of the car, he took a shot at me."

I sat down hard on the chair beside his bed. "Oh, my God."

"The fall in your house, though." He frowned. "That one has me puzzled. I don't know how anybody got inside to put a toy truck on the stairs."

"I can't believe this is happening. When exactly did my life start including gangland murders?

"It's not a murder."

"Not yet!"

"Hey, we've got the situation under control."

"So everywhere you and I go now, we need bodyguards? You call that under control?"

"Yes. And I don't want to hear arguments, either. Trying to snatch you was outside the rules of engagement. Which means somebody's not playing fair."

"Do you hear yourself? This isn't a game, Michael!"

"Sweetheart, don't be scared." He reached for my hand.

"What about the next time?" I got up from the chair and moved out of range.

"There won't be a next time. We're taking steps."

"Taking steps? What does that mean? More retaliation? Somebody tries to—to rub you out, so you're going to rub him out instead?"

Michael laughed.

"Don't make fun of me!" I cried. "I'm frightened!"

He sobered fast. "I know. I'm sorry. But look, I wouldn't be marrying you if I thought you were truly in danger. Everybody knows you're out of bounds."

"Obviously not everybody. Those two hulks who grabbed me—"

"That won't happen again. I'll make that very clear. Please, Nora, take a deep breath."

I did. And held it. I looked at the diamond on my left hand.

"What are you thinking?"

I said, "I'm rethinking my options."

He smiled. "What can I do to make the case for marrying me?"

I went over to the bed again and took his hand. "I'm afraid for your safety."

"Hey, the worst thing that happened to me this week had nothing to do with the Pescaras and everything to do with walking around in the woods with you."

I finally took an inventory of the patient and realized he had only one IV tube in his arm. Gone was the heart monitor. Someone must have brought him a clean shirt, because he was wearing a faded T-shirt that advertised the fishing shop he owned. He had propped up his good leg in the bed, which gave him the appearance of more vitality than a man in his condition ought to have. I glanced down the length of his left leg, covered by the sheet.

"How is it?" I asked.

"It looks like I got caught in a steel trap. But it'll heal. They're giving me antibiotics by the gallon."

"And the broken bone?"

He sketched a waffling motion with one hand. "They showed me the before-and-after X-rays. It's ugly. But I'll walk. They had me up on crutches this afternoon between the soap operas. You ever watch those things? Man, that's some sexy television."

It was my turn to apologize. "I'm sorry you're hurt. It's all my fault."

"It's my own fault. I should have stayed out of the weeds. Stayed in the car." He squeezed my hand. "But you could help me feel better."

I allowed him to pull me until I perched carefully on the side of the bed farthest from his broken leg. "You must be on the road to recovery if you think soap operas are sexy."

He kissed my forehead. Then my cheek. Then I turned my head and kissed him on the mouth, which turned into something longer and more potent that warmed my cold thoughts.

He smoothed my hair away from my face. "What did Bloom say when you told him about the tigers?"

"Actually, I—I didn't tell him."

"Why not?"

"Because he dropped the contract-on-your-life bombshell, and even tigers slipped my mind. I'll tell him tomorrow."

"Tell him tonight."

"Michael, there's been a development in the Penny Devine murder."

He nodded. "The autopsy was today, right?"

"They're not sure about the exact cause of death yet, but there was definitely a gunshot wound. Through the hand."

"Defensive wound," Michael said, demonstrating by raising both hands, palms out. "She put her hands up to deflect the bullet. It's an instinct. Poor old lady."

"Actually," I said, "it seems the hand we found didn't belong to Penny after all."

That surprised him. "Whose was it?"

"The police don't know. They're sending it off to be tested for drugs and whatnot. I suppose DNA, too. But get this. The hand belonged to a man."

"The guy who disappeared from the estate?" Michael guessed. "The gardener?"

"Kell Huckabee. It makes sense, doesn't it?"

Michael raised a skeptical brow. "He had a pretty fancy manicure for a gardener. Somebody wanted to disguise him, maybe? Then they planted the hand at the polo match, hoping everyone would assume it belonged to Penny."

"That's what I figure, too."

"So unless a complete stranger came along and dropped the hand on their grass, the Devines have some explaining to do."

"Yes. And perhaps the most important question . . . ," I said.

"Is, where the hell is Penny Devine?"

"Exactly. If it's Kell who's dead, and Potty and Vivian concocted the suicide note and planted the wristwatch . . . is Penny actually alive?"

We thought about things together for a moment. I wasn't sure where Michael's mind went, but I found myself thinking about Crewe. I didn't want him to be involved in the whole mess, but I couldn't help thinking he was connected.

Michael reached for my hand. "You look scared again. The police are going to solve this, Nora. You don't have to worry about it anymore."

I tried to wipe my face clean. He needed to get well, and stewing about Crewe or Ben Bloom's revitalized interest in stopping the Abruzzo family would only keep him agitated. I said, "I'm sorry."

He pulled until I was folded against his chest. "Hey, be happy. The good news is that there's no Blackbird curse."

I smiled, arms around him and my ear tuned to the steady thump of his heart. "You sure about that?"

"Fairly sure."

In the trash can, his cell phone chirped.

"Let me guess," I said. "It's not your stockbroker calling."

"I doubt it."

I sat up. "Shall I answer?"

"It can wait."

"Is it something legal?"

"I'm buying some Super Bowl tickets, that's all."

"The Super Bowl is over."

"Uh, tickets for an upcoming Super Bowl."

"You don't even know who's playing next year." A thought struck me. "Or do you?"

"They're not for next year. And no, I don't know. What do you take me for?" He was smiling.

I pulled the phone out of the trash and handed it over. Within a minute, Michael had negotiated for the purchase of two hundred tickets to a game that was years away. While he concluded the deal, I decided I didn't want to speculate about what he planned to do with tickets he couldn't possibly use himself.

I heard a commotion outside the door.

And my sister Libby burst in, laden with shopping bags and trailing a long white scarf from around her neck.

"Darlings!" she cried. "I'm here to help pass the time!"

I put my forefinger to my mouth and indicated Michael on the phone. "Libby," I said in a lower voice, "you didn't have to come."

"Hospital stays can be so dull, Nora, and I knew you'd need a distraction this evening. So I toodled over with a zillion magazines! This is the perfect evening to work on the wedding plans!"

Michael disconnected his call, and I thought I heard him stifle a groan.

Libby dropped two enormous shopping bags on my lap. "Tuxedo choices! Centerpiece ideas! What better time to take care of these details than right now—to take your mind off the pain and suffering?"

I bobbled the bags and Michael made an instinctive grab to prevent them from hitting the floor. He managed to come up with a magazine with a half-naked woman on the cover. She wore tiny threads of virginal white lace, but flaunted enormous, nonvirginal breasts.

Michael blinked. "Whoa."

"Wedding-night lingerie." Libby patted the magazine. "It's a crucial choice. It might very well set the tone for the whole marriage. I thought you might want some input."

Michael flipped open the magazine approvingly. "Good call."

"I know some men get squeamish when it comes to planning a wedding," Libby went on. "It's natural, I suppose, for the male of the species to second-guess his decision to give up his bachelor rambles and cleave to one woman for the rest of his days—not to mention giving his bride complete creative control of the wedding just to make her happy. But let me tell you, it's the first step on a slippery slope. First you allow your future wife to choose 'We've Only Just Begun,' and the next thing you know, you're agreeing to scatter your ashes together over Graceland."

"Uh . . ."

"What I mean," Libby said firmly, "is that the wedding isn't as important as the marriage. But if you can't communicate your needs now, you might as well resign yourself to a sad excuse for a marriage. Assert yourself, however, and I promise you'll be setting the tone for a long and fruitful partnership that will be the most fulfilling."

Sometimes my sister managed to blurt out philosophy that made surprisingly good sense.

I said, "Thank you, Libby."

"Okay," Michael said. "After the television this afternoon, I feel like I'm getting a whole new—you know, perspective into the female mind, so I'm ready."

"What television?" Libby plopped prettily into one of the chairs and fluffed her hair. She had come to the hospital in a voluminous dress that made the best of her curves. A silver belt with a gigantic buckle cinched her waist, drawing attention to her cleavage. Her pointy boots had high heels. She rubbed her toes through the leather. "You mean daytime drama?"

"There's a guy dying in a girl's ski chalet, but he seems to have enough energy to—"

"Oh, that's my favorite!" Libby cried. "Isn't it a poignant story?"

"Uh—"

"He faked his own death to be with her, you know. The police think he drove off a cliff and killed himself. And doesn't he look fabulous without his shirt? I understand the actors lift weights before those scenes so their muscles are plumped up. Would you like to see some bridesmaid dresses? I'm partial to this one, see?"

While Libby opened magazines and displayed photos of slender teenagers in revealing bridesmaid dresses—all the while filling Michael in on the convoluted backstory of a soap opera—I sat beside him and let myself relax.

A male nurse came in at nine and made polite remarks about letting the patient get some rest. Libby made note of the nurse's wedding ring and didn't wheedle for a longer stay.

We left Michael in the nurse's capable care as well as the protection of his cadre of Abruzzo musclemen, who seemed content to pass their time in various corners of the hospital.

Libby drove me to Blackbird Farm, and when I went into the house, I discovered that my kitchen had been commandeered by Rawlins and three of his high school friends. They sat at the kitchen table frowning at the playing cards they held in their hands. An open book lay in the middle of the table—*Poker for Dummies*. At the head of the table lounged Emma, grinning confidently. They were all drinking Mountain Dew from cans.

Beside Emma, Ignacio still looked shell-shocked from our tiger adventure.

"C'mon, girls," Emma said to Rawlins and his pals. "Ante up!"

The boys all slurped from their cans of soda and continued to frown at their cards.

"Hello?" Ignacio said to me.

I patted his shoulder. "Michael's doing fine. Thank you for asking."

"While these ladies contemplate their losses," Emma said to me, "you should take a look at what's in the living room. A couple of movers stopped by this afternoon."

I had forgotten about my windfall from Penny Devine. I went into the sitting room and saw large wardrobe boxes and a steamer trunk stacked among the furniture.

Cautiously, I opened the steamer trunk and found a mound of garments, each carefully wrapped in acid-free paper. I glimpsed a flicker of sequins, and intricate embroidery on a white linen cuff. I sat back on my heels to look at the row of wardrobe boxes and wondered how many beautiful designs could be inside. Hundreds of thousands of dollars' worth, no doubt. But if Penny wasn't dead after all, did these beautiful things still belong to me?

The phone rang.

I assumed it might be Bloom calling, so I went into the butler's pantry to tell him about the tigers. But when I picked up, I heard the voice of Dilly Farquar. He said, "Nora, dear heart, tell an old gentleman your secrets. Is it true? Did Penny Devine bequeath all her couture to you?"

"How on earth did you find out?"

"Smoke signals." Dilly sounded very pleased. "So it's not a wild rumor?"

"I can't believe it, Dilly."

"Obviously, she had a soft spot for you. She was fond of your grandmother."

"Yes, but—well, I'm flabbergasted. Surely her collection belongs in a museum."

"Some of it, certainly. Now, listen," he said. "You know I'm not a man who asks many favors, but this is huge for me, Nora. Penny Devine's collection must be one of the most comprehensive in the nation. She started buying clothes from Chanel in 1949."

I found myself laughing dizzily. Exhausted yet relieved about Michael, I allowed myself a moment of pleasure. "What's the favor you want, Dilly?"

"Dear heart, you must let me help you unpack the collection. If I see those clothes, I can die a happy man."

"Done," I said.

"I should warn you. *Vogue* is going to call. So will the Metropolitan Museum. They'll all want a peek."

"You're the man for me, Dilly. The stuff arrived a little while ago."

"You have it now?" He was startled. "I'll bring breakfast tomorrow. I'll bring champagne!"

Which is how I found myself entertaining the *crème* of Philadelphia's fashionistas the following morning.

# Chapter Eighteen

$B$ut not before telephoning Ben Bloom to tell him that Vivian Devine kept tigers on a piece of rural property in Bucks County. I finally reached him just as I finished brushing my teeth that night. Bloom said, "Say that again."

I tapped my toothbrush on the sink and repeated my information.

"Tigers?" He sounded dumbfounded. "You mean, like tigers from a zoo?"

"I don't know where Vivian got them. Judging by the way she collects abandoned house cats, I assume she thinks she's rescuing them from abusive circumstances."

"Wait a minute. Tigers?"

"Yes," I said patiently. "I can give you the address, and you can look for yourself."

Bloom spoke to someone with him—I thought I heard the sound of traffic, too—and then he came back on the line. "Okay," he said. "Anything else?"

"You mean about the murder, or about the attempt on Michael's life?"

"Listen, Nora, I thought I was doing you a favor when I told you about that."

"You did. I didn't like hearing it, but," I said slowly, "I'm glad you told me."

"I figure if you know what's going on, you might take better care of yourself."

Drily, I said, "Thanks, Detective. I appreciate your concern."

"Nora?"

I waited.

He said, "How about forgiving me? So I made a mistake today, telling you the way I did. Everybody's entitled to be forgiven once. And I'm trying to do the right thing."

"I'll take that under advisement," I said.

I hung up. My feelings for Ben Bloom were hard to define most of the time, but tonight I didn't like him one bit.

I considered phoning Michael's hospital room to say good night. I missed him. I missed his laugh. I missed his warm body in my bed. I didn't want to wake him, however, if he was already drugged and asleep.

Peeking out the window curtains, I noted that Michael's crew remained on alert at the end of my driveway. Nothing short of an army was going to get past them.

I climbed into bed and turned out the light. I knew I'd been taking out a lot of aggressions on Michael lately. Misdirected anger, perhaps. Sometimes we made tender love, but at other times it was something very different. I had a lot of emotions about losing our baby, I knew. And about the complexities of Michael's life and his unwillingness to put his family business completely aside to make a future with me. I wished he could be good.

I had often wished he could be a clean-cut cop, like Ben Bloom.

Except Bloom didn't seem all that clean anymore. Once again, I'd let him manipulate me.

In the morning, I phoned the hospital early and spoke with Aldo, who said Michael was talking with his doctor at that moment and couldn't take my call. I got dressed in jeans and an old white dress shirt that had been my husband's. I made myself some oatmeal and ate every bite. I observed that Emma had left already. No note in the kitchen, of course, but her truck was long gone.

In the sunshine, I went out to the barn to check on her livestock and discovered four adorable ponies grazing in the paddock. They trotted over to the fence to meet me and poked their inquisitive noses through the rails. Emma's leggy jumper, Mr. Twinkles, ambled over, too, and he nuzzled my hair.

"You'll always be my favorite," I told him as I patted his neck.

At nine thirty, a sumptuous get-well-soon gift basket arrived with a card to Michael from Lexie. The basket was heaped with fruits, exotic vegetables, two bottles of wine and a box of chocolate truffles—all tied up with an elaborate ribbon.

At ten, Dilly showed up carrying a wooden case of cold champagne. Fashion icon Kaiser Waldman gamboled into the house on Dilly's heels, swinging a walking stick and wearing a tweed jacket in a flamboyant shade of green, riding boots with elaborate buckles and a pair of trousers that bloused at his knees. The designer removed a pair of square and very dark women's sunglasses to look around the foyer of the house. The gilt mirror that had been a gift from Ben Franklin to my great-great-something grandmother particularly caught his attention. Then his gaze fell to the worn Persian rug on the floor.

Kaiser said, "*Mon Dieu*. My uncle had the château with the floor that tilted exactly like this one. The whole place fell down four years ago, like the house of cards."

Following Kaiser bounded a slim younger man I didn't know. He carried a large folding piece of furniture and had luscious blond hair layered to reveal a pair of diamond earrings. His face was beautifully sculpted, with a generous, full-lipped mouth curled catlike at the edges. He wore Seven jeans that had clearly been purchased in the misses department, and the message printed on his T-shirt said I'M AN OPRAH SHOW WAITING TO HAPPEN.

"Nora, this is Arturo."

He put down his burden and shook my hand with a flutter of eyelashes. "Call me Artie, doll."

"How nice to meet you."

"I look familiar, don't I? I'm an actor. But today I'm just obliging Kaiser. I mean, who could say no to the master?"

Over his shoulder, Dilly said, "I don't know about his acting, but Artie's the best tailor in Philadelphia."

Then Dilly found his way into the sitting room, and we heard him cry, "Gentlemen! In here!"

The three of them froze in reverential poses as they gazed at the altar of Penny Devine's wardrobe boxes. Then they took a synchronized pace forward to peer down into the open steamer trunk and the cascade of lace that tumbled out of it.

"Nora," Dilly rasped. "Champagne glasses! At once!"

I supplied glassware, and Artie conjured a gallon of orange juice and a bottle of Cointreau. He mixed mimosas in a handy flower vase and poured for everyone. Kaiser reclined grandly on the sofa, unbuttoning his tweed jacket to get comfortable for a long stay. He tucked a pillow under each elbow.

"You may begin," he announced when he was ensconced.

At which point Dilly and Artie took turns pulling one garment after another from the wardrobe boxes.

Kaiser winced at a yellow silk dress from Dior. "How can the woman look anything but foolish in that shade? You see? Even Dior was fallible!"

"But a turning point in his career, don't you think?"

"The downturn," Kaiser said darkly.

Dilly nodded with resignation and draped the yellow dress over a chair. To me, he said, "That one doesn't belong in your closet, dear heart. Granted, some of these things should probably go to a museum. I know a curator here in the city, definitely the best person to take charge of the clothes and make something lasting out of them. But you should keep a few pieces. You'll wear them and treat them right. Penny knew that."

Artie gave a cry of rapture as he found a black number twinkling with rhinestones and beading.

Which sent Kaiser into a fit of headshaking. "No, no, no, no! Too much with the sparkles! Gaultier had no sense of propriety in his early years!"

"Who wants propriety?" Artie demanded.

"What was de la Renta thinking?" Dilly plucked up a dress of orange organza. "For a woman of Penny's years?"

"During the fat phase," Kaiser said knowingly. "You see the ploy? Focus on the décolletage, and the eye will not wander elsewhere. Penny was always fighting the fat."

Dilly located a long wisp of peach-hued silk embroidered with delicate fronds and appliquéd fruit.

Kaiser clasped his hands in ecstasy. "There she is! Carolina Herrera at the pinnacle of her artistry! I must see it on the body!"

Dilly and Artie turned to me.

"The body?" I asked. Involuntarily, my hand strayed to the open collar of my shirt and closed it tightly. This particular body had been through a pregnancy and a miscarriage and an emotionally triggered weight loss that made me feel flabby, not slim. The last thing I wanted to do was play fashion model.

"Dear heart," Dilly said with great kindness, "it's not like we haven't seen our share of women, you know."

"And it's not you we're interested in," Artie added. "No offense, doll."

"Strip down," Kaiser commanded. "We must see the Herrera!"

At which point Artie began unbuttoning my shirt and I found myself slipping into an evening dress that weighed no more than a summer nightgown. Unwillingly, I wiggled my jeans down underneath the dress and kicked them across the floor. The Herrera felt like gossamer floating around me, though, and my heart lifted.

I had, of course, worn my grandmother's couture so frequently that I had already experienced the phenomenon of fine workmanship on the human body. My spine straightened to the posture my childhood ballet teacher had insisted upon. My shoulders went level. My chin somehow lifted to a point in space slightly above normal. And my breath caught high in my throat.

Artie cleared away my coffee table and set up a folding mirror with three panels. I stood in the middle of it and looked at myself.

Kaiser frowned. Dilly and Artie stood back to eye me critically.

"The breasts," Kaiser said.

"Hm," said Dilly, nodding.

Artie leaped forward. He had slipped a pincushion on his wrist, and he plucked a pin from it. In an instant, he lifted my right arm and began nipping pins into the fabric as fast as an expert typist tapping the keys of a typewriter. He worked his way under my breasts and emerged on my left side before jumping back to study the result.

The dress met with Kaiser's approval. He waved his hand like a dauphin. "The Herrera is salvageable. Keep it. What's next?"

For the rest of the morning, I stood on the wooden champagne case in my tallest Jimmy Choos while Dilly and Artie fluttered around me like a couple of Disney bluebirds.

"Good Lord!" Dilly cried when he whipped out a purple spandex number with an outer-space theme. "Didn't Penny wear this to the Oscars?"

"The year she knocked Joan Rivers on her ass!" Artie clapped his hands at the memory. "Oh, how I prayed for a catfight! But in a wonderfully ironic moment Russell Crowe broke them up before the fur could really fly, and— oh, sweet Carol Burnett, it's a Bob Mackie! Do you think it might fit me?"

"You're seven feet tall in heels," Dilly said. "Of course it won't fit you. Besides, the color is so garish we'd have to help you write a suicide note if you actually got the thing to zip. But Nora, do try it on. Humor us."

"I'll look like a drag queen, Dilly."

"Better you than Artie," Dilly said. "He's got the shoulders of a line-backer."

"I *was* a linebacker, I'll have you know," Artie said. "Take off your bra, doll. Bob Mackie is all about built-ins."

Artie helped me writhe into the slippery, sequined creation. It was one of the Cher-inspired dresses with a neckline that plunged to Panama and a back that showed nearly every single vertebra in my spine. The eye-popping purple made me think of electrified grapes.

I hitched up the skirt and climbed onto the champagne box to display the final product.

Dilly said, "I can't imagine Penny Divine buying this horror."

From his crouch on the floor, Artie said, "The morning papers say Penny may not be dead after all. The tabloids will go crazy."

"So who," asked Kaiser, "is really the dead woman?"

I wondered if my information from Bloom was supposed to be a secret, but I decided probably not. "Actually, it's not a woman at all."

Artie looked up from my hem, intrigued. "The papers didn't say anything about that! It's a man?"

"In drag," I said. "Acrylic nails, lady's watch—Penny's watch. Someone wanted the police to believe it was really Penny."

Dilly had been watching me. "Who do you think it is, Nora?"

"My bet's on Kell Huckabee, a man who used to work at Eagle Glen as the caretaker. He disappeared a while back, and—"

"Kell?" Artie's eyebrows rose.

"Huckabee?" Dilly was just as startled. His glass slipped from his grasp and shattered on the floor, sending a thin spray of champagne across the floor. "Oh, how clumsy of me!"

He got down on his knees and began mopping up champagne with his handkerchief. "I'm so sorry! I've broken one of your lovely glasses."

"Don't worry about it, Dilly. How do you know Kell Huckabee?"

Kaiser and Artie exchanged a cautionary look.

"The suspense is unbearable," I said. "How do you know Kell?"

"Drugs," Artie admitted.

That surprised me. "Cocaine? Heroin?"

"No, no, Kell Huckabee sold performance drugs in gay clubs. A little

Ecstasy, but mostly that new underground drug called MaxiMan. All the young guys love it. Makes us hard for a whole weekend."

Dilly finally glanced up from collecting broken bits of glass, looking pained. "Don't be crude, Artie. You promised to behave if I brought you along."

"Sorry, but it's true. You pop one MaxiMan at a club on Friday night, and you're good to go until way past *60 Minutes* on Sunday. It's the latest thing for gay men. That, and a swing in the shower."

Confused, Kaiser said, "Only sixty minutes?"

"No, no, the whole weekend!"

"Dilly, you've cut yourself!"

He stared at his finger, which was oozing a tiny drop of blood. "So I have."

Kaiser passed Dilly another handkerchief, which he used first to dab the tear of pain that had squeezed out of his left eye. Then he wrapped it around his bleeding finger. He had turned pale at the sight of his own blood.

"Are you all right?"

"Fine, fine. Don't let me spoil the festivities. It was a silly accident. Let's see the dress again. Spin around for us, dear heart?"

I obeyed, but asked, "Was Kell Huckabee gay?" Recalling my hot afternoon with Nuclear Winter, I asked, "Or bisexual?"

"Not that I know of." Artie stuck a pin between his teeth and spoke around it. "But he obviously knew his most interested customers would be. I mean, does your average hetero really want to admit his problems to the corner pharmacist, let alone a drug dealer? For us, though, it's just recreation. MaxiMan makes a good time."

"Where did Kell get his supply?"

"I have no clue."

But I could make an educated guess. Kell Huckabee got the drug from Potty Devine, who seemed to be passing it out like breath mints.

Dilly squeezed the handkerchief on his finger. "What are you thinking, Nora?"

That Potty Devine suddenly sounded like a man who could have wanted to keep Kell Huckabee quiet. If Devine Pharmaceuticals was trying to buy another company, they'd need everything to be spick-and-span. Which made me think of another Devine scandal avoided.

"Dilly, tell me again about the child Penny had."

"It was many years ago, dear heart."

"Did you ever hear what became of the baby?"

"Not a word."

Kaiser rooted in the pockets of his jacket for a cigarette case. He opened it, then reconsidered smoking in the presence of the beautiful clothes and snapped shut the case again. "In the old days, the bastard children were given away. Adopted by servants."

"In books," Artie said, "an inconvenient child went to distant relatives, remember? Very *Jane Eyre*. It was best to send the baby far, far away."

"Nora," Dilly said, "you'll make yourself sick with all this worrying. Why not spend a day concentrating on these beautiful clothes?"

Before I could better explain my thinking, we heard a door slam and voices from the kitchen. I was trapped on the champagne case while Artie fiddled with the hem of the Mackie dress, so I turned awkwardly to see who was arriving.

"Woohoo!" Libby cried, barging into the room with her baby in arms and various scarves flowing from her neck. "Look who I found in the driveway!"

# Chapter Nineteen

It was *The Sopranos* meeting *Project Runway*. Aldo came first, followed more slowly by Michael on crutches, and a couple of his hangers-on, including Delmar. They all stopped dead, staring at me on the champagne case with a flamboyantly gay man at my feet and the purple dress practically pulsing with garishness.

Dilly, Kaiser and Artie stared back at the mob crew, just as speechless.

"My goodness!" Hefting the baby on her hip, Libby was the embodiment of heterosexuality run amok. "Nora, you look like a starlet who picked the wrong stylist."

"Hi," I said to Michael, perhaps too cheerfully. "I didn't expect you until later this afternoon."

"A bunch of reporters showed up, so we took a back door." Although stunned by my appearance, Michael pulled himself together and managed to hobble closer, clumsy with the crutches. His left leg was encased in an inflatable cast, and it hardly appeared substantial enough to protect the broken bone. His attention, however, was fully captured by the purple dress. "You," he said, "look fantastic."

Kaiser covered his mouth. Dilly managed to keep silent. Artie coughed.

The rest of the wiseguys stared at me as if I'd just strutted off an Atlantic City stage with the rest of the showgirls.

Aldo swung around and clouted Delmar upside the head. "Whadaya think you're lookin' at?"

"It's nothing special," I said firmly, already aware of Dilly's amusement at the common man's taste in women's fashion. "Should you be in bed?"

"From the looks of things," Artie muttered, crouched at Michael's feet and gazing up at his tall figure, "he won't be much good in bed for a long time. What a waste."

I remembered my manners and introduced everyone.

Dilly, Kaiser and Artie couldn't help staring at the notorious man in their midst. They took turns shaking his hand.

Libby said, "Kaiser, do you make bridesmaids' dresses? Because I'd love to have a consult with you. I'll nurse the baby and then we'll discuss, okay?"

Kaiser choked, and I said, "Libby, would you mind making coffee when you're finished—uh, taking care of little Max? Some of us are going to have blinding headaches soon."

Dilly insisted Michael sit down and even jumped up to ease him into one of the leather chairs. Artie pulled the footstool close to make him comfortable. Aldo fetched a pillow. In seconds, Michael managed to have half a dozen people doing him services.

Libby went off to nurse her child, and Aldo dragged the two bodyguards into the kitchen.

Kaiser studied Michael with intent interest from the sofa. "You are the mafioso, yes?"

"No," Michael said. "That's my father. And you're—what? Some kind of dressmaker?"

The world-famous fashion designer lifted his hands humbly. "The simple tailor, like my father, that is all. You are wanting to marry this nice young lady?" Kaiser waved at me.

"That's the plan."

Kaiser nodded. "It has chemistry, this match."

Libby returned long enough to deliver a Ziploc bag full of crushed ice cubes to Michael. "For your hand," she said. "It will stop the swelling. Next I'll bring you some toast."

"What happened to your hand?" I asked.

"Bumped it," Michael said. "Go ahead with the fashion show."

Artie held up a short black cocktail dress. "This one next!"

With Michael watching, stripping off the Mackie dress brought a stinging blush to my face. But he seemed distracted—probably from more pain than he admitted. In two minutes, I was back on the box, this time decked out in a short cocktail frock with a Chanel label basted discreetly inside.

Dilly sighed. "The quintessential little black dress."

It was sleeveless with a simple round, topstitched collar, a cunningly nipped waist with a demure grosgrain ribbon, and a gently flared skirt that suggested my hips and skimmed my kneecaps. A good tailor could make it fit properly, but the bones of the dress were perfection.

For the first time, Kaiser got to his feet and made a sedate circle around me, staring at the dress with fixed attention. "Hmm."

"Exquisite," Dilly murmured.

"Drop-dead gorgeous," Artie agreed.

"What do you think, Michael?"

He shrugged, cradling the ice pack in his hand. "It's good."

"It *is* good," Kaiser proclaimed. "I will fit you myself! The garment must not be damaged by imbeciles."

"Hey," Artie protested.

Kaiser snatched the pins and set to work, tweaking, tucking, perfecting. He muttered in French and German, frowning, pursing his lips in aggravation. Artie watched closely.

"There's something scratchy inside," I said, wriggling.

"Nonsense."

"No, really. I can feel it."

At last Kaiser grabbed my bottom with both hands, making me jump. "What is this?"

I craned around. "It's my—well—"

"It is something inside the dress!"

"I know!"

I turned the hem inside out and reached up inside the dress lining. My fingers struck a hard bit of metal that had snagged on a seam. With a struggle, I worked it free and held it up to the light.

A wristwatch.

A delicate one, made of white gold with PIAGET stamped on the tiny face. "Good heavens," I said. "It must be Penny's watch."

Michael leaned forward. "Like the one we found at the polo match?"

"Not quite." I tossed it to him. "Maybe the other watch was some kind of knockoff. That one is the real thing."

Dilly said, "She must have lost the watch in this dress the last time she wore it."

"But," Michael said, turning the watch over in his hand, "her family said the other watch was hers."

"They claimed it was," I agreed, meeting his gaze.

"Time to phone Detective Gloom again?"

"I think so."

Kaiser objected. "Not yet! The fitting is not complete!"

He attacked the dress again with expert fingers—first snatching pins from Artie's hand, then slipping them one by one into the seams of the Chanel.

At last, he finally stood back in triumph. "Good!"

A little black dress by Chanel.

Fitted by Kaiser Waldman.

I could die a happy woman. Or at least a well-dressed one.

Libby arrived with more mimosas and toast. "Is that ice helping?" she asked Michael.

He flexed his hand. "Sure, thanks."

Libby went to the CD player and turned on some music, so the party really began to swing. I used the chance to excuse myself and slip into the butler's pantry between the kitchen and the dining room to phone Ben Bloom with my discovery of Penny's watch.

I dialed Bloom's cell phone, but got his voice mail. I left a message about the watch and told him to call me at home.

When I put the receiver back on the cradle, I found Dilly standing behind me.

He said, "I'm sorry about the broken glass, dear heart."

"Oh, Dilly, think nothing of it." I gave him a fond peck on the cheek. "It was nothing special. I'm so glad you came this morning."

"So am I." He took my hand and looked down at the gargantuan ring on my finger. "This is my first opportunity to meet your intended. He's— not quite what I expected."

"What did you expect?"

Dilly smiled apologetically. "Something brutal. But he makes an effort to be pleasant."

"He's not brutal at all. And he's more than pleasant."

"I'm sure you're right." Dilly touched my gaudy ring. "Nora, I hope you know what you're getting into. Sometimes we—all of us—experiment in times of stress. We want to see how the other half lives."

"Dilly, are you warning me off?"

"Just giving you permission to change your mind if you need to. One youthful indiscretion doesn't have to alter your life."

I stiffened. "Do you mean *ruin* my life?"

"Don't be offended. I'm clumsy at this, but—look, I'm trying to tell you that you can make mistakes and learn from them." Suddenly Dilly had tears in his eyes, and his hand trembled. "I know you suffered a loss recently, so maybe you're not yourself." Dilly paused before saying, "But perhaps you lost your child for a reason. Perhaps it was for the best."

Coldly, I said, "You have no idea how much I wanted that child, Dilly."

"Maybe you did. But think, Nora. Any child you have with that man will always connect you to his—his family. Are you sure you want that?"

I said nothing.

Dilly went on. "Think about what you're doing, Nora. Think about who you are. Who he is. Who your children will be."

At once, I thought of the two thugs who had grabbed me in the street. Men who wanted to hurt me.

"Think of your children, Nora."

We heard the front doorbell ring. Dilly gave me a kiss on the cheek and left me in the pantry. I heard Aldo go to answer the door. When he came back, he had Crewe Dearborne in his wake.

Crewe arrived in the sitting room, looking downright startled to find such a crowd. I wasn't sure if Aldo playing the role of my butler shook him up or the presence of the fashionistas in the living room did it. He carried a flat canvas package, tied with string, and a grocery bag.

"Nora," he said when he'd kissed my cheek. "There is a carload of gangsters checking ID at the gate. What kind of house party do you have going on?"

"They're not gangsters, they're—well, how nice to see you, Crewe." I introduced him to Kaiser and Artie. Michael got up from his chair, precariously balancing himself on one crutch.

"Mick," Crewe said, "what the hell happened to you? The morning papers all have different reports. What's going on?"

"Long story," Michael said. "The short version is, I broke my leg taking a walk in the woods."

"Jesus." Crewe looked respectfully down at the cast. "Does it hurt?"

"Like a son of a bitch."

"Here's your toast!" Libby sang, coming into the living room with her baby on one shoulder and a plate in the other hand. "Hello, Crewe."

Crewe glanced at the slice of slightly burned bread improved only by a skim coat of strawberry jam. "That's all you're giving him to eat?"

"He's an invalid!"

Michael mustered his most dangerous scowl. "I am not!"

Libby was unmoved. "A full stomach will only slow the healing process. I also brought a tea that strengthens bone. It tastes a little like mung beans and cabbage, I'm told, but it works."

"You poor bastard," Crewe said with feeling. He took off his coat. "I brought you some real food. It's surely better than mung beans and cabbage. Where's the kitchen?"

Crewe had never been in the kitchen at Blackbird Farm, and he was taken aback by the huge space with its antiquated stove, the French chandelier and the tile floor where an eighteenth-century scullery maid reportedly had her way with one of George Washington's lieutenants.

But Crewe got to work and was soon whipping up a meal worthy of Julia Child. Libby gave little Max to Michael and went off to browbeat Kaiser into designing her bridesmaid dress. And I began to wonder why Crewe really had come. For all his expertise in the kitchen, he seemed a little high-strung.

Michael cut to the chase. "How's Lexie?" he asked, flat out.

Crewe's hands paused in the act of unrolling his knife kit and selecting a very sharp deboning knife from the collection displayed within the canvas pockets. "She's fine," he said. Then, "Well, not so fine, I guess."

Michael nodded. He had little Max balanced on one shoulder, and the baby hiccoughed drowsily and slept. Crewe opened a package of white butcher paper that had been wrapped around a rack of lamb. "Fact is," he said, "I'm hopelessly in love with her, and she's got more passion for the stock market."

Michael nodded again.

"I don't know what to do," Crewe went on. "I think about her all the time. And she wants nothing to do with me."

More nodding.

"It's probably time to just give up. I mean, who needs the hassle? I'm doing fine on my own. I've got as many dates as I want, although, okay, I admit going out to dinner alone every night gets old fast. Most women just don't interest me. But I have a challenging career. And my mother needs me. I see her quite a bit. Sure, that sounds ridiculous, but—look, I don't need Lexie to make my life complete, you know?"

I shot Michael a glance, but he didn't say a word, just continued to listen.

"But," Crewe said, "she's a lot of fun to be with when she's not all strung out on business. She's brilliant about art, you know. She blew me away at the Dalí exhibit a few years back. The way she talked about the pictures— she was more insightful than anyone I'd ever heard. And, see, I've been wanting to go to the Guggenheim Bilbao, but once I had the idea for that trip, I couldn't imagine doing it without her. Even a weekend in New York, doing the galleries—how great would that be with Lexie?"

Pretty great, I thought.

"And she's beautiful. You can see that, right? Not to mention altruistic. The amount of time and money she gives to charity? It's incredible. It goes to show how big her heart is."

I knew exactly how big Lexie's heart was.

"But," Crewe said as he began to neatly slice individual chops from the rack of lamb, "every time I speak to her, she gets this look on her face like I'm spoiled milk. Like I need a bath. And God forbid I bump her hand with mine."

I opened my mouth, but Michael sent me a quelling look.

Crewe worked efficiently. His knife flashed through the tender meat until he had gone through the whole rack. Then with a quick flick of his wrist, he twisted each chop into a perfect pink lollipop. "She's touchy. So damn touchy. It's frustrating. I know I should take my time. Get her to trust me. But I don't know how to do that."

He checked the flame and laid a pan onto the burner. "Surely she doesn't want to be alone the rest of her life, right? So she's got to learn to trust somebody eventually. I just need to find the way to do that. A creative way. A way she'd respect."

With Michael and me listening, Crewe frowned and said, "I can't just hang around the museum hoping she'll wander past. There's got to be— you know, I heard she rows on the river. For exercise."

*Every morning,* I wanted to say. Lexie took her kayak out on the Schuylkill around dawn.

"I've got a canoe of my own. It's in storage at the moment, but I could get it out, maybe put it on the river to see if it leaks. That wouldn't be too obvious, would it?" Crewe dashed some olive oil into the pan and tossed in a sprinkle of herbs he'd quickly diced with another one of his knives. He followed the herbs with the lamb, dropping each chop into the hot oil to sear. The contents of the pan sizzled, and an aromatic cloud swirled up. "Even if I never actually bumped into her, it would give us something to talk about. I could ask her advice about buying a new canoe. Couldn't hurt. Right?"

Crewe used a set of tongs to flip each of the chops and finally turned around. "What do you think?"

Michael shrugged. "Doesn't sound so hopeless to me."

Crewe nodded. "No, it doesn't. Thanks, man. I appreciate your input."

I wanted to shriek at them. With any one of my female friends, we could have spent the entire day reaching the same conclusion—after examining every nuance of word and action. I still wasn't sure they had come to a truly well-considered decision.

Crewe slipped the pan under the broiler and stood wiping the blade of his knife.

Michael said, "You're pretty good with that thing."

Crewe looked at the knife in his hand. "This? Oh, I've taken a few classes. I wanted to do the whole Cordon Bleu course, but—well, newspapering seemed a little more useful. You cook?"

"Not like you."

I thought the conversation might continue in that personal vein, but Michael said, "How'd the Phillies game turn out last night?"

"You missed it? It wasn't bad. Tight score. They pulled it out in the end."

For the next few minutes we watched Crewe assemble a salad. He took a pear from the gift basket Lexie had sent and sliced it into paper-thin wafers with a few more expert flashes of his knife. He opened a bottle of wine, diced some garlic and mixed it with an apple vinegar from my pantry to make a vinaigrette. Then he smoothly grabbed a plate and, with a graceful motion, slid two perfect lamb chops onto it. He flicked them with pepper, then snapped a sprig of basil from the pot Michael had been growing on the windowsill and tucked it neatly around the lamb. He carried the plate to the table and set it before Michael. "Try this. It'll be better than burned toast."

I took the baby so Michael could eat his meal. Crewe went back to the stove and set to work preparing food for the rest of the group and me. After he'd taken plates to the living room, he came back and sat down at the table. He sipped from a glass of wine and watched us eat.

"So," Michael said when he'd finished the last atom of food and pushed the empty plate away, "I don't think you came all the way out here to cook my lunch."

Crewe stared at the table without really seeing it. A rush of color appeared on his cheekbones. "No."

"What's up?"

"I don't—I feel like a heel for coming now." Crewe looked unhappy. "I shouldn't have even considered it."

"What are you talking about?" I asked.

I had seen Michael's expression—a new one, to me. Watchful, yet emotionally detached. He was several chess moves ahead of Crewe. And even more ahead of me.

He said, "What's going on?"

Crewe began shaking his head. "I can't ask. I thought maybe you—but now I know it's wrong to even talk about it."

"What do you know?" I asked.

Michael said, "Nora."

Crewe looked up at me. His face had flushed, and his hand was so tense I thought he might accidentally snap the stem of his wineglass. "I'm in some trouble."

"We can help," I said at once. "Crewe, we're your friends."

"And I want to keep it that way. I value you, Nora. And Mick—look, we haven't known each other long, but I get it now—I shouldn't impose, should I?"

"Impose? Sure," Michael said with studied ease.

Crewe shook his head.

I reached for his hand. "Crewe, tell us what's going on. Has something happened?"

"It happened last summer," he said slowly, still unable to meet Michael's eye. "I was doing a story for the paper. I reviewed several restaurants that served the same high-end veal from a specialty farmer. It was excellent, so I decided to do a feature piece on the farm. I asked the chefs where the veal came from. The farmer turned out to be Kell Huckabee, using some property owned by Vivian Devine to raise the calves."

I held my breath.

"So I went out to Eagle Glen," Crewe went on. "I found Huckabee, and I started to ask him about the veal, but he—well, he went ballistic. He didn't want to be interviewed, said I'd ambushed him."

"He didn't want to advertise his product?"

Crewe shook his head. "He was furious. He had wanted to keep his enterprise a secret from the Devines, I guess. Then Vivian Devine showed up, and she figured out right away that Huckabee had been raising animals on her property against her wishes."

Vivian hated any cruelty to animals, I thought. Of course she'd object to raising calves for the restaurant market.

"Anyway, she and Huckabee got into an argument with me standing right there. Huckabee was—I've never seen a man so angry. He was small, but he looked dangerous to me. So I—look, I'm not proud of what I did. I thought he was going to hurt Vivian, so I took a swing at him. Honest to God, I thought he was going to beat that old woman. I knocked him down."

Crewe rubbed his face and continued ruefully. "A day later, the police came to my place and arrested me for assault. It was very embarrassing. My mother was there. I hated humiliating her. She's very—you know, Nora. Very conservative. So when Huckabee telephoned later and made me an offer, I—I accepted."

"An offer, Crewe?"

Michael said, "Huckabee said he'd drop the charges if you paid him."

Crewe sighed miserably and nodded. "I should have recognized it for what it truly was. Blackmail. But at the time, all I wanted to do was spare my family the embarrassment. So I paid."

"And he came back," Michael said.

"Yes. Twice. Each time he asked for more money."

Michael didn't ask how much money. It didn't matter. The salient point was that Crewe had a connection to Kell. And worse, a motive for murder.

Little Max began to stir in my arms, and he rubbed his eyes with his tiny fists. I stood up to soothe him back to sleep by walking him around the table.

Michael said, "How much do the cops know?"

"I'm not sure. They came to my house this morning, very early. I had just come from the gym and—well, it doesn't matter. Now that they believe the remains you found aren't Penny's, they think it's probably Huckabee. They asked me a lot of questions about my relationship with him."

"Did you call a lawyer?"

"I didn't think I needed one."

"Did they have a warrant to search your place?"

"I—no, I don't think so."

"Did you let them inside?"

"We talked on the stoop."

"They didn't ask to see your bank statements? Phone records? Stuff like that?"

"No. But they said they'd come back later. If they had more questions."

Michael nodded. "They'll have more questions."

By that time, little Max had awakened to discover himself in my arms, not his mother's, and he began to fuss. I put him against my shoulder and tried to quiet him.

Michael shifted his leg, but didn't speak while the baby cried. He considered the options.

Crewe misunderstood Michael's silence and continued, "I don't know what to do. I thought maybe—is there a way to make this go away somehow? I was thinking you might—"

Michael put up one hand. "Don't say it. If you say anything more, we're talking obstruction of justice. If you ask for help, it's solicitation. And we become a conspiracy."

"Oh, God."

Michael had intentionally sharpened his tone to make Crewe understand the gravity of the situation. But now he gentled his voice. "There's a lot going on here. If we knew what the cops know, we'd be in a better position to decide what to do. Nora could talk to Bloom, but then she'd become an accessory."

Crewe looked horrified. "No, no, I can't ask anyone else to get involved in this. It's my mistake. All I want—"

"Don't say it out loud. You have a problem and you want it to go away."

My friend's expression became even more shocked. "But—how?"

Michael shrugged. "You could turn this thing around so Huckabee is the bad guy. Without causing—what do you call it? A social scandal that'll upset your mom?"

Crewe flushed again. "It's ridiculous, isn't it? I'm ridiculous. I should take my punishment like a man and quit whining."

Michael shook his head. "Nobody said anything about whining. It could be done, that's all I'm saying. There's probably a way to put all the heat on Huckabee. And he deserves it, right? Threatening an old lady? Blackmailing you? So he's not one of the good guys. First priority is to get you in the clear." Michael checked his watch. "When did the police see you this morning?"

"Around nine, I guess."

"So they could have a warrant by now, easy. How did you pay Huckabee? Cash?"

"Yes."

"Withdrawn in a lump sum the day he took the money? Or in smaller withdrawals, at different intervals?"

Miserably, Crewe said, "Lump sums."

Michael shrugged. "Water under the bridge. Did you save any paperwork? Blackmail letters? Messages on your cell phone? Answering machine?"

"He never left messages, just called me on the phone, and we talked."

"Okay. Do you own a gun?"

"Michael," I said, "please—"

"Yes," Crewe said hoarsely. "I live in the city. When I bought my house, before I renovated, it wasn't entirely secure, so I bought a—"

"Is it in your house now?"

Crewe nodded, struck dumb. But both his hands were trembling.

"It's okay," Michael soothed. "Look, it's possible to put this whole thing back on Huckabee. Shouldn't be too hard. And he's probably dead, right? So who's going to care? You just have to figure a way."

Crewe blinked as he absorbed the full meaning of Michael's words. "You mean change the facts? Make him look guilty?"

"He *was* guilty, right?"

"Yes and no. I don't know. I mean, I did hit him. I feel . . ."

It was obvious that Crewe felt rotten about the whole mess.

"Look," Michael said just as bluntly as before. "Your problem can go away. But I can't promise you'll come out of it with a clear conscience. You're the one who'll have to live with what happens."

"With twisting the truth."

Michael smiled, although he did not appear to be amused. "What do you reporters call it? Spin. We'll be spinning the truth."

Crewe swallowed hard and looked down at the table again. Quietly, he said, "I don't know if I can do that. Huckabee may be dead, but I—it would be wrong, wouldn't it, to dodge blame? To put it all on him."

"Depends," Michael said, "on your definition of wrong."

I turned from the table and walked Maximus across the kitchen. He let out a more full-throated yowl, a demand for his mother.

I glanced over my shoulder. Crewe ran his hand through his hair and sighed unsteadily. Michael met my gaze from the table.

I had brought my friends and Michael together. I had hoped he could blend in, become a part of my social life. But I hadn't expected my two worlds to collide like this.

Dilly had warned me. Lexie had tried, too. Even Libby had recognized that things were maybe too different between us.

I just hadn't expected this.

Michael watched me and said nothing. I held the baby close and left the kitchen.

# Chapter Twenty

Upstairs, I telephoned Reed to pick me up for my nightly round of social engagements.

"Can you be here in an hour?" I asked him.

"You're the boss," he said.

I had slipped away from the party to change my clothes. And to gather my wits. I used the bedroom telephone to make another quick call. Then I put on a Calvin Klein sheath dress with a silk jacket that I could slip off later. Simple and versatile. I swept my hair up, suitable for evening.

When I came back downstairs, Dilly, Kaiser and Artie were still going through Penny Devine's red-carpet dresses. They appraised my change of clothes.

"You look marvelous," Dilly said, giving my cheek a kiss. "Just change bags, dear heart. The proportion is all wrong."

I patted his face fondly. "Stay as long as you like."

Libby was asleep on the sofa with her shoes off and Maximus snoring on her chest. I didn't disturb them. When Reed arrived, I kissed Michael good-bye in the kitchen.

"You're leaving already?" he asked.

"Sorry." I could barely meet his gaze. "There's an afternoon tea and then a cocktail thing and a charity dinner that starts at six. I'll be home before midnight, though."

"Be careful what you drink."

"I will."

"Got your cell phone?"

I grabbed it off the counter. "I do now."

Crewe helped me with my jacket. "My mother's invited to a tea this afternoon. Maybe it's the same one you're attending?"

"Maybe," I said, giving his cheek a quick kiss before heading out the door. I didn't want to linger. I didn't want to hear more. "Bye."

Reed didn't question me when I gave him directions, and in half an hour we pulled into a Wawa convenience store.

At the edge of the parking lot idled a police car, its windows down and radio squawking. Leaning against the rear bumper was Ben Bloom, slugging from the straw of a large fountain drink.

As if sinking a three-pointer, he threw the paper cup into a nearby trash can and came over to the town car. He opened the rear door for me, and I got out. A large truck rumbled past, making it hard for Reed to hear our voices, but I walked away from the car anyway. I didn't want him reporting back to Michael this time.

Bloom slipped one hand under my elbow. "Hey. You sounded agitated on the phone."

"No more than usual," I said. "Did you find the tigers?"

"Animal Control went over a couple of hours ago. They're delighted to have a project that's going to be so high profile. They're working on their press conference notes right now. It's going to be all over the six o'clock news."

"Is that good?"

He shrugged. "I managed to mobilize the state-police forensic team, too. They took one look at the blood in the carport and acted like they'd won the lottery. It'll be nice to have some expert help on the case now."

"Do you think—I mean, did the tigers—?"

"Eat Penny Devine? Maybe. I don't know how they're going to figure it out, but the blood-spatter geeks can't wait to try."

I shivered despite the warmth of the sun. "What about Kell Huckabee? Was he attacked by the tigers, too?"

"Do you think the tigers sawed off his arm nice and neat?"

We had stopped beside the patrol car, and I hugged myself.

"Sorry." Bloom looked more closely into my face. "Is something else wrong? You don't look so hot. What's going on?"

"I'm fine."

He smirked. "Just wedding jitters, huh?"

When I didn't answer, he opened the passenger door of his car. "Get in."

"No, I just wanted to know about the tigers. There's no need for—"

"Get in, Nora," he said more gently. "I have something you need to see."

I obeyed and slid into the front seat. I knew immediately why he'd left the windows rolled down. Despite its clean exterior, the car smelled slightly of vomit.

He left the door open, too, went around the patrol car and got in behind the wheel. He left his door gaping wide and reached to turn down the volume on the police radio. On the seat between us lay a manila folder. He picked it up.

He said, "Abruzzo's out of the hospital?"

"Yes. But he's in a lot of pain."

"Good. Maybe he'll stay close to home for a little while."

Michael had never told me his history with Ben Bloom. I understood they'd met in some kind of juvenile jail, where Michael's behavior had convinced authorities he needed a little more time in captivity. Bloom, by contrast, had been a perfect angel—or so I was led to believe—and walked out early. His criminal record had been expunged, thanks to the intervention of a family friend, and he'd turned his misspent youth into a life of crime fighting.

That was as much as I had pieced together. There was more to the story, but neither Michael nor Bloom wanted to tell me what had happened between them while in custody. I knew only that they now disliked each other intensely. And that seemed to have grown into Bloom's rekindled fire to put Michael back in jail.

I said, "You're talking about the man I'm supposed to marry."

"Supposed to? That's an interesting choice of words."

I shook my head. "That was a slip of the tongue. I am going to marry him."

Bloom tapped the manila folder on the steering wheel. "Maybe you'll come to your senses first. What time did he get home today?"

"In time for lunch."

"Eleven? Twelve? Or was it a late lunch at your house?"

On my guard, I said, "Why are you asking?"

"Because I think he made a stop after leaving the hospital."

"He's on crutches, you know. Hardly capable of sticking up a liquor store or whatever you think he's done."

"It wasn't a liquor store," said Bloom. He held up the folder for my inspection. "You know those guys who tried to grab you the other day? Can you identify their faces?"

"I'm not sure."

"I've got some pictures to show you."

I held out my hand. "Let me see."

"I'll warn you. They're not pretty."

From the folder, Bloom removed two Polaroid-style photographs. I accepted them and looked at the two faces in the pictures. I recognized the first immediately by the shape of his head, the cut of his sideburns and the angle of his nose. The second man—younger, with more hair— could have been one of my would-be abductors, but it was hard for me to be sure.

Because most of his face was covered in blood.

He was dead.

I dropped the photos on the seat. Instinctively, I covered my eyes as if I could prevent the images from penetrating my brain.

"No," I said. "Oh, no, no, no."

Bloom waited while I fought to catch my breath. Grimly, he picked up the photographs and put them back into the folder. He said, "I guess that's a positive identification?"

"What happened?" I asked when I could speak again. My voice broke. "Who—who are they?"

"One's Benny Cartucci. The other's James 'Torchy' Pescara."

"Pescara?"

"Yeah," said Bloom. "Torchy's one of Lou Pescara's unlimited number of nephews. He's been working for the family, doing little arson jobs here and there, some petty crime, a couple of minor convictions. Not anymore, of course, since he got whacked this morning. Somebody killed him down on the Delaware. Just half an hour from the hospital where your boyfriend checked out early, without a doctor's permission."

"Michael has a broken leg! He couldn't possibly—"

"It's got to be Abruzzo," Bloom reasoned.

"Why would Michael do such a thing?"

"Because of you, Nora. Because you were threatened. That's how it works," Bloom said, as patiently as if he were explaining multiplication ta- bles. "Somebody grabbed you, and Mick had to do something or they'd do it again, using you against him. I figured he'd just beat the crap out of those two mutts, but I was wrong, wasn't I? He decided to kill them so nobody would ever touch a hair on your head again. He left Torchy's body out in the open, real brazen. An obvious message."

*I'll make it very clear,* Michael had said. *What they did to you is outside the rules of engagement.*

And his hand. I'd seen the bruise on Michael's hand. How had he explained the injury? *I bumped it,* he'd said.

"No," I said.

"So your wedding jitters should be all for nothing." Bloom fastened the catch on the envelope. "He's made sure you'll never be harmed. It's more than his father would have done in the same situation, I've got to admit. That's why Big Frankie's still a mediocre mobster. Mick, though, he's got the right stuff. He knows how to make a statement. How to make people afraid of him."

"Stop it," I said.

"Trouble is, the one who's still alive—at least we assume so—is Benny. Benny's not small-time. His expertise is shooting. He's a sniper. Very good at it, too."

I got out of the car. The harsh sunlight slammed against my head, and I reeled. Leaning against the car's door to catch my balance, I put one hand up to dash the tears from my face.

Bloom came around the car to me. He took my forearms, but I wrenched out of his grasp. He waited until I had my weeping under control.

At last, he said, "I'm sorry."

"No, you're not."

"I'm sorry to hurt you, Nora. Abruzzo belongs in jail, but you—you shouldn't have to suffer like this."

"He didn't do it! He came home! He has a broken leg!"

"He was there, and we're going to prove it. Mick's a smart crook, the most dangerous kind. But we're going to get him on this one, Nora. It's almost impossible to commit this kind of murder and get away without leaving some tiny clue behind. And there's a whole lot of cops who want to make sure he goes to jail one way or another."

I fished a handkerchief out of my handbag and used it.

Voice tight, Bloom said, "I hate seeing you like this."

He tried to touch me again, but I pulled away.

"Let me help you, Nora."

I looked up into his face. His smirk was long gone. In its place was an expression that looked a lot like genuine concern. His dark eyes met mine and didn't waver. He put one hand on the roof of the car and leaned closer to me.

"No." I turned my head away.

He sighed. "Forget about the Devine murder. Or the Huckabee murder, whichever it is. Why don't you stay with a friend for a few days? Calm down so you can think rationally again."

"I don't need to leave my home to think rationally."

"You should get away from him."

"Michael would never hurt me."

"Maybe not physically." With a light touch that was almost a caress, Bloom let his fingertips slide down my arm. "You could stay at my place, if you like."

I could not imagine staying with Ben Bloom.

Nor could I imagine Michael killing anyone. It was beyond anything I believed about him. I had seen glimpses of his dark side. Perhaps I'd been attracted by that part of him, too. But this—murdering men who'd threatened me—I did not want to think he was capable of that kind of horrific act.

I stepped away from Bloom. "I have to go," I said.

"Nora—"

I left Bloom and tottered unsteadily across the parking lot to the town car. Reed had gotten out and opened the back door for me.

"You okay?" He saw my face. "You're not gonna pass out, are you?"

I shook my head.

He opened the door to the front seat instead, and helped me slide inside. A moment later, he got behind the wheel and turned to me.

"Oh, Reed," I said. And I burst into tears.

"Hey, now." He sounded exasperated. "Don't do that!"

"I'm not crying."

"Then what do you call it? Just cut it out. What'd that cop say to you? You want me to call Mick?"

"No! Don't tell Michael," I said into my handkerchief. "You can't tell him about this."

"Oh, man." He put his hand awkwardly on my shoulder. "Come on, now," he coaxed. "Take a deep breath."

I did, and I felt a little better.

"You want to go home?" Reed kept his hand on my shoulder.

"No." I sniffled. "There's a tea I have to attend. I'm meeting a photographer there."

"You can't go to nothing looking like that. Fix up your face."

He drove in silence the rest of the way into the city, while I tried to rescue my makeup. Periodically, Reed sent nervous glances my way. But he didn't say more.

There had to be another explanation for the killing of Michael's cousin. I couldn't imagine what it was, but surely there was more to the story than what Bloom had told me.

Then it hit me that Aldo hadn't come along with me today.

Because he knew one of the men who'd tried to hurt me was dead. Maybe the other one was, too.

We arrived at the small restaurant near upscale Rittenhouse Square, and Reed pulled next to a fire hydrant. But I didn't feel like attending anything, let alone a gracious tea with my mother's friends.

"You look better now," Reed said. "You can do this."

I sat for a moment with my hands in my lap. "Thank you, Reed. You're very kind."

"I'm not kind—I'm talking the truth. You look better."

"I mean for not telling Michael about this afternoon."

He took a deep breath and held it, promising nothing.

I got out of the car and went into the restaurant.

It had been a French bistro last time I'd been inside, but a zealous party planner had transformed the space into—well, hell. The restaurant was draped with long panels of diaphanous red fabric, with neon thunderbolts strung from the ceiling. Cauldrons of "flame" billowed behind the bar, and the bartender wore horns and a forked tail. The stools were jammed with middle-aged women wearing pearls and slurping strong drinks with glow sticks floating in them.

"Nora!"

A tall woman in a citron green Chanel suit hailed me from a throng near the coat check. She waved. "Over here!"

It was Nelly Barton-Flagg, my mother's best friend and the afternoon's hostess. For years she had been the faithful, dignified president of a charitable trust that raised money for Hodgkin's research, but today Nelly's triple strand of long pearls had gotten caught in the stem of her cocktail glass, and she'd lost one earring. Her glazed eyes told me she'd already consumed at least one drink before I'd arrived.

She air-kissed me with enthusiasm. "Look at you!" she cried. "So grown-up and pretty! I'm glad you could come to my exorcism!"

"Nelly, I thought this was a tea to raise money for—"

"Oh, the hell with that! It's my divorce party! The papers came yesterday, so I decided to bag the tea and throw a shindig instead! I'll write a check to the charity myself. Today I'm partying! Look, the band is just getting started! Have a mojito!"

On a raised platform, the restaurant staff had cleared a space for the musicians to set up. They were a wedding band, I could see, dressed in campy turquoise tuxedos, but also wearing devil horns in honor of the occasion. The pianist thumped the keys and burst into the opening lines of "Hit the Road, Jack."

Nelly burst into throaty laughter, and her friends cheered. Many manicured hands were raised in applause. I saw drinks slosh over designer suits and drip onto sensible pumps. The exorcism was in full swing.

"Nelly, I had no idea you and Jack had—"

"He dumped me," Nelly bellowed over the thunder of the band. "He found himself a girlfriend who's younger than you! So I got the best lawyer in town, and now I'm free as a bird and rich as Croesus!"

"I'm so sorry—"

"Don't be sorry," she said. "Jack was a good provider, and that's about it. Lousy in the emotional department, and no great shakes at picking up his socks, either. I was getting damn tired of being his mommy, so that little chick he's found can take over—at least until he goes to jail."

"Jail!"

Nelly laughed again. "My lawyer found out he'd been hiding investments from the IRS as well as me! So who wants to be married to a crook? I wasn't going to spend the rest of my days in a cell because of his fancy accounting tricks! So no sad faces. Help me party, okay? Hey, Mary Ellen!"

Nelly pushed her way to greet another friend—this one holding a dozen balloons printed with the word CONGRATULATIONS! in cheery letters. I leaned against the bar and immediately found a mojito in my hand.

The devilish bartender winked at me. At my elbow lay a pile of voodoo dolls dressed in business suits. The woman next to me picked up one of the dolls, dug a large hatpin out of a bowl and gleefully jammed the pin through the doll's heart.

Turning away, I found myself next to the *Intelligencer*'s photograper, one of the older guys, best known for shooting pictures from the sidelines of the football field. With his nylon jacket open to show a rumpled shirt that barely stretched over his belly, he was grinning broadly and popping beer nuts into his mouth. "Hey, Nora."

"Hi, Hank." I had to shout over the noise.

"Great party! I'm going to ask for these assignments more often. All these bitter women looking for rebound sex? Even a guy like me could get lucky!"

I winced. Nelly was making a spectacle of herself when she probably wasn't thinking straight. "You've taken enough pictures here, Hank. I don't think I'll be writing up this party in my column."

He shrugged. "Okay, but maybe I'll stick around a little longer. I want to see what develops. That's a photographer joke, y'know." He laughed.

I edged away from Hank, wondering if I should warn Nelly about him.

On the wall next to the bar someone had tacked up a large poster of a donkey, and two more tipsy women were playing "Pin the Crime on My Ex."

The band concluded their first song and segued into a rock-and-roll version of "Let's Call the Whole Thing Off" amid much cheering. I saw Nelly's arm pumping over the crowd.

I slipped my way along the bar until I found myself face-to-face with Nelly's daughter, Jacqueline. She stood alone, sipping from a glass of what looked like plain tonic. Younger than me by about eight years and still in graduate school, she clearly felt ill at ease among the rowdy crowd of older women.

I touched her arm. "Jacqueline?"

She turned, her face frozen into a polite expression. Then she recognized me, and melted. "Oh, Nora! How nice of you to come!"

I gave her a hug and found she'd lost weight. Jacqueline had always been slightly built, but now she was hardly more than a bundle of matchsticks. I said, "I'm so sorry to hear about your parents. I had no idea."

She nodded glumly. "I know. It's a shock."

"Your mom looks happy with her decision, though."

"She might look happy now, but they're both miserable. You'd think two smart people who'd been married for thirty-five years could figure a way to work things out."

"I'm sorry, Jacqueline." My heart went out to her. "Why don't we get together for lunch someday soon?"

Before she could answer, we were jostled by the rambunctious crowd, then separated entirely.

In a matter of minutes, I came upon Crewe's mother—an unlikely guest at such a party.

Karen Dearborne's thin face was strained as she stood clutching her Chanel quilted handbag in front of her functional blue suit. Her hair—thinning, but still a determined shade of blond—was contained by the same black ribbon headband she'd worn for years. A double string of pearls did a good job of camouflaging the wrinkles around her throat. Best known for being afraid of catching germs, Karen also wore her trademark pair of old-fashioned white kid gloves.

"Hello, Karen."

"Nora," she said. "How nice to see you."

Her tone said otherwise, but I smiled. "And you, Karen. I had dinner with Crewe Sunday evening."

"Did you?"

I could have mentioned that her son had come to my house to plot a criminal conspiracy, but instead we made meaningless small talk about Crewe and his eating habits and his devotion to exercise, all the while trying to ignore the bacchanal around us.

At last I decided to seize the bull by the horns before we were separated. "Karen," I said, "I'm very concerned about the Devine family. I don't know if you've heard today's news."

She stiffened. "I try to ignore the news. I'm sorry to say so, Nora, because I know you're related to those people. But I never liked them. Penny especially. She was a very crude woman."

"The police are starting to dig into whether or not Penny had any children. I wonder if you—"

Karen paled. "I have nothing to say in the matter. It has nothing to do with us anymore. Topper was adamant about that."

She rushed away from me, but collided with a busboy's tray full of dirty dishes and glassware. A plate overturned and slid off the tray, ricocheting off her skirt before hitting the floor near her shoe. Gooey bits of deviled egg smeared her clothing.

Instinctively, I pulled out my handkerchief to help clean up the mess, but Karen took one look at my crumpled, tear-soaked hankie and recoiled as if it contained plague spores.

"Sorry," I said, and reached for a handful of cocktail napkins from the bar. I handed them to her. "Karen, was Topper the father of Penny's child?"

Karen glared at me. "How do you know that?"

"I don't, but there are tests that prove whose DNA is whose. Eventually, someone's going to figure it out."

Alabaster pale, she bent to clean the worst of the egg from her skirt. "Why does anybody need to know? It's been a secret all these years, and Topper paid every dime that woman asked for! He financed that boy's life from the very beginning and never asked to see him once."

"Never—? Karen, who are you talking about?"

Crewe's mother gave up cleaning herself and threw the dirty napkins on the bar. "That woman never wanted him around, and when she found a home for him, Topper paid. He paid until the boy was twenty-one, which was more than fair."

"Who? What boy?"

"How should I know? Penny gave the child away! To servants, she said. To people she trusted. And she sent Topper's money to them so they could raise him properly. I have no idea who the child is."

But I knew. Suddenly I understood Kell Huckabee had been Penny's illegitimate child. Not Crewe, but Kell, who had grown up as the child of employees at Eagle Glen. Crewe's altercation had been with his own half brother.

Karen was no longer shaken, but angry now. She glared at me. "I don't know what kind of person you've become, Nora, but you're nothing like your grandmother. She was a great lady, and I'm sure she'd be embarrassed about how you've turned out. You've utterly ruined your family's good reputation by consorting with that—that shady character."

Karen walked away, dodging contact with other women as she headed for the door.

I decided I'd seen and heard enough, too. I gave Karen a head start, then followed her out into the street.

"Where to next?" Reed asked, clearly relieved to see I wasn't bawling.

Although I wanted nothing more than a trip home, I gave him directions to one of the city's most elegant hotels. I stared out the window at the stores and restaurants we passed along Walnut Street, and wondered if I'd ever walk into my old haunts again without people whispering. Was my reputation dying at that very moment?

Reed dropped me at the hotel and promised he'd be waiting nearby when I was ready for him to pick me up again. With his cell phone number memorized by now, I went into the hotel.

The charity dinner was one of those swishy affairs for "fogies and farts," my father used to call the aristocratic crowd—with long gowns for the women and evening clothes optional for gentlemen. Old jewelry that probably spent most of its time in vaults sparkled on elderly throats and arthritic wrists and fingers. I looked around and decided that if the guests donated as much money as their ancestors had spent on diamonds, the charity could probably quintuple its annual budget.

The cocktail hour was well under way, with solemn waiters in uniform carrying drinks and extravagant nibbles on Lucite trays. A pianist, hidden on a balcony above us, played lively Gershwin, barely audible over the hum of cultured voices. Small knots of guests strolled around, meeting and greeting.

I took a deep breath and plunged in.

"Nora." A slim, silver-haired matron in a stunning voluminous skirt suitable for a presentation at the Court of St. James's looked startled to see me. "What a surprise."

"Hello, Carol." I had already taken my notepad from my bag. "The party looks wonderful. I know you're on the committee. Can you tell me about the decorations? For my column?"

Carol Hamilton, chairwoman extraordinaire, and a tastemaker in the city's most conservative circles, held a slender glass of champagne before her and allowed five ticks of her watch to go by before she managed to find a proper response. "Yes, of course, dear. Why don't I send you into the dining room to have an early look for yourself? Peaches and Petals did the flowers. They're still doing final touches. I'm sure they'll have all the details."

Carol was the mother of one of my good school friends, and I'd spent many an adolescent night under her roof, even traveling to their Bermuda home a few times for holidays. I had been made to feel like one of the family, especially during the years when my parents misbehaved.

But now Carol looked through me to an oncoming guest, clearly asking me to step aside and make way for someone she preferred to be seen talking to. I realized that the murder of Torchy Pescara had already hit the five o'clock newscast. The whole city probably knew that Michael was the prime suspect in a gangland killing.

My face warm, I slipped into the hotel ballroom in search of the florist.

Forty tables had been decorated with swoops of pink linen and centerpieces that were six feet tall—great poufs of pink and yellow flowers exploding from the tops of tall glass vases balanced at the base by thick pads of moss dotted with elaborately painted eggs and butterflies. It was spring in full bloom, with huge clouds of white chiffon suspended from the ceiling. Around the perimeter of the room, six waterfalls sent streams of water cascading over artfully arranged umbrellas. The effect was astonishingly beautiful.

Instead of the genius florist, I found the banquet captain, Joe Carmello, who managed all the big benefit dinners at the hotel and often provided insider information to use in the newspaper. He was a barrel of a man, hardworking and always calm even during the maelstrom of an extravagant event.

But Joe's expression slackened when he caught sight of me. "Miss Blackbird! I was hoping to catch you before the dinner service starts."

He had been calling me Nora for six months, but now we were back to formal names.

He drew a folded piece of paper from his jacket pocket—the notes he made for himself before every event. He lifted his bifocals from the chain around his neck and consulted the paper with a frown. "We've had the usual last-minute rush of cancellations and additions to the guest list. The committee was forced to change the seating arrangements. You don't mind, do you? I've found a spot for you at Table Twenty."

The dreaded Table Twenty. Hidden in an alcove, it was better known as Social Siberia—the place to hide guests known for getting drunk, who embarrassed their friends with lewd talk or who just plain didn't belong.

"Thank you, Joe," I said with all my composure. "But I'm afraid I'm going to upset your applecart again. I can't stay. I'm just here to get a few quotes, and then I must dash."

Joe's honest face could not hide his relief. "I'm sorry to hear that. We're serving a delicious veal with pesto-stuffed mushrooms this evening. But I'm sure you're busy."

"Yes," I said. "I—Joe, wait a minute. This is an odd question, but can you tell me where the hotel buys its veal?"

Accustomed to all kinds of bizarre inquires about the hotel, the service, the food, the wine, Joe didn't bat an eye. He said, "Of course. We acquire our meats from high-end sources, usually organic farms. Our lamb, for instance, is flown in from Virginia. The veal comes from a gentleman in upstate New York—very high quality. I'll e-mail you the information."

"Thank you. Have you always used the upstate New York farmer? I mean, have you ever considered a local source? Kell Huckabee, for instance?"

Joe frowned. A man who prided himself on keeping all important details in his head, he nodded. "I remember that name. Did he approach me once? Yes, I believe so, last summer. He wanted the hotel to try his product, but he could not provide the quantity we require. We serve a great deal of veal at our special events. He was just getting started and didn't have enough supply."

I did not ask more. Instead, I thanked Joe, excused myself and headed back to the cocktail party. There, an *Intelligencer* photographer—a petite woman named Jeanie, who often met me at society parties—was already taking pictures of the well dressed. As I consulted with her, I noticed the crowd edging away from us. Unusual, because normally partygoers wanted to have their photos taken for the newspaper.

It was me they were avoiding, however, not Jeanie.

She said, "I've already taken a dozen shots of dresses. What else do you want?"

"Some members of the committee. See that woman in silver?" I pointed out Carol, who had studiously avoided catching my eye.

"Sure." Jeanie glanced up at me, curious that I didn't lead the way. "Want me to approach her?"

"That would be nice," I said.

I stood back, making murmured suggestions to Jeanie, who followed my directions to organize some important donors to pose for pictures. I knew charities relied on such advertising to encourage more people to give to their cause, so I forced myself to choose wisely among the many guests who mingled nearby.

When we'd snapped several more photographs, Jeanie said she had another stop to make before the evening was over. I decided I'd seen enough, too, and we went out to the street together. We waved good night and I paused to root in my bag for my cell phone.

Three taxis pulled up in front of the hotel in quick succession, and Lexie Paine got out of the second one, alone.

She wore a slim midnight blue dress with a diamond choker. A white wrap trimmed in rabbit fur slipped down one bare shoulder. She was clearly on her way to the charity dinner. But she saw me and headed straight over. Her face was stricken with sympathy.

"Sweetie!" She grabbed me hard in a hug. "I just saw the news. Are you okay?"

"No," I said, teetering on the edge of control.

"Oh, honey, I feel so terrible for you! Is Michael—? Has he been arrested? The news report said he's the prime suspect in that ghastly shooting this morning. You must be devastated."

"This morning Michael was discharged from the hospital. He couldn't possibly have killed anyone."

I gave her the short version of what I knew about the murder of Torchy Pescara there on the sidewalk under the hotel marquee. Lexie listened closely, making sympathetic noises as I outlined what had happened with Michael since I'd seen her.

"I don't know what to do," I said miserably. "I'm exhausted and upset and—and—the thing is, Lex, I don't want to go home." It was wrong, I knew, but I didn't want to hear Michael's explanation of the killing.

Lexie understood. "Oh, sweetie. Let's go to my place." She put her arm around my shoulder. "Let me whisk you away. I wanted to skip this stupid dinner anyway."

I tried to rub the tension from my forehead. "I know Michael's innocent. I do. But—oh, Lex! Sometimes I think we're so different—and I—I can't understand why his life has to be the way he's made it."

My friend pulled me to the curb. "Let's get a cab. We can be at my house in a few minutes. Then you can have a good cry."

"We don't need a cab. Reed is right around the corner. I'll call him."

I opened my cell phone and found the small screen blinking. I had turned off the ring tone while I was at the party, and someone had tried to reach me. "Oh, damn, I've got messages. Six."

"Who from?"

I clicked through the screens to check. "Four from home. Two from Libby."

"Do you think there's some kind of emergency?"

No. Michael had tried to call me from the house, I guessed. To explain, perhaps, or to ask me to come home so we could talk rationally about the murder of Torchy Pescara. And heaven only knew what Libby wanted to talk about. Maybe she'd found a deal on marijuana nosegays for the wedding.

My thumb froze on the keypad of the phone.

"Don't return the calls," Lexie said, seeing my hesitation. "Not if you don't want to hear what they have to say."

I stowed the cell phone in my handbag again, and we walked around the corner. A whole line of limousines and chauffeur-driven cars stretched for the next three blocks—illegally parked, but nobody seemed to care. Most of the drivers were standing on the corner talking together beneath a streetlamp. We walked a block before we found Reed sitting behind the wheel of the town car, diligently reading a book by the light of a small flashlight.

He jumped, startled, and dropped his book when I tapped on the window. He scrambled out of the car.

"Reed, this is my friend Lexie Paine."

"Hello, Reed." Lexie surprised Reed by shaking his hand.

"We'd like to go to Lexie's house. On—"

"I know where it is," he said, regaining his usual testiness. He helped us into the backseat.

When we pulled into the street and made a right turn into the flow of traffic, Lexie said, "Do you want to talk? Or should I divert you? Take your mind off your troubles?"

I leaned my head back against the seat to avoid the glare of oncoming headlights. I felt enormously tired, but I was glad for a diversion. "Divert away, please."

On the dark seat between us, she dropped a beaded evening bag in the shape of a dolphin. "I did some checking. This is all off the record, of course. I'm in violation of a terrifying number of regulations by telling you any of this, but I know you'll use it only for your own reasons. And you'll have to find a secondary way of confirming the information." Lexie glanced at the back of Reed's head, the universal sign that he should close his ears. "My firm manages some investments for a certain pharmaceutical baron."

Potty Devine, I thought, and I straightened.

She nodded at my unspoken comprehension. "I discovered he'd been withdrawing large sums of money from his accounts over the last two years."

"How large?"

"More than his living expenses should be. But not enough to purchase any significant stock or real estate. Usually, there's something to show for cashing in investments like that. In this case, however, the money simply disappeared. I've seen the same pattern before, remember? Last year when another of my clients was being blackmailed."

I nodded. "I remember. Exactly how much money are we talking?"

"Escalating amounts. Starting with five thousand, then ten, finally twenty-five thousand dollars. As time goes on, I've noticed the average blackmailer gets greedier. Last autumn, he withdrew nearly fifty grand."

I wondered whether the amounts were similar to the payments Crewe Dearborne had made to Kell Huckabee.

"But get this," Lexie went on. "There must have been a glitch. My pharmaceutical gentleman redeposited that fifty thousand just a couple of days later."

"In October or November?"

"Yes, November. How did you know?"

Potty claimed he'd fired Kell Huckabee in November, I thought. Which meant Kell could have blackmailed Potty earlier in the fall.

Had Kell blackmailed Potty as well as Crewe? Had Potty redeposited the money because he knew Kell wasn't around to accept his blackmail payment? Because he knew Kell was already dead?

"This is significant," Lexie said, watching me connect the dots. "Isn't it?"

"It's possible that the blackmailer died between the time your client withdrew the money and put it back again."

"Good Lord." Lexie drew her wrap closer around her shoulders. "You don't think the silly old man could have actually murdered somebody?"

"If he was being pressured by a blackmailer, yes."

"Tell me, why would anyone blackmail my pharmaceutical gentleman? I thought it must have been one of his girlfriends. But his love life isn't a secret he wants to keep, is it? In fact, the old fool is damn proud of his sex life."

"A man by the name of Kell Huckabee was an employee at the estate for many years. In addition to the work he did for the family, it seems he made a few extra bucks selling MaxiMan in gay nightclubs."

Lexie raised one brow. "Where did he get his supply?"

"He had to get it from an insider. A very inside insider. If I had to guess, I'd say his source was your pharmaceutical gentleman. Who is still very free with his samples, I must say."

"He'd get into trouble with six different kinds of regulators for allowing MaxiMan to get out of the lab like that."

"Hence the blackmail."

Frowning, Lexie said, "Would Huckabee demand a supply of the drug, then turn around and blackmail his source for giving it to him?"

"I don't know. I think we need to talk to your pharmaceutical gentleman."

Reed glanced into the rearview mirror. "Don't you even think about that."

"You're not supposed to eavesdrop, Reed," Lexie chided.

"I'm not deaf," he said. "You're talking about that old man, Devine."

I said, "We need to find a way to learn if Kell was really blackmailing Potty."

"Without getting ourselves killed," Lexie added.

Reed said, "You're not getting killed, 'cause you're not talking to no-body."

Lexie pretended she didn't hear him. To me, she said, "If Potty bumped off Huckabee, how did he do it?"

I reminded Lexie about the tigers and told her about the gunshot wound to the hand.

"He might have been shot. The police have no way of knowing for sure. But chances are, the rest of his body is—well—"

"Oh, God, Nora! You don't mean he was eaten? By Vivian's tigers?"

My cell phone suddenly buzzed in my handbag, and I sighed. "I think I liked life better before I was so available."

"Take a look," Lexie urged. "Maybe it's Michael again. Maybe you should talk with him, Nora."

I read the incoming number on the phone's screen. "It's Libby."

"Go ahead," Lexie said. "See what she wants."

Libby was barely coherent.

"The police," she babbled. "They came and took them both! I was never so humiliated in all my life, Nora! Why, they even wanted to search my diaper bag! And when the police found all those jars the twins left in your refrigerator, they went crazy! It was awful! Horrible!"

"Libby," I said sharply. "Calm down. The twins were arrested?"

"No, of course not the twins!" she said. "They came for That Man!"

"The police arrested Michael?"

"Yes!" Libby shrieked. "And Crewe, too!"

"What are you talking about?"

"Aren't you listening?" my sister demanded. "The police arrested Crewe Dearborne! For the murder of Kell Huckabee! Nora, the police say Crewe killed a man!"

# Chapter Twenty-one

"That's ridiculous," Lexie said, highly offended by the suggestion. "Of course Crewe didn't kill anyone."

"The police have been under pressure to make an arrest," I said. "I didn't think that meant they'd grab the first possible suspect."

My cell phone buzzed again in my hand, and I answered without thinking.

In my ear, Emma's voice said, "Have you heard the latest bulletin?"

"Which one? There are so many."

"Mick's in custody."

"Old news."

"You sound pretty heartless. Aren't you worried?"

I sighed. "Of course I am. Is he—does he have his lawyers with him?"

"Yeah, Cannoli and Sons met him at the state-police barracks. The cops put him in the squad car with his hands cuffed behind his back. With that broken leg of his, it sure looked like police brutality to me."

My heart lurched. "Oh, Em."

"Where are you?" she asked.

"In the city."

"Me, too. Where can I find you?"

"We're heading over to Lexie's house."

"I'll meet you there," Emma said. "I've got something to show you."

We arrived at Lexie's home within a few minutes. Reed was helping us out of the backseat when Emma's pickup bumped into the driveway and rocked to a stop.

Instead of wearing her usual grubby riding clothes, my sister surprised us all by walking around the hood of the truck in a black, very short sheath dress made of some stretchy fabric that clung to her like dew on a ripe peach. Around her shoulders she had thrown a man's dinner jacket. The silk lapels gleamed in the moonlight. Even Reed couldn't stop himself from staring. She looked like a movie star.

"What?" Emma demanded when the three of us failed to greet her. "What's wrong?"

"Nothing," I said, the first to regain myself. "You look very nice, Em. Where have you been?"

"I was supposed to have dinner with someone, but I changed my mind."

"Dinner with whom?" Lexie asked. "Calvin Klein? Emma, you clean up beautifully."

She snorted. "I ditched my date when I found somebody more interesting to spend the evening with."

"What's going on, Em?"

She jerked her head back at the truck. "Take a look at my passenger."

Lexie and I followed Emma to the truck door, which my sister opened to reveal a slumped male figure sprawled on the seat. As the dome light came on, I gasped.

"Raphael! Em, what have you done?"

"He's fine," Emma said. "He was in the bar of the restaurant, and we got to talking. The slick son of a bitch tried to slip me a Mickey."

I leaned into the truck and instinctively reached for his throat to check Raphael's pulse. His head lolled away from me, but I could see he was breathing. Someone had painted a matador's mustache on his upper lip with a ballpoint pen. Dressed in a white tuxedo shirt with the collar open, elegantly cut trousers and a pair of Italian shoes that had been polished to a high sheen, he could have been a male model on his way to an important fashion shoot. If he'd been conscious. His pulse felt steady under my fingertips.

His eyes—only slits of awareness—did not register any recognition as I leaned close. He slurred something in Portuguese.

"What's wrong with him?" Lexie's voice was tense behind me. "Shouldn't we get him to a hospital?"

"He'll be fine in the morning," Emma said. "I swapped drinks on him. He drank his own magic potion."

"Oh, my God," I said. "You let him swallow a roofie?"

Emma laughed, sounding pleased. "Serves him right, don't you think? When he wakes up, I hope he has a hangover as bad as yours."

"What are we going to do with him?" Lexie asked.

"Oh, I've already had my wicked way with Mr. Braga. I'm thinking I'll just toss him out on the street."

"Em, what did you do to him?"

My little sister grinned without apology. "I took him up to a parking garage and we fooled around a little. Not long, because he lost his head pretty fast. So we talked. And he told me all kinds of secrets. It was better than truth serum."

"Em, you shouldn't have drugged him."

With another laugh, Emma leaned against the filthy truck, smudging dirt on Raphael's expensive dinner jacket. "Among other things, I got the lowdown about his relationship with Penny Devine."

I forgot about the moral implications of drugging a man. "What did he tell you?"

"That he slept with Penny. Many times. Command performances. Turns out, the Braga family isn't as wealthy as it used to be. Raphael's been depending on Penny for income for a long time. He takes MaxiMan to help him get through the weekends with Penny."

"Where did he get the MaxiMan?"

"From Kell Huckabee."

"What a snake." Lexie glared at Raphael's inert body. "Why don't you take off all his clothes and dump him at Independence Hall?"

"He also told me why he drugged you, Sis. And it kinda surprised me."

I met my sister's steady gaze.

She said, "He's scared to death of you. After he saw you at the polo match, he got the impression you wanted to stake a claim. He thinks you're going to steal his kid."

Lexie covered her mouth. "Oh, dear."

"He drugged you for information, Nora. He borrowed the roofies from one of his slimeball teammates. And he tried the same trick on me tonight. He wanted to know what you planned to do about—what's her name? Mariel?" Emma gave me a long, measuring stare. "You've been keeping secrets, Nora. Does Mick know you have a little girl in Brazil?"

"It's not Nora's little girl," Lexie said.

"No? Is that how you see the situation, Sis?"

"You should take Raphael to a hospital," I said, fastening the seat belt around his inert body.

Now that I understood Raphael's point of view, I felt terrible. How had I miscalculated so badly? And did that mean I had made other errors in judgment?

Emma promised to take care of Raphael. I kissed Lexie good night and went home with Reed. On the way, I tried to sort out everything I knew. And I found myself thinking about Mariel. For the first time, I let my imagination conjure up her face. Would she look like Lucy? Did she have Lucy's Blackbird temperament? Or did she look more like her father? My head spun with details.

When we reached Blackbird Farm, Michael's crew was once again guarding my driveway. Reed slowed, and I rolled down my window to speak to Aldo.

"Is he home yet?" I asked.

"Not yet. But don't you worry," Aldo said. "He's got his lawyer with him. He'll be home in no time."

"Tonight?"

Aldo made the waffling motion with his hand. "Maybe tomorrow. This one could take some time."

I didn't want to hear any more. I punched the button, and the window rolled up again.

Reed escorted me to the back door, stepping gingerly over the charred floorboards of the porch. He paused, shifting uncomfortably on his feet as I fished in my handbag for my keys. "You going to be okay?" he asked finally.

"I'll be fine." I was touched by his concern. Although I'd known him for nearly a year, it had taken this most recent crisis to force Reed to show his true, caring nature.

"Don't worry so much," he said, lingering on the porch. "I know a lot of bad dudes. But Mick—he's been good to me and to my old lady. He's just got a lot of—you know—pressures."

This was more of a speech than I'd ever heard from Reed.

"Don't tell him I said this," Reed added, "but he's the closest thing I have to a dad, you know? He made me go to school and go to London—

stuff I wouldn't have done if not for Mick. So the other stuff he does—it's okay with me."

"Thank you, Reed."

He shrugged, already heading for the car. Over his shoulder, he said, "No problem."

I watched him leave, wondering if Reed was a better judge of character than I.

Michael did not come home that night. As I filed my story via e-mail, I tried not to think about him or where he was. Or what he might have done.

In the morning, I showered and dressed and went downstairs around nine.

The living room was still a shambles, with Penny Devine's dresses hanging from all the doorjambs and the empty wardrobe boxes yawning open untidily. A carton of evening bags had been upended on the coffee table, like the booty of a shopaholic after a spree on Rodeo Drive.

In the middle of the mess, Michael slept on the sofa. Usually a light sleeper, he'd normally have heard me before I reached the bottom of the stairs, but this morning he slept soundly, his nose buried in an embroidered throw pillow. Someone had wrapped a frilly evening cloak fetchingly around his tall frame. His leg and cast were propped on the coffee table. The dark smudges under his eyes gave my heart a jolt.

I should have felt sorry for Michael. He was in pain. He'd been through a terrible night.

But a part of me was furious with him.

I studied his crutches. They didn't match. One was decidedly newer than the other. And the bruises on his right hand did not come from any small incident while he'd checked out of the hospital.

I slipped quietly into the kitchen. Someone had already made coffee and it was steaming on the counter. An empty cup sat in the sink. Aldo, I thought.

I made oatmeal for my breakfast and sliced a banana on top. I ate half the bowl standing at the scullery, but the sight of Michael's crew hanging around my mailbox at the end of the driveway dulled my appetite. I put the unfinished bowl into the sink beside the coffee mug, and I thought about how my life had changed.

The phone rang, and I grabbed it on the first ring. I carried it out onto the back porch so Michael's sleep wouldn't be disturbed.

Libby cried, "I sold Tom Cruise on eBay!"

"What?"

"For nine hundred dollars! Can you believe it?"

I had forgotten about Libby's latest crackpot scheme. "No, as a matter of fact, I can't."

"I think I could get at least as much for Julia Roberts, so I need to do more baking right away." She barely paused for a breath before asking, "Have you seen the morning papers yet?"

"I watched the local news while I got dressed."

"So you saw all the pictures of those poor tigers."

All the TV stations had helicopters circling Vivian Devine's ranch house, where Animal Control was busily shooting tigers full of tranquilizers in preparation for hauling them out of their enclosure and trucking them to other sanctuaries where they would presumably get better care.

"And you know," Libby continued, "the police are absolutely convinced That Man of Yours killed a person yesterday morning between the time he left the hospital and when he arrived at your house. Nora, I know it's hard to call off a wedding once plans are in motion, but I have to ask. Is your heart set on going ahead with this marriage?"

"I'm not making any plans at all, Libby. You are."

"Listen," said my sister. "I'll be the first to admit I don't trust him. Except when it comes to you. Nora, I don't see him doing anything to hurt you. I think he'd protect you with his last dying breath."

"I know," I said. That's what I was afraid of.

"So the wedding's on?"

"I'll get back to you."

I phoned Emma next, and asked her to pick me up as soon as possible.

When I put the phone on the cradle in the kitchen, I heard a distinct groan from the sofa.

I poured a cup of coffee and carried it into the living room.

Michael had propped himself up on one elbow and was rubbing his forehead as if it throbbed. He needed a shave, and his hair was a tangle.

I brushed aside the heap of evening bags and sat on the coffee table in front of him, cradling the cup of coffee in my hands.

In a raspy growl, he said, "I dreamed I threw up."

"Very nice," I said. "Good morning to you, too."

"It's morning?" He winced at his watch. "Jesus."

"When did you get back from the police station?"

"About five."

"You couldn't manage to get upstairs?"

"I didn't try." He heaved his leg onto the sofa, tried to get comfortable, and gave up.

I handed him the cup of coffee. "Is it time to take some pain pills?"

"I took some before I went to sleep. I'm good for another couple of hours."

"Do the pills help?"

"Not much." He sniffed the coffee warily, still without meeting my eye. "Are the twins in the basement? And what about Emma?"

"We're alone in the house. The twins are conducting their experiments elsewhere. And Emma made other sleeping arrangements."

He seemed to relax a bit. "She with that Ignacio guy?"

"Emma doesn't keep a man around very long—especially one with so few faults as Ignacio. Last I saw, she was with Raphael Braga."

Michael looked at me finally, interest sharpening. "Oh, yeah?"

"Listen," I said. "You're not feeling well, so I'm going to give you the short version of a very long story, a story I should have told you before."

Hearing my tone, he waited.

"I told you already that while I was in college, a friend of mine married Raphael Braga and moved to his family's home in Brazil. His parents were very wealthy, an old family, and it was important to everyone that they have children right away. But my friend, she couldn't. There was a problem. She was desperate to have a baby, so she asked me to help. And I did. The two of us went to a hospital in New York, Michael, and I gave her some of my eggs."

I took a deep breath and continued, keeping my voice as steady as I could manage. "I donated my eggs to my friend. They were fertilized in a lab and implanted in her, and she had the baby. A little girl, who was perfectly healthy—just what the family wanted. She's in Brazil, living with Raphael's parents now."

Michael paid close attention, watching my face for every nuance he could glean.

I said, "My friend and Raphael have separated, but the child—her name is Mariel—she lives with her grandparents while Raphael pursues his career in polo. I don't know how much she sees her mother, but Raphael tells me she is—that's she's happy."

"Nora."

I went on, speaking more rapidly. "I didn't tell you before because I wasn't sure how you'd feel. That maybe you'd be angry with me, especially now that we—that I lost our baby."

"But you're telling me now."

"Yes."

"So this is some kind of confession? You want me to absolve you of your sin?"

I looked at him at last. "You think what I did was a sin?"

He said, "You gave away—"

"I helped a friend."

Automatically, he lifted the coffee to his mouth, but he didn't drink from the cup and lowered it again. "Did you ever consider maybe your friend and Braga weren't meant to have kids?"

"I didn't stop to consider a lot of things. And anyway, that's not the way I think. Someone needed my help, so I did what she wanted."

"That's you, all right," he said quietly. "Jumping in to help anybody who asks."

"She wasn't anybody. She was my friend."

"What's next, Nora? If somebody wants a kidney, you'll be first in line?"

"If someone needed it, and I could provide something to save a life, yes."

He shook his head, as if marveling at my foolhardy nature. "What about now?"

"Now?"

"You're thinking about this little girl in Brazil, right? That maybe she needs you."

I shook my head. "No."

"You're her mother. The other woman is out of the picture, and her father is all over the world instead of taking care of her. So she needs you. And," he said, "maybe you need her."

"I don't—"

"You want her."

I shook my head again.

"You'd like to have this child you made with Raphael Braga—because ours didn't live."

"That's not what I'm thinking."

"No?"

But of course it was. Deep in my heart, I wanted to know Mariel, the little girl I had never met but who was mine, at least partly. There wasn't any sense denying how I felt. Maybe this part was the sin. But I couldn't help the way I ached inside.

Michael set the coffee cup on the table beside me. "I knew there was something between you and Braga. I thought you were afraid of him, and you are a little, aren't you? But you're attracted to him, too."

"No, not attracted. Not the way—well, the way I am to you. But he and I are connected in a strange way."

He settled back against the cushions again, putting one arm behind his head and looking up at the ceiling. "Well, this explains a few things."

I discovered I had been clenching my teeth, and I made an effort to calm down. "Like what?"

"Like what we've been doing in bed lately. I thought you'd gone a little nuts because of losing the baby, but it's Braga, isn't it? Part of you is angry I'm not him."

"No. No, I'm sorry if I—if things were too rough, but—"

"Hell," he said with a shrug, "I liked it. I like it all—when you're sweet or when you're an animal."

My face flushed hot. I had done things with Michael—primal things— that I'd never even contemplated with my husband. It had been passionate and exciting and sometimes frightening. And yes, perhaps angry, too.

He said, "Were you thinking about him? In bed with me?"

"Of course not. What we have is—it's ours."

"A little twisted, sometimes, but always hot, right?"

"Don't joke, Michael."

"Okay," he said after a moment, "what have you decided to do?"

"To tell you the truth." I had come this far, and I needed to go the rest of the way despite the racing thrum of my heart. I said, "I wanted you to know the whole story because I—we need to have the truth between us. Even if it changes how we feel about each other."

He looked at me, his face controlled.

I said, "Michael, we can't be together if we lie."

"Now I get it."

"I want to know the truth."

He shook his head. "My truth is different."

"Will you tell me what happened yesterday?"

"Nora, you already know who I am. That should be enough."

I took a deep breath for courage. "Are you afraid I'll leave you? If you killed a man?"

He didn't deny it. When he didn't answer, I spoke again with a voice that was barely a whisper. "What happened to your hand?"

He glanced at his bruises, unconsciously flexing his fingers despite the pain he must have felt.

I said, "That didn't happen the night you broke your leg. That injury happened yesterday. Yesterday before you got home with two crutches that don't match. Were you in a fight? Did you . . . hurt anyone?"

He said, "If I hadn't done something, you would always be in danger."

As if he'd punched me, all the air went out of my body, and I instinctively curled up and covered my ears. "Oh, God."

He sat up with a grunt of pain and swung his good leg to the floor. He grabbed my forearms and pulled me up until we were face-to-face, inches apart.

With his blue eyes burning into mine, he said, "This is the way things work in my world, Nora. My Pescara cousins took a run at you, and they would have kept coming, again and again. I did what had to be done."

Suddenly I was shivering so hard, I might have been abandoned on an ice floe. "Oh, God."

He released my arms. "You honestly think I killed them."

"Did you?"

"No." His voice was flat. His expression went blank, a practiced masking of his emotions. "I hurt them. But I didn't kill either one of them."

I got up from the table and walked away, still shaking so much, I had to hug myself. "I'm sorry. I'm sorry I had to ask."

He did not acknowledge my apology. "We tracked them down, and I told them to leave you alone."

"You beat them up."

"Whatever. What happened to them afterwards, though, I wasn't there. But now one of them's dead, and it's on my head. Even if I didn't pull a trigger, I'm the one who set it all in motion."

I turned back to him. "Set what in motion? Who did kill him?"

He ran one hand through his unruly hair. "I don't know yet. Two guys who work for my father, maybe. Or somebody who works for me. I'll find out. Whoever it was, though, did it with us in mind. That man was killed to protect you. To protect our life together."

I gripped the back of the leather chair and held on tight to keep my balance. "So it's my fault, too."

"No." He shook his head. "No, it's me."

"Who you used to be," I corrected. "That's all in the past, right? Your life of crime is over."

He sighed. "It's complicated, Nora. More complicated than you think."

"I know. I saw that yesterday when Crewe asked you for help like you were the Godfather or something."

"Not help. Advice, maybe."

"And look where it got him."

Michael glanced up. "What?"

"Crewe. His situation is even worse today."

"What do you mean?"

"Weren't you here when it happened? Or nobody told you?"

Of course not, I realized at once. Michael had been in police custody when Crewe suffered the same indignity. I said, "Crewe was arrested late yesterday. For the murder of Kell Huckabee."

Michael let out a string of curses. "How the hell did that happen?"

"Ben Bloom's department was under pressure to make an arrest. Crewe had the most evidence against him."

"The cops are going to look like idiots." He rummaged in the clutter of beaded handbags to find his cell phone. "Bloom should know better. Does Crewe have a decent attorney? He probably doesn't even know a criminal lawyer, does he? Never mind, I'll make some calls." He gave my body a quick, unsmiling perusal. "You're dressed to go out, I notice. You're going to do something for him, aren't you?"

"This morning I must see Julie Huckabee."

"Who are you taking with you?"

"Emma."

He gave a short laugh. "Take Aldo and a couple of his guys instead."

"We'll be okay by ourselves."

With an irritated glower, he said, "Call Bloom if you don't want Aldo. I mean it, Nora. I don't want you and your sister investigating a murder all by yourselves. Dammit, I'll go myself—"

"I'll call Bloom, if that will make you feel better. You should stay here. Let Aldo look after you. He does it very well. Go back to sleep. Take more pills. I'd take care of you myself, but I need to speak with Julie."

"Is she dangerous?"

"She's a bird-watcher."

"Did she kill anybody?"

"I doubt it. But maybe Potty Devine did."

"That's one screwed-up family."

We stared at each other then, Michael on the sofa with his phone in his hand and me behind the chair, holding on for dear life as new emotions swarmed between us.

I said, "I love you."

He stayed where he was, looking at me. "Is that enough?"

Neither of us could answer the question.

And Emma arrived before we could say more. We heard her slam through the kitchen door.

I had time to say to him, "Please be here when I get home."

Then Emma breezed in, talking about something that made no sense.

Finally, she stopped in the middle of the floor and said, "Damn, what's going on here?"

Neither one of us answered.

"Oooo-kay," Emma said. "Good to see you out of jail, Mick."

"Thanks. You going to be careful today, Em?"

"You bet, big guy. Don't worry about a thing."

# Chapter Twenty-two

*E*mma had Lucy in her pickup. Our niece was playing with the foil again, but had exchanged her tutu for a pair of camouflage overalls with a shirt underneath that was appliquéd with bullfrogs and lily pads. She was eating a granola bar. I gave her a big hug, and she wrapped her arms tightly around my neck.

"What are you doing out of school?" I asked.

"It's teacher-conference day." Lucy pulled granola crumbs from my hair. "Mummy said I could play with you and Aunt Em."

Emma got into the truck and reached for the ignition. "Libby thought the conference with the twins' teacher would run a little long—like maybe the rest of the week—so I said I'd take Luce today."

"I don't think this is a good idea."

"You want me to leave her with Mick?" Emma started the truck and was already backing up.

"No," I said.

Emma heard my tone and glanced at me. "You think maybe you ought to take it easy on Mick for a few days, Sis?"

I didn't feel like talking about Michael. Lucy played with the radio, punching buttons and putting sticky fingerprints all over the dashboard.

Had Michael and I reached a breaking point? Had our differing values clashed one last time? Perhaps we had finally hit the last crossroads. I knew which road was mine, but I wondered if he could take the same one.

Over the blare of the radio, I asked, "How's Raphael? Did you take him to a hospital?"

"Nope. I drove him over to see a friend of mine—a doc I used to date, who said he'd sleep it off. So I took him back to his hotel and put him to bed. I debated about tying him to a bedpost just to give him

254

something to worry about when he woke up, but I took pity on him in the end."

"Was he okay when you left?"

"Sure, he was fine. I stayed until morning, just to be on the safe side. In fact, after I left, I gave him a wake-up call bright and early, too, so he could get a head start on the same hangover you had."

"You talked to him today?"

"I talked, he groaned. But he was alive. You don't need to worry about him. I made a few calls while I watched him sleep it off, and the cops arrested a bunch of polo players early this morning—caught them red-handed with roofies. They're all going to be deported. Raphael, too."

"I don't know what to say, Em."

"Hey, you're not the only one with the strict moral code."

"What about Ignacio, Em?"

"Iggy?" Emma lit a cigarette. "He's not getting deported. But I kicked him out. He's good in bed, Sis, but maybe he doesn't belong with me. He's too nice a guy."

My heart twisted. "Oh, Em. You deserve somebody really wonderful. More than even Ignacio has to offer."

She blew smoke out her rolled-down window. "Yeah, okay. When I get some free time, maybe I'll start looking for something else." Too much confession time made her testy, and she said, "What the hell's our plan today, anyway?"

"We'll talk to Julie," I said. "I think she's the one who knows the most."

We arrived at the Devine estate shortly before noon. At the gate, the television vans were long gone, but Vivian's truck had been abandoned with one tire sunk into the mud. Farther up the drive, a hired landscaping crew had just finished mowing the vast lawns, and they were loading their equipment onto trailers. We found Julie Huckabee frowning at the top of the driveway behind the mansion. Beside her on the grass crouched Vivian's shy Brittany spaniel, Toby. The dog wriggled his hindquarters and ducked his head when he saw me.

"Hello," Julie said when the two of us got out of Emma's pickup truck. "You're not going to make more noise, are you? After all that mowing, the birds won't be back for hours."

"We'll be quiet," Emma promised. She leaned down and gave the spaniel a friendly pat. He was so surprised that he collapsed on the ground, prepared to be beaten. When the blow didn't come, he turned his pale eyes up at Emma, shivering.

Lucy clambered out of the truck, dragging her foil with her. Julie didn't appear to be surprised by Lucy's weapon.

I said, "Julie, is Vivian here? I want to thank her in person for giving me Penny's clothing collection."

"She's not here. The police. They took her away last night."

"To talk to her about the tigers?"

Julie's trancelike state wavered, and she bit her lower lip, nodding. "The police made her leave the truck at the bottom of the driveway. I tried to move it, but I got stuck in the mud. Uncle Potty will be angry it's down there. He doesn't like things to look cluttered. He gets real upset with Aunt Vivian about her messes."

"Want me to move it?" Emma asked.

Julie agreed Emma could drive the truck up from the gate, and Emma set off walking back down the drive. The landscaping crew whistled as they passed her on their way off the property. Emma gave them a one-fingered salute and kept walking.

The spaniel got up and watched Emma depart. He trembled and gave a little whine, which prompted Lucy to get down on the ground and try to pet him. The dog edged away, then held still and let Lucy touch his back. She made crooning sounds to calm him, and he crouched down on the grass, permitting her to stroke him again.

Lucy said, "I like your puppy."

"He's not mine," Julie replied. "He belonged to my father."

Like the frightened dog, Julie wore the same hunted, nervous look in her eyes.

"Julie," I said, "I'm sorry Vivian is in so much trouble right now. I know you're fond of her. She's been like a grandmother to you. Especially since your mom's been gone."

Julie regarded me askance, as if afraid to meet my gaze.

With the same soothing tone Lucy had used on the dog, I said, "The police are wondering if she—if her tigers had anything to do with Penny's disappearance. And your father's."

At the mention of her father, Julie looked away.

I said, "Maybe there's something I can do to help. You seem very alone right now."

Quietly, she said, "Vivian was only protecting me, you know."

"From your father?"

Lucy had begun to rub the spaniel's stomach, and she didn't appear to be listening to us.

Julie nodded uncertainly. "They'd been arguing for a long time. She was upset when she found out he had the calves in the back enclosure. It's very cruel, how he raised calves for restaurants. But I don't think she meant to shoot him. Not really."

I made a supreme effort to control my astonishment. "Vivian shot Kell?"

"He was going to shoot the tiger, but Vivian took the gun away."

They had argued, I guessed, when Vivian discovered Kell had gone against her wishes and kept calves on the property. Of course Vivian had been furious to discover her employee was being cruel to animals. And when their argument escalated, kindly Vivian had shot Kell. Everything in Julie's expression told me how it had happened. "And afterwards," I said, "Vivian needed to get rid of the body."

"Y-yes."

Julie shivered and hugged herself tighter. "They're always hungry. Always. But Uncle Potty said—well, he wanted to find a way to make it look like Aunt Penny was the one who was dead. He thought they could fool everybody."

He'd staged Penny's death so he could railroad the corporate vote on Devine Pharmaceuticals' patent problem. Potty had been the one who'd fed Kell to the tigers. But he'd kept a piece of the remains in hopes of tricking everyone into believing it was Penny who had died. No wonder he had pushed so hard to have the remains returned to the family for burial before an autopsy could be performed. I wondered if he'd figured out a way to frame Vivian and her wild animals for the murder now that she had been arrested.

Tears had begun to shine in Julie's eyes, and then she was trembling.

"I shouldn't have told you," she said. "Aunt Vivian told me never to tell."

I put my arm around her bony shoulders. "It's okay, honey. You're not the one in trouble here. You're going to be okay. You're not alone."

"I can show you," she whispered.

"What can you show me?"

"It's in Vivian's trailer."

"Something important?"

She nodded and pulled away from me. "This way," she said.

I followed Julie, not sure what it was the girl wanted to show me. She was so strange and ethereal—like a mental patient or an abused animal. But I went along with her, heading into the ragged, abandoned vegetable garden. From beneath a straggling bush jumped the serval cat. It paused to study us, and I pulled Lucy close. Behind her, the spaniel froze.

Then the serval cat leaped away, and we continued toward the trailer. All but the dog. Toby suddenly stopped on the grass and refused to follow us farther.

We arrived at the door of Vivian's trailer. I could smell the cats from outside, but this time I couldn't hear any mewing. The sickly kitten lay on the step—only now it was dead.

"Lucy," I said, "you better stay outside."

With her hand on the door latch, Julie said, "It's inside."

She opened the door, and I went up the step.

"Aunt Nora!" Lucy ran up the steps to me, unnerved by the dead kitten.

I decided in a heartbeat it was better to have Lucy by the hand than outside where I couldn't see her.

I said, "Leave your sword outside, Luce."

"Go on," Julie said.

I thought Julie was coming inside with us. But she wiped a big tear from her face and closed the door. I heard a thunk from outside. When I turned and tried pushing against the door, I realized she had locked us inside the trailer.

Lucy took one breath of the fetid air and immediately glued herself to my leg. "Aunt Nora—"

The trailer had clearly been home to dozens of cats. Their smell hung in the air. A thick layer of sodden newspapers covered every inch of the floor. The cats had destroyed all the furniture; the upholstery hung in filthy shreds. Everywhere else, heaps of junk showed that Vivian had hoarded so much stuff that there was hardly room to walk.

I tried the door handle. It turned, but the door was barred from the outside. I threw my weight against it. "Julie!"

I knocked on the door, but Julie didn't answer. Around us, the air was hot and thick with the smell of cats and death. But no animals slid around the room. No kittens mewed. The furniture was jumbled and broken.

I saw a cluttered hallway to my left, and a door—presumably to Vivian's bedroom—was half-closed. But we heard a movement in that room, and the door edged wider. "Vivian?" I said. "Potty?"

Then I realized it was a paw that opened the door.

A large paw.

A tiger's paw.

In another moment, the animal appeared in the doorway—less than ten feet away from us.

A year might have ticked by, or ten seconds, while we stared at each other.

His head was huge, his mouth open and panting, teeth clean white. He had an absurdly pink nose. The stripes of his mask angled away from his yellow eyes and blended into the powerful muscle of his shoulders. His ribs moved rhythmically as he breathed.

The rest of him was rail thin—too thin to be healthy.

He looked hungry.

I pushed Lucy to put her behind me. But her body was too rigid. I stepped in front of her instead.

The tiger watched me move and snarled—a horrible hissing snarl that rattled me down to my bones.

Lucy had been holding her breath and suddenly gasped out a sob.

He listened to her sound, ears pricked forward, and that yellow gaze flicked from me to Lucy and sharpened. He moved sideways to get a better view of her.

"Lucy," I said in a rasp, "we're going into the kitchen. Okay?"

She began to release a thin, high-pitched wail.

I edged her backward, nudging her and feeling for solid footing while keeping my gaze fastened on the animal. He came forward a step, and then another, matching my every move.

With my pulse thundering in my ears, we reached the kitchen, separated from the rest of the trailer only by an L-shaped counter. My foot struck and overturned an empty metal water bowl. I bent quickly and picked it up, then threw it into the living room. The clang of the bowl distracted the tiger for a split second, long enough for me to seize Lucy up in my arms. I flung her onto the kitchen counter. Beneath the hanging cupboards in the corner, there was two feet of space, and I wedged her there, then grabbed a broken kitchen chair from the floor and jammed it in front of her. Lucy gripped the chair with both hands, and I caught a glimpse of her face—white and frozen with fear.

I had only enough time to grab the other chair and hurl it against the kitchen window before the tiger leaped over the counter. The window didn't break, and the tiger landed in the rubble that had once been the kitchen table. Lucy screamed. The giant cat turned toward her.

There was nothing in the kitchen to fight him off with, no furniture, no knives, no utensils.

I skittered sideways and with slippery hands opened the refrigerator door. Inside, I found a few plastic containers, and I threw them at the animal. They bounced ineffectually off his matted hide, but he forgot about Lucy and swung on me. I forced my body into the small safe space created by the heavy enamel door.

All the while, I realized I'd been screaming for Emma. Emma and Julie.

Suddenly from beneath the refrigerator burst a small, filthy cat, flushed out from its hiding spot by all the noise. Terrified, it streaked across the kitchen floor, cutting a path directly beneath the tiger's hind feet. The tiger turned with a predator's precision instincts and pounced. The house cat was too quick, though, and shot into the living room. The tiger charged after it.

I grabbed the chair that protected Lucy and tried to yank it from her, but she fought me, holding fast. I don't know what I said to her, but she looked me in the face, trusting, and let go. I swung around and smashed the chair against the kitchen window, once, twice, and then it shattered. Shards fell outward, and I used my fist to break the remaining piece. Then I had Lucy in my arms, and I threw her out the window.

I don't remember going out the window myself, but suddenly I could breathe fresh air, and my hands were full of grass. Lucy was clinging to me, climbing around my neck in hysterics.

I hugged her fast and scrambled to my feet. I'd lost my shoes somehow, but didn't stop. With Lucy in my arms, I ran across the garden, sure the tiger would be following me out the window any second. Julie stood spraddle-legged in the garden, shocked by what she'd done. Then she turned and ran for the carriage house.

I lugged Lucy as far as Emma's truck and grappled with the door handle. The spaniel was at my heels, and he jumped up against the door, yelping. In another moment, all three of us were inside the truck, and I slammed the door behind us, safe.

The driver's-side door opened.

"Oh, Em," I said. "Get in, and hurry—"

But it wasn't Emma who climbed into the front seat of the pickup.

It was Potty Devine. He got into the truck and slammed the door. In his lap, he held a shotgun. The double barrels were so long they struck Lucy's knees. I pulled her tighter into my arms.

"Cousin Nora," Potty said. "Ha-ha."

Lucy buried her face, wet and hot, against my neck. She was crying so hard I could barely hear Potty.

But I could see the look on his face, and it frightened me.

He said, "How much did she tell you?"

"Potty, please—"

"Julie's not very bright, you know. And probably deranged. She doesn't understand the consequences."

"Potty—"

"But she's a good girl."

"She told me what happened, Potty," I said. "That Vivian was the one who shot Kell."

"It wasn't me," he said. "That stupid Vivian has been such a do-gooder all her life. Funny she was the one to pull the trigger, right? Ha-ha. Good thing the police arrested her. She'll go to jail."

I wanted the whole story, but the presence of the gun stopped me. He might not have killed Kell Huckabee, but Potty looked capable of killing me. Or Lucy. Toby whined beside me.

"So," Potty said. "What are we going to do, Cousin Nora? Now that Julie has spilled the beans?"

I didn't have a clue.

Then Emma, behind the wheel of Vivian's truck, drove up the driveway.

"Oh, hell," Potty said. "What is it with you Blackbird girls?"

He wrestled the shotgun up onto the dashboard as if to point it at Emma. I reared back in my seat and kicked at the gun. Potty cursed. Lucy screamed.

Emma downshifted and pointed Vivian's truck at her own pickup. I had just enough time to snap the seat belt around Lucy before Emma gunned the engine, and the larger truck surged forward. I braced myself for the impact—one hand against the dashboard, the other against the seat.

The crash was so hard I cracked the side of my head on the window. Lucy cried out. I saw Potty's head slam against the steering wheel. The dog hurtled through the air and struck Potty's shoulder before landing in a squirming tangle in Lucy's lap. The pickup spun, then came to a rocking stop.

I grabbed Lucy, unsnapped the seat belt and dragged her out of the pickup. The dog followed us, and half a minute later, we were inside the second truck with Emma.

"What the hell?" Emma cursed as the dog clambered into her lap and peed on her leg.

We watched Potty climb out of the pickup, holding one hand to his bleeding forehead and the gun cradled clumsily in the crook of his elbow. His walk was unsteady, but he launched himself in our direction.

Which was the moment the tiger came stalking out of the garden. He halted, nose to the wind, and watched Potty lurch toward us. Slowly, he sank into a pouncing position.

"Oh, hell!" Emma put the truck into gear again and tried to maneuver the vehicle between Potty and the hungry animal.

The tiger flinched back from the truck.

Potty finally realized he was in mortal danger. He staggered in place and tried to shoulder the gun. But he bobbled it, saw he was doomed, then turned and ran clumsily for the safety of the carriage house. In three long, loping strides, the tiger was on him.

Emma swore. I hid Lucy's face in my lap and held her there for a long time.

I remembered to use my cell phone a little while later. I called 911. We stayed in the truck until help arrived. Later, they took us to a police station.

It was hours later when Libby finally came. Her daughter, who had clung to my neck since I'd landed on the grass outside the trailer, finally caught sight of her mother and let go of me. Lucy ran across the parking lot of the suburban police station and threw herself into Libby's arms, weeping.

Emma patted my shoulder. "Don't worry, Sis. You did great. Lucy's been through an ordeal, and at times like this, a kid just needs her mom."

Yes, I thought.

Detective Bloom came over and told Emma she could leave. "We've got to keep your truck overnight, though," he said. "We're collecting evidence."

"Doesn't look like it's drivable now anyway," she said grimly. "Guess I'll hitch a ride with Libby. You coming, Nora?"

Bloom said, "I'll see that Nora gets home."

Emma gave him an appraising stare. At her side, the spaniel looked as if he had decided to become permanently attached to my sister. He hung at her knee, watching her face for clues that she might abandon him.

"I'll be fine," I said.

"Don't be long," she warned. "Somebody's waiting for you at home."

She strode over to Libby's minivan, her new companion hot on her heels.

When we were alone, standing on the asphalt beside a bench that was surrounded by cigarette butts, Bloom said, "As a matter of fact, that somebody needs your help."

I sighed and rubbed my forehead to dispel the headache that thumped behind my eyes. I was very tired. But Bloom appeared to be full of untapped energy. "Can you put it in plain English, please?"

"It's Mick," Bloom said. "He's figured a way to draw the Pescaras out in the open."

"What?"

"He's put together a little sting operation, and tonight's the night. We're going to tag along and make an arrest. He's cooperating with us for once."

I processed all that information and felt what small supply of adrenaline that was left in my body give my heart a kick. I tried to fathom what Bloom's agenda could be, but my brain was fuzzy.

"Is it safe? Will he—he's going to be all right, isn't he?"

Bloom shrugged. "Mick made all the arrangements. And if I know him, he's thought through all the possible angles. I figured you might like to come along. Watch your boyfriend in action now that he's doing the right thing. Are you up for it?"

"Ben," I said.

I felt all my self-control waver.

"He'll need you there," Bloom said.

He put one arm around me and pulled me close. Beneath his superhero coat, his striped shirt smelled of coffee and pencils like a college freshman's. Against my hair, he said quietly, "You can do this."

His lean body had more tensile strength than it appeared to have, and I let myself absorb that. He shared a bit of calm with me in that moment, and I took it. Whatever Michael did always had complications. But Ben had the law on his side. Surely he would make the right choice.

"Okay," I said. "Let's go."

We drove for more than an hour in rush-hour traffic, finally reaching New Jersey just as the cars began to thin out on the highway. We stopped at a state-police barracks and met up with two more cops—one from Pennsylvania, the other from Jersey. Ben went inside to talk with them, and I waited in the car with the window rolled down.

What was Michael up to now? It would be like him to take matters into his own hands, to find a way to solve his own problems. But a persistent voice in the back of my mind insisted an alliance with the police was not in Michael's nature. And he'd never want me around for some kind of showdown.

Ben came out looking eager for action, and he handed me a package of crackers with orange goo layered between them. I dropped them onto the seat between us. We got into a convoy of cars with a total of five police officers.

"Tell me again what's going to happen," I said.

"It's simple. We're going to arrest some of the Pescaras. Mick set it up for us. He arranged the meeting, and all we have to do is swoop in and make the arrest. He'll be a hero."

"Why am I here?"

Bloom reached for the radio and spoke to the officers in the other cars. They talked in coded numbers that made no sense to me. He never answered my question.

At last we reached a long, flat plain that ran alongside the Delaware River. To the north I could see a stretch of water ideal for fishing, hung over with leafy trees. To the distant south stood the shapes of warehouses and a faraway silver skyline of city skyscrapers. The water was shallow and ran swiftly over flat rocks.

On a sandy berm alongside the road, a lone man in biker leathers hunkered beside a motorcycle, tinkering with its engine.

When he straightened up, I realized he was Michael.

I got out of the car and ran to him.

He caught me by my wrists. "Oh, my God," he said. "What happened to you?"

I had forgotten that both my forearms were bandaged. Breaking the window of Vivian's trailer and climbing out through the shattered glass had cut me. Even the sleeves of my sweater were slashed and stained with blood.

"It's nothing," I said. "I'll tell you later."

"Where are your shoes?"

I had lost them, of course, and Emma had loaned me a pair of her riding boots, dug out of the back of her truck. I made a ridiculous fashion statement, but Michael guessed the worst.

"I'm fine," I said. "But Potty Devine is dead."

"Jesus. What happened?"

"It doesn't matter now. Vivian Devine killed Kell Huckabee, and Potty helped cover up the crime. He and Julie made—oh, it really doesn't matter. What are you doing here? Please, Michael, don't tell me you're doing something dangerous."

Michael's face was deeply carved with lines that told me he was still in terrible pain. The pants of his biking clothes had been slit up one side to accommodate the cast on his leg. He had zipped his jacket up tight to his throat.

He looked over my shoulder and said in a growl, "Take her out of here, Bloom."

"We'll make sure she's out of the line of fire."

Ben came to stand beside us, and I was aware of the other cops climbing out of their cars, too.

"This isn't what we agreed on," Michael said.

"It'll be fine," Bloom replied. "Give us a few minutes to take up positions and clear the cars out. We'll hang around until your family reunion starts, and then we'll move in."

"To pull that off, you should have been here hours ago. They're way ahead of you."

"We were a little busy." Bloom manufactured a smile. "Since when did you get so jumpy?"

I said, "What's going on?"

To Bloom, Michael said, "You brought Nora along as some kind of insurance to make sure I do everything right. Well, you couldn't be more wrong."

Bloom shoved his hands into the deep pockets of his coat. "Okay, I don't trust you. What's so surprising about that?"

"I'm the one who came to you, remember? I said I'd bring Pescara in, but I had to do it my way. If he knows you're here, this powwow is going to get ugly. And you'll lose your promotion."

"Since when did you start doing me favors?"

"I don't care who gets credit." Michael was impatient. "I just want this whole situation over."

"Family trouble is getting bad for business, isn't it? Know what I think? This is your big power grab. If you can settle matters with your cousins, suddenly you're the top dog. No more pretending your old man is in charge."

"Take Nora out of here," Michael snapped. "I can't negotiate anything as long as she's at risk."

"Take a deep breath, Mick. We just came to watch you in action. Hell, today could be some kind of historic moment. You can get rid of all the Pescaras *and* put your pop on the back burner. And it all happens with police approval. Nicely strategized." Bloom glanced at me, with no apology. "Wait here, Nora. I'll be right back."

When he walked away, I said, "I'm sorry. I should have known Ben was using me. I'll go now."

"Get in the car," he told me. "Stay low."

My voice cracked. "Michael—"

"It'll be okay. Some of the Pescaras are coming, that's all. It's not as complicated as Bloom says. We're going to talk. It's the only way to settle this mess without anybody else dying. If Bloom doesn't screw up, we may finally solve the cop killing—"

"But you're in danger. You're putting yourself in jeopardy to make things right."

"Sound familiar?"

I heard the edge in his voice, and he glanced away—sorry, perhaps, to have let his true thoughts slip out. He reached for the helmet that swung from the handlebar of the motorcycle.

A lot of things made sense then—what made us so alike, for one. And what frightened both of us the most about each other. We were always going to barge around helping other people. No matter what the cost.

"Look," Michael said, "you and I could be happy sailing around on a yacht, putting suntan lotion on each other and drinking champagne in bed every night, but that's not reality, is it? Not for us."

Our whole relationship seemed to hang in the air between us. It was as if we had spent a year together waiting for this very conversation. My heart hurt in my chest, and I reached for his hand.

He didn't smile. "I've been thinking. If the cops still aren't convinced about Huckabee's death, we could change things."

"What do you mean?"

"We could spin it. We have enough information to make Braga look guilty. It wouldn't be hard to convince the police that he killed Huckabee as some kind of favor for the Devines."

"Why would we do that?"

"If he went to jail for murder, Nora, we could get the kid. It would take some work, but we could make it happen. You could have your daughter."

I stepped back.

He said, "We could raise her ourselves, you and me."

Hope—or some insane imitation of it—rose in me. For a brief moment I indulged in the fantasy. I could see it clearly. The three of us a family. Together and happy.

And just as quickly, the truth of what he suggested hit me hard. Here it was at last—the difference between his moral code and mine. The fact that I even considered his proposition made me flinch. Who was this person I had become? I didn't recognize myself anymore. He had presented me with a deal with the devil, and the wrongness of it didn't matter to him as long as he achieved his end result.

"We'd be lying," I said.

"Does it matter?"

"Michael—"

"Braga's no angel. Is he fit to be your daughter's father?"

"But—"

"We could do it," he said.

How different we were. Our compasses pointed to opposite poles. My friends and family had told me over and over that we came from different worlds, and I had resisted their arguments. I loved him, yes. But here, at last, was the dividing line.

He said, "You could have your child back."

*She was never mine,* I nearly said. The words were in my mouth.

The trees around us were suddenly silent, and the voices of the police behind me hushed. The water of the river paused, and the earth stood still.

A single sound cracked the air—a pop, a bang or a shot—whatever it was, I'll never forget the sound it made coming from behind me in the woods.

A spout of water jumped up from the river. Just as I felt the air part beside my ear.

Then three more—very fast. Three shots, and they struck Michael squarely in the chest. His Pescara cousins had chosen not to talk. The police presence blew Michael's plan.

The force of the bullets hit him hard. Enough to throw him back, head snapping, off his feet, propelled into space. I saw the shock in his eyes, fleeting as the last breath that left his lungs, before he was knocked down into the water. He landed on his back against the rocks, arms thrown wide. I saw him there, my own heart stopping with the force of impact.

And then the river moved over him, washing across his body.

# Chapter Twenty-three

*I*n June, I was nearly able to function again. And I was finally permitted back at work after a six-week suspension for taking a bribe from Potty Devine that I had not been able to explain adequately. My suspension was punishment for perhaps the worse sin of giving the silly story of Penny Devine's couture collection to a rival newspaper.

So I was back at square one, trying to prove I could do a job I was never trained to do. But I needed it. And I had decided to learn how to do it right.

I thought I could manage attending a small event, so I went to a fund-raiser at the museum where Penny's collection would have a permanent home. Dilly's curator friend chose a few of the important pieces and put them on mannequins, then invited some of the city's better-dressed benefactors to ask for money to finance a real show for the public next year.

My friend Jill Mascione's catering company provided the food—mimicking the menu from the Academy Awards dinner to enhance the Hollywood theme of the evening. I didn't taste any of it, but many of the guests raved. Instead of bearing flowers, the tables were decorated with miniature Oscars standing in swirls of golden sand. Three different large screens projected movie clips of Penny Devine's career. Two women in gold lamé dresses passed out programs at the doorway to the museum's garden room, where the clothing was on display. Guests mingled among the mannequins, admiring the clothes.

I wore Penny's little black Chanel with a long silk scarf around my neck, black opera-length gloves to hide the still-visible gashes on my forearms, and Audrey Hepburn-style dark sunglasses in case I lost my composure. I had wanted my donation of Penny's collection to be anonymous, but those sorts of secrets were hard to keep, and many people whispered kind remarks in my ear.

Lexie Paine found me in the crowd and kissed me gently. "Sweetie, you look ten times better. Almost yourself again."

"Thanks, Lex. You look like a million, of course." I admired her white dress—a copy of the famous Elizabeth Taylor white chiffon from *A Place in the Sun*. Her escort looked nothing like Montgomery Clift, although just as handsome in a summer-weight dinner jacket. "Hello, Crewe. Thank you for sending the steaks last month. They were delicious."

"I wanted to come and cook them for you myself, but I figured—well. Anyway, I owed you something for everything you did in April. I'm a free man, thanks to you."

For the first time in public, I found myself capable of talking about what had happened. I said, "It was Julie Huckabee, really, who told the police everything they needed to know. That Vivian shot Kell for his mistreatment of animals."

"I can't believe Julie really helped Potty dispose of Kell's remains and try to fake Penny's demise." Lexie shivered. "The poor kid."

"She was a very mixed-up girl," I conceded. "Years of verbal abuse at home from her father, and then her strange relationship with Vivian, too. It was only a matter of time before she had a breakdown."

"How ironic, then," Lexie said, "that she's going to inherit everything—Eagle Glen and Devine Pharmaceuticals, too, now that it's clear Kell was Penny's son. It's like the end of a Chekhov play."

"Julie is Penny Devine's only living relative. So that made her the sole heir now that Potty and Vivian go to jail."

"At least the estate will be worth something. The company stock took a terrible dive. Even if they manage to get MaxiMan on the market, it's going to take a miracle to get Devine Pharmaceuticals back to where it was."

"I think Julie's primary concern is keeping the birds happy at Eagle Glen. As for the company—I don't imagine she cares much."

"Hm," said Crewe. He'd been listening to us while studying one of Penny's dresses—a girlish red pinafore from her younger days in musicals. "Strange that among all those bones the police found at the tiger sanctuary, none of them belonged to Penny."

Lexie said, "Do you think the tigers ate Penny?"

"I don't think Vivian was in the habit of feeding anything but roadkill to her tigers," I said. "But after her final argument with Kell—after she shot him, and Potty hatched his plan—I think it just made perfect sense to Potty to dispose of the body by giving it to the tigers. If the forensics team hadn't found evidence in the carport where Vivian prepared all their food, I don't know if anyone would have ever believed such a gruesome ending to that family saga."

"But," Crewe said, "is Penny really dead, Nora?"

"Even the police think she'd have come forward by now if she were alive."

Lexie shook her head. "What a crazy story."

Without thinking, Crewe put his hand lightly on Lexie's back. It was an intimate gesture, I thought, and I noted that she didn't flinch away from him. I wondered if perhaps they were spending more time together than just the occasional social engagement. Lexie seemed downright comfortable with him. Still her prickly self, of course, but comfortable.

Crewe said, "We're just glad to see you back at work, Nora. The *Intelligencer* didn't fire you after all?"

"No, they suspended me for a while." I managed a smile. "But apparently readers missed my column. So this week I'm back full-time. I've got to prove myself all over again."

Lexie gave my hand an encouraging squeeze. "You'll do it, sweetie."

"Would you like to come to dinner with us tonight, Nora?" Crewe asked. "We're headed to Boater's to try their gazpacho. We were thinking of sitting outside under their umbrellas. What do you say?"

"Do come," Lexie said. "Otherwise, Crewe will make me order six entrées by myself."

"Sorry," I said. "I've got to finish up here, and then I have another appointment."

"Another time," Lexie said, giving me a kiss.

"Soon," I promised.

They strolled away, and I went in the opposite direction, admiring the clothes one more time before they were whisked away to be properly preserved. At the end of the line of mannequins, I was surprised to find Ignacio, of all people.

"Iggy," I said. "I thought all the polo players had moved on to Florida for the season."

The handsome athlete turned his sunny smile on me. He was still just about the most attractive man I had ever met—so tall and elegant in his fine clothes, but managing to convey a certain Brazilian manliness at the same time that his cheerful innocence shone through. With enthusiasm, he clasped one of my hands in both of his. "Hello!"

"So nice to see you," I said.

"Hello?"

"Emma's very well, thank you. I think she misses you."

"Hello," he sighed.

"I'll tell her you said—well, hello."

He turned to his companion, a matronly woman in a nondescript gray pants suit and a large, unbecoming picture hat. Beside Ignacio, she was so colorless that she might have blended into the woodwork if I hadn't recognized her face.

"Run along, Ignacio," she said crisply. "I'll catch up with you shortly."

"Hello," he murmured to me one more time before slipping away.

"He's so attractive that I don't mind that he can't speak English," Penny Devine said. "I do love having a good-looking young man around."

I stared into her face, struck dumb by the fact that she was standing in front of me. It was undeniably Penny. Her sparkling eyes and pert face—although coarsened with a little bit of jowl and a few wrinkles—were undimmed by her plain choice of clothing. She wore no jewelry at all. Her new, chunkier figure would not have squeezed into her old wardrobe, but she appeared to be healthy and very much alive.

She took off her hat to give me a shrewd glance. Her hair was white and cut sensibly short, but not styled. She said, "You look fine in that dress, Nora. I had the good sense to give it to the right person. Not that clothes matter, you know. I've given up on my looks, you see."

"Penny," I gasped at last.

"Keep your voice down," she snapped. "After all the trouble I've gone to for the last year to get myself a new life, I don't want some hysterical ninny ruining everything."

"But—but—you're alive!"

"And I want to keep it that way."

"I—I don't know what to say."

"So shut up and listen," she said with all the hostility I remembered. "I only stopped by to look at my clothes one last time. Then I'm leaving for good."

"But—you could have Eagle Glen, take over Devine Pharmaceuticals—"

"And do what with them? Forget it, I have everything I need—a bank account in the Caymans and plenty of young men who don't mind keeping company with a rich old lady. Ignacio might be the best of the whole string, don't you think?"

"He's adorable," I admitted.

"I wanted to see my granddaughter," Penny said, still brusque, but with a different tone. "I figure I owe her a little something, but I can't get into the hospital where they're keeping her."

"I'm sorry. She's still being treated. If you wait a few more weeks—"

"Have you seen her?"

"I visit every few days, yes. Dilly does, too. He's—well, I think he's anxious to try to help her, too. The court gave us permission."

"I tried to see her a few times myself. Without going to Eagle Glen."

"You did?"

She gave me a cold smile. "You didn't recognize me, did you? I went to my own funeral—the polo match. I stayed with the horse trailers, did you notice? And I went to the ballet fund-raiser, too. Julie used to take dance lessons, I heard, so I thought maybe that bastard Potty might have treated her that night. I danced with a man who smelled like mothballs. You saw us."

"Aldo," I said. "He's gone now."

"Gone? Where?"

"He committed a crime and disappeared. A mob hit—that's what the police call it." For my part, I wasn't sure what to call Aldo's execution of the man who'd tried to kidnap me. Just thinking of it made my stomach roll.

"Too bad. He was a hell of a dancer." Again, Penny's expression slipped and I saw something kinder show through. "But Julie. Will she get through everything that's happened?"

"She's receiving wonderful care. I have an acquaintance who's a very good doctor. And Reed, a young friend of mine, is visiting her often. We're doing everything possible to make sure Julie recovers and learns to live on her own—that's our goal. We hope she'll be capable of independently living. But she's a very disturbed girl."

After the final ordeal at Eagle Glen, Julie had retreated into a near-catatonic state. Even now, several weeks into her treatment, she could not be unsupervised for more than a few minutes. For hours, she watched the birds that flocked to the feeder Dilly had installed outside her window.

Penny grunted. "She's a mess, isn't she? When I get settled, I'll send you an address where you can reach me if you ever need money for her."

"Financially, she'll always be fine."

"Good. Money can make up for a lot of other losses in life."

I took a deep breath. "Do you truly believe that?"

"Yes. Yes, I do. I've been buying love for a lot of years, and it works. Maybe if my brother and sister had figured that out, they wouldn't have had so much time to resent me." She pierced me with another hard look. "You're one of those softhearted types, aren't you? Classy and cool on the outside like your grandmother. But with a real heart inside, just like her. I knew it." Penny collected herself again. "Well, you can't help everyone in the world—not even your own child sometimes."

"You're thinking of Kell," I said. "Your son. Are you . . . ?"

"Sorry he's dead?" The aging actress shook her head. "I was the wrong mother for him. I gave him life, didn't I? I even made sure he grew up with a decent family. My maid took him and did her best, which was a hell of a lot better than I could have done. What he did with himself after that was his business. No matter what you think, young lady, you can't live your children's lives for them."

"But you can give them skills and the emotional stability to cope—"

"Emotional stability?" Penny barked a laugh. "What kind of emotional stability do you think I had? I came of age on a soundstage! The only emotion I ever knew was the kind a director told me to dump on command. My own mother was my boss, not a loving parent. All I knew was hard work, how to get a job done. Lose weight for a role? Okay, I did that when I had to. I made some bad movies along the way, sure. But—" Aware that her train of thought had drifted, she said, "Your grandmother understood all that. She had a practical side under those pretty clothes of hers. She was a good friend to me. Maybe the only friend I ever really had."

"I'm sure she was fond of you, too, Penny."

"Too bad she married that stick-up-his-butt Charlie Blackbird. What a drag. He was all wrong for her. She needed someone with fire, and all she got from him was opera tickets and his granddaddy's silver. You have a man in your life? A real man?"

"No."

"Well, find one. That's my advice. Find one who lights your fire and to hell with proprieties. You don't have kids, either, right?"

"No," I said. "I don't."

"Well, think about it long and hard before you do, that's all I have to say."

"Penny—"

"Yeah?"

I wanted to ask her many questions. About her sister Vivian's love of animals that took the place of affection for anything human. How she felt about her bullying older brother. How she could have abandoned her own child.

But suddenly I realized Penny had been the one who escaped. She had fled a miserable life for one that at least appeared to be happy and fulfilling, even if she had been acting through it all. Now she seemed comfortable with the disaster she left behind—comfortable knowing that she didn't have the wherewithal to change it. I didn't need to ask her any questions. Her actions spoke enough.

So I said, "I'm glad you came today. You've explained a lot."

She snorted again. "Don't expect much explaining in life, young lady. Each one of us has to figure things out for ourselves."

She jammed the unattractive hat back on her head. "Now, where's Ignacio? He's coming to the Caribbean with me. We're going to start a horse ranch of our own. Where I can get as fat as I like. Fast horses and strong young men—that's what I want for the rest of my life. I deserve it."

She waddled off into the crowd, and that was the last anyone saw of Penny Devine.

Reed drove me home that afternoon, and in the car I wrote up my report of the museum party, determined to be diligent about my job.

At Blackbird Farm, I found Emma and Libby lugging cardboard boxes down the newly repaired steps of my back porch. For hard work, Emma had dressed in her scruffiest jeans and a sweatshirt, while Libby had put on another too-tight velour tracksuit, unzipped to show her cleavage.

"Don't mind us," Emma said, balancing two heavy boxes under her chin. "We're dismantling the laboratory the twins set up in your basement. You don't want to know what we found down there."

"It's important to encourage creativity in children," Libby added. "But not homicidal tendencies."

In the box Libby held, I caught a glimpse of *Gray's Anatomy* on top of a microscope and a jumble of plastic bags filled with dark, gelatinous substances.

"I've canceled their forensics-camp registration," Libby said. "I'm thinking a few weeks of Bible school is a much better idea."

Emma's phone rang in her hip pocket.

Libby and I waited for her to answer the call.

But she shook her head. "I'm out of business."

"Exactly what kind of business?" Libby asked frostily.

"Poker games," our little sister said. "I was organizing poker games for—well, for Mick. Setting up games, get it? For a cut of the pot, of course."

"Illegal gambling!" Libby cried. "It's a wonder you didn't get arrested!"

"What, like selling stale cake to rubes on eBay isn't a criminal act? How much money did you make with that scam?"

"Enough to pay for Bible school."

Emma lugged the boxes down the porch steps and didn't look back. Her new dog Toby, the shy Brittany spaniel, wagged his stumpy little tail at me, but he didn't hesitate to follow Emma out to her truck. If he could help it, Toby never let Emma out of his sight.

As Libby lingered on the steps, I said, "Why don't the two of you stay for dinner? I have some tuna to grill. We could make a nice salad."

Libby hefted the box on her hip. "I don't think so." She withdrew a small plastic vial from the pocket of her velour jacket. She placed it in my hands. She was blushing.

"What's this?"

"I know it was wrong," she said. "I should have asked permission first, but you know that nice insurance inspector man who came around while the carpenters rebuilt your porch? Well, let's just say his performance was—okay, it needed a little help. And I thought of these MaxiMan pills going to waste—you know, the ones Potty gave you. Why should they sit on your windowsill losing their potency when some deserving couple could put them to good use? So I—well, I should have asked before I borrowed them, but I wanted to slip them into his chocolate pudding last night when he—"

"Libby, you gave MaxiMan to the insurance adjuster? Without his knowing about it?"

Libby looked affronted. "Nora, I'm not the kind of woman who goes around injuring a man's self-esteem! Why should I hurt his feelings? Shake his confidence? Why not just let a man enjoy the first good sensual experience he's had in years?"

"Libby!"

"Well, it worked!" she cried. "He was wonderful! He enjoyed himself! What's the harm?"

"You can't go around drugging people against their will! Promise me you won't ever do such a thing again!"

"Too late," she replied.

"What?"

Hastily, my sister rushed down the steps, carrying the box full of her sons' grisly experiments. Over her shoulder, she said, "It was an accident! I thought they were his pain pills."

"Whose pain pills?"

"That Man of Yours! He's upstairs packing his clothes. He was looking for some Advil for his leg, because they took off his cast this morning. So I grabbed the first blue pills I saw and—look, it was an honest mistake, Nora."

"Libby! Michael has moved out! We're not together anymore! We agreed—"

"Maybe he hasn't taken them yet. Bye!"

"Dammit, Lib, if you—"

"Just let me warn you," she called, already halfway to her minivan. "The proper dose is one tablet, but I handed him two. Maybe you'd better try to stop him before he swallows them."

*"Libby!"*

She scrambled into the minivan, and my sisters disappeared down the driveway. Over Toby's barking, I thought I could hear both of them laughing their heads off.

I could have waited for him downstairs. But there was still a chance he hadn't ingested Libby's drug of choice, so I went up the stairs two at a time to save Michael a long weekend of discomfort.

"Hey," he said, in the act of tossing a shirt onto the bed from the closet doorway.

"How was the museum?"

"Strange," I said.

"Feel good to be back at work?"

"Yes," I admitted. "Very good, in fact."

Having him in my bedroom after such a long absence felt very strange. The size of him startled me all over again. But seeing him alive and mobile lifted my heart. His Pescara cousin Benny, the sniper, had failed to kill him, and most of the other cousins were in jail—for the moment at least. Michael must have felt his family situation was under control if he had come unprotected to Blackbird Farm again.

"I'm glad you're back on the job." He returned to the closet and said through the open door, "It's time you stopped spending every waking minute looking after Julie Huckabee. It'll be good for you to work again."

"You're not the only person with that message today." I sat on the edge of the bed.

He heard my tone and stepped out of the closet with a laundry basket in hand. He had come in jeans and a comfortable old flannel shirt, and I noticed he had a pair of boots on, not the walking cast he'd been wearing the last few weeks. With relief, I saw that he wasn't limping much, either.

If not for the body armor worn beneath his biking leathers, he'd have been dead. As it was, he'd suffered broken ribs, which were just now healing. Although he'd lost weight, Michael was looking more like himself at last. The color in his face told me he'd been fishing lately. He needed a haircut, too, a strangely comforting sign that his life was getting back to normal.

I said, "Penny Devine came to the museum."

His eyes widened.

I told him everything, and he listened without moving from the doorway.

"Damn," he said at last. "So she wasn't dead after all."

"No," I said. "She was more alive than I thought she'd be. It's very strange, though. She had no remorse about her son Kell's death. But she expressed interest in Julie. I guess that's something."

"Nora."

"I know, I know." I closed my eyes and rubbed my face with both hands. "I need to stop worrying about other people and take better care of myself."

"But that's not who you are," Michael said.

I put my hands in my lap. "No, it isn't."

Michael stayed in the doorway, carefully keeping an agreed-upon amount of distance between us.

He leaned one shoulder against the doorjamb. "I took care of those jars the twins left in the refrigerator."

"Oh, thank you! I've been afraid to open the door."

"Oh, and your sister brought a bunch of drawings from Lucy for you. I left them on the kitchen table. You're going to need an art gallery if she keeps it up."

I said, "We can't be together, Michael. You have to realize that I'll always help a friend, even if it hurts me."

He gave up trying to make idle conversation. "I know."

"And I—I still don't understand who you are. Or what the people around you are capable of doing. Aldo killing the man who grabbed me— it's just more than I can cope with."

"I know that, too. But I miss you."

"I miss you, too."

"That's good to hear." He smiled a little. "Because I'm not going to stop loving you."

Maybe he was not as beautifully handsome as Ignacio or Raphael Braga or even Crewe Dearborne. But his heart was there in the open between us, and his body had all the qualities to make most women forget a few character flaws. Here in the bedroom where we'd made love and said things I'd never tell another soul, I felt my heart skip. Because I couldn't stop loving him, either.

But his moral code was so very different from my own.

He read my thoughts and said, "Listen, I left the telescope on the dining room table. It's still in pieces. I'll need a couple of boxes to get it out of here. Do you mind if it stays a little longer?"

"Not at all. Some of your puzzle books are in the nightstand, though."

He found the Sudoku books and dropped them into the laundry basket, followed by the shirt and the boots he'd left under the bed. When all his things were gathered, he took the basket in one arm and kissed the top of my head. "See you around, Nora," he said.

And he left.

I heard him go down the staircase.

I kicked off my shoes, got up from the bed and slipped off my dress. I hung it in the closet and came out into the bedroom to look for my jeans.

I had made mistakes in the past. No doubt I was going to make a lot more. The trouble came with making choices that felt so right or so good while they were in progress. I had helped Carolina ten years ago when she wanted a baby, and it still felt like the right choice. I no longer thought of that child as something of mine. Maybe my hormones had calmed down enough to let me understand the truth and see the situation from Raphael's point of view. I'd been his worst nightmare, yes. The woman who wanted to steal his child away from her home. I saw that now.

Someday, if I was lucky, I'd have my own family. To raise and keep safe and love.

Back at the doorway, Michael said, "Look, I know I've done some things that are wrong in your world."

I turned around.

He said, "But they're right in mine."

"Michael—"

"It's going to take more than that telescope for me to see things differently, Nora. Hell, I can't even get the damn thing put together by myself. I need your help."

Even though I knew he wasn't talking about the pieces on my dining room table, I said, "I don't know anything about telescopes."

He almost smiled. "I don't want to be apart. I'll move out, if that's what will make you happy. But if you can forgive me first, maybe we can work on everything else."

"Michael," I said, "did you take the pills Libby gave you?"

He looked surprised. "Yeah. Why do you ask?"